DELICIOUS SURRENDER

"Get away from me!" Illyana cried. "Let me go! I'll have Papa kill you for this!"

She tried to pull her hands from Clay's grasp, but he was far too strong. He kept her hands pinned to the wall above her head.

"Have him kill me?" Clay taunted, his eyes dark with want. "Well, then, as long as I'm going to die anyway, it's only right that I do something worthy of execution."

Yana's mouth trembled, but she said nothing. Clay moved even closer to her, and everything, every subtle touch, heightened her awareness of him.

"Tell me you want me to stop . . . or I'll continue," he said in a softly rasping tone.

"W—wait," she managed to say. But before she could say more, Clay's mouth was over hers, kissing her fiercely. She felt trapped between Clay and the wall and her own responsive body, trapped by a rising passion she could no longer deny. . . .

Passion's Tender Embrace

ROBIN GIDEON

ZEBRA BOOKS
KENSINGTON PUBLISHING CORP.

ZEBRA BOOKS

are published by

Kensington Publishing Corp.
475 Park Avenue South
New York, NY 10016

First printing: February, 1990

Printed in the United States of America

For Don & Lucy,
and for
Arv & Ruth,
Ernie, John & Jeanette,
Amanda, and Albert.

rg

Chapter 1

"I don't want this man anywhere near me!" Illyana Zacarious shouted, pointing a finger at the broad chest of her newly appointed bodyguard. "Do you hear me, Papa?"

Nico, Illyana's father, had seen his daughter's temper on too many occasions. Headstrong and willful, she had been determined to write the rules for her own life ever since she was a toddler. But this time, with her health and his wealth at stake, he could not allow his daughter's spirit to run free. Besides, Nico could not afford to lose face in front of the son of the man he hoped to make his new business associate.

"Yana, please, this is for your own good, your own protection," he said. "We are in a new country. If Mr. McKenna feels that we—"

"*Opa!*" Yana snapped in mock laughter. Her eyes, dark and shining like twin jewels of glittering onyx, danced from her father's troubled countenance to the stranger's handsome face.

Yana suspected the stranger did not speak Greek. He looked vaguely bored with her outburst, and this piqued her curiosity.

"Yana, I'll not have you talking back to me here and now," Nico said, his tone taking on a harsher edge, his voice just above a whisper.

"Streets paved with gold! That's what I was told I would find here in America! But what do we find instead, Papa? We find ourselves in need of a bodyguard!"

"He's only escorting us so we won't get lost. That's—"

"Look at him!" Yana shouted. "Just look at him!" she continued in her native tongue, pointing once again at the tall, lean man who stood impassively with his arms crossed over his chest. "He looks like someone we should be protected *from!*"

Yana's eyes locked with the stranger's, and when they did, she felt a strange flutter in her stomach. For a moment, her voice faltered. "He has the look of . . . oh, what do those storybooks call them? Yes, I remember. He has the look of a common gunslinger!"

Even as Yana spoke the words, she knew she was lying. Lying not only to her father, but to herself. There was nothing at all common about the young man who had met them at the New York City pier when they arrived in America.

His face was lean almost to the point of being

8

gaunt, his cheeks hollowed slightly, making the high cheekbones more pronounced, the angles and planes of his face acutely sharp. His eyes were ebony-black, so dark that the pupils could not be distinctly seen. His nose was straight, rather long, and hawkish, with a slight rise at the bridge. Despite his sinewy leanness, lines ran from the corners of his nose, arching downward in a half circle to surround his mouth.

Yana studied the man's mouth. When she had first seen him, she'd thought he was scowling. Now she realized the fierceness of his expression was his natural state. His mouth had an unconscious sneer to it, his lips somewhat Cupid's bow in shape, curling fractionally downward at the corners.

Yana turned away from the stranger. When she looked at him, she felt uncomfortably warm inside, as though the proximity to him had heated the blood in her veins. He made her feel in danger, though she couldn't say why or how she felt this way.

"Papa, please," Yana said softly. She stepped close to Nico, moving away from the handsome, silent stranger. Though she continued to speak Greek, her voice dipped to a protective whisper. "He was sent here to be your bodyguard, not mine. I'm nineteen years old now. I can take care of myself."

Nico raised his eyes heavenward despite the fierce noontime sun.

"Yes, Yana, you can take care of yourself. You don't need a man in your life. You've told me all that before. Haven't we gone through this same discus-

9

sion every time some fine young man from a good, reputable family has to tell me that he simply cannot marry you?"

Yana smiled a little, though she knew this was a tender subject with her father. In Greece, fathers arranged marriages for their daughters. To break such an arrangement was to lose respect.

"Then just stop arranging marriages for me, Papa. Then these nice young men won't disappoint you."

"It's not the men who are disappointing me."

Nico shook his head sadly. Yana's eyes misted with unshed tears, knowing how deeply she'd hurt him. He placed his hands lightly on his daughter's shoulders, leaning closer so he could look directly into her eyes.

"Yana, most women your age already have a family to take care of. They've settled down with a nice young man and made their fathers into proud grandfathers. Is that such a bad thing? Of course not. It is the way it has always been."

"But I don't *want* to get married, Papa. I love you, but I don't want a husband." She paused a moment before adding, "Certainly not one that is chosen for me."

Nico raised his dark, bushy eyebrows. This was an ongoing argument, and as she knew he would, he rose to the challenge.

"Do you think that I would betroth you to a bad man, an evil man, a poor man? Alexander comes from an old family, a proper family. He is worth millions. And with your dowry, he would be worth

10

even more millions. Yana, he could take care of you. He could give you everything you could ever want. He could give you children. And it would be so beneficial for everyone to have the Zacarious family and the Nader family united in marriage.''

Yana tossed her hands up, huffing in indignation.

''Business, Papa! That's all you think about is business! You think because you give me away to a rich man that will make me happy? No! You use me as a pawn to become partners with another powerful family!''

Nico and Yana began shouting, their faces almost touching, their love for each other made stronger by their respective stubborn wills binding them together with silver chains.

Clayton McKenna leaned back against the pier railing and crossed his boots at the ankle as Nico and Illyana Zacarious continued their argument. Though he didn't speak a word of Greek, he had a pretty good idea of what had made the fiery daughter of the shipping magnate so angry.

Another selfish, spoiled little chit, thought Clay, studying Illyana surreptitiously out of the corner of his eye. *She can't have her own way so she's throwing a tantrum.*

Clay reached into his jacket pocket and extracted tobacco and paper. He rolled a cigarette, scratched a wooden sulphur match against the pier, then inhaled deeply. As he exhaled, he received a cross look from

11

Illyana. Clay just smiled slowly at her, and he was pleased with himself when her eyes narrowed in anger. With renewed zest, she resumed her argument with Nico.

Though he appeared at ease, Clay's mind was alert, his ebony eyes never resting anywhere long. His father, Sorren McKenna, had sent him to watch over Nico Zacarious. After Nico had finished his discussions with the New York bankers, Clay was to see him safely south to Virginia, where the truly serious business negotiations would begin between Sorren and Nico at the McKenna family country estate.

The plan was simple enough, provided personal egos stayed under control and everyone remained honest. As the turn of the century approached, the United States was in the midst of a huge surge in industrial productivity. The population was booming, both with native-born children and with those from foreign lands seeking the opportunity for a better life.

Everyone needed everything, or so it seemed. The plan was first hatched late one night in Sorren's library, while imaginations were being liberally lubricated with French brandy. Clay was bored, he told his father. He needed a new challenge, something other than just overseeing the considerable interests in cotton. What Clay would like to do, he explained, was to expand the market for cotton overseas.

Sorren's idea for expanding the family fortune was to diversify into shipping. The Greeks, Sorren said, were the best shipbuilders in the world. The Greeks made the fastest, surest ships anywhere. With a small fleet . . . well, there would be a fortune waiting in transporting the goods everyone wanted.

Clay countered that the Germans made the finest optics in the world. Perhaps importing the fine optics from Germany would be a money-making proposition, especially since high-quality, high-powered optics were so critical in surveying, mapping, and for a thousand other uses necessary to the new cities and factories that must be built.

It was Shadow, Clay's strikingly beautiful, mixed-blood mother, coming into the library to retrieve the brandy decanter, who in an offhanded way had come up with the idea.

"If you two hadn't spent so much time with the brandy, you'd see that the real money is to be made in overseeing the whole operation," Shadow said, her loving eyes a bit stern. She didn't like it when Sorren and Clay had more than a drink or two of brandy. She'd never seen either of them really drunk, but once in a while her husband and her oldest son would get together with a bottle, talk far into the night, and drink a little too much. Shadow's Kiowan blood distrusted liquor, and she worried that her son would grow to like it too much.

"How's that?" Sorren asked.

"If what you say is correct, the United States needs the optical instruments that are made in Germany. The Greeks build the best ships in the world—not surprising, I suppose, considering they've been at it

13

longer than anyone else. And Clay is saying that the price of cotton isn't what it used to be because there's so much of it here. Why not bring all the best together?"

It was later, after much discussion and many cups of steaming black coffee, that the plan really began taking shape. Europe needed cotton, which the vast, fertile fields of the southeastern United States could provide. Europe also needed tobacco, another product that grew thick and plentiful in the rich soil.

America needed the superior-quality optics that were being made in Germany.

If a ship could be outfitted to bring optics from Germany to the ports in the United States, and cotton *back* to Europe, the profits would make everyone rich. The only trouble was that ships weren't designed to carry bulk items such as cotton and tobacco, as well as small, fragile items like microscopes and telescopes.

Enter Nico Zacarious and the Zacarious Shipping Company. If the McKennas and Zacarious could come up with a suitable plan to design and build ships that could be altered, in port, to carry the appropriate items back and forth from Europe and the United States, the potential profits staggered the mind. That was why Nico had come to New York.

Clay found the businessman's feisty daughter to be a somewhat annoying but stimulating surprise. The fact that Sorren had given the job of protecting Nico to his son was silent testimony to the potential dangers. But Clay had strenuously protested this "babysitting" assignment. It was a job better suited for one of the hired men, Clay had argued. He relented to Sorren's wishes in the end, however, because Clay realized that he was the only man his father truly trusted. If Sorren was so adamant that Clay take the responsibility, there had to be a reason.

"Excuse me, Mr. Zacarious," Clay said when there was a momentary lull in the argument. "Do you think we could get a move on? I'll take you to your banks, but first I think a stop at your hotel suite is in order. Standing here with you two"—he searched for a delicate word—"*talking* so loudly in a foreign language is drawing attention to us. Surely you understand that this is not wise."

Nico looked at Clay. The old man's mouth was pressed into a tight, severe line. "Of course, Mr. McKenna. You are absolutely correct. Please, lead the way."

Yana said something in Greek, giving her head an angry toss in Clay's direction, sending jet hair flying around her shoulders and down her back. Nico replied, "It is rude to speak a foreign tongue, Yana. When we are in America, we speak only English."

Yana's dark eyes locked with Clay's. She had expected him to break the contact first; men always did with Yana. But she was the one who, almost demurely, cast her eyes down.

"Of course, Papa," she answered quietly. Then, to Clay, she added, "I wouldn't want to do anything to offend the sensibilities of our American friends." She drawled the word *friends* out like an insult.

15

Clay led the way through the crowd. Men moved out of his way when they saw him approach. Women looked on at the dark-haired young man in a tailored silk suit appreciatively, some covetously. The women noticed the breadth of Clay's shoulders and how he carried them squarely. They noticed his powerful thighs and his long-legged stride. They did not notice the high-caliber revolver secured in a hand-tooled holster under his left arm. The weapon's presence was artfully hidden by Virginia's finest tailor. Nobody had to see a gun, though, to sense that Clay was too much danger to trifle with.

They walked through the pier to the waiting four-horse carriage. Even to Nico Zacarious, who had inherited millions from his father and had turned those millions into many more millions, the large carriage was spectacularly opulent. Everything about it, from the taut, gleaming leather siding to the polished spoked wheels and gilt-edged trimming, whispered less than quietly of hand craftmanship, detail, and money.

"Mr. McKenna, it is beautiful!" Nico exclaimed with a touch of envy. Even before he stepped inside the carriage, Nico promised himself that he would find out who had made the carriage and order one for himself, to be shipped back to his palace in Pirias.

"Please . . . Mr. McKenna is my father," Clay replied, opening the door for Nico. He extended his hand to Yana, but she refused his help as she stepped up into the carriage.

"I'm just Clayton," Clay said. "My friends call

me Clay.''

Nico, genuinely warmed by the young man's lack of pretense, asked, ''And what shall I call you then?''

''Clay, I hope.''

''Clay it is then.''

Clay looked at Yana, who had slid across the burgundy-colored leather seat to the far side of the carriage. She was staring out the window. Clay could feel the heat of her anger. Obviously, she didn't like the fact that he and Nico were getting along quite nicely.

''I get the feeling that to your daughter,'' Clay said, his voice low, yet loud enough to carry to Yana's ears, ''I'll always be Mr. McKenna.''

Yana's head snapped around, her dark eyes bright and alive. ''Nonsense! Why should I be so formal with the hired help? I'll just call you the same as I do a stable boy! I snap my fingers!''

Yana snapped her fingers like a gunshot, then turned back to the window.

Clay shrugged his shoulders, stepping away from the carriage door as, once again, the argument between Yana and her father came to life in virulent Greek. It seemed, to Clay's ear, to be a magnificent lauguage to curse in. The words all seemed to flow together rhythmically. Even though he knew—or at least strongly suspected—that Yana was cussing him out royally, he found it interesting to hear the repartee between father and daughter.

Stepping up so he could quietly instruct the coachman, Clay gave the name of the hotel Nico and

Illyana would be staying at. The coachman nodded, saying nothing. Clay had hired him that morning, paying him handsomely for his services. Since the coachman had had no time to set any plans and did not know who his employer or passengers were, he could not be a threat to Clay.

The McKenna family had many vicious, patient enemies. There were those who would pay extraordinary sums to see a McKenna cut down to size or end up facedown in a street with a bullet in the back. Consequently, Clay McKenna was a man who trusted very few people and made even fewer mistakes.

As soon as Clay got into the carriage, a brooding silence developed between Nico and Yana. The two sat quietly, each fuming in silent rage at the other, staring out opposite sides of the carriage at the scenes of streetlife in New York City. The temporary truce in the battle of wills—and Clay was quite certain it was only temporary—provided him the opportunity to at last get an unhurried look at Illyana Zacarious.

At first glance, Illyana was spine-tinglingly beautiful. It was on closer inspection that Clay decided she had a more exotic type of beauty than classic beauty, though this revelation did nothing at all to quell his agitated male senses. From the moment Clay had seen Yana walk off the ship with her head held high and an imperious aura that surrounded her so completely the force of it was textural, his body had been distinctly and distractingly aware of Illyana Zacarious's vivacious and blatantly feminine charms.

She wore her wavy midnight-black hair down, letting it flow down her back and over her shoulders, the curling ends coming to a stop six inches below her shoulders. Clay's eyes scanned slowly and appreciatively downward to Yana's breasts, which were very full and round, pressing against the blue silk of her dress. Her waist narrowed dramatically. Her hips were delectably rounded, like her breasts. Unable to see her legs beneath the dress, Clay saw in his mind's eye a vision of dark-hued flesh, smooth as the silk of her dress, trembling slightly with want. He saw the tips of his fingers tracing lazy circles against a velvety inner thigh as he . . .

Stop thinking that way! thought Clay angrily. *She's spoiled beyond redemption, and selfish, too! Selfish women out of bed are invariably selfish and disappointing in bed.*

Clay tried to concentrate on the chaos of New York City as it rolled by his carriage window, but his gaze was drawn inexorably back to the tempestuous Greek woman who, if his father's reports were correct, was the sole heir to the Zacarious Shipping Company fortune, said to be worth millions, and light of her father's life.

Yana had a high, wide forehead. Clay wondered, as his half-Indian mother claimed, if a wide forehead indicated high intelligence. Clay wondered if Yana's mind was as sharp as her tongue.

Yana's nose, thought Clay with some sense of relief, was a bit on the small side. He tried to

19

concentrate on the fact that her nose was too small, but when his eyes drifted downward to Yana's mouth, he felt a fist tighten inside him. Yana's mouth was medium-wide and rather full, with the lower lip plumper than the upper. Just above the right corner of her mouth was a dark beauty mark, and though Clay wanted desperately to think of it as a flaw in her perfection, his trustworthy inability to deceive himself whispered that the beauty mark was exactly that—a beauty mark. It wasn't a flaw at all, but instead added to Yana's allure and heightened her devilishly exotic aura, which filled the lavishly appointed carriage and suffused itself into every pore and nerve in Clay McKenna's body.

His eyes went down once more to Yana's breasts. He watched them tremble softly as the carriage rattled over a rough section of the cobblestone street, fascinated as a teenager in spite of his considerable experience with the fairer gender.

The carriage came to a stop in front of the hotel, and Clay breathed a sigh of relief. As soon as he had Nico and his enticing daughter securely tucked away in their suites, he could relieve himself temporarily of his duties and find a woman to quench the desire Illyana Zacarious had brought to flame.

It was a fine though slightly obscure hotel, and Yana found herself feeling a little disappointed. She had hoped the accommodations—all prearranged by the McKennas—would be substandard. Such a transgression on Clay's part would make it much easier for her to find his presence intensely disagreeable.

The trouble was that Yana had found her eyes drawn to the roguish Clay McKenna. She didn't like his attitude, but he did remind her of her own femininity. He conjured up feelings inside her that Yana preferred remained dormant.

Yana stripped out of her traveling dress. Though it was lightweight—cool against the stifling, humid New York heat—the dress was now clinging to her arms and legs. She tossed the garment onto the bed disdainfully. Perhaps she'd give it to her church in Pirias, to be subsequently cleaned and then donated to a needy woman. Idly, Yana wondered if there were any organizations in New York that performed such tasks. She hoped so. Yana was rich enough and cavalier enough with her father's money to have no intention of ever wearing the dress again, yet she was aware enough of the world around her, of the masses who toiled in poverty, to want the dress to be of use to someone else.

Such deeds helped Yana justify her inherited wealth and the extravagance it spawned.

She deposited an embroidered petticoat atop the dress, then walked to the window and looked out. It was nearly five o'clock, and the streets were quickly crowded with workers going home. The city was certainly exciting, but it wasn't nearly as glamorous as she had imagined it.

A cool breeze filtered through her fifth-floor

window, caressing Yana's heated flesh. She sighed. Though the breeze was most welcome and smelled faintly of the ocean, the air just wasn't the same as the invigorating salty breezes that flowed easily through her huge bedroom windows in Pirias.

Clayton McKenna. Clay.

Did she like the name? Yana wasn't sure. The man who owned the name didn't treat her in a manner to which she was accustomed. She much preferred the wealthy, hungry, desperate young men who were so happy to do whatever she asked, to give her whatever her heart desired. In a word, Yana liked her men obedient. She liked them to be generous, too. A suitor who brings gifts, Yana believed, shows that he is genuine, his intentions honorable. Of course, Yana would never let any gift, no matter how outlandishly extravagant it was, sway her will to stay out of a man's—*any* man's—bed. Her affections—and certainly her virginity—were not for sale. Nevertheless, she enjoyed the gifts, even if she didn't really need them.

Clay hadn't given Yana a gift when he had met her and Nico at the pier. He had given her nothing more than an appraising look and a handshake, a slight tip of his hat, and a half smile. It was the half smile, Yana decided, that made her body respond inwardly to Clay.

Yana leaned forward so her palms rested on the window ledge. She closed her eyes and breathed in deeply. Her breasts swelled outward, straining against the French lace trimming of her corset. She felt the pressure against her breasts and, with her eyes still closed, could feel Clay's cool yet deeply warming gaze upon her.

A tremor passed through Yana. In her mind's eye, she could see Clay as clearly as if he were standing right in front of her. Only now, in the unreality of her fantasy, she could look at him without fear that he'd notice her stare or the approval that shone in the twilight depths of her chocolate eyes when she looked at him.

He's too handsome, really, for his own good, thought Yana. *His physical charms have made him arrogant, conceited. I hate his type. They're always selfish. So unrelentingly sure of themselves. But they're hollow inside. Or simply too full of themselves.*

And though, with a casual toss of her hair over her shoulders, she tried to dismiss Clay, his presence— starkly masculine and distinctly predatory—remained in the forefront of her mind.

She saw Clay's half smile. She saw the way nothing seemed to affect Clay personally. In her mind, Yana saw how Clay's expression was impassive, almost bored. But yet his eyes always darted from here to there, constantly searching for trouble. The rapid workings of his mind could practically be felt even though Clay said nothing, just like the strength in his body could be felt even when he was motionless.

"Stop it!" Yana hissed under her breath. She did not want to think about Clay or even admit that his masculinity affected her.

At nineteen, Illyana was at least three years into marrying age. As her father's only daughter and only child, she had been told from early on that it was her responsibility to bear Nico a grandson. A man had to run the family business, and blood ties were always better than marriage vows.

But Yana had other ideas on such matters.

Her mother had died giving birth to Yana. Though Nico never realized it, he let Yana know that he had been lonely ever since the death of his wife. Yana, he said, was his only love. Though Nico had intended for such comments to be taken as endearments, they reinforced Yana's silent belief that she was responsible for the death of the only woman that Nico truly loved—his wife, her mother.

She vowed, at the tender age of thirteen, that she would stay away from men. It was the only way to prevent tragedies from happening. She saw her world, from that point forward, through the eyes of a woman who had destroyed her father's happiness.

So Clay McKenna's reminding Yana that she was no longer thirteen was most unwelcome. Her tender, sensitive body had never been touched, never been caressed, never even been held tenderly by anyone other than her father, on the few occasions when her fears had overwhelmed her to the point that she had to turn to the one man in the world she knew would not hurt her, the only man whom she did not want to feel pain but knew had been hurt grievously himself.

Turning away from the window, Yana stretched her arms above her head, working the cricks and kinks out of the muscles in her shoulders and legs. She needed a good ride to loosen up her body and free her from the tension that had slowly been knotting tighter and tighter in the pit of her stomach since she had met Clay. The only trouble with that idea was that Scirocco, her mare, was at home in her stable.

Yana put a foot on the bed and unclasped the corset holding up her left stocking. As she rolled the stocking down the tapering length of her thigh, there was a soft knock at the door.

"Come in!" Yana called out. She and Nico, living together for so many years and having only themselves to worry about, were not overly modest with each other. Yana rolled the stocking down her leg and off her foot, then started with the other stocking as the hotel door opened.

Clay McKenna took one step into the room and froze dead in his tracks.

Chapter 2

If Clay had been able to see himself and the look of utter astonishment on his face, he would not have believed it. Clay McKenna, after all, was a ladies' man *par excellence*. He had, by all accounts, enjoyed the amorous companionship of far more than his fair share of women. *Too* many women, worried fathers said.

But none of his previous dalliances had prepared him for what he saw when he was beckoned into Yana's hotel bedroom.

She was leaning over, calmly unfastening a garter from a silk stocking. Dressed only in pantalets, a trussed corset, and a single stocking, Yana was more vividly erotic than any woman Clay had ever seen. Though she had clothes on, she was more brazenly sensual than a dozen naked women combined. And the effect Yana Zacarious's dishabille had on what many women and all men thought of as the unflappable Clayton McKenna was to leave him dumb-struck and openmouthed, speechless.

"At least the hotel is nice," Yana said, rolling the stocking down past her calf to her ankle. "Still, this probably isn't the best hotel in New York."

From his position, with Yana bending over at the bed, Clay was able to see her cleavage in full, erotic bloom. Full, rounded breasts were held high, pressed together by the bodice of the corset. The lace trim of the ivory corset, pressing against her darker flesh, caught Clay's attention. As she slipped the neatly rolled stocking off her foot, the speechless young man watched Yana's breasts moving with a gentle firmness that gripped his insides in a painful stranglehold.

In those half-dozen seconds that Clay was able to look at Yana without her realizing it wasn't Nico who'd entered her room, a thousand different things flashed through his mind. His mother's teachings whispered that he should turn his back and exit quickly, giving his apologies to Yana later, when she was more suitably attired. His masculine instincts said he should rush across the brief expanse of floor space that separated him from Yana, take her into his arms, toss her onto the bed, remove what few articles of clothing she wore, and make glorious, passionate love to her until both of them experienced a satisfaction that was heretofore unknown. His father's voice sternly whispered in Clay's mind that he was making a terrible transgression against the daughter of an intended business associate.

But his mind was numbed by Yana's curvaceous magnificence. All those voices in Clay's head fell on deaf ears. Even if he wanted to move, to rush out of the room and think of some elaborate apology that might be acceptable to Yana (and what would Nico think?), Clay McKenna was frozen in one place.

Finally finished with the stocking, Yana placed both feet on the floor and turned toward the window. *She's even beautiful facing away from me*, Clay thought.

"What do you think of the McKennas now, Papa? The son seems dangerous somehow. I can't really put my finger on it. There's something in his eyes, in the set of his mouth, that tells me he's danger. Have you noticed how he never really sits completely still? There's always a foot tapping, his fingers drumming." Illyana looked down at the carriages moving far below. "I don't trust him, even though he seems to have cozied up to you pretty quick. And that surprises me, Papa. You usually are more cautious than that."

Clay knew this was the time he could, with silent feet on the thick rug, walk backward through the door he had just entered. Yana might not even know that he was the one who had walked in. He could deny everything. God knows, there were enough times in Clay's life when he had needed to deny his actions.

But he couldn't move. He was helpless against Yana's innocently beguiling allure. Had she *tried* to look this sexy, the effect on Clay would surely not

29

have been as powerful. But she wasn't trying to be anything but herself, a nineteen-year-old woman comfortable in the company of her father. That, as much as her stunning body encased in a corset that Clay felt was entirely unnecessary for her feminine curves, was what made Yana at that moment the most provocative woman in the world.

As though the world had suddenly slowed down so that movements were snail-like but mental alacrity maintained its usual pace, Clay watched the slow transition as Yana turned to face him. He saw her in profile, and then the momentary look of confusion in her large dark eyes. He saw the fire explode in her gaze as she sent visual daggers sizzling across the room to cut him to ribbons, laying him bleeding and dying on the floor with just a look alone.

"What do you think you're doing in here?" Yana hissed, keeping her voice low enough so she would not draw the attention of her father, who was in the next room. It would later bother her that she had made a point of not alerting Nico.

"I'm sorry," Clay responded. The sound of his voice was strange in his ears. Did he really—*could* he really—sound that . . . *contrite?*

If Clay had been shocked at walking into the hotel room and finding Yana scantily dressed, he was amazed at what happened next.

She didn't dash madly for her dress to cover herself. She didn't even cross her arms over herself in a futile attempt to hide those glorious breasts. What Yana did do was to follow her instincts.

30

Illyana Elani Despina Zacarious . . . attacked.

The speed at which Yana came at Clay surprised him, but she was not fast enough to draw blood. A hand raking at his face, fingers curled and long nails slashing, never reached his eyes. Clay sidestepped smoothly. When Yana wheeled and tried a second time, he caught her wrist, his fingers firm as steel bands around the tender skin.

"As tokalo!" Yana hissed through clenched teeth, looking at the tanned fingers surrounding her wrist. She locked gazes with Clay, then went for his eyes with the fingers of her left hand.

"Stop it!" Clay said, a hint of a smile curling one corner of his mouth as he captured Yana's left hand before she was able to blind him. "It was an accident!"

But Yana would not be so easily soothed. She tried to jerk herself free from Clay's grip, but his large hands held her secure. When Yana pulled away from Clay a second time, all she succeeded in doing was pulling his muscular, sinewy lean body against her own.

Wild with rage but not with fear, Yana tried one last time to pull herself out of Clay's grip. She used all her might, literally throwing herself backward. The wall stopped her progress but not Clay's. Having been pulled forward, his body pressed against her, the solid surface of his chest compressing her breasts. The heat of his body, pressed against her own however briefly, sent shock waves of a strange, new excitement sprinting through Yana's system.

31

There was a moment, a space of time lasting perhaps less than a second, when Yana and Clay stopped fighting. In that instant, Yana looked up into Clay's face. She saw the gleam in his eyes, the twinkle of mischief. This boyishness pleased Yana but infuriated her at the same time, because it was clear that Clay did not take her attack seriously. Yana also felt Clay's leanly muscled chest pressing against her bosom. Even through the fabric of her corset and his shirt and jacket, the heat of his body was transported spontaneously to Yana. The warmth of a soft, voluptuous body pressing against Clay registered in his eyes. He wanted her.

Fear now exploded in Yana's brain. Clay wanted her as a man wants a woman. And unlike her other suitors, those silly Greek boys with their inheritances and their flowers and their wheedling pleas to do nothing more than hold her hand, Clay wanted all of her, body and soul. And Yana's body reacted to him. Her nipples had grown hard inside her bodice, becoming taut and sensitive. Yana's body, long denied the pleasures that other women her own age knew, responded to Clay's animal virility. For this reason, Yana hated and feared Clay. He made her femininity respond to his unmistakable masculinity, the instinctual attraction of sexual opposites. It was an attraction as ancient and mysterious as time itself.

"Get away from me!" Yana whispered, her tone tremulous and yet defiant.

"Stop fighting me. I won't hurt you," Clay responded.

But each second of the clock heightened Yana's sensitivity. Her breasts felt overfull and heavy in the bodice of her corset, fiercely and painfully constrained, even though the garment had been tailored by her personal dressmaker to her precise measurements.

The heat that had been generated by Clay now traveled throughout Yana. If she did not end the physical contact between herself and her tormentor soon, that heat would turn to flame, burning so hotly and brightly that she doubted she could extinguish it before she was consumed.

Had Yana tried to calmly reason with Clay, he would have released her wrists and stepped away so she was no longer trapped between him and the wall. He would not *want* to let her go, but he would.

But she didn't give Clay the chance to reason with her or vice versa, because every nerve in Yana had become hypersensitive to his touch. The voices in her soul that had been silent for so long were now shouting joyously at the touch of animal man, of Clayton McKenna.

Yana's eyes darkened with hatred spawned by fear. Her knee lanced upward toward Clay's groin.

She had not yet missed her target before Yana realized she would fail. *He moves like lightning,* thought Yana. Clay had leaped backward, just far enough so the bent knee could not strike him. He continued to hold tightly to Yana's wrists.

"You bitch!" spat Clay.

Clay kicked his right foot between Yana's knees and, in a wrenching move, forced her feet wide apart. He leaned into her a moment later, his body pressed intimately against her. The move had been intended by Clay to be defensive. With his body between Yana's thighs, it was impossible for her to success-fully knee his groin. Whatever his intention, when Clay found himself nestled against her, a thousand images, all of them deliciously erotic, flashed across the surface of his mind.

He pushed Yana's hands together and up, holding both wrists in one large hand, trapping them against the wall above her head. With his right hand, Clay grabbed Yana's chin, forcing her face up. His fingers and thumb pressed painfully deep into the flawless flesh of her cheeks.

"Don't you ever try to do that again," Clay said, his voice icy calm, yet carrying an undercurrent of thinly controlled rage. "Ever. Never."

Clay relaxed his hold on Yana's chin. She turned her face away so that she wouldn't have to look into his dark, angry, frightening eyes.

"I'm sorry," Yana said. Inwardly, she cursed herself for apologizing. She had done nothing wrong. After all, *she* hadn't barged into *his* hotel room, had she? "You scared me."

She heard his deep, steady breathing and felt Clay's chest expanding and contracting against her breasts. She no longer struggled to free her hands.

"I didn't mean to scare you." There was a tight-ness in Clay's throat that made his voice hoarse.

"I knocked. You said it was okay to come in. I was just checking on you. I was only trying to do my job."

"I thought you were my father."

Clay's smile was warm, with a touch of the devil in it. His eyes went from Yana's face and down to her bosom, which was pressed firmly against his broad chest, her breasts swelling out, straining against the delicate lace trimming of her bodice. When his eyes came back to lock with Yana's, she shivered.

"Did you really think it was your father?" Clay asked softly, sarcastically. "Or did you know it was me? Is that why you were taking your clothes off when I came in? Most women wouldn't be so . . . immodest in front of their fathers."

Yana's anger flared anew. However much her body enjoyed the touch of Clay McKenna, her mind despised it.

"Opa! Such an ego you have, Mr. McKenna!"

Yana tried to pull her hands from Clay's grasp, but he was far too strong. He kept her hands pinned to the wall above her head. She struggled a little more. Yana's struggles made her more vividly aware of the fact that Clay's slender hips were between her thighs. This whole strange encounter had to end *now*.

"Get away from me! Let me go! I'll have Papa kill you for this!"

In Greece, such a threat would have turned any man pasty-faced with fear. The Zacarious family was not one to cross. And everyone had heard of how old

35

Nico doted on his fiery-tempered, darling daughter. But Clay McKenna was neither impressed nor frightened. He had received death threats before. The Zacarious family was a power in Greece. In America, it was the McKennas who owned vast sections of Virginia and various businesses from Boston to San Francisco.

"Have Nico kill me, eh?" Clay taunted, his eyes still dark with want. He leaned a little closer to Yana, pressing his lower body into the juncture of her thighs. The pressure against Yana's flesh made her moan softly. Her eyes closed briefly. When they opened again, the pupils had dilated. "Well, then, as long as I'm going to die anyway, it's only right that I do something worthy of execution. That seems"— his face twisted into a handsome though thoroughly evil grin—"*proper*, doesn't it?"

"Stop this!" Yana snapped, but there wasn't the anger in her voice that had been there earlier. There was, in its place, a pleading quality. Though this quality was very faint, almost unnoticeable, it did not go undetected–by Clay's ears. He had heard similar sounds from women in his arms many times in the past.

"Do you really want me to stop, Yana?" Clay asked, and with his words he added an extra ounce of force behind his hips. He moved, rocking slightly from side to side, rubbing himself intimately against Yana. "Are you absolutely sure you don't want this?"

Yes, thought Yana. *Yes, I want you to stop this*

insanity this instant.

No, Yana's soul whispered. *I want this to continue. I want to know what other women know. I feel alive and frightened, and you scare me but excite me, too!*

Yana's narrow, full-lipped mouth trembled. She said nothing. Clay rubbed himself against her, and everything, every subtle touch, heightened Yana's awareness of him. From inside the smooth silk of his slacks, she felt the muscles in his legs against her inner thighs. The contact was a strange and sensual caress. She felt his maleness, straining against his slacks, pressing hungrily against her. Though there were several layers of clothing separating Yana and Clay, the heated passion that burned between them seared them both. The touch of their bodies was as though they were naked.

"Tell me you want me to stop . . . or I'll continue," Clay said in that softly rasping tone that Yana now realized was just another of the considerable sexual skills he used to gently tear down a woman's resistance.

"W—wait," Yana managed to say. But before she could say more, Clay's head dipped down and his mouth was over hers, kissing her fiercely.

Clay used the tip of his tongue tentatively at first. Yana did not want him to kiss her deeply, but what *she* wanted was not what her *senses* wanted. Her lips parted, just slightly at first, and she felt the warm, intimate invasion of Clay's tongue in her mouth.

His tongue danced and searched, tasting and

probing. Yana had never been kissed this way before, but the fire that burned through her and made her tremble set off warning bells inside her. The few men she had allowed to kiss her had left her feeling fouled somehow, as though her lips could not possibly taste any pleasure when pressed against a man's mouth. Now she knew it was not the act of kissing that she didn't like, but rather the men she had kissed. Had she kissed Clay McKenna before, her attitude would have been different.

She opened her mouth a little more, hesitantly inviting Clay's tongue in further. She got what she wanted, and Yana's head began swimming dizzily with conflicting emotions and devilishly arousing feelings charging through her.

Clay's right hand, which had been lightly at Yana's throat, inched slowly downward. Yana felt his fingertips moving gently over her skin, branding her as his with a touch that was demanding and yet soft as a feather.

"Beautiful," Clay whispered, leaning away from Yana so that his eyes could take in what his hand was doing. With the tip of his finger, he followed the outline of Yana's corset, simultaneously touching lace and skin. The fingertip moved from one breast to the other. "So . . . beautiful . . . Yana!"

Yana kept her eyes closed. Her hands were still above her head, held against the wall by Clay's left hand. Yana did not try to free her hands. She tried to calm her ragged breathing but couldn't. His finger, sliding back and forth over her breasts, riding along the top of her corset, was all she could think about, all she could feel. That, and the pressure of Clay's groin against her own. She turned her face aside, catching a trembling lower lip between her teeth to bite on, preventing herself from moaning softly. She did not want Clay McKenna to know how traitorous her body was or how deeply he was affecting her. When his finger disappeared into the tight, soft cleavage, Yana sighed again, almost sobbing with want.

"Stunning," Clay whispered, a reverence in his tone as his hand moved lower to cup the lush fullness of one heavy, firm breast. He squeezed, and Yana moaned. Clay heard a sound and was oddly surprised to discover that he, too, had moaned.

How many times had Clay McKenna been with a woman in a hotel room? How many women had there been? Too many, to be sure. Most of them were now just vague images in his mind, hazy faces in the fog of yesterday.

So why, with all his experience, wasn't Clay more calm, more aloof? Why, as he watched his hand gently massaging Yana's left breast, were his fingers visibly trembling? She was beautiful, but so were most of the women Clay had slept with.

"You are . . . exquisite," Clay said, his tone husky. He searched his addled brain for an appropriate word to let Yana know exactly how beautiful she was and how desperately, even painfully, he needed her. "Exquisite," he whispered. And then, using a word his father used to describe his mother, he said, "Precious."

Yana tilted her head back. She moistened her lips with the tip of her tongue. She felt trapped between Clay and the wall and her own responsive body. She invited Clay to kiss her, but he did not.

Kiss me, damn you! she thought. And though she ached with the need to have his mouth against her own, to know once again the sweetly intimate pleasure of his exploring tongue, she could not *say* what she wanted.

An eternity later, Clay's mouth came down to cover Yana's. She sighed deeply, no longer putting forward the pretense of resistance. The hand and fingers massaging her breast, manipulating her nipple into a state of such intense arousal it actually hurt, had exposed her charade for the lie it was.

Between the hand at her breast, pinching softly her aroused flesh through her corset, and the heat and hardness of Clay's erection, pressing against her, and the mouth that devoured her lips, and the tongue that probed and teased her so . . . it was all much, much too much for a nineteen-year-old virgin who had denied herself so completely and for so long.

Clay's fingers curled inside Yana's bodice, sliding between ivory lace and soft, smooth flesh. With a slow, steady pull, he brought the bodice down to expose one breast.

"Ohhh!" Yana sighed, again turning her face away from Clay. Her mouth opened as though she were about to speak, but no sound could escape her passion-constricted throat.

For long moments, Clay stared at Yana's breast, letting his eyes drink in her beauty, looking at her as though he'd never seen a woman before. Again, from somewhere deep in his mind, the question was asked why Yana affected him so strongly, but Clay was no longer interested in knowing the answer. He accepted, without regret, her power over his senses as a matter of fact, and as such, it was something he had no control over.

"Precious," Clay said in a breathy whisper.

He kissed Yana's nose, her lips, her chin. Moving down, he kissed the smooth, taut perfumed arch of her throat, and then the hollow. Baring his teeth, he nipped lightly at her flesh, causing Yana to squirm.

Regrettably, since the friction between them had affected him strongly, Clay had to take a half step away from Yana to bend down further. He broke the invisible bond at their waists that had kept them together. Then, sighing, he cupped Yana's breast from the underside.

"Beautiful," Clay said in a voice that seemed like it should belong to someone else.

The areola was round and naturally dark in color, darkened even more with passion. Clay ran his thumb over the elongated tip and watched it grow fractionally. Yana trembled.

"Clay . . . don't," Yana managed to say.

"Shhh! I won't hurt you."

Yana felt the warmth and moisture of Clay's tongue along the upper slope of her breast. With

41

agonizing patience, Clay tantalized her, circling the risen peak with the tip of his tongue without ever touching the core of her sensation. She rolled her head from side to side, her skull against the wall. Yana was oblivious to everything but the presence of this handsome, virile, dangerous man who held her hands above her head with one of his, and played her body with consummate skill with the other. Yana wondered if she could go delirious with want.

And then, at last, Clay captured her nipple between his lips. He sucked gently on the bud, flicking it with his rasping tongue.

Yana cried out softly. The warmth of Clay's mouth mingled with the heat generated from deep within her. Her knees trembled and unconsciously Yana arched her back, pressing her soft bosom more firmly against Clay's ravenous mouth. His soft lips, moist tongue, and sharp teeth all caused distinct sensations, each one even more pleasing than the last.

"Beautiful," Clay whispered, his nuzzling lips brushing against Yana's sensitive flesh as he spoke. His breath felt cool against the moist crest of her breast where his lips and tongue had been. "See how you rise up for me, Yana?"

But Yana did not see. Her eyes were closed. Her breath was trapped in her burning lungs. She could not relax sufficiently to exhale. She waited, tremulous with anticipation, for Clay's mouth to again force the sweet esthesia that she had never experienced before. To Yana, that was all that mattered. Her fears and doubts, the promises she'd made herself—they were all forgotten. Everything she knew and everything she believed in was forgotten in this single, frightening, exhilarating moment of pure . . . *feeling*.

"Look at me, Yana," Clay purred, stroking her breast with the fingertips of his free hand. "Look at your beauty . . . and watch me."

Yana could not. She didn't want Clay to talk to her. When he did, she was taken away from mindless feelings and her brain was forced to think. Thinking, here and now, was the last thing in the world Yana wanted to do.

She felt the soft pad of one slightly callused thumb pass lightly over her eyebrow. Clay was whispering to her, telling her she must open her eyes. Yana resisted. If she opened her eyes, reality would come flooding in. This was all just a dream, she told herself. A wonderful dream that she wanted to continue.

Clay caught Yana's chin between a curled index finger and his thumb. He turned her face toward him, kissing her lightly and briefly on the mouth.

"Open your eyes, beautiful girl. I want you to see."

Yana was helpless against Clay. She opened her eyes just slightly, just enough to see his roguishly handsome face. A look of burning hunger showed clearly in his dark and suddenly expressive eyes.

He kissed her on the mouth again, the tip of his tongue briefly tracing the outline of Yana's lips. Then, as though her eyes were inexorably drawn by

43

some mysterious force, Yana watched as Clay bent over again.

"Don't," she whispered, frightened and excited as she watched and felt Clay raise her exposed breast.

For a second, with his lips close to the moist, brown peak of Yana's breast, their gazes met and held. Clay gave Yana a half smile. Then Yana watched the naughty and erotic sight of Clay's tongue circling her nipple briefly before he opened his lips enough to take her breast into his mouth.

"Oh, God!" Yana gasped.

Her legs shook, and for a moment Yana wasn't sure she could remain standing. She pulled her hands free from Clay's grasp. Her arms slipped around his head as she hugged his face to her bosom, pulling him in tighter as she leaned toward him. Her body was hungry for the pleasures that this dangerously erotic man could force upon her.

She felt a hand sliding up the back of her thigh. Strong fingers spread across her bottom, cupping her, squeezing her. Yana's long ebony hair trailed over her shoulders. When she looked at Clay again, she saw tendrils of her satiny hair against his cheek as he, with an artist's touch, used his lips on her breast.

"I must have you," Clay said, the words coming out slowly, as though it were a strain to force them from his throat.

He stood upright, his hands sliding around Yana's waist. He pulled her roughly against the solid length of his body, looking down at her with eyes that shone with a need that was at once both tender and wild.

Yana looked up at him, placing her hands lightly against his chest. This chance encounter had gone too far. *Way* too far. What had happened to her resolve to stay away from men? She hardly knew Clay McKenna at all, the self-protective part of her mind insisted.

As though choreographed in advance, both Clay and Yana looked to the big bed that awaited them just fifteen feet away. For long, silent seconds, they just stared at it, one of them knowing what pleasures would be theirs on that bed, one of them wondering if the sensations could get even better.

When their gazes met once again, Yana's eyes were filled with fear.

"Don't be afraid," Clay said soothingly. He brushed the backs of his fingers against her cheek. "You are beautiful. Making love will be beautiful. It'll be magnificent. It'll be . . . precious."

There were a thousand things that Yana wanted to tell Clay. She wanted to say that she was a virgin and that she had never once thought she would ever be anything but. She wanted to tell Clay that she was scared and that, more than anything else in the world, she hated looking to a man for support when she was frightened. Yana wanted to tell Clay that he should leave her room that instant, because he was the one responsible for making her think and feel the way she now did.

But Yana could find no words to say to Clay. She glanced at the bed, knowing that the mysteries that had tormented her troubled sleep in the past would come unraveled there, in Clay's arms, under his sweet, sensual, expert lovemaking.

"Clay . . . I'm scared," Yana finally said. She felt defeated somehow, though she had no idea why she felt that way.

"There's no reason to be scared," Clay said. His hands tightened around Yana's trim waist. He pulled her to him again, towering over her, looking down into her eyes. "Trust me, Yana. I will make this beautiful . . . so beautiful for you . . . for us."

Yana had always kept her sensitive emotions in check. She was afraid of anything tender, because tenderness represented closeness, and such emotions had somehow made her responsible for her own mother's death and her father's unhappiness. But looking up into Clay's dark, unfathomable eyes, she felt that for once she could allow herself to be under a man's control, even if that control were only temporary. Clay understood the mysteries that tormented Yana's fitful sleep. He could show her everything she needed to know, everything she needed to feel.

The word *yes* had just formed in Yana's mind when there was a knock on the door leading to her father's adjoining bedroom.

Yana's eyes burst open wide. Clay's hand came up with catlike swiftness, the palm clamping tightly over her mouth. Clay stepped into Yana, flattening her against the wall, his body pressing firmly against her, trapping her. His ebony eyes were fierce, and in one blinding instant she was quite certain that Clay McKenna was a man who had known violence personally.

"Yana, are you in there?" Nico called through the door.

Yana's heart was pounding, thudding against her ribs. She looked into Clay's eyes and knew—knew with absolute, frightening certainty—that he had used violence against others before.

She pleaded with her eyes, silently telling Clay that she wouldn't warn her father he was in the room with her. She, as much as Clay, did not want Nico to know what had been happening. The shame that Nico would feel, Yana was sure, would be even greater than her own.

"Yana, are you all right in there?" Nico asked, louder than before.

Clay took his hand away from Yana's mouth. She moaned softly, fear and the knowledge of what she had allowed to happen overwhelming her.

"Yes, *Mbambaky*," Yana said finally, her voice trembling. "I'm . . . not decent." The truth to her words burned little holes in Yana's heart. "I'll come to your room just as soon as I get dressed."

Clay stepped away from Yana. He looked at her, but the smile that was on his lips never quite reached his eyes.

"Good. Thank you," he said in a whisper.

Yana turned her back to Clay, suddenly self-conscious of her apparel. She adjusted her bodice, then strode quickly to the bed to retrieve her dress,

47

which she held modestly in front of her.

"Get out of here," Yana said, hissing the words through clenched teeth. Her eyes showed the confusion and betrayal she felt. But the betrayal had come from her own body, from her own dormant needs that had been brought to the surface by Clay McKenna.

"No need to get angry," Clay said, taking a step closer to Yana. "It wasn't my fault your father interrupted us."

"Get out, you arrogant bastard!"

Clay's eyes narrowed. It was the wrong epithet to use on him. His mother, half-Indian and half-Caucasian, had been born out of wedlock. Clay had heard the stories of how she had been treated by her Kiowan tribe and by the white community.

"I'm a lot of bad things in this world, Yana, but a bastard isn't one of them." Clay was choosing his words all wrong, but anger was making his brain function erratically. "From now on, when you insult me—as I'm sure you will—please keep your insults directed at *me*, not at my family. Understand?"

"Just get the hell out of here," Yana said, her voice just slightly softer now. "Leave before I call my father."

Clay was out of the room a second later. He moved, Yana saw, with a fluid grace and absolute silence that she hadn't noticed at first. He moved like a predatory animal, a nightcat that stalks his prey in deadly silence, keeping in the shadows, seeming to appear and disappear at will.

48

Alone in her room, Yana stretched out on the bed, facedown, cradling her head in her arms. Her whole body trembled softly from the aftershocks of Clay's passionately thrilling, yet thoroughly frightening caresses. He had made her body come to life. He had touched her, kissed her, as no man ever had.

I must never be alone with him again, Yana promised herself. *He can destroy me.*

Chapter 3

Clay was in a foul mood the following morning, though he was determined to keep his emotions hidden. He had spent the night lying flat on his back on the big hotel bed, left forearm over his forehead, his eyes staring sightlessly at the ceiling.

He hadn't been able to get Yana out of his mind. The notion of finding a substitute to douse the fire that Yana had started inside him came to mind often but was always discarded quickly. Clay McKenna, out of principle and not moral conviction, refused to purchase his female companionship. He'd never found it necessary. Besides, what woman could he possibly find in a bordello that would compare to Yana?

He thought, too, of drinking enough bourbon to smooth out the sharp edges of his need. It was his duty, his familial obligation to keep Nico safe from harm, that prevented him from seeking the temporary solace of liquor. Now was not the time to let his senses become dulled.

The night had been long, with nothing and no one to keep Clay's thoughts from lingering on those brief, breathless moments when he had held Yana in his arms, felt her body pressing warm and soft against his own, tasted the subtle sweetness of her full-lipped mouth.

"Good morning!" Nico said enthusiastically, his smile open and unaffected, seeming to brighten the entryway of the hotel. "Did you sleep well, Clay?"

"Yes," he said, forcing energy into his reply. He fought to keep his eyes on Nico so he could prevent them from straying to Yana, who stood at her father's side. "And you?"

"Me?" Nico patted his stomach. "I slept like a king! I feel good things ahead for us. Our families will both become greater with this venture." Nico turned toward Yana, touching her forearm lightly. "And you feel that way too, don't you?"

Only Clay could hear the undercurrent of turmoil in Yana's tone when she replied, "Yes, Papa."

Breakfast was at a nearby restaurant, though Clay had suggested room service would be safer. Nico, anxious to see as much of New York as he could during his brief stay in the city, could not be refused.

The silence between Yana and Clay was filled by Nico's insistent chatter. He drew Clay into conversation by asking questions. Clay's answers were polite but minimal, without detail.

"Where is the coachman?" Nico asked when Clay

ordered the carriage.

"We won't be needing him today," Clay said. "I thought you might appreciate the privacy as we make our stops."

It was half truth, half falsehood. Clay didn't trust the hired coachman. With Yana, he already had one more person than expected that he had to keep an eye on.

Nico stepped into the carriage, whistling softly, leaving Clay and Yana outside. For the first time that morning, Clay looked directly at Yana. When he did, his heart skipped a beat. She was stumming in a green dress of lightweight fabric, which molded tightly to her contours from the hips upward. The billowing skirt hid her legs, but Clay's mind filled in what his eyes could not see. She went, in Greek fashion, without a bonnet. Her luxurious mass of dark, wavy hair was held away from her face with gold combs inlaid with emeralds to match the color of the dress.

"Good morning," he said finally, feeling as foolish as an adolescent and as guilty as a sybarite.

Yana's night had been as sleepless as Clay's, as troubled with doubts and dreams and unfulfilled wishes. The anger she had managed to hold vanished when Clay gave her a half smile, his ebony eyes changing from distant to impish.

"Good morning," she replied and, after a moment, added with as much sweet malice as she could muster, *"Mister* McKenna."

Undaunted, Clay extended his hand to assist Yana

53

into the carriage. When Yana placed her hand in his, Clay squeezed and whispered, "At least you didn't snap your fingers."

Yana's eyes widened, and had Nico not been there to hear her, she would have told Clay exactly what she thought of his attitude.

The door closed behind Yana and she sat down opposite Nico, reminding herself once again that she must never allow herself to be alone with Clay. The temptation of pleasure was too great, the final cost of that temptation too dear.

"I do wish you wouldn't be so rude to Clay," Nico scolded mildly as the carriage started in motion. "He's only trying to be helpful."

"I wasn't rude," Yana said, putting on her most innocent, wide-eyed expression for her father. "I've scarcely said five words to him this morning."

"That's what I'm talking about. Would it be so bad to give him a smile, Yana? To show him a little kindness? He only wants to make us happy, that's all."

That's what you think, Papa. You don't know Clayton McKenna like I do. He wants much more than just a smile from me. If you knew Clay like I do, you'd know he is not a man who is easily satisfied . . . and never until he's taken everything.

After a lengthy silence, Yana said, "Papa, must I go to the banks with you today? I would much rather see New York."

Yana couldn't believe her luck when Nico gave his consent. Not even in Pirias was she allowed to go out

54

without an escort! And here she was in New York, with the whole city to explore on her own!

The rest of the trip to the first bank, Yana chatted happily with her father, smiling often, doing the things she knew made him happy, all the while expecting him to come to his senses and tell her that roaming New York on her own was too foolish to even consider.

The carriage came to a halt. Yana braced herself, knowing Clay would object to her going off alone. Could Clay change Nico's mind? Would he try?

The incredulous look on Clay's face spoke volumes, but his words came out precise and controlled. "Sir, you can't really be serious about this."

"But I am, Clay. And what's this *sir* for? I thought we were to be friends."

"We are, and that's why I must insist we all stay together. Clay's gaze stole over to Yana, staying with her longer than he wanted. "Nico, with all due respect, your daughter does not know this city. She doesn't know this country. A lot of bad things can happen. Please reconsider your decision."

Nico nodded his head, his expression grave. "I know all of these things, Clay. That is why you must go with Illyana. Stay with her. Never let her out of your sight. That way I will know that she will be safe. She will always be safe with you."

A flashing moment of egotism made Clay wonder if Yana had put Nico up to this. One look at Yana, though, told Clay she wasn't any happier about this development than he was.

55

Yana wheeled on her father, her eyes dark and angry. "Papa, when I said I wanted to see New York, I meant that I wanted to see it *alone.*"

Nico's heavy brows pushed together. "Alone, Yana? Here? In a strange country? You make fun of your poor old papa by saying such things. What kind of father would let his daughter do such a thing?"

Clay cleared his throat to get Nico's attention. "You needn't worry about your conversations with the bankers. Your privacy will be maintaned. I won't even be in the offices with you."

Nico looked at Clay and shook his head minutely. "I leave her with you, Clay. Unless these bankers are violent men, I will be safe in their stuffy offices most of the day. I am safe; you have done your job. Go with Yana. She means everything to me. Guard her with your life."

Clay was caught between his father's orders and Nico's wishes. He nodded his head, then tipped his hat back. Casting a slow look at Yana, he smiled coolly before his attention went back to Nico.

"This is the Morgan Bank. From here, the Merchants' Bank is just down the street," Clay said. "And the First Port Bank is across the street from that. Those were the three banks you wanted to see."

Yana looked out the carriage window, a grim smile turning up the corners of her mouth. She was not entirely displeased with the events of the morning. It bothered her that she now had Clay with her at all

56

times. He had shaken her to the soul with his sensual kisses. The responses he had drawn from her frighteningly receptive body still tormented her thoughts. He could make her feel and act in ways she never thought possible.

But now she had Clay McKenna exactly where she wanted him. He was her servant, and from a very early age Yana had learned how to handle servants who cast longing looks in her direction. It wasn't necessary for Yana to have her father dismiss the butler's son or the stable boy when he looked covetously at her. All Yana had to do was teach the imprudent wretch his proper place in her world, and that was the last trouble she would ever have with him.

With Clay McKenna, it might be a bit more difficult, Yana conceded. Clay certainly wasn't a stable boy. But he was a man—essentially, just a man—and Yana knew how to deal with men.

Yes, thought Yana with a smile. It will be grand fun to teach Clay his proper place in her world. By Yana's calculations, that place was two or three steps behind her and a little to the left. Close enough to attend to her every whim without being underfoot.

"Thank you," Yana said sweetly, placing her gloved hand into Clay's as she descended the steps of the ornate carriage. "Now that we're here, I won't be needing you anymore." Clay's eyes narrowed on Yana, but she just smiled back. "What I mean, of course, is that I won't be needing you right at my side. You understand, I'm sure."

Clay tried to keep his anger from showing. He said nothing. Yana's arched brows over condescending dark eyes rankled the sensibilities of a young man who had never spent a day in his life when he wasn't worth at least a million dollars.

The diamond district was abuzz with activity. Clay knew the area from experience; Yana had read about it.

"Please keep your distance," Yana instructed quietly, warming to the new role she had adopted for Clay.

"Distance, Yana?" Clay replied. He took a step closer to her. A pulse throbbed in her throat. Very huskily, he added, "Are you afraid someone will think we're together?"

For only a second, Yana's imperious expression changed to self-doubt. She took a step backward. Yana used Clay's arrogance, as well as his willingness to openly show her that he coveted her, to fuel her anger and regain her composure.

"Just keep your distance, Mr. McKenna." Then, before Clay could say another word, she turned her back on him and ducked into the nearest doorway.

The rings that Yana first inspected would dazzle even the practiced eye, but she refused to let her feelings show. She knew her business here, and displaying too much interest reduced one's bargaining position.

"It just doesn't seem quite right for me," Yana said in a blasé manner. She slipped the heavy marquise-cut diamond ring from her finger, placing it gently on the heavy black velvet cloth the jeweler had placed on the glass countertop. "Perhaps you have something in a necklace that might catch my eye."

The jeweler smiled politely, folding the ring inside the cloth, then tucking it into his jacket pocket to be returned to the safe later, after the promising customer had made her decision. Such jewels as the marquise-cut diamond ring were not left on display for just anyone to see.

He was certain he'd never seen the woman before. The jeweler would have remembered such a striking young female. There was something about her posture, about the way she carried her head, that signaled the jeweler she would accept nothing less than his finest baubles. However, the man who followed the woman—tall, silent, with dark eyes that took in the world at a glance and, apparently, didn't much care for what he saw—seemed somehow familiar. Perhaps the man had once been the bodyguard for another young ingenue.

"Very nice," Yana breathed, lifting the necklace out of the tray.

A single rectangular-cut jade stone was fixed to a heavy gold chain. The gold links were thick, too solidly cast to be worn by a delicately boned woman. For Yana, wide-shouldered and wide-hipped with a full bosom, the necklace seemed tailor-made. It would highlight both her femininity and her strength.

Turning toward the gilded mirror to her left, Yana held the necklace up. The green of her dress did not show off the color of the jade to its fullest, causing Yana to issue a small moue.

"For you, eight thousand," the jeweler said quietly. "There is not another stone like it in all the world. It is as unique as you are."

Clay grimaced. Yana was swallowing the old man's compliments with big greedy gulps. He started forward, intent on protecting his sheep from the avuncular wolf, when he checked himself.

Who am I to say she can't waste her father's money?

After a few second's perusal, Yana gave her shoulders a little shrug, then let the necklace dangle from a thin finger in the jeweler's direction. She now looked impossibly bored.

"I think not," Yana breathed, waiting for the old man to retrieve the necklace from her outstretched finger. She was also listening carefully for a second, lower price.

"I think so," Clay answered from nowhere, plucking the necklace from midair.

The jeweler barely suppressed his smile.

Yana's heart was thudding against her ribs. She looked at Clay's reflection in the mirror. He seemed to tower over her as, with careful deliberation so as to not touch her, he opened the chain, holding it by the ends.

"It is beautiful," Clay said, his ebony eyes looking into Yana's in the mirror. "But you knew that right away, didn't you? You've got a taste for the finer things in life. So do I, Yana . . . so do I."

Clay's hands slipped beneath Yana's heavy fall of

hair at the back of her neck. He worked the clasp of the heavy gold links with deft fingers, his eyes never leaving Yana's, the half smile on his lips reminding her of the pleasures she had found in his embrace.

"Look at it, Yana. See what it does for you."

Yana's eyes went down to the massive jade stone. It had twisted so the gold back was toward the mirror, the stone hidden, resting directly in the tight cleavage of her bodice.

And then, into view, came Clay's hand, long-fingered and infinitely capable of stealing away a woman's better judgment, dark by heredity, darkened more by the sun, impeccably manicured . . . and moving toward her breasts.

Yana's heart stopped beating. Unconsciously, she inhaled deeply and held her breath, causing her breasts to strain against the lace trim of her décolletage. Crazy thoughts ricocheted through her mind.

He's going to touch me! He's going to touch me with that silly old jeweler standing right there!

Yana did not want Clay to touch her. At least she did not want to *want* Clay to touch her. She did not, however, do anything to prevent his hand from moving toward her.

But Clay's fingers touched only the stone as he gently turned the face of the gem outward. He never said a word. He set the jewel back against its inviting resting place.

Yana exhaled. No matter how condescending she wanted to be toward Clay, she could not deny the feelings he inspired.

"Look, Yana," he whispered, his voice low and intimate. He cast a sidelong glance at the jeweler, who made a silent exit. He placed his hands lightly on Yana's shoulders, leaning forward so that his face was nearly level with hers. "See how beautiful it is . . . there . . . against you, touching you. One beautiful jewel enhancing the beauty of another."

Was he mocking her?

Yana could feel his eyes on her breasts. The gem seemed to have been heated by Clay's fingers, warming her flesh. She closed her eyes briefly, fighting to maintain control of her rioting senses.

The tip of her tongue played over her lips, moistening them. She swallowed, then said in a hoarse whisper, "I do not want it."

"Yes you do, Yana. Not only do you want it, but you need it. You may not *want* to need it, Yana, but you do."

Yana was not sure exactly what Clay was talking about. She wished she could block his words out of her mind so she could think clearly.

Clay's breath was warm against her cheek, fluffing tendrils of her rich auburn hair as he spoke. All Yana had to do was turn her face toward him and the invitation to be kissed would be there. That's all she had to do to once again taste the delicious, illicit pleasures that Clay had taught her, in one chance meeting, to crave.

"No," Yana said. Then, with more conviction, "No! Please take it off. I want to leave now."

"You're making a mistake," Clay said, a smile playing on his lips and the corners of his eyes. He slipped his hands beneath Yana's hair to unlock the clasp. This time, though, his fingertips grazed lightly against her silky flesh.

As soon as Yana heard the snick of the clasp unlocking, she twisted away from Clay and the mirror. *How does he work his magic on me?* she wondered.

A kind of vague terror gripped her. She could think of nothing more than to run away from Clay and the United States, going back to Pirias where Scirocco waited for her, back to the land where everyone knew her name and the young men were all diffident and so easily controlled by nothing more than a stern look.

Yana headed for the door without a backward look, intent on putting distance—as much distance as possible, and her father's orders be damned—between herself and Clay.

Clay grabbed her elbow as she marched with long strides down the sidewalk. "Wait a second," he said, pulling Yana around. "Don't be in such a hurry."

Yana looked up at Clay and realized once again that it was her fault her father had lived a long, lonely life.

"Listen, I want you to stand right here," Clay said. His eyes held questions, but the smile was still playing with his mouth. "Just for a moment, okay? And for once in your life, please stay out of trouble."

Yana just looked at Clay, saying nothing, mentally cursing herself.

"I'll be right back. Don't go anywhere."

As soon as Clay gave his name to the jeweler, a line of credit was established. Clay's father had done business with the jeweler before, buying gems for Shadow. If the son wanted to carry on a similar tradition, the jeweler was only too happy to oblige.

With the jade necklace clutched in his hand, Clay left the jeweler, stepping onto the boardwalk just in time to see Yana pausing to look backward during her escape. For a second, over the three blocks that separated them, their eyes met. Not even the distance could hide the fear Yana felt.

"Damn her," Clay muttered, starting out at a brisk walk in Yana's direction.

Yana ran around the corner. At a dead run, Clay took off after her, praying silently to Kiowan and Christian gods that he wouldn't lose her.

Nico felt young again, sitting in the smoke-filled tavern, waiting. Nico had always been a deal-maker first, a shipbuilder second. He loved trying to understand how people think and then making money from that understanding. But it had been many years since he'd involved himself directly in the dark aspects of running a company such as the Zacarious Shipping Company.

Antoli Pacca arrived a few minutes late. He sat down opposite Nico in the booth. The men nodded their heads in greeting but did not shake hands. They drew little attention from other patrons, who were primarily seamen more concerned with their drink than any strangers.

"The trip went well?" Antoli asked, folding his arms on the table.

"Passably well. Yana was not pleased with the duration, but she is bored quickly."

"Perhaps in time that will change," Antoli said, doubting his own words.

The bartender shouted to Antoli that if he wanted a drink, he had to come to the bar to get it himself.

"I must get something," Antoli whispered, the Greek words tasting good on his tongue after spending a month speaking English. His distaste for the English language and the American people was evident in his tone. "Here it is always necessary to buy. It is not enough to talk."

When Antoli returned, Nico pushed him for the information. He wasn't sure how much time he had alone, without his daughter or Clay McKenna interfering in his business plans.

"Sorren McKenna is much more powerful than we first thought," Antoli began. He took a sip of the rye, grimaced, thought how much he would enjoy an ouzo, then continued. "I have found that McKenna owns much more than he let us believe. He has companies owning companies and owns other companies. His wife oversees many of these."

Nico raised his eyebrows. "He lets a woman run his business? Hmmm. Shadow, yes. Odd name. Some sort of Indian, correct?"

Antoli nodded. "It's not easy to follow what

65

McKenna's been doing or where he got all his money. His western holdings were born rich, so he must have been paid handsomely for his government work. Since then, he's made some good business acquisitions and profited from them greatly. But the original source of his money is unclear. He still seems to have some connection with the government . . . or illegals. It's hard to tell which."

"The illegals and the government are often one in the same," Nico said softly.

Nico sat back in the booth, his expression impassive. It did not particularly bother him that Sorren McKenna's past was murky and possibly illegal. He had done business with men he had not trusted in the past. But it was always best to at least have a clear vision of the character of the man one did business with.

"Financially, he is in good standing. He's worth more than his expenses. Much more."

"His word? His honor?"

"He's got his enemies. No doubt about that. But his word seems good. And no one I spoke to said anything against his honor."

"Children?"

"Three in private schools. Except for the oldest, Clayton. He's part of the family business."

Nico digested the information. Antoli hadn't learned much more than Nico already knew, but he was glad nevertheless that he'd sent his aide to the States a month early. Nico Zacarious had not become a rich man by blindly trusting those he went into partnerships with.

"What do you know about Clay . . . Clayton?"

Antoli shrugged his shoulders. "I didn't ask many questions about the boy."

Nico smiled to himself. Clay was older than Antoli. He couldn't imagine anyone knowing Clay and still calling him a boy.

"He is a ladies' man," Antoli continued. "Much sought after. But that is to be expected, I suppose. He is unmarried and rich. Women find that an attractive combination."

Clay's personal fortune did not dissuade women from wanting to share their lives with him, Nico knew. But to dismiss his charm with the ladies as merely a side effect of his personal wealth was an easy but inaccurate assessment.

"Go south," Nico said when Antoli had relayed everything he had learned. "See what you can find out there. Be especially careful. The closer to McKenna's home you go, the more dangerous it is."

"Do you think he suspects anything?" Antoli inquired.

Nico's eyes took on a brilliant hue. The blood in his veins seemed fresh and new, invigorated by his actions. "Sorren McKenna would be a fool not to suspect. Sorren McKenna is not a fool, therefore he suspects. It is up to us to keep his suspicions just suspicions and nothing more. Eh, Antoli?"

"Yes, Nico Zacarious," Antoli said formally, knowing his place on the social structure. "You may sleep well. I will do everything you ask."

67

Antoli left the same way he had arrived, without a word. Nico Zacarious leaned back in the booth, letting his mind drift to Sorren McKenna. And there was Clay to think about. He had suspected the young man had an eye for the fairer sex. Would Clay's eye drift in Illyana's direction?

Clay was trying to control his panic. He felt it growing inside him, deep in his soul, in the marrow of his bones. It was a feeling he had to fight whenever he was not in command of a situation.

Yana was an unknown to him. She was, in many respects, his adversary. But unlike his other adversaries, he knew virtually nothing at all about how Illyana thought. Was this a game she intended to win or lose? Where would she run to? She didn't know New York. At least that's the impression she had given. But Yana had already surprised Clay once today; he dared not make any more assumptions.

If cornered, by Clay or anyone else, what would she do?

Now, as Clay zigzagged through the crowd, searching for a dark-haired woman in green, he doubted everything that he thought he knew about Illyana Zacarious.

He had closed the distance to less than thirty yards when Clay saw a flash of green disappearing around a brownstone building. Breaking once again into a full sprint, his long legs ate up the distance. But when he rounded the corner, fully intent on shaking

Yana until her teeth rattled, she was nowhere to be seen.

"Hey, did you see a young woman in green a second ago?" Clay asked a boy in his teens who was pushing a cart laden with bolts of cloth.

The boy shrugged his shoulders, his eyes saying that for a price his memory might improve. Clay grit his teeth, understanding the teenager's assessment—that by Clay's clothes, he was a man of wealth—and dug into his pocket. He produced a five-dollar bill, the equivalent of more than a week's pay.

"Where?" Clay demanded, holding the bill out to the boy. The boy reached for the money, but it was moved away before he could get it. "Answers first."

A scrawny arm was extended. "She went into the back of old man Fisher's shop."

"You'd better be telling the truth." Clay gave the boy the money, and a moment later he stepped into the back of what was commonly—and accurately—called a sweatshop.

Rows upon rows of men and women were huddled over sewing machines. The workers were mostly Caucasian, though there were some Orientals mixed in. The air had a strange odor to it, part perspiration, part fresh linen. Clay wrinkled his nose, his dark eyes searching for Yana.

The few people who looked up from their work cast worried looks in Clay's direction. From one woman Clay thought he saw understanding.

"Where is she?" he asked, quietly and with menace, towering over the woman who continued to

69

sew frantically. "Where?"

The woman trembled violently with fear. Clay hated himself for frightening her so. He dug into his pocket for money to soothe his conscience, though he knew it wouldn't work completely.

"Hurry, damnit! Where did she go?"

For a moment, Clay thought the woman was going to cry. She tilted her face up slowly until her eyes met his. He knew what she thought of him—that he was another evil man chasing a frightened woman who wanted nothing more desperately than to be rid of a violent husband or lover. The seamstress was trapped, wanting to protect Yana from Clay, yet wanting to protect herself.

"She went out the alley door," the woman said in a quivering voice, heavy with an accent. "It leads to the alley in back."

Clay would have gladly given her more money, but there was no telling if he would have to bribe anyone else for information on Yana's whereabouts. He dropped fifty dollars on the sewing machine near the woman and was not yet out of the sweatshop when he heard her thanking him tearfully for his generosity.

What had started out as a reluctant twosome had turned into a cat and mouse game that Yana found rather amusing. She felt the childlike enthusiasm of being chased by someone. And what could be better than playing hide-and-seek with all of New York City as the playground?

Best of all, there wasn't anything Clay could do once he caught her. He didn't want to play this game, but he didn't have any choice.

Yana closed the door behind her, stepping into the alley.

It was, she realized instantly, a terrible mistake.

There were four of them. Three men in worn clothes and one man nicely dressed in a suit. The well-dressed man appeared to be buying something from the other three. When he look at Yana, a dark, violent scowl spread across his face.

"Grab her!" he said in a low, menacing voice, extending an arm, pointing a finger like the barrel of a revolver at Yana.

"But she ain't seen nothin'," one of the other three muttered.

He took a second look at Yana, his attention now centered on her beauty and vulnerability rather than the money he was about to receive. He spit a brown stream of tobacco juice into the dirty alley and nodded his head. This was his favorite kind of entertainment.

"Do as I tell you," the rich man said, his eyes never leaving Yana.

The three unkempt men fanned out, spreading themselves across the breadth of the alleyway, blocking any escape. Yana had seen men like them before. On the dockyards in Pirias, such men were common, but Yana's social standing had kept her isolated from them.

Yana turned toward the door through which she'd

71

entered the alley. To her dismay, there wasn't a knob. She wheeled around and the three men had moved closer now, advancing slowly.

Their approach was unhurried, cautious, their movements warning Yana that they'd done this kind of thing before. No matter how helpless she looked, they weren't going to take needless chances.

"Stay away from me," Yana whispered, wishing her tone sounded more forceful than it did.

It was a dead-end alley. The only escape for Yana was to get past the three men advancing on her, then past the one rich man who remained further back, waiting.

"Please . . ." Yana said, hating the sound of her voice, feeling a cold, forbidding sense of doom flooding over her, insinuating itself into her senses. "Somebody will hear."

The leader of the three grinned crookedly, revealing missing and yellowed teeth. He spit a stream of juice to the ground again, very nearly hitting the toe of Yana's slipper.

"Ain't nobody gonna hear nothin'," he said. "An' if they do hear somethin', people around here know enough to mind their own business. People who stick their noses in other people's business got a way of gettin' their nose cut off."

As though to emphasize the point, the man reached behind his back and produced a stiletto-bladed knife. He spit again.

Their collective smell hit Yana like a wave. She felt nausea well up inside her. Taking small steps backward, retreating at the same speed the three men advanced, she searched her mind frantically for some plan, some route of escape, some clever lie to tell.

"I didn't see anything," Yana said, her tone quivering more now. She took another step backward and felt the cold brownstone wall against her shoulders. She could retreat no further. "Please don't hurt me."

The three men were grinning now. Their eyes, bloodshot and filled with lust, seemed to tear at Yana's dress, ripping it from her body.

From behind the outlaws, the well-dressed man said in a low, almost casual tone, "I want her first. Then you can do with her whatever you wish."

Yana thought she was going to be sick.

Suddenly, the alleyway door burst open, swinging wide to bang against the side of the building. Yana moved to her right, her back still against the wall, and saw Clay leap into view. He crouched at the waist, his dark eyes like those of a nightcat, fiercely bright, dangerous-looking.

"Clay!" Yana shouted. "Look out!"

What happened next went so quickly that Yana was hardly aware of what Clay had done. The tobacco-spitter made a move for her, apparently intent on grabbing her, perhaps wanting to use her as a hostage. He hadn't touched Yana yet before pistol shots echoed through the alley. Two shots, the second coming so quickly after the first they almost sounded as one.

The man was thrown against the brownstone wall

beside Yana, his eyes wide, fear gagging in his throat. He slumped to the ground, still leaning against the wall, the stiletto knife still in his hand as he died.

A second man was reaching into his jacket pocket when Clay's revolver roared again and spit out vengeance. The outlaw did a violent pirouette, clutching his shattered elbow.

The well-dressed man was running for the open end of the alley like death was snapping at his heels.

"Choose your next move carefully," Clay said quietly, his voice as steady as the Colt that was pointed squarely at the chest of the third outlaw. "Your life depends on your next move."

The man was white-faced with fear. "L—let me take him with me," the unharmed outlaw sobbed in a squeaky voice.

Yana was transfixed by what she had just seen. In her sheltered life, she had never seen a man shot to death. The men who had been about to attack her, she realized, were the lowest form of humanity, capable of unspeakable violence and cruelty. But equally true was that Clay's skillful use of violence had saved her.

"Don't kill him," Yana whispered to Clay.

"See! Please, mister, she don't want you to shoot me. We didn't mean no harm. We were just funnin' your lady. Honest, mister, we wasn't gonna do nothin'."

"You are a liar," Clay replied slowly. He raised his revolver, sighting over the barrel, aiming at the man's face. "But I will allow you to live . . . for now. Take your friend and get out of here. Leave this city.

And believe me as you have never believed anyone in your life. . . . If I ever see you again, I'll kill you. Do you understand me?"

The trembling man looked to his left, past Yana, to the corpse in the alley.

"Mister, you let me and Petey go an' you ain't never gonna set eyes on us again. I promise you that."

As soon as the two men left, Clay rushed to Yana. He continued to hold the revolver in his right hand. With his left, he cupped Yana's chin in his palm, forcing her face up to his.

"Are you all right? Did they hurt you?"

Yana looked into his eyes. She saw honest sympathy and concern, and it warmed her heart. With Clay at her side, she was safe. She began to tremble uncontrollably, and he held her close.

Tears of relief glistened on her lashes. "They would have . . ." Her words got choked off with emotion. "Thank you. Thank you."

Awkwardly, as they began to respond to each other, they gently pushed themselves apart.

"We've got to get out of here," Clay hissed, his tenderness vanishing. When he grabbed her hand, he crushed it inside his fist. "Congratulations, Miss Zacarious. You've been in the city less than one day and already one man is dead and another maimed for life."

Chapter 4

"I'm sorry," Yana said as Clay helped her up into the carriage.

"I don't want to hear it."

Yana sat and looked out the carriage door at Clay. His eyes were hidden in the shadow under his hat brim, but she felt him staring through her to a place far away. She wanted Clay close beside her, close enough so that she could feed off the strength that emanated from him, becoming stronger herself because of his proximity.

"I'm sorry," Yana said again in a feathery whisper. "I didn't mean for anyone to get hurt."

The look on Clay's once-handsome face was impassive, and Yana knew now why strong and brave men could become frightened by a look from him. He looked at Yana as though she weren't even there. Then, slowly, his mouth turned downward at the corners. He shrugged his broad shoulders.

"I wouldn't worry about those men," he said. "Maybe you've kept someone else from getting hurt. Those men were criminals."

Clay was about to close the door when Yana's hand flashed out, stopping him.

"Don't leave me alone." The words shot from Yana's mouth without her really thinking about them. "I don't want to be alone."

Clay studied Yana for a moment with eyes that held no expression. "You won't be alone. I'll be right outside. Somebody has to drive the carriage."

"Can't we just sit here?"

"There is a dead man in an alley a couple of blocks from here. He's got my bullets in him." His eyes took on a quiet cruelty. "Doesn't it make sense that we put some distance between us and the carnage?"

Clay's sarcasm tore at Yana's soul. She turned her face away, not wanting Clay to see the tears she was afraid would soon spill.

"Please, Clay . . . don't make me ask again. I'm scared . . . and I don't want to be alone. More than anything else in the world, I hate feeling alone."

The silence between them lasted only a few seconds. But for Yana, the time it took for Clay to respond was a torturous eternity.

"Stay here. If you leave this carriage, I swear to God I'll throw you to the wolves." His tone softened slightly. "I'll be back as soon as I can."

The carriage door closed. Yana, still with her face turned away, finally opened her eyes. Fresh memories of what had happened in the alley—and thoughts of what *would* have happened if Clay hadn't found her—came flooding back. She wiped away tears of fear and frustration, and waited. She waited for Clay to return, because in a deep part of her mind she knew he wouldn't abandon her and let anything evil touch her.

When the carriage door finally opened again, Clay gave Yana a half smile. He sat down beside her.

"I hired a man," he explained coldly. "We've got an hour or two before you'll see your father. I suggest you take the time to collect yourself."

Yana looked away from Clay. There wasn't any sympathy in his dark, brooding eyes. She realized that it was her act of foolishness—running away from Clay when he'd gone back inside the jeweler's— that had caused this problem. Nevertheless, she couldn't help but think that a gentleman would show her at least some semblance of kindness in her moment of need. Certainly, no matter *what* she did in Greece, her suitors there would have been more than happy to do whatever was necessary to comfort her.

Clay wasn't like them though. He didn't care about what she wanted. Clay McKenna didn't care if she was scared or felt lost.

Yana's mind took an abrupt swing. She hadn't really been responsible for those men in the alley getting hurt, she decided. Clay had been the one to shoot them, and from what she knew about those unwashed thugs, they more than deserved the punishment they'd gotten.

"What are you afraid of?" Yana asked, her tone

79

displaying her sense of hurt at Clay's callousness. The sarcasm was thick, laced with petulant cruelty. "Afraid my father will find out you were negligent in your duties?"

"How in hell was I supposed to know you'd run like a rabbit?" Clay found it difficult to control his ire when he was close to Yana, when his eyes could caress her face, when he could smell the freshness of her body that he once held close against his own. Quietly, he asked, "What were you trying to do, anyway?"

"Get away from you."

"Why?"

What could Yana say? That she needed to put distance between herself and him because every time he was near she felt all crazy inside? Could she tell Clayton McKenna that he alone had, with what seemed like effortless skill, sparked the dormant feminine desires Yana had kept hidden and protected, even from herself? Could she tell him that every time she closed her eyes she still saw his chiseled features, still felt the passion in his eyes? Could she say that she could still feel his caresses on her body, could still feel the sweet sensations of being touched tenderly?

"Well?" Clay prodded.

"Can we change the subject?" Yana stared out the window as the carriage rattled down the cobblestone street. She suspected the coachman was simply going in circles around the same group of brownstone buildings.

"I can't make you talk," Clay said. "However, I

might be able to bribe you."

The notion that Clay presumed he could bribe her infuriated Yana, and she twisted around sharply in the carriage to face him.

"What do you—?"

Yana's words were cut off abruptly by what she saw. Clay held the gold and jade necklace in his hands. The smile on his face made Yana melt inside.

"I bought this for you," he said, his tone not only softer than it had been before, but warmer, too. "It looks perfect on you. With another woman, it just wouldn't look right."

"Why?" Yana asked. Her suspicions ran high with Clay McKenna. She didn't trust him, and she certainly didn't trust herself when she was with him.

"Call it a peace offering."

Yana almost asked if a peace offering had something to do with an Indian custom that she knew nothing about. However angry she was with Clay, though, she didn't want to offend his heritage or show her ignorance of it.

"Please, you must accept this," Clay continued, his voice like a warm blanket that surrounded Yana. "I want you to have it."

"No." Yana looked straight into Clay's eyes and, with honest anger, said, "I can buy my own jewels, Mr. McKenna. I don't need your handouts."

Clay was taken slightly aback by Yana's anger, but not for long. When he was determined to have his way, Yana noted, he could be a very persistent man.

"Who else could wear such a necklace?" Clay

asked rhetorically.

Yana didn't know what to say to Clay or what to think of him. One minute he was furious with her, and the next he was giving her extravagant gifts. In one sentence he let her know that, to him, she was a selfish child. In the next, with words and actions, he made her feel like a woman.

"Why?" Yana repeated, her eyes roaming over Clay's face. She was flattered and impressed by the extravagance, but wary.

"Because."

"The things I said to you . . ." she began.

Clay's dark eyes became smoky with recent memories. "Not everything we said to each other has been so bad." Clay moved closer to Yana, holding the necklace by the ends of the heavy gold links. "Let me put it on for you."

Yana was mesmerized by the eyes that looked straight and unflinchingly into her own. So many things—some exciting, sensual, and enticing, some violent and horrifying—had exploded into her life from the very moment she had first set eyes on Clay McKenna.

Very slowly, Yana turned her back to Clay. She dipped her head down at the same time she lifted the thick, heavy spray of hair away from her neck and shoulders. Yana closed her eyes, waiting . . . wondering . . . sensing she was on the threshold of something splendid and new, something that would touch her heart in a way she would always remember.

"The jeweler had you in his heart when he made

this necklace." Clay's voice blotted out all other sounds, though he spoke barely above a whisper. "He hadn't met you, of course. But still . . . when he created this necklace, he had to know in his truest heart that it should only be worn by one woman." Yana felt the weight of the jade touch her bosom, then heard the snick of the clasp being secured. "One very special . . . one unique . . . very, very sensual woman . . ."

Yana wanted this moment to last forever. Clay's words were intimate, arousing. When he released the necklace, his hands spread out over her shoulders, heating her skin, making the surface of her body as warm as his words had made her inner being.

"You've been fighting me since we met," Clay continued, his cheek nearly touching Yana's, his lips close to her ear. "Did you ever wonder why that is? Is it because I make you angry? Or is it because I inspire other feelings in you, Yana?" Clay's hands moved down from Yana's shoulders to her upper arms. He pulled her toward him, just enough so that her back was against his chest. "Be honest with yourself. Listen to what your body is telling you. Can't you hear it whispering to you? Can't you feel what it's trying to tell you?"

Yana could hear what her body was telling her, all right. But her body was no friend. Her body had quite mysteriously become an ally of Clay's, and together they were working to destroy her, to tear down her resistance.

"The necklace . . . is just a symbol . . . of a new

beginning," Clay said in that deep, resonant voice. His left hand moved slowly up Yana's arm, over her shoulder and neck, to push her hair away from the nape. "A new beginning for you"—his breath was warm against Yana's neck, the heat transmitting itself throughout her system—"and me." He kissed Yana's perfumed neck softly, swiftly, his lips teasing more than satisfying. "It's a new beginning for us, Yana . . . sweet Yana . . . precious Yana."

There was enough logic left in Yana, enough barriers around her heart, for her to believe that Clay was only telling her the words he knew she wanted to hear. He had, no doubt, rehearsed and refined the words over many years and with many women. His words could not be trusted.

The things Clay McKenna said, however honeyed, were nothing more than traps and snares that would entangle her. Words were the lures he set to capture unwary women.

Clay pushed himself a little away from Yana. Passion had not made him so delirious with want that he did not know what he was doing or was unaware of the ramifications of his actions. No, indeed. Clay knew all too well that Yana was forbidden fruit—the kind he enjoyed the most. But she was also—and this is what ate at him—his *responsibility*. Clay had given his word to Nico that he would defend Yana with his life.

But who would defend her from him?

With her shoulders still twisted around so that her back was to him, Clay sensed that he had a slight advantage. When he looked into Yana's eyes, big pieces of his resolve seemed to fall away from the carefree yet rock-solid facade he showed the world.

With a smooth tug on the silken cords, he dropped the curtains over the windows of the carriage.

Clay felt Yana shudder softly. He knew that she was not unaffected by his caresses. He knew, too, that he was violating his own personal code of conduct by wanting Yana so badly. And perhaps Clay would have found the inner strength to push himself away from Yana had she not turned just then to look over her shoulder at him.

"Those men . . . they frightened me so," she said, but Clay knew when he looked deep into her brown eyes that the hoodlums in the alley were not on her mind.

Clay placed his palm softly against Yana's cheek, gazing into her eyes, drawing her to him, trying desperately to tell himself that Yana was actually no different from any other woman he had lusted after in the past.

"You're not alone now," Clay whispered. His right arm slipped around Yana's shoulders, turning her, forcing her to face him more directly.

She is so beautiful, thought Clay with a sense of wonder. *If she weren't so beautiful, I would be stronger.*

Clay looked at the jade stone resting against Yana's bosom. He delicately lifted the gem, and in a move that made no sense to his conscious mind, he dipped his head down and kissed the stone. He placed the gem back upon its resting place, but his hand did not leave Yana. As his gaze traveled up to her face, his hand spread over her breast. She drew in her breath sharply but could not protest. He watched her passion bring a rosy hue to her high cheekbones. His fingers pressed more deeply into her silken flesh. Her eyes drifted shut. When they opened a moment later, Clay knew that he was powerless against the passion that Yana incited in him, a passion that was stronger, more demanding, than anything he'd ever known.

"You are intoxicating," Clay said as he pulled Yana closer.

His mouth came down upon hers, the kiss almost harsh in its intensity. Yana moaned softly as Clay's tongue forced her lips apart, entering her mouth. The hand kneading her breast sent a flush of warmth spreading through her limbs, centering finally in the moist core of her desire.

In a move that was somehow symbolic of her surrender to Clay, Yana turned on the carriage seat so that she faced the dark-eyed young man. She looped her arms tightly around his neck, pulling him closer yet keeping her elbows high enough so that his hands could move over her without hindrance.

With the outward sign of Yana's acceptance of the desire that had blossomed between them, Clay moaned softly. His lips feasted on the delicacy of Yana's mouth. His fingers sought the peak of Yana's nipple. Not even the layers of cloth that separated Clay's hand from her flesh could conceal her erectness. He pinched the nub and Yana made a sound of passion against his mouth.

"My God," Clay whispered when the kiss finally ended. With startling ease and swiftness, the buttons of Yana's dress came unfastened. Clay's hand slipped inside the dress as he amended, "My *goddess . . .*"

The bodice of her chemise was tugged down to expose her breast. The areola was darkened with her hunger, the bud in its center raised and heightened to the sensitivities of passion.

Yana could not tell if she was being guided or if she was simply falling. It wasn't until she rested her head against the wine-colored leather carriage seat that she realized she was now prone. Clay's hands and mouth seemed everywhere, kissing her deeply until she was breathless, exposing her breasts, touching her, caressing her until she burned with an inner fire that seared her senses.

She felt the drawstring of her pantalets come loose. A hand, warm and tender, touched her. Yana gasped, shocked at the intensity of the feeling that coursed through her. She felt moist where Clay's fingers touched her, and she was naively embarrassed by this.

Is it wrong, her passion-fogged mind questioned, *to be so wet?*

Yana wondered if Clay was offended by the way her body was reacting to him. Was it right? She wished that she'd had someone in her life, a sister or female friend, whom she could have gone to for information on such subjects. She knew so little about these things, and Clay knew so much!

For Yana, fantasy and reality became indistinguishable. There was a part of her mind that could hear the fragments of conversations from people as the carriage passed them by.

So many people so close, thought Yana in an oddly disembodied way as Clay's tongue traced slow, deliberate circles around the lust-hardened nipple of her left breast. *Can they see us? Can they see what Clay is doing to me?*

For a young woman of genteel heritage and disposition, allowing a man to do more than kiss her hand in public was unthinkable. But with Clay, inexplicably, this maiden voyage into the world of the sensual unknown was given greater dimensions by the danger of discovery.

"Yessss!" Yana heard herself purr. She pushed her fingers into his ebony hair, hugging his face against the plush extravagance of her breast.

His mouth worked magic on Yana's breasts. How and when Clay had bared both of them, she did not know. She didn't care to know or even question. All that mattered was she was feeling things she had felt only once before . . . but the sensations were so much stronger this time.

"Ohhh!" Yana sighed, rolling her head slowly from one side to the other on the carriage seat.

She felt her pantalets being tugged down. Yana raised her hips to assist Clay's quest. Moments later, the warm tips of Clay's fingers were working their way slowly up the inside of her thigh while his lips continued their heavenly assault on her breasts.

When he touched her again, Yana let out a soft,

high sound of pleasure. Nobody had ever touched her there, like that, before. It was as though she could feel her pulse, her very heartbeat, right there beneath Clay's fingers. And her pulse was racing, her heart pounding with the deliciously naughty feelings that Yana was certain she would one day be damned for.

But that day of damnation wasn't now, and *now* was all Yana cared about.

"Beautiful woman . . . sometimes a child, sometimes a woman . . ."

The words rang soft and true in Yana's ears, mixing with the feelings that Clay was drawing from her with his hands and mouth. A finger probed deeper and Yana squirmed.

I must stop this, she thought.

But Yana did not act on the thought. She pushed it aside because it was getting in the way of the beautiful colors that seemed to shine just at the backs of her eyes.

She felt Clay moving her legs, positioning her as he wanted. Yana felt vulnerable and exposed, her dress bunched around her waist, one foot up on the carriage seat, the other on the floor.

"Release yourself . . . relax . . . just relax, precious Yana," Clay was saying, his words reinforcing the directives of his hands and mouth.

Dimly aware of her surroundings and of what exactly was happening, Yana complied. She could not think, much less ponder the rightness or wrongness of such wanton behavior.

When she felt Clay's lips against the inside of her

89

thigh, she thought it an odd place for him to kiss her. Then the slick, warm tip of his tongue eased along the seam of her stocking. When the tongue moved higher still, inching slowly, tasting and tantalizing along the brief expanse of flesh that separated the top of Yana's stocking from the core of her desire, awareness burst upon the young woman's consciousness.

"Don't!" she gasped, pushing an elbow beneath her to look at Clay.

"Relax . . . just relax and let me take care of everything," Clay said, a half smile on his lips, his broad shoulders wedged between Yana's trembling thighs.

Clay reached out to take Yana's wrist. When he pulled it, he straightened her arm. Yana fell backward, lying prone again. She did not have the strength or the conviction to put forward another protest. A large hand came down over her breast, pressing it to her body, heightening her already-overpowering want. And then she felt his lips against her body, kissing her tentatively at first, and then more boldly, invading her very soul.

"Clay . . ." she said in desperation.

Yana squeezed her eyes tightly shut, concentrating only on her body, only on the things that she felt. She had never even dreamed of such things before.

This ecstasy took hold of Yana with tidal wave force. She reached for Clay, fully intent on pushing him away. But her hand could not do the bidding of her mind. Her slender, trembling fingers pushed into

Clay's hair and pulled him toward her as she writhed beneath his exquisite caresses.

It started in the pit of her stomach, or so it seemed. A tension, a knotting of all her muscles. Breathing was impossible. Time stood still. Pleasure became so intense, so powerful, that it danced along the thin border between pleasure and pain.

Then Yana was tumbling down from that tumult in a wave of emotion, white fire coursing through her veins. She felt as if she really were in space, falling through the air, falling . . . falling . . . falling . . . until she landed softly, safely back on earth, back with Clay.

Yana blinked her eyes until they focused on the ornately detailed roof of the carriage. Her body tingled from head to toe.

It occured to her that her position was monumentally unladylike, but she didn't have the strength to move.

"Yana . . . I knew we would be like this," Clay said huskily, rising from the floor of the carriage. He spread himself out atop Yana, kissing her mouth briefly, a smile in his eyes. "So passionate . . . so"— Yana looked uncomprehendingly into his eyes as he searched for the right word—"unrestrained."

Clay moved his hips sensually, and Yana felt the hard length of him pressing against her. The haze fantasy of what she had just lived through was replaced by the cold reality of what she knew Clay wanted next.

"Don't," Yana said weakly. She pushed a hand

between their bodies, balling it into a fist against his chest. Her breasts felt unusually sensitive now. Her pulse seemed centered between her trembling thighs. "Please, Clay . . . I'm serious. Don't . . . this is wrong."

"No, precious, this is right as rain."

Clay kissed Yana again, but she did not kiss him back. She turned her face away the moment the kiss ended. When Clay moved his hips, rubbing himself against her, fresh excitement blossomed inside Yana, frightening her more than arousing her.

"Stop it, Clay. This has gone too far."

I can't think straight . . . What happened? . . . What happened? . . . Think, Yana, think. . . .

She pushed against Clay, but there was no strength left in her arms. Clay kissed her again, harder than before, forcing his tongue between her lips. He reached between them, but instead of touching her, he worked to unbutton his trousers.

"No, Clay . . . please, dear God, I'm begging you . . . *stop!*"

The final word was almost a shout. Panic gripped Yana, erasing the golden feelings she had basked in only moments earlier. She twisted sharply beneath Clay, struggling mightily to get out from under him.

She had expected Clay to force himself upon her. She had no real experience in such matters, yet Yana knew—or at least thought she knew—about the nature of men. Didn't they reach a point of no return, a point where they could not, even if they wanted to, stop themselves from satisfying their basest instincts?

As he had so often in the short time that Yana had known Clay, he surprised her. He sat bolt upright, a hint of a smile curling his lips. His eyes, though, were dark with hunger, flinty with anger.

"You want me to stop? Fine. I don't have to resort to rape to have the"—his eyes danced over Yana's body as she pushed her dress down and struggled frantically to pull the bodice of her chemise over her breasts—"companionship of a woman."

Yana turned away from Clay, closing her eyes. The reality of what she'd just done shocked her. How had it happened? Why was she so incapable of denying Clay?"

"There'll come a time, my lady, when you'll say yes to me . . . but maybe then I won't want you. Maybe then I'll let you know what it feels like to—" Clay made a huff of pure indignation that cut into Yana. "Aw, to hell with it! This really doesn't surprise me. I guess I should have seen you for what you are from the very beginning."

Yana's hands were shaking so badly she could hardly button her dress. Her pantalets, wrapped around one slipper, were an incongruous sight, shaming Yana somehow. She could not put them back on without embarrassing herself further. Yana pulled them from her foot and stuffed them quickly into her purse.

"You don't know me, Clay," Yana said in a whisper.

She turned toward Clay, needing his support and understanding, needing him to realize that he'd taken her into a world she'd never been to before, one that thrilled her but scared her to the marrow of her bones. But when she looked at Clay, she saw him in stony profile, his eyes narrowed to slits, his jaw set angrily.

He could never understand what this has meant to me, thought Yana. *He doesn't understand fear . . . and he could never understand love. It is all just physical to him.*

Chapter 5

Yana was alone in her room, but that didn't mean she felt safe. She couldn't feel safe, not as long as she had to remain in her own skin, her body like a stranger to her.

All she wore was a silk wrapper, stretched tightly around her body and knotted at the waist. She lay facedown on her hotel bed, her head cradled in her crossed arms, her traitorous breasts pressed into the softness of the mattress.

Her behavior in the carriage, she had decided, was not really her fault. She was certain there *was* fault, blame to be laid upon someone's doorstep—namely, Clay's. It was his smooth talk, his glittery eyes that seemed to see straight through all of Yana's fears and weaknesses. It was his mouth, pressing against her own, teaching her the ecstasy of intimacy.

Yes, thought Yana, that was it. It was all Clay's fault that she had behaved with such wanton disregard for propriety.

But there was more blame to go around, Yana reluctantly admitted. Her own body had played into Clay's hands, in more ways than one. If she hadn't been so susceptible to pleasure, she would have been able to deny Clay. Had her *mind*—her *will*—been stronger than the desires of her *body,* Yana would have told the brash young man how wicked he was.

The events that had happened in the carriage— Yana wasn't really certain what exactly *had* happened—kept playing over and over in her mind. She could still taste Clay's tobacco-laced tongue playing erotically against her own, could still feel his passion seeping from his body into hers. She could still feel the warmth of his moist mouth touching her breasts . . . and elsewhere.

Surely, what Clay had done was wrong. It *had* to be terribly, terribly wrong. Sinful, even.

It must be wrong to take so much pleasure— pleasure that makes my whole body and even my hair feel tingly—from something so wicked.

The thought made Yana tremble. She tried to prevent such thoughts from entering her mind, but they continued, taunting and tormenting her.

And afterward, when I felt strangely empty and alone, yet mindlessly satisfied, as though an answer had been given to a question I've never asked . . . what was that? It's all so confusing!

Yana's breasts still felt sensitive, as though Clay's hands and mouth were caressing her even in his absence. She rolled onto her back, releasing her weight from them. And though the physical pressure was gone, the memory of what had happened in the carriage—and how she had responded—continued to weigh heavily on her mind.

So many questions—questions without answers—haunted Yana.

Why had her body suddenly become so traitorous? Why had she suddenly been unable to control her own desires and feelings? Why was Clay the man her body desired, not one of the rich young suitors her father wanted her to marry?

What would her father think if he knew what she had allowed to happen? However much Yana argued with her father, she still desperately sought his approval and respect. Could he have any respect for her if he knew how sinfully she had behaved? And if he did know, would his pride foolishly demand he challenge Clay to a duel? Yana knew that her father was no match for Clay's deadly prowess with weapons. Clay had demonstrated his proficiency in the alley with lethal, frightening clarity.

Yana closed her eyes, groaning softly, wishing for the solace of sleep.

Clay cleaned his revolver, even though he had already cleaned it once since the shooting. It gave him something to do with his hands, though his mind continued to wander . . . always back to Yana.

For the first time in his life, he felt cowardly. He had done nothing cowardly, but that did not matter to his guilty conscience. He had gone against his father's wishes, against his word of honor that he'd given to Nico, and quite probably against Yana's wishes. All that was more than enough to convict him of *something*.

Clay had been able to convince too many young women that the many rewards of pleasure were far preferable to the lonely comfort of chastity for him to believe that his seduction skills were not finely polished. Too many times in the past he had been able to turn a "Please, stop!" into a "Please, *don't* ever stop!" by his words and his caresses.

Whether he had seduced an unwilling Yana or she had willingly allowed herself to be seduced mattered little to Clay's conscience.

I've got to get Nico and Yana to Virginia. I can turn them over to Papa and Mama, and then I can find a willing woman who won't waste my time or try my patience.

But the thought of being with one of the women he usually had casual sex with lacked its usual appeal. Clay was painfully aware that it was Yana who had made the others obsolete, who had turned their once-considerable charms into something that was vaguely gray and lacked color or excitement. And Clay, ever restless, required excitement and intrigue in a woman.

He could not figure out what Yana wanted. Once Clay could categorize a woman, figure out exactly what she wanted from him—and, being a McKenna and one of the richest bachelors in the United States, they *always* wanted something more than just *him*—then he could see them clearly, coldly, objectively. He played his own games much more effectively and skillfully once he understood what his bedmate's game was.

Was Yana an experienced harlot, playing coy, stringing him along until she got what she wanted from him—whatever that was?

Or was she, as she sometimes appeared, a sharp-tongued virgin covering up her fear of men with false bravado?

Either one was a possibility, he suspiciously concluded.

She responded in a way that suggested she was no stranger to carnal pleasures, to the illicit desires of the flesh. But at other times she seemed so . . .

And round it went in Clay's mind. He made his decision, decided it was final, then changed it again.

She was an experienced seductress who was playing with him, pulling him close and then pushing him away, exercising her power over Clay like a queen over the jester.

But then, as soon as Clay was convinced that the real Yana was an arrogant temptress, he saw her as a confused innocent who did not know how incredibly beguiling she was.

Clay closed the lid on the walnut cleaning case, tucked the revolver into its form-fitting holster, then blew out the kerosene lantern on the bedside table.

Sliding beneath the bed sheet, he closed his eyes, hoping that he would be strong enough to keep his distance from Yana until his obligations to his family were complete.

Once Yana and Rico were safely at his home and he had found some worthy excuse to tell Sorren and Shadow, he could ride away and maybe, just maybe, find satisfaction in another woman's arms.

Clay hoped it was possible.

Nico sat on the edge of the hotel bed, a smile on his lips. His meetings with the bankers had gone about as expected, perhaps a little better. And though his meeting with Antoli Pacca hadn't garnered much information on Sorren McKenna and the McKenna business empire, Nico was sure that his assistant would have much more to tell him when he arrived in Virginia.

Spread over the bed were the proposals that Nico had shown the bankers, along with the figures and percentages they had given him. America, Nico decided, was not paved with gold, as the rumors had said. But it was definitely a rich country, one where a healthy profit could be made with enough planning and the right ideas.

Nico thought about what Antoli had told him concerning the reputation of Clayton McKenna. Once Nico had learned of Clay's history as a ladies' man, he was relieved that his daughter was not getting along very well with McKenna. The day Clay and Yana had spent together had apparently fueled a mutual resentment. During dinner, though Nico had tried to involve everyone in the conversation, Clay and Yana had never said a word to each other. They had hardly even looked at one another.

Yana is a smart girl. What father wouldn't be proud of her? She knows a lecher when she sees one, and she's smart enough to keep her distance from Clay.

As Nico carefully arranged the papers and placed them in folders, he began thinking about the eligible young men in Greece. There simply *had* to be one wealthy young man back home whom Yana wouldn't object to marrying.

For two days, though Yana traveled through the city of New York and saw sights that should have captivated her curiosity, all she could think of was Clay and how she had so wantonly responded to him in the carriage. Her father, apparently oblivious to Yana's emotional unease whenever she was in Clay's company, continued to insist that he stay with her every minute of the day, acting as guide and body-guard.

If there was any saving grace to the situation, at least as far as Yana was concerned, it was that Clay seemed very nearly as nervous about their private, personal history as she was.

Yana was pondering these things as she neatly folded the last petticoat and placed it in one of three steamer trunks she had taken with her from Pirias. She closed the lid with some difficulty, sat on it, fastened the three latches, then hopped off to fix the lock into place.

Yana was savoring some pleasure at having packed on time—her tardiness in such matters was a continuing annoyance to Nico—when a rap of knuckles against her door sounded.

"Yes?" Yana called out warily. Nico was making one last excursion through New York, this time to buy gifts for her, so she doubted it was him. And the thought of being alone in her bedroom with Clay made her heart pound. Seconds ticked by. Yana felt anxious. "Yes . . . come in."

The door opened, but Clay did not step fully inside. He kept partially hidden behind the door.

"Yana, it's me. I think we should talk. Are you dressed?"

"We have nothing to talk about," Yana said. After a beat, she added maliciously, "Why not just barge in, like before? Don't tell me you're learning manners at this late date?"

Clay stepped into the bedroom. His gaze met Yana's. The room was so quiet that the sound of the door closing behind him seemed magnified, as though he'd slammed it. Yana turned her eyes away from Clay, willing herself to be immune to the dangerous allure that he exuded.

"Whether either of us likes it or not," Clay began, "our families will, with any luck at all, soon go into what should be a very profitable business venture. That is going to require that you and I put aside our differences and act civilly to each other."

"Mr. McKenna, I have been nothing less than polite to you in front of my father."

Despite herself, Yana noticed once again how immaculately tailored clothes defined Clay's broad chest and narrow waist. The slight scowl on Clay's face, which turned the corners of his mouth down, was his natural expression of concentration. Yana realized she was not the only one to carry personal demons because of her abandonment to Clay's desires.

"You cannot accuse me of being uncivil to you," Yana said. A dark brow arched meaningfully over her right eye. "If anything at all, I'd say I've been far too lenient with my . . . *civility* toward you."

Clay felt the tenuous hold he had on his anger and guilt weaken. For perhaps the first time in his life, Clay was afraid that he was not in control of himself, that another person—Illyana Zacarious—could control his emotions with nothing more forceful than a raised brow over eyes that twinkled with such stubborn spirit.

"Don't you get glib with me! You haven't said five words to me since—" Clay hissed through clenched teeth before boiling anger cut his words off. He crossed the room in several long strides. "You weren't civil, you were selfish!" He took Yana by the arms, his long, bronzed fingers clutching just above the ruffled cuff of her off-the-shoulder dress. "I'm not accustomed to being left behind, shall we say? And I've got to tell you, I don't like it very much."

Yana was shocked at Clay's forcefulness but not

103

frightened by it. She did not truly believe Clay would hurt her, no matter how angry he got.

"What's wrong, Clay? Did I offend your inflated pride by refusing you?" The words shocked Yana. She had been raised to never speak of such things. Was it actually her talking about *that?* "And take your hands off me!" Yana squared her shoulders defiantly, looking unflinchingly up into Clay's jet-black eyes. Coldly, quietly, she added, "You are not to touch me unless I tell you to. And trust me, Clayton McKenna, that day will never come!"

Clay knew that he was, more than anything else, angry with himself for what had happened in the carriage. As he looked at Yana, the sense of his own vulnerability to her beauty was so strong that he wanted to lash out at her.

Since their time together in the carriage, she had treated him as a total stranger. Clay realized guiltily that he had probably treated one-time lovers exactly as Yana was treating him now. He suspected that if there was some balance in the world, he deserved to be treated so indifferently by Yana. But for once, it was Clay who could not casually dismiss the encounter as meaningless, carefree entertainment.

"Damn you, Illyana! I wish to God I'd never set eyes on you! I wish you'd never come into my life!"

"You're lying, Clay."

Yana issued the statement softly, with the certainty that it was true. The effect on Clay was shattering. His tempestuous spirit flared, fired by the horrifying knowledge that he had met a woman who had captured a piece of his soul, exposing a part of him that, until recently, Clay had not shown anyone.

The strangled cry of rage was issued by Clay a moment before his mouth came down over Yana's. He kissed her punishingly hard, spurred on by passion, goaded on by a fear that he was not immune to Yana, that he was unwillingly drawn to her needs, wishes, and charms.

With an understanding beyond her experience, Yana sensed why Clay was so brutish. And in that split second of comprehension, she understood why she had taunted him so mercilessly.

Her arms wrapped tightly around Clay's middle. She molded her body to his, feasting on his mouth, kissing him with matching fury.

"Damn you!" Clay hissed, his hand covering her breast, squeezing hard.

"I hate you!" Yana spat back, furious with herself for wanting Clay to take her where she had not gone, hating him for making her want to go there.

She caught his shirtfront in her hands and, with all her might, ripped it apart, sending the ivory buttons bouncing across the polished wooden floor.

When Clay pushed Yana backward, she held tightly to his ruined shirt, pulling him with her until they both tumbled to the bed. His fingers curled into the low bodice of her gown and yanked downward, exposing one trembling breast.

"Kiss me!" Yana cried out, pulling Clay upon her.

Clay was not as Yana had, on those rare occasions when she allowed herself fantasies, dreamed he would be. And she certainly did not behave as she had thought she would. Frightened and yet fierce, Yana pulled at Clay's clothes, tearing them, biting at his shoulder as her dress was forced upward and her petticoats pushed aside.

She heard rather than felt her pantalets being torn from her.

She reached for Clay, squeezing him through his trousers. Clay was thick, fully aroused, supremely ready for her. For only a moment, fear forced Yana to take her hands away from him. But then, stronger forces urged her on. With trembling, clumsy fingers, she struggled with the buttons of his fly as Clay tugged frantically at his belt.

He sprang free, filling Yana's hand. She squeezed firmly, drawing a rumbling groan of pleasure from Clay.

The heat and hardness of his masculinity shocked Yana. She did not know exactly what she had thought a man would be like, but whatever notions she'd had, they weren't like this.

She felt Clay's hands sliding between her thighs, pushing them apart. His fingertips pushed over her stocking top, touching naked flesh, then pressing intimately against her, pushing experimentally, then entering slowly.

Yana cried out, arching her back, shocked at the feeling that his fingers created, stunned at the sensation that jolted her system with brutal pleasure. She sensed that she had spread her legs wider for Clay's hand, and this realization shocked her but in no way altered her behavior.

Clay's hips moved, pumping his shaft through Yana's fingers. She felt the heat of his desire and his pulse, and knew this time that she could not possibly stop him or herself.

Clay kissed her avariciously, forcing his tongue between Yana's lips. She lost her hold on him. She sucked hungrily at Clay's mouth, then pushed her fingers into his hair and forced his head down to her one exposed breast.

"Kiss me!" Yana whispered, frantic with need as experienced fingers sought and found her most sensitive spot.

Clay's mouth was warm and moist when it closed over her breast. His tongue flicked across her blunt, erect nipple. Yana cried out in ecstasy, her body twisting violently as she hugged him to her bosom.

Yana sensed, then, the force and power of her own sensuality. The needs that she had denied and subjugated had been brought to the surface by Clay. And now those needs—marrow-deep and coursing in her blood—had come rushing to the surface, unbidden and uncontrollable, sweeping her along with the current of passion.

She reached for his manhood again. She touched him and moaned softly with her own pleasure. The heat of Clay's body—not merely the secret places where he touched her or she touched him, but his totality—suffused every pore of her skin, missing nothing, flowing like molten gold to gild every contour of her body and soul with priceless pleasure.

107

Clay slid upward on the bed until his face was over Yana's and she could look into his dark, searching eyes. In that instant, Yana read his mind with heart-shattering clarity, seeing the questions that he asked of himself and of her but could not put into words.

Have I gone too far? his ebony eyes beseeched. *Have I destroyed whatever chance I had of winning your trust, your love?*

He would go no further, his glittering ebony eyes said. The next move was Yana's to make, the decision hers.

"Gently . . . gently," Yana whispered, answering the unspoken questions. She pulled him to her.

Clay settled into the smooth valley of her silk-sheathed thighs, resting his weight on his elbows. The feral need that had consumed him only moments earlier had been brought into check, suddenly harnessed by his oath to never force himself upon a woman and his need to never hurt Illyana.

Yana felt him, solid and heated, filling her hand, pressing against her midriff, branding her flesh with a possessiveness that curled upward through her. For long moments, Clay just looked into Yana's eyes, questioning her, doubting himself and his own self-control.

A gentle nudge, a slight twist of his hips, let Yana know both what Clay wanted and that, if this moment were to progress to its culmination, she would have to initiate the next step.

Clay kissed her mouth, and in retaliation for his brutal treatment, she caught his lower lip between

108

her teeth and bit hard enough to taste blood.

"Ouch!" Clay gasped. He licked at the blood on his lip, and in his eyes was a new respect for Yana, "I suppose I deserved that."

Yana's eyes blazed fire. "I'm glad I hurt you," she said, her senses battling between the anger that Clay caused and the passion he ignited. "You deserve worse than that. Much worse." But as Yana spoke, she answered the final unspoken question by twisting her hand around Clay's manhood and guiding him to her moist entrance. "Gently, Clay," she whispered, her voice so soft he could barely hear her. "Very, very . . ."

". . .Gently," he finished for her, pushing between her fingers, sliding slowly and tenderly upward into Yana.

She issued a short cry of pain, and when Clay stopped his motion, it was Yana who urged, "Don't stop, Clay! Please don't stop!"

The feel of Clay buried deep inside her, moving within her, filled Yana with a sense of awe, of wonder. Pleasure curlicued through her, making her moan and tremble. She clung to Clay, her arms wrapped tightly around his neck as his breathing and movements rapidly became more frantic, more feverish.

"Yes, Clay," Yana purred into his ear.

The aggressiveness Clay had shown earlier, when he'd first taken Yana into his arms and thrown her to the bed, had returned, though he was no longer dancing on the threshold of violence. Each hard thrust filled Yana, sending her senses reeling, her heart soaring. Each second brought a new understanding of pleasure to Yana and, even more mystifying, a sense of being *a part of Clay*.

A strangled gasp of ecstasy ripped from Clay's throat. Yana cried out in pleasure, reaching a summit with him as Clay drove deep within her. Reaching deeper still, his passion flowed out in a torrent, and together with Yana, kissing her lips softly between labored breaths, they drifted slowly and unwillingly back to the real world.

Chapter 6

Clay stood at the window, leaning against the sill, watching Yana as she gingerly tugged at her chemise and bodice to cover her breasts.

Clay felt like a beast. Never before in his life had he ever been so forceful with a woman. Never! Seeing Yana disheveled, her skirt bunched at the tops of her thighs, her hair a mess, looking decidedly like a victim, made Clay want to shout apologies at the top of his lungs. He wanted to tell Yana that he had never been so coarse before and would never be that way again. If only Yana could see it in her heart to forgive him—just this one time—he would make sure he never did anything again that would warrant an apology.

The guilt was tangible. Clay knew its foul and acrid taste would not soon fade—if ever.

Yana sat at the edge of the bed. She smoothed her dress down over her legs. She hadn't looked up yet, hadn't given Clay a chance to see into her eyes. And what would he see when she did? Would her soft brown eyes be hard and filled with hatred for him?

The thought made Clay's insides tighten painfully.

He followed the direction of her gaze, and when he did, a fresh wave of anxiety shredded his soul. There on the floor were Yana's white silk pantalets—torn. More than anything else, it was the clearest reminder to Clay of his unconscionable behavior.

"I believe," Yana said, her voice strangely cool and emotionless, "that you owe me one pair of pantalets. I have all my lingerie specially made by a couturier in Italy. All the other ladies tell me Paris is the best place for lingerie. I don't tell them about my couturier. If I did, then everyone would use him and he wouldn't have so much time for me."

Yana raised her face. Her eyes were clear and shining, and for the life of him, Clay could not understand why she was discussing her couturier at a time like this. He was quite convinced she was in shock. A fresh wave of guilt assaulted his conscience.

"Yana, I'm so sorry." His voice cracked with emotion.

She picked the pantalets off the floor, inspecting the waistband that had given way to brute force. Clay, unaccustomed to apologies and ever more so to guilt, moved away from the window, getting down on one knee before Yana. He took her hands in his, bending at the same time to look up into her face.

"Yana, I can't begin to tell you how sorry—"

"It wasn't how I imagined it would be," Yana said

112

simply, cutting off Clay's apology.

In the aftermath of lovemaking, with golden sensations still tingling through her, Yana realized that she had wanted to make love to Clay—wanted desperately to do so. She just hadn't anticipated it happening quite the way it had.

"I always thought that when you and I would make love, it would be at night, in my bedroom in Pirias, with a fire in the fireplace. There would be lots of good food and maybe just a little too much good wine." She gave Clay a small, rather dreamy smile. "That is how I thought it would happen, anyway. It's the dream of a little girl, I suppose. That's what you must be thinking now, isn't it?"

"I'll make it up to you," Clay replied quickly, holding Yana's hands as delicately as he would a child's.

A lifetime of limitless wealth had given him the power to order the world around him to suit his every need. It was only natural for Clay to think he could buy whatever happiness—and forgiveness—Yana might want or need.

He was a second away from making an even bigger fool of himself by promising to buy Yana everything but the moon and stars if she'd only forgive him. Just as those words were about to pass from his lips, Yana looked Clay squarely in the eyes and said, "Make it up to me now."

"What?"

"Make love to me like I dreamed you would."

The words were issued with such utter simplicity, such guilelessness with just a hint of imperiousness—Yana, too, was long accustomed to ordering the world to suit her whims—that Clay could not keep from laughing softly.

"Now?" he asked, sweet pleasure singing in the single word.

"Yes. Now. So that when I remember this day, I remember everything—the forceful and the gentle, the wild animal in you and the sensitive man." Yana's full-lipped mouth, still a little puffy from the harsh kisses she had received minutes earlier, curled into an impish smile. "And you can begin by taking my clothes off, Clay. All of them. And if you ruin any more of my clothing, I shall take serious offense."

Clay looked down at his naked chest. His own shirt was still minus the buttons. He stripped it off and dropped it to the floor, the muscles in his chest and upper arms rippling smoothly beneath the surface of his bronzed skin.

"Whatever you want, milady," he said as Yana turned slightly on the bed, exposing the buttons that ran down the back of her dress. "Your wish is my command."

This time, Clay was tender to the nth degree, coaxing every last bit of pleasure with maddening skill from Yana's responsive body. And not until Yana was certain that she would go mad with desire if Clay did not enter her, did he consummate the lovemaking. Together they danced the sweet dance of Yana's secret dreams until their passion was spent.

*   *   *

The hatred in Edward Danzer had been brewing for years. He could not actually remember the first time he realized the McKennas had to die. He only knew that they were a blight on the land. Each day the McKennas were allowed to breathe, more good southern gentlemen would be deprived of the land and income that was rightfully theirs.

He closed his eyes and thought, fighting to keep his mind working logically. No matter how much he hated Sorren McKenna, he couldn't let emotions dictate his actions. That was how mistakes occurred. He had to keep his mind clear for the meeting with Antoli Pacca.

Danzer's hatred for McKenna had started back during the war. Sorren, rumors had it, had worked as a spy and assassin for the Union against Danzer's beloved Confederacy. Though Danzer himself had been too young at the time to have any solid memories of the war, he had heard all the gruesome stories from his mother and sister, the only other surviving members of his family.

When the Union army had marched into Virginia, almost the very first thing they did was to free the slaves. The stories Danzer's mother told of what it was like to see slaves she had owned running free still made Edward shiver with revulsion.

And, of course, the conquering army had had their way with the southern women. The fact that Sorren McKenna was not among the rapists and looters, or among soldiers who freed the slaves, mattered little to Danzer. What did matter was that in 1880, Sorren

115

McKenna had purchased every last acre of land that had belonged to the Danzers and erected a new mansion that put the old Danzer plantation to shame. And Sorren McKenna and his half-breed wife didn't stop there. They bought more land all around, and it wasn't too long after that that their son, Clayton, was running around like he owned the entire county.

A muscle flicked in Danzer's jaw. He had to consciously relax to keep from clenching his teeth in rage. He opened his eyes, scanning the crowd at the saloon. Nobody paid any attention to him, and this, too, irked Danzer. When his father would enter a tavern, the stories his mother told him went, nobody would say a word until Old Man Danzer greeted them. If *he* was in a jovial mood, then *everyone* was in a jovial mood. If Danzer was in one of his dark, surly moods, the tavern cleared out so he could drink his whiskey in peace and quiet.

That was the kind of respect and deferential treatment that was due Edward Danzer. If it weren't for the cursed McKennas, Edward Danzer would probably be getting the respect due the son of Old Man Danzer.

His thoughts focused on Clayton McKenna, who was the spitting image of Sorren and just as wild, according to the stories about the elder McKenna's escapades prior to his marrying the Indian woman, Shadow. Even Danzer's second cousin had been seen with Clay McKenna. And everybody knew that a woman seen in public with Clay was sleeping with

116

him in private.

They've all got to be expunged from the face of the earth. Sorren, the Union spy who steals land and has so little dignity he marries a squaw. Shadow, walking around like a queen, pretending she's just as good as white folk. Clayton, just another Sorren only younger, flaunting his money to have his way with the ladies, infecting them with his Indian blood . . .

As Antoli Pacca approached the tavern in Virginia, he had an eerie sense of déjà vu. Hadn't it been less than a fortnight earlier when he'd met with Nico Zacarious to discuss what he had learned about Sorren McKenna?

But this meeting, with Edward Danzer, would be much different. He'd never met Danzer, though they were men with common interests.

A smile curled his thin lips. Everything was falling into place so much better than he had hoped. The expedition into Virginia to spy on Sorren McKenna had given Antoli the names of McKenna's enemies. With that information, more pieces of Antoli's personal plan for redemption and revenge began falling, as naturally as rain, into their rightful places.

When he entered the tavern, Antoli paused to let his eyes adjust to the dim light. At first he saw only the silhouettes of the customer. Then, as his pupils dilated and things became clearer, he noticed one man with curly red hair looking at him straight on. This was not the type of establishment where a man

117

looked directly at another unless the look held a challenge. Antoli pushed his hat back on his forehead, then almost imperceptibly raised and lowered his shoulders. The red-headed man barely nodded—an equally obtuse move.

Antoli crossed the room and sat in a straight-backed chair across from Edward Danzer.

"Good afternoon," Antoli said, slightly annoyed that he had to once again strain himself by conversing in English. "I understand we have some things in common."

Danzer heard the accent but kept the disdain from his face. "Perhaps," he said with just a trace of contempt. "We mustn't make hasty conclusions."

For nearly an hour they talked quietly, jousting in the way that men do when they want to know what the other one knows without giving up any information of their own.

"Then McKenna is vulnerable?" Antoli asked, his eyes lidded, looking over the rim of a glass. "He can be destroyed?"

"McKenna is dangerous. Whether he is vulnerable has yet to be seen." Danzer leaned slightly toward Antoli to subtly indicate the importance of his words. "But he *must* be destroyed."

"Sorren, or the son?"

"Both of them." Danzer's eyes, gleaming with feverish anticipation, met with Antoli's. "*All* of them. The squaw . . . the father . . . the children. They must all be destroyed. There must be no trace left of them."

Antoli Pacca smiled coldly, his lips pulled tight

across his teeth. Nico Zacarious had destroyed Antoli's father, and for that, he would die. If Edward Danzer could assist in Nico's destruction and in doing so kill the McKennas, it didn't bother Antoli at all.

"I believe it is time we decide how to kill the McKennas," Antoli said, finding it very difficult to contain his excitement.

It wasn't exactly vanity, but the plantation did look spectacularly good, and both Sorren and Shadow McKenna knew it. Extra help had been brought in to supplement their regular staff of twelve in polishing all the hardwood floors, adding to their special luster. Emma, the snowy-haired, rotund black woman who had been the McKenna children's nanny, had kept a close eye on the new help, sensing that something special was about to happen, wanting the home to be as spotless as a hospital ward and as cheery as a nursery.

"They's a'comin', Mister Sorren," Emma said, standing on the porch beside the master of the house. Sorren was leaning against one of the twelve marble columns that ran along the front of his mansion. "Stan' straight now, Mister Sorren," Emma tut-tutted, giving Sorren a stern look. "Our boy's comin' home, an' he's bringin' business with him."

A half smile curled Sorren's lips. He glanced at Shadow. She, too, had a smile on her mouth and a brightness in her eyes.

"It'll be good to see Clay again." Shadow slipped

119

her hand inside Sorren's. "It's been so long." She gave her husband's hand a squeeze. "How do you think Clay's been getting along with Mr. Zacarious's daughter?"

The question seemed innocent enough, but all of them knew it wasn't. Clay's reputation with the women in Virginia—and along most of the eastern seaboard—was almost legendary and certainly scandalous. It had been said, to Shadow's absolute horror, that Clay could seduce any woman he wanted. Shadow dismissed such talk as jealous gossip, but she knew there was at least a grain of truth to it. After all, she had fallen in love with Clay's father, and to look at her son was to look at Sorren one generation later. Though Sorren was not quite as lean as he had once been, he was still the handsomest, most attractive man Shadow had ever seen. This opinion, to her occasional consternation, was shared by many other women.

The crunch of steel-rimmed wheels along the gravel drive drew the attention of the people on the porch, so no one answered Shadow's question.

The carriage was not yet at a complete stop when Clay, looking splendid though not entirely well-rested, leaped out, a wide smile creasing his face.

"Papa! Mama! Emma!" he shouted, taking long strides toward them.

Clay shook hands with his father, hugged his mother, then bent low to embrace the much shorter Emma.

"You've gotten skinny," Emma said disdainfully,

120

patting Clay's hard, flat stomach. "You ain't been eatin' right an' don't tell me no different!" Emma, her eyes glistening at the reunion—she loved Clay as much as his parents did—toddled off, muttering, "I'll go fetch somethin' from the kitchen. Dang fool boy's wasted away to nothin' but skin an' bones."

"She'll never change," Clay said of Emma to his parents.

Shadow said, "Thank God for that" as she stepped off the porch, following Sorren to the carriage.

Nico was about as Shadow expected him to be. He was polite with her, almost to a fault. He bent low to lightly kiss the back of her hand, drawing a soft, pleased laugh from her. Such formality was still common in Virginia, but not among the men who knew both Sorren and Shadow. Though it was unfounded that Sorren could burst into a jealous rage, no man dared challenge his wrath by being in any way forward with his wife.

Nico's eyes, Shadow noted, had that bright, intelligent gleam in them, the kind that so many successful men have. Shadow, possessing not nearly as suspicious a nature as Sorren, decided on the spot that she liked Nico Zacarious and hoped her family could do business with him.

But when Nico's daughter stepped out of the carriage, accepting her father's hand to steady her as she descended, Shadow's heart did a little leap. Illyana Zacarious wasn't simply attractive, she was ravishing. One didn't have to be a man to take notice of how stunning she was.

Her auburn hair was combed back away from her face, revealing the delicate line of her jaw and her small ears. Arranged gracefully and held in place with ivory combs, Illyana's hair seemed to radiate the sun instead of simply catching it. She wore a small, stylish mint-green velvet hat which matched her dress. Shadow's experienced eyes told her the velvet hat and dress were of the highest quality, tailored by a superior couturier.

Shadow McKenna had seen her son, from the age of fifteen on, pursue women. She accepted this as a natural part of life. Sometimes she could not quite understand what her son found attractive in a certain young woman. At other times, she knew quite well what had caught his eye. With Illyana Zacarious, it wasn't just pretty eyes or a full bosom—which Clay seemed particularly drawn to; it was the sum total of her, each individual feature attractive if taken separately and utterly devastating to the male of the species if taken as a whole.

Introductions were made and everyone stepped into the McKenna mansion. But Shadow, who loved her son with all her heart and tried to accept and see his faults as well as his strengths, was worried. In some ways—in the ways of the flesh—her son was not a disciplined man.

Silently, Shadow hoped that Illyana had more strength of will than her son.

Sorren sat in his office at the ranch house, his

gaunt features eerily illuminated by the thin yellow light emanating from the kerosene lamp. He hadn't bothered with gas jets, choosing instead to use just the single reading lantern on his desk. Even that was turned down low. For clear thinking—the kind of thinking Sorren had to do right now—he preferred almost total darkness.

His initial meeting with Nico had been cordial enough. Nico Zacarious, Sorren's intelligence reports said, had been known to have ties with what the men in Greece had written were *extralegal professionals*. In less polite terms, that meant they were criminals, but not the bandit variety that bothered with holding up banks and trains. *Extralegal professionals* might hire other men to rob banks and trains. They planned such thefts, but they never risked prison terms by doing such tawdry work themselves.

What disturbed Sorren more was the rumor he'd heard that someone had been in the area near his home—near his *family*, for God's sake!—and in Washington, asking questions about his past.

As Sorren's final payment for his many years of faithful services rendered, the friends he had in and around the government had spent countless dollars and endless hours wiping out every trace of his and Clay's involvement with the War Department and the Special Branch.

"We must get to know each other better," Nico had said, a full, guileless smile shimmering on his mouth, Sorren's best cognac in a snifter in his hand. "I am a businessman, Mr. McKenna, and I do not like doing business with strangers. Therefore, we *must* become close friends. Don't you agree?"

Sorren had agreed, but his ebony eyes were hard and fathomless. Only Shadow, who knew Sorren better than anyone else, saw him raise his shield of self-protection.

The seeds of suspicion had been planted and had quickly taken root.

It wasn't merely that Sorren suspected Nico Zacarious of hiring men to do a background check on him. That much Sorren expected. He'd done the same to Nico, hiring men in Greece to give him the inside information that no man likes revealed about himself. What was truly damning to Nico, as far as Sorren was concerned, was the *type* of questions that had been asked.

Do the McKennas have any enemies? Who would profit by seeing them die?

It was the inclusion of Sorren's family that worried him so much. He'd lied to others and been lied about by others. But never did it involve a man's family. A man's wife and children are sacrosanct; even the most unscrupulous businessman understands that. Certainly a man with ties to the euphemistically titled *extralegal professionals* would understand that.

So why would Nico Zacarious, a man who otherwise appeared to be a gentleman bandit, essentially no different that Sorren himself, hire a man to search for such damning information about his family?

The meeting with Nico, the first of what would

surely be many, had held a second disturbing surprise to Sorren. There was the girl, Illyana.

Sorren knew better than to think of her as a girl. At nineteen, she was older than his own wife had been when they'd first met and he'd gloriously, intractably fallen in love with her. Still, he saw the world through the eyes of a man with several daughters, so she looked like a girl to Sorren—young, to be sure, but possessing a woman's body, her charms much too evident.

Sorren shook his head dejectedly. He resisted the urge to roll another cigarette. It was a habit his wife disapproved of, and for the past twenty years he'd been trying to give it up.

Clay. He was a problem. A potential problem, anyway.

Sorren had no delusions about Clay. At least he tried to see his son as objectively as any proud father could. Clay was intelligent and dedicated. He could, when he put his mind to it, accomplish just about anything.

These were the things about Clay that made Sorren sit back in the office chair some nights, glass of whiskey in one hand and cigarette in the other, and smile to himself. *Not bad, Sorren,* he would think. *You've raised a good son and helped him become a good man.*

At times like these, Sorren shared the credit with Shadow. After all, she had remained at home with the children far more often than he had.

It was the other times that Sorren cringed inwardly

and scowled outwardly at his son. Times when yet another young woman's heart was broken by the discovery that being the recipient of Clay's practiced charm was only an ephemeral lesson in pleasure.

"Papa, I'm telling you the truth," Clay would say earnestly when confronted with such news. "I never promised to marry her. I never promised her anything! She was the one running after me, not the other way around. All she really wants is to get her fingers into the McKenna bank account."

More often than not, after Sorren had done his own investigation into the allegation, he learned that his son was telling the truth. But there was still the matter of responsibility—*shared* responsibility, no matter who chased whom—and this could not be denied.

Most galling of all to Sorren was that in his own heart, he grudgingly admitted that Clay was a chip off the old block, a tauntingly accurate copy of himself. Though Sorren did not see himself as a bad man, there were events in his past—dealings with the women he'd known prior to meeting Shadow—that he did not care to dwell on.

The hunter, Sorren McKenna, was now the protector. And he was about to go into business with a proud, stubborn, willful man from Greece, who had foolishly brought with him his extraordinarily beautiful daughter.

Sorren loved Clay, he just didn't trust him around women in general and certainly not around someone as arrestingly alluring as Illyana Zacarious.

126

What would happen if Clay decided to turn that cursed charm of his on Illyana?

At times like this, Sorren took full responsibility for how his son had turned out. Shadow was blameless.

Sorren rolled a cigarette and lighted it. He had a lot to worry about.

Chapter 7

Yana let her fingertips run along the intricately embroidered edge of the bedroom curtain. For the remainder of her time in the United States, she would be staying in this bedroom.

Has Clay slept here? In this bed? A sly and wickedly mischievous smile tickled her full, sensual mouth. *Has Clay slept with anyone else in this bed?*

Her smile vanished. Yana pushed the thought away. She had guessed that Clay was not the most monastic man she'd ever met, but that didn't bother her—at least she tried hard to tell herself that she didn't care about his past. All that really mattered was whom Clay slept with in the future.

She stepped away from the window, stretching her arms languorously over her head, then fell comfortably backward onto the large goosedown mattress.

Under other circumstances, the railroad trip from New York to Virginia would have been unendurably boring. But that was B.C.—Before Clay.

Clay hadn't simply made love to her, he had changed her life and the way she saw herself and everything else. On the train, with her father beside her and Clay on the other side of the private cabin, she had cast flirtatious glances at her lover. Occasionally, he smiled back. Sometimes he frowned, saying with his eyes, *Are you crazy? Your father is sitting right next to you!* At other times, he didn't react to Yana at all, and she found this most disturbing. She hated it when Clay acted as though nothing had transpired between them.

Though Yana wasn't entirely pleased with having to hide her affection for Clay—she'd kept such feelings securely locked away for so long, waiting for Clay to come along, it seemed terribly unjust to her that she had to deny them now—there was a devilishly exciting element in having to sneak around, flashing amorous looks at her lover whenever she thought her father wasn't watching, touching Clay on the arm or the back of the hand whenever the opportunity presented itself.

Yana sighed, staring at the brocade ceiling of the guest bedroom. *When,* she asked herself, *would be the right time to tell Papa?*

This was not something she could just drop in her father's lap like the morning newspaper. These were extraordinarily delicate matters, and for all Illyana Zacarious's schooling in etiquette and propriety, she knew that *delicacy* was not always her strongest character trait.

130

When she heard the knock at her bedroom door, Yana crossed the room slowly, her hips swaying slightly. She recognized Clay's knock by this time. His knocking on her bedroom door had opened a whole new world for the young Greek heiress. It had been Clay, back in that hotel in New York, who had freed Yana from the choking constraints and fears that had imprisoned her for so long.

Yana opened the door halfway and swung around it, one leg on either side. Her eyes were dark and smoky, smoldering with a newly ignited fire.

"Hello," she purred to the surprised Clay. "I was wondering how long it would take you to come here." Yana reached for Clay's hand. "Clay, it is a little late for you to be shy," she said when he resisted, caught off guard by her blatant behavior. "This isn't the first time you've been in my bedroom."

Yana pulled Clay into the room, closing the door behind him. A quick inspection of the door latch proved disappointing; there wasn't a lock. Yana, who had friends that had been married for years now, felt she had a lot of catching up to do—lock or no lock.

"Yana, I've got to talk to you," Clay began, his voice smooth and modulated, his tone serious. He pulled his hand out from inside hers. "It's important. *Very* important."

"Yes, I'm sure it is. But it can wait until later. . . ." Yana moved close to Clay, her body nearly touching his.

"Yana, this is serious."

131

She looked into Clay's eyes. They were expressionless, cold, the lines in his face etched hard and
unyielding. She didn't like it when Clay was this
way, especially now. She felt scandalous for being so
bold, but there was a little voice inside her that
whispered Clay did not want her anymore. Yana
could not easily dismiss the teachings of her youth—
that once a man sleeps with a woman, he no longer
respects her. She needed confirmation that making
love had meant something special to Clay in New
York and that it would here in Virginia, too.

She unfastened one button of Clay's shirt. When
she went for another, he stopped her. A cold shiver of
apprehension went through Yana, making her more
determined and just a little more fearful.

"We've stayed away from each other all the way
from New York," Yana pouted prettily, pushing her
full lower lip out. She was not unaware of how Clay
responded to her impish moods. "Our parents are
busy. Can't you give me just one little kiss?"

"No."

Clay spoke the single word like a muffled gunshot,
and Yana flinched inwardly as she felt its heavy
impact strike her. The nagging doubts she had had of
herself and Clay—seeds of dread that had been
planted long ago by puritanical tutors and nannies—
instantly came to full bloom.

"What's wrong?" Yana whispered, her tone a
mixture of hurt and anger. "Don't I interest you now
that we've—?"

Yana stumbled for words, wanting to say *made*

love but not entirely certain that was the case. She looked into Clay's eyes, hoping to see a refutation of her unspoken fears. Instead, she saw only his confusion.

"What are you talking about? Yana, I came here to—"

"—give me a polite brush-off?" she interjected, cutting his words off. Yana glared hatefully at Clay. *"As tokalo!* That's what I say to you and all your empty words!"

Clay took a step backward, not understanding the Greek words or the Greek woman. This sudden change in Yana shocked him. Of all the moods he had anticipated, this wasn't one of them. When Yana took another step away from him, Clay followed, closing the distance, reaching for her. She slapped his hand away. She was a total stranger to him now.

"What's this?" Yana hissed violently. "When I want you to touch me you won't, but if I don't want you to, you can't keep your disgusting hands off me?" Yana's eyes glittered with escalating rage. "That must make it difficult for you to be happy, Clay. Only wanting what you cannot have. Or maybe a strong woman threatens you? Is that it?"

"It's not like that." Clay's face was expressionless, but the corners of his eyes were pinched with tension. He was getting angry with Yana, her words affecting him more strongly than he liked.

"Afraid you're not man enough for a strong woman, Clay?"

The verbal slap in the face was more than Clay

could take. He pulled Yana to his body, feeling the suppleness of her breasts against him. As she wriggled, fighting against him to free herself, Clay groaned as a rush of memories and heat, triggered by this voluptuous spitfire of a woman, took hold of his senses.

"Shut up and listen to me, damn it! You don't have any idea at all of what I think or feel!" Clay hissed the words through clenched teeth, ever cautious of the servants who just loved to talk among themselves about his sexual escapades.

"You've got nothing to say to me. I understand you perfectly well, *Mister* McKenna."

"I've got everything to say to you, and you don't understand one damn little bit about me or yourself!" Clay wound his arms more tightly around Yana, enjoying the feel of her pressing against the length of him. "Now, for once in your life, just shut up and listen!"

Yana, too, was distractedly aware of the contact of their bodies. Old fears mingled with new sensations. Fears collided with desires. She tilted her head far back on her shoulders to look up into Clay's fierce, dark eyes.

"Tell me what you have to say, if you must," she whispered, fighting for a tone of dejected resolve. But the blush to her cheeks was not from anger. "But must you squeeze the breath out of me in the process?"

Clay fractionally relaxed his hold on Yana. He could not find the strength of will to release her completely, not when the warmth of her voluptuous body permeated all his senses, reminding him with painful clarity that Illyana Zacarious was off-limits to him.

"Whether you come to me or run from me has nothing to do with how I feel about you," Clay began, aware of Yana's heart beating against him, knowing she was nervous and realizing he had to choose his words with infinite care if he was to avoid a messy scene. "In fact, you and I aren't really what's important here. What's important is that your family and my family do business together, so that's what must be most important to *us*. Think of—think of what your father would think . . . what he would say."

"In other words, we can't do anything that might upset business?" The accusation was thick in Yana's tone, but this time it wasn't directed at Clay. She was tired of her father's quest for money always influencing what man she was supposed to marry.

"Exactly."

Yana's mouth curled into a frown, and all Clay wanted to do was kiss it away. Each passing second made him more aware of her heady, feminine allure. He knew that he was hurting her with his words—he was hurting himself with them, too—but he felt they were necessary.

"This isn't the place to talk," Clay said, sensing Yana's temper was about to explode. "Too many ears around."

Yana, well versed in having servants talking about

her behind her back, nodded her head. Her eyes, however, did not lose any of their hardness. Besides, now that it was clear Clay wanted nothing more to do with her, the last place she wanted to be was in her bedroom. Too many memories were associated with bedrooms and Clay. Combined with that was the horrid reality that the one time in her life she had been so bold as to flaunt herself in front of a man, openly seeking his seduction, she had been resoundingly rejected. Her humiliation was physical, and she felt it burning inside her.

Later, standing at the entrance to the stables, looking at Clay's home a hundred yards away, she thought, *This is a grand, lavish place to live. I can tell why Clay takes so much pride in the glittering mansion.*

"We've got some of the finest riding horses in the territory," Clay was saying, trying to hurry Yana into the stables. He had inherited his father's love of horses, as well as his skill with them. "You can ride, can't you?"

"Yes—yes, of course, I can ride," Yana replied, a touch of irritation in her tone. She was still angry and confused at what had been said in her bedroom, and leery about Clay's further explanations for his behavior. Moreover, Clay's question made her understand that she really did know very little about him, and he knew possibly less about her.

Clay showed her his prized stallion and the two mares that would foal in a few months. When he talked of his horses, stroking their noses, he seemed so different from the cold-blooded, machinelike man who had rescued her from the criminals in that dirty New York alley. As Yana watched him, his eyes gleaming, his whole countenance that of a proud father, she found it almost impossible to see him as the person who had, in the blink of an eye, killed one man and seriously wounded another.

"I knew you had a soft spot," Yana said quietly, leaning toward King, the ebony stallion with a mane as dark as Clay's. She fed King an apple from her open palm. "It's your horses."

"I haven't got a soft spot." Clay was smiling, though he said the words in a tone that was stony serious. "And I'll deny having a soft spot to my death's breath."

"I don't doubt that for a second," Yana replied, giving Clay an honest, slightly troubled smile. "That doesn't make it any less true, mind you. It just means that you won't admit to it."

The tenderness she saw in Clay sparked a small fire inside Yana. But it was not the type of fiery passion that would flare out of control. Rather, it was a slow burning fire, the kind that never is completely extinguished, even when passion is sated and the body fulfilled.

"Is it really that bad?" Yana asked. Clay looked at her, and she saw the trouble, the confusion he felt, show clearly in his eyes. "Because our fathers want to stuff their pockets even more than they already are, you and I have to pretend that we mean nothing to each other?"

Clay looked away, staring into space. Yana thought, *Tell me I'm wrong, damn you! Tell me I've got this all wrong and that you haven't meant a word of what you've said! Tell me that making love meant something special to you, Clay!*

"So it was all just a mistake, eh?" Yana's tone was deceptively calm. Her soul ached with the knowledge that she had turned her back on a dozen good men, and the one man who had sparked something loving and tender inside her had now, with cavalier disregard for her feelings, decided that business must come before everything else. Nothing must stand in the way of the Almighty Profit!

"No, Yana. It wasn't . . . yes, I suppose it was a mistake. It was my mistake. Your father and I have talked. He's got expectations of you. High expectations. He wants you to marry a good Greek man and bear him plenty of heirs to the Zacarious throne. And my father . . . if Dad knew—" Clay shook his head. The notion of his father discovering that he had seduced Yana was painful. "My father expected me to be a gentleman. And believe me, I never had any intention of letting—of letting what happened happen. It just happened, Yana. That's all I can tell you."

It was a feeble explanation and Clay knew it. He felt sick at heart for having—even unwittingly—deceived Yana. And worst of all, he knew that every word he spoke hammered home another nail into the coffin of Yana's affection for him. He had ventured into a golden, ecstatic, mysterious land with Yana for one glorious afternoon. And that one afternoon of lovemaking was all that Clay would ever have with Yana. From this point forward, he felt certain, Yana would remember him only as the man who had seduced her, then given her a mealymouthed excuse for deserting her.

"What do you think would happen if my father ever found out what you did?" Yana asked, rubbing King's velvet-soft nose, keeping the horse's thickly muscled neck between herself and Clay. When Clay looked at her, she had a malicious, bitter smile on her face.

Clay's face went blank as he gazed deep into Yana's eyes. "I don't even want to think about something like that. He doesn't know, does he?"

"What would your father say?" Yana continued, a wicked, delighted gleam in her eyes. "Sorren seems to be a very proud man, much like my father. I just wonder what he would think if he knew his son—"

"Don't even think that way. It's not healthy."

"For you? No, I don't suppose it would be. In fact, I'd wager that your father would be very nearly as angry as mine." Yana's brows raised and lowered in hard amusement. She was almost enjoying taunting Clay. For the first time she felt she had some power over Clay, and Yana was angry enough to use it. "Makes a certain amount of sense, don't you think?"

"If I had any sense and if I'd done any thinking, I wouldn't be in this mess."

"So that's what I am to you. A mess? Perhaps you can get Emma to clean me up? She has been cleaning

139

up your messes for a long time—your whole life, fact. Yes, maybe Emma can just sweep me under the rug." Yana looked seriously at Clay for a moment. "That is the right American expression, isn't it?"

"Yes. No! I mean, yes, you used it correctly, but that's not how I see you, Yana. It's not like that at all."

"So you say . . . so you say."

However much Yana was enjoying this game, Clay saw the underlying potential for ruin unless discretion—after his lamentable but thoroughly pleasurable lack of discretion—was maintained. He knew full well that he deserved whatever malice Yana threw at him, but an inner voice whispered angrily, *This damn girl is toying with me!*

"Dinner should be ready soon," Yana said, feeling the inner reserve of strength, which had allowed her to be chipper and coy with Clay, failing her quickly. "I'm going back to the house. And, Clay, you won't come barging into my bedroom here, will you?"

Dinner was not quite what Yana had expected. Instead of the servants standing stiffly at attention, waiting to fulfill the master's every whim, there was only one servant present, the indomitable Emma. And even she was a surprise to Yana. Emma, Yana noted, was more inclined to give orders than take them.

"Here you go, missy," Emma said, ladling rich roast beef gravy liberally over a mountain of mashed potatoes on Yana's plate. "You eat this now while my cookin's still hot." Then to the others, she said, "Eat now! I don't want you folks jawin' while my good cookin' gets cold!"

Emma, whose round body showed that she practiced what she preached as far as food went, waddled out of the dining room, mumbling that if anyone got indigestion, it was because of "business talk," not her cooking.

Yana stared a bit numbly at her plate. Three thick slices of roast beef were crowded in with a heaping mound of buttered, cooked carrots, along with an even larger helping of potatoes.

It was enough food for three meals.

Shadow, seeing Yana's look of dismay, said quietly, "Just eat as much as you like. Don't feel you have to finish everything that's on your plate. That's just Emma's way."

Sorren added, "Emma has a way of running this house the way she sees fit. And unless every man, woman, and child has a figure like hers, she thinks they are emaciated."

Yana laughed lightly. Emma reminded her of her own grandmother in that respect. Grandmama Zacarious immediately began cooking whenever there were two or more people in one room at one time.

The memory of Grandmama Zacarious was fresh and poignant, bringing a sweet-sad smile to Yana's lips. She had lost her grandmother two years earlier.

Emma soon returned from the kitchen with a silver

coffeepot in hand. As she filled the cups, she tut-tutted about how little food had been eaten. She left the dining room again, still muttering under her breath.

Though Sorren and Nico had agreed to put business aside during dinner, their attempts at casual conversation were dismal. Both were more men of action than of words, each anxious to enter the fray. The gentleman's agreement was forgotten. The main topic of discussion became the future shipments.

"It was Clay's idea, actually," Sorren was saying, sitting at the head of the table with Shadow to his right and Clay to his left. "He had been running some of our smaller companies and was getting bored." Sorren smiled, glancing over at Clay, undisguised pride showing on his face. "He gets bored easily. Always has. He needed a new challenge, so he created his own."

"You have a fine son," Nico said. "He will carry on the family name and your businesses. Long after you and I have gone to a better place, your son will be making you proud. He will never disgrace the McKenna name. I can tell this, Sorren. I could see this in him on the pier in New York." Nico's voice had been steadily rising as he spoke. He pointed a finger skyward in emphasis. "I could see he was a young man of character from the very first moment I set eyes on him!"

Yana was surprised to hear the plan to ship cotton to Greece and optics to the United States was Clay's.

He'd never seemed the businessman type to her, and it made her wonder what else about him she did not know.

Nico continued singing Clay's praises. When Yana looked at Clay, he was studying his mashed potatoes intently, not looking up.

He's embarrassed. He likes attention, but only if he can control it. Papa compliments him and Clay starts looking for a place to hide.

At first, Yana found this particularly amusing, and she was pleased that Nico continued—to Clay's obvious and growing displeasure—to tell Sorren and Shadow what a fine son they had, and how pleased they must be to know the heir apparent to the McKenna business empire was so capable. Then another thought tickled its way into Yana's mind, and it was her turn to stare unseeingly at the food on her plate so no one at the table would notice the hurt in her eyes.

Does Papa miss not having a son? Does he blame me for not being a man? Mama died giving birth to me. If it hadn't been for me, maybe Papa would have a son now—someone to carry on the family name.

"Is something wrong?" Shadow asked under her breath, touching Yana's forearm lightly.

Yana put on a quick smile, though it was empty. "No, everything is wonderful. I just thought of something, that's all."

Yana smiled again, but she saw that Shadow's concern did not diminish. A moment later, when Shadow was asked a question concerning financing for the customized ships to be built, Yana was pleased that attention was diverted from herself.

As the conversation droned on, Yana's mind continued to wander. Clay's admission that he could no longer have anything but a business relationship with her continued to haunt Yana's happiness. In her heart of hearts, she did not truly believe that Clay could dismiss her so cavalierly. She had felt their closeness, felt *something*—whether it was love or not, she couldn't be sure, but it was definitely something—when they had made love. Especially the second time, when Clay was so tender with her, touching her with feather-soft caresses, gently questioning her, finding all the secret, hidden places that brought the most satisfaction, places that Yana herself had not known existed.

I know he wants me as more than just a friend, thought Yana with the certainty of a woman who had been denied very little in her entire life. *He may say different, but I know what I feel. If he won't touch me, even though he wants to, I'll punish him for his damnable sense of family duty!*

The next time Clay reached for the sugar to sprinkle over the strawberry dessert Emma had served, Yana reached out, too, her fingertips brushing lightly against the back of his hand. The contact, brief as a blink, could have been an accident. But when Clay's dark eyes met Yana's, she let him know with a flash of her eyes that it was no accident.

Yana eased her foot out of her slipper and touched Clay's foot beneath the table. He moved his foot.

144

Yana raised her foot, touching Clay's knee. His whole body flinched in a slight tightening of all his muscles, unseen by all but Yana. Her foot slipped inside Clay's knee. He pushed his chair farther away from the table, moving out of range.

I hope he's miserable! He's jumpy as a frog. Good! It's time Clayton McKenna feels as nervous as he makes other people feel.

Yana took the greatest joy in teasing Clay, boldly flirting with him while maintaining an outward appearance of listening to the business that was going on. She wanted Clay desperate for her, starving for her. And when he came for her, as she was quite convinced he would, she would turn him away as cruelly and embarrassingly as he had turned her away.

That'll teach the high and mighty Clayton McKenna a lesson he won't forget! I'll never let him touch me again!

Yana doubted her own conviction, but at the time it pleased her to be defiant of her traitorous body's desires.

"Missy, I want you to sit down an' listen to me now," Emma began, wringing her hands absently on the apron stretching tightly around her more than ample girth. She waited until Yana sat in one of two chairs near the bedroom's bay windows that overlooked the breeding mares's pasture. "You seem to me like a right fine an' proper young lady. That's

145

why I gots to say to you what I got to."

Yana, her hands folded in her lap, swallowed dryly. When Emma had suggested they have a "little talk," she was not at first alarmed. Yana had taken an instant liking to the old woman, even though Emma seemed to be continually hovering about, getting into everyone's affairs. Now, seeing Emma's nervous gestures and the serious look on her face, Yana felt cold dread pool inside her.

"Like I was sayin'," Emma continued, "you seem like you was brung up real fine by your papa and mama." Emma licked her lips to moisten them. She hardly knew Yana, and it certainly wasn't her responsibility to protect the young Greek woman, but Emma had never been one to keep her opinions to herself.

"Please, Emma, just tell me what you have to say. You're beginning to scare me."

Emma inhaled deeply, then plowed forward, doing what she felt was her God-given duty.

"I know that Mr. Sorren and Mrs. Shadow didn't see nothin' goin' on tonight at the dinner table. An' I know your papa didn't see nothin', neither. But I saw. Yes, missy, Emma's eyes are old, but they don't miss nothin'." She cleared her throat. Such topics were difficult for her. "I saw the way you was lookin' at Mr. Clay, touchin' him when you thought nobody was lookin', carryin' on with your eyes all lovesick like. An' I don't blame you none, missy. Mr. Clay's one fine, handsome man. That he is. But what you don't know, darlin', is exactly what that kind of tomfoolery

146

can do to a man like Mr. Clay. He ain't sweet an' innocent like you is, Miss Yana. Mr. Clay's a real fine man an' I love him like my own, but I knows that boy as well as his own mama an' papa, an' I know he's got a powerful dark side to him."

"Dark side?" The sense of dread was just as strong in Yana as before, though now she was confused about Emma's intention. "I'm sorry, Emma, but I don't understand. Is that American slang, this dark side?"

Emma shook her head, her dark round eyes grave. "It ain't slang, missy. It's jus' the way it is." Emma sat in the chair facing Yana's so they could be level with each other. "I know what it's like for good young ladies these days. In my day, there weren't no such thing as flirtin'." Emma realized this was a lie, but it was a little one, and for her purposes, she felt it was justified. "Maybe I'm jus' an old busybody, but I know what flirtin's for an' what it leads to. Mr. Clay, he's a good boy. He truly is. But he's a wild boy. Near as I can figure, he's just too good-lookin' and too slick with his sweet words. He's got a powerful dark side to him."

"What . . . *exactly* . . . do you mean by that, Emma? I know you mean well, but you're frightening me."

Emma, flustered, nervous, hating the topic yet driven forward by a maternal instinct that was much stronger than any sense of protocol, reached out to take Yana's hand into her own.

"I'm tellin' you, missy, that if you keep foolin' with Mr. Clay the way you was at the dinner table, the

147

dark side is jus' gonna swallow him up whole! Ifin you was married to Mr. Clay, then I can't see as how no harm would come of it. But I can see you are a proper young lady! Now, the only reason I'm tellin' you this is 'cause your mama ain't here now to warn you 'bout what men can be like. They be mighty easy gettin' started and powerful difficult gettin' stopped!"

At last Yana understood what the lovely old woman was trying so desperately to say without actually saying it. She smiled and squeezed Emma's hand in return. She couldn't admit to having succumbed to Clay's inimitable charms, and though lying was not by nature something she did well, she knew a lie was in order.

"Don't worry, dear Emma, I won't let anything go too far," Yana said. "Clay . . . well, he's been so cold with me, so distant . . . I just couldn't resist seeing if I could break through that shell he's got around him. I meant nothing by it and Clay knows that." And then, hating herself for lying, she concluded, "Actually, Clay and I haven't gotten along very well. We've sort of been at odds with each other since we first met."

Emma was obviously still suspicious, but she was willing to accept Yana's words as fact. She nodded her head as though she knew what Yana was going to say all along. "Your mama did you proper, missy. She surely did."

"It wasn't my mother, it was my father who raised me. My mother died"—the words were choked off for a second as guilt and loss flared in her breast—"she died long ago."

148

"You ain't got no mama?" Emma exclaimed, wide-eyed in outrage at a world that could be so unjust. "No mama at all?"

Yana shook her head. The conversation had gone from bad to worse. She certainly did not want to explain to Emma how her mother had actually died—giving birth to her.

"Don't you worry 'bout nothin', missy," Emma said, her words laced with maternal indignation. "You got a mama now! You surely do! I raised me a passel of my own children. I raised Clayton and LaTina and the other little girls, too. Miss Shadow and Mr. Sorren they he'ped me, but I brung up Mr. Clay like he was my own an' no different. So from now on, you think of me as your mama. Well, maybe as your gran'mama." Emma chuckled, her enormous body trembling and rolling all over from years of her own hearty cooking. "I'm too old to have young'uns your age!"

The words both pleased and disappointed Yana. She wanted her own mother—her real mother. But since that was impossible, what more could she ask for than to have Emma, with her noble heart, as a surrogate grandmother?

"I'd like that, Emma," she said after a moment, her voice a whisper.

"It's settled then, chil'. I'm your gran'mama now, so you got any trouble, you jus' come and tell me. I know more 'bout troubles an' how to get rid of 'em than anyone God put on this good earth. You don't believe me, you just ask Mr. Clay or Mr. Sorren or

149

Mrs. Shadow. They'll tell you I'm right." Emma pushed herself with some difficulty out of the chair, then patted her stomach. "Now that we got that settled, how 'bout if I bring you up a little somethin' to eat?"

"We just ate!"

"Not a meal like," Emma said, shaking her head slowly in dismay. "Jus' some milk an' maybe a few o' my cookies. I make real fine cookies."

"But, Emma, we ate not thirty minutes ago."

"Yes. An' we been talkin' since then. People work up an appetite when they talks about important things like we jus' done. I'll bring you up a little somethin', jus' so you can keep your strength up."

Yana, realizing that arguing with Emma was futile, just smiled.

Chapter 8

It had been the strangest week of Illyana Zacarious's colorful life. She had alternated, sometimes in the same hour, between loving Clay and despising him. The trouble was, she had plenty of reasons for hating Clay, and as many reasons for wanting to spend every waking moment with him, wanting to be—and do—everything he could ever want from a woman.

So around and around her mood went. Sometimes she craved Clay, wanting nothing more out of life than to see his face; at other times, there wasn't enough room in all the world—let alone Virginia—for both of them to exist.

But Yana was in a happier mood now, sitting in her bedroom where she spent so much of her time. Spread out before her on the bed comforter that Emma had made with such infinite care was Yana's gift to Clay. The gold necklace caught the morning sunlight, its brightly polished surface glittering warmly. It was nothing more than simple gold links attached together. Perhaps at another time, Yana could get Clay something to hang from the necklace. But for now the chain was enough. Though its simple elegance didn't match the extravagant jade necklace that he had bought for her, it was enough— at least temporarily—for Yana to feel on an even ground with Clay. She didn't want him having the upper hand with her on anything.

This he will like, thought Yana with conviction. *It's clean, simple, masculine. Every time he looks at it, he'll be reminded of me.*

Antoli Pacca leaned back on the carriage seat. The springs, rusted and old, squeaked noisily. The rented horse and carriage were less than Antoli was accustomed to. Though he hated Nico Zacarious, the Greek businessman did keep Antoli in a style that exceeded the rickety contraption he had rented.

Below him, in the valley and stretching beyond the hills, were the McKenna tobacco fields. To the north, barely visible, were the cotton fields. From these fields, Nico hoped to make another king's fortune to add to his considerable wealth.

It will be death you find here, Antoli thought savagely, *not greater wealth!*

Nico's death was a comforting thought. Knowing Nico would be dead soon gave Antoli a renewed sense of purpose—and with it, patience.

152

He had waited so long, toiled so many years as Nico's right hand . . . but soon, that would be all over! Soon—not soon enough, but soon—Nico would be dead and Antoli's family honor would be restored. And in the process, Antoli's personal fortune would be secured.

Antoli could almost taste Nico's blood on his tongue. He licked his lips, mentally savoring the taste. Far below, men worked the fields. Antoli watched them working, despising them, hating their stupidity for laboring so long and so hard to line the pockets of another man.

"What do you think of Illyana?" Shadow asked, standing at Emma's side in the kitchen. They were baking bread, as they did together every Saturday afternoon. It was the only day of the week Emma would allow Shadow into the kitchen.

"What'cha mean by that, Mrs. Shadow?" Emma's pudgy black hands were caked with flour as she kneaded dough.

"You don't play dumb very well," Shadow said mildly. "You've seen what's been going on between Clay and Illyana, just the same as I have. Do they have something special going for each other, or are they just getting on each other's nerves?"

A wide grin spread across Emma's face. She kneaded the bread dough with renewed vigor.

"Near as I can tell, there jus' ain't no tellin'. I looks at them young'uns and I thinks the good Lord jus' set them down together on this earth to be together. Then they fights like cats and dogs an' I jus' know they'd commence to fistin' if we hadn't brung up Mr. Clay to know better than that."

Shadow, busy greasing a bread pan, nodded, then pushed a dark lock of hair off her forehead with the back of her wrist. "That's about how I see it, too, I'm afraid."

"What about Mr. Nico?"

"I can see a problem there." Shadow's lovely, aristocratic features—the Kiowan blood in her clear and present—took on a grave countenance. "I don't think he'd like having Indian grandchildren, however slight the Kiowan blood is. For that matter, from talking with him, I think he's got a Greek man in mind for Yana. In Greece, it is customary for the father to select his daughter's husband."

Emma's gray brows pushed together. "You really think Mr. Nico would hold you bein' Indian against Clay? He seems too smart a man to be that plumb stupid."

Shadow, having been an outcast of both the white and Indian cultures her entire life, shrugged her shoulders. She had grown accustomed to otherwise intelligent men holding deep fears of "tainted" Indian blood. Emma, the child of a Negro mother and father, did not have the same cultural insecurity.

"You can never tell," Shadow said after a long pause.

"I suppose. Jus' the same, that Yana's a right strong young lady, an' it jus' seems to me Mr. Clay needs hisself a woman like her."

"Now, Emma, don't get started matchmaking."

"Didn't do so bad with you an' Mr. Sorren, did I?"

They laughed together, old friends enjoying each other's company. But beneath the laughter, there was concern for Clay, for Yana, and for the impact their possible romance could have on their lives, and on McKenna Enterprises and the Zacarious Shipping Company.

"You don't like it?" Yana asked. Then, as a statement of fact, said, "You really don't like it."

"I didn't say that."

"You didn't have to."

Clay held the slender gold chain between spread fingers. "It's beautiful, Yana. It really is. It's just that—"

Yana crossed the room, hating herself for being so naive as to think she could do something that would please Clay.

"It doesn't have to mean anything. You bought me a necklace, so I bought you one. It's not like we're engaged, or anything like that." Yana looked out the window at a mare nursing a young, hungry spindly-legged foal. Such scenes had suddenly begun to tug painfully at her heartstrings. "The necklace doesn't have to mean anything at all."

Clay reached into his shirt pocket for tobacco and paper. When he had a cigarette going, he inhaled deeply, studying Yana's profile, wondering how much he knew about her, how much she meant to him. The chain was a gorgeous gift. More than that, it perhaps indicated a thawing of the underlying tension between himself and Yana that had been triggered by his attempt to put some emotional distance between them.

But what strings were attached to the chain? Would it be so bad to have a permanent tie to Yana?

Clay had spent most of his adolescence and all of his adult life avoiding permanent ties with women. Affection, allegiance, sometimes even some amount of transitory responsibility were acceptable. But never any ties. Nothing binding. Nothing that Clay couldn't get out of or away from.

"Does it offend your sense of masculinity," Yana asked, intruding on Clay's disturbing thoughts, "to receive a gift from a woman?" A hard edge crept into Yana's voice. She continued looking out the window as she spoke. "I should think you would have received many gifts from your lovers, Clay." *There, I've admitted it. Lovers. Do lovers have to be in love? Once a lover, always a lover?* "It surprises me to see you accept this with such . . . ill grace." Yana turned away from the window to stare into Clay's slitted eyes. "What is it, Clay? Why can't you accept a simple gift from me?"

Because you're not like any woman I've ever known, that's why. Because in the past week I've discovered much more about you, and everything I learn makes me want you more. Because if I wear this chain, I'll always be reminded of you, Yana. And if

156

I've got to do anything, it's forget all about you. I can't accept this necklace, because soon you'll be on your way back home to Greece and you'll be out of my life forever.

"It's a flaw in my character" was Clay's glib reply in an ill-chosen attempt to lighten the atmosphere.

"As tokalo! Damn you! Damn everything about you!" Yana hissed, giving Clay the full force of her rage. And when all Clay did in response was give her his casual half smile, it took all of Yana's consummate will to restrain herself from physically attacking him. "What's so damnably funny, Clayton Mc-Kenna? Certainly, humiliating me cannot be that amusing."

"I'll make a deal with you. I'll accept your gift and I'll wear it. But there are conditions."

"Conditions. I buy *you* a gift and you give *me* conditions."

Clay raised his hands placatingly. "I think you'll like these conditions."

"I don't like *anyone* putting *any* conditions on me."

Undaunted, his smile still confidently in place, Clay said, "The first condition is that you must wear the necklace I bought for you. It's perfect for you, so you must wear it. And the second condition is that you must allow me to buy you some dresses. At least one. You really do need some American fashions."

Yana looked at Clay, eyeing him warily. She didn't trust him—or his seemingly innocent conditions—at all. But his smile never wavered, reaching all the way

157

up to his jetty eyes, and Yana had never been able to deny Clay anything when he looked at her that way.

"All right," she said, a smile playing with her lips. "But I don't trust you one little bit, Clayton McKenna."

"Objection noted."

Yana did a slow pirouette in front of the mirror, looking at herself critically from all angles. The gown, suitable only for evening and very formal occasions at that, was made of yards and yards of the tightest woven midnight-black silk, liberally tailored at the cuffs and plunging neckline with white Italian lace.

Through the mirror, Yana stole a look at Clay, who sat in one of the three high-backed, overstuffed leather chairs arranged in a half circle around a small table, upon which a carafe of port wine rested. In the second Yana had allowed herself to look at Clay, she could not tell whether he approved of the gown or not.

"Turn around, missy, and let Mr. Clay have a look," Emma suggested. "He's got a real fine eye for ladies' fashion."

If only you knew Clay like I do, Emma!

Emma was unaware of how angry her words were making Yana. This was the fourth dress Yana had tried on, and though every one had looked stunning on her, she had rejected them all. If Clay approved of a dress, Yana was determined to not like it at all.

But Emma was patient. Yana was one of those rare women who made every dress look spectacular.

Yana spun halfway around, looking over her shoulder at how the dress draped on her. She ignored Emma's request, just as she had ignored the previous ones. Yana didn't need Clay's approval to make her decision.

Emma pursed her lips, displeased with Yana's behavior. She had seen pretty young women get skittish and act strangely in Clay's presence before, but she still could not understand why Yana would not try to do a single thing to make Clayton McKenna like her.

She moved closer to Yana, stepping up behind her so she could whisper without Clay hearing. "Listen, missy, I'm going to step into the other room for a cup of tea. If you make a decision or if you need anything, you just give ol' Emma a holler." Emma put her hand lightly on Yana's shoulder. "Maybe without me bein' here, you and Mr. Clay can have a little talk."

Yana wanted to tell Emma to stay, but she remained silent as the kindly black woman disappeared behind the door.

"Turn around, Yana." Clay's timbre was warm, friendly, yet hinting at past intimacies. "Let me take a look at you."

Yana turned slowly to face Clay. When his ebony eyes raked over her, a shiver worked its way up her spine. As much as she would like to believe otherwise, she was not in the least bit immune to the magnetism of Clay McKenna.

"Don't you think it's time we had a walk . . . as Emma suggested?" Clay's brows rose questioningly. "We do seem to have unfinished business." Clay's devastating half smile played across his mouth. "Yana, we really don't have to hide . . . at least, not from each other."

Yana didn't like the tone of Clay's voice. His gaze, roaming casually over her, touching her with invisible caresses, should have made her livid. But it didn't. Instead, Clay's look conjured up feelings that had thrilled Yana beyond words, sensations so exquisite her body had first turned against her, then seemed to turn inside out as liquid fire raced in her veins.

"I—I don't know what you're talking about." Yana cleared her throat. Her gaze locked challengingly with Clay's. "You can be so boring when you talk in riddles." Yana's tone dripped cultivated haughtiness, which pleased her and bolstered her courage. "Don't be that way. I simply hate being bored."

Clay's throaty chuckle rumbled through the dressing room. "You really are something! I can remember a time"—Clay paused meaningfully, sipping port, looking at Yana over the rim of the glass—"when you didn't find my company all that boring."

Clay set the glass down, placing his hands on the arms of the chair. Yana, seeing he was about to rise, took a step backward. Clay smiled. "In fact, if memory serves me well, I recall you being rather . . . *entertained,* shall we say, by my presence."

Yana was confused, but she refused to let her mental agitation show in her expression. Was this the same man who had not long ago said mixing personal and private lives was impossible?

Yana issued a short, false contemptuous laugh. "Who are you trying to fool, Mr. McKenna? I tolerate your company because my father says I must. That's the only reason I even talk to you."

Clay pushed himself to his feet. In a dimly-lighted corner of his mind, he realized that he was going against his own personal conviction to stay away from Yana. He pushed the thought back into darkness, promising to come to some understanding of it later.

"You flatter yourself too much, Mr. McKenna."

Yana's words had no outward effect on him. The right side of his mouth curled upward mirthlessly.

"You have a rather selective memory, *Miss* Zacarious." Clay glanced at the door through which Emma had disappeared. When he looked back at Yana, his piercing gaze told her that she was alone with him, and that no mater what happened in the dressing room, no matter what improprieties occurred —Emma would turn a discreet, blind eye to it.

He stepped toward Yana slowly, purposefully. "You've also got a selfish streak in you that I find most displeasing. You don't want to displease me, do you, Yana? After all I've done to make your stay here in the United States as . . . *satisfying* as possible."

161

Yana refused to give up any more ground to Clay. She squared her shoulders, feeling the heat of Clay's passion touching her in a thousand different places with feathery caresses that made her tremble softly. Her hands were balled into small, white-knuckled fists at her sides.

"Don't talk that way," Yana said, her voice cracking, her fleeting courage and conviction slipping from her grasp. "Don't tease me about what has happened between us." Clay kept advancing. Yana's words, more honest than before and now less taunting, had to be forced through dry lips. "What has happened . . . I don't know what has happened . . . it just . . . but must never happen again . . . you said so yourself . . . truly never . . . nothing like this has ever happened before. . . ."

Clay stepped up to Yana. She put her hands on his chest, the fingers spread, to prevent him from moving closer. What she had to say was too important for her to stop now, even though her thoughts and the words that followed them were disjointed, indistinct. "What's happened has happened, Clay, but we must forget that it did. And it must never happen again. Never, ever again. It was— *is*—wrong. You said so yourself. Remember what you told me? You said we can't . . . mustn't . . . what happened was . . ."

Yana's fingers were very lightly kneading the sinewy muscles of Clay's chest through his shirtfront. She caressed him without even thinking about it, her words saying one thing, her hands telling quite a

162

different story.

"I disagree." Clay looked down at Yana, his eyes dark, glowing with an inner fire, his expression impassive. "I doubt you believe your own words, but that's no matter. Say what you must. Believe what you must. We both know where the truth is, what the truth is."

Resting on the inner slope of Yana's breast was a small gold cross on a necklace. Clay touched the cross with a fingertip.

"I thought we had an agreement."

Yana looked at Clay, saying nothing, her heart pounding.

"You didn't like my gift?" Clay's eyes danced with amusement. He touched the slender gold necklace at his throat. "I liked your gift. And I also follow through with my agreements. It's a point of honor with me."

In a whisper, Yana said, "You have no honor."

"Perhaps. Perhaps not. Who is to say?"

Yana swallowed dryly. Clay was standing too close for her to think logically. She felt his steelish pectorals through his silk shirt, the feel of his body against her palms heating her senses from the inside.

"Why don't you like the necklace I bought you?"

"It's beautiful. I love it. I haven't worn it because I was afraid my father would—"

"—ask questions?" Clay finished for her. "Yes, I suppose you are right." Clay's words were casual; the way his eyes touched her was not. "You know, I was very angry with you after we were in the carriage together. I'm not used to . . . well, let's just say that I believe in *mutual*"—he drawled the word out slowly—"satisfaction. It's best that way."

Clay touched Yana's cheeks lightly with his fingertips. Then the fingers trailed slowly down her throat until, once again, he touched the gold cross. His eyes never left Yana's as his hand moved slowly sideways to close over her breast.

"I've been told that many men are only concerned with their own pleasure, so I've always been careful to never be that way," Clay said, his voice warm, seductive, promising. "But there comes a time when a man simply must insist upon his own satisfaction. After all, it's only fair."

Clay's left hand slipped under Yana's hair at the nape of her neck. His face was now only inches from Yana's. Her heart hammered in her chest. Her nipples throbbed with tension. She remained silent, unable to look at anything but Clay's lips, waiting and wanting his arousing kisses.

"It's only fair," Yana heard herself say.

The kiss started out gentle, hesitant. But then, like a fire that had suddenly become full-blown, heightened by the current between them, it became stronger, deeper, more intense.

Yana had not yet actually made a decision, and she was too inexperienced in such matters to know that Clay had made the decision for both of them. Had she known, perhaps she would have fought against Clay with greater determination. Maybe she would have cried out for help, believing that Emma would

164

summon Sorren and Shadow to put shackles on Clay and cart him away.

But she didn't know, and perhaps it was best that way, because it allowed her to accept Clay's warm, probing kisses without fear or hesitation, believing she knew what would happen next, looking forward to another journey into that forbidden land of eroticism where only Clay could take her.

She parted her lips, inviting Clay's tongue. When she received it, Yana purred softly, leaning forward as she tilted her head back, giving herself freely to the delicious sensations he could draw so easily from her.

"I haven't been able to think of anything but you," Clay breathed. His fingers pressed deeply into Yana's breast, his lips brushing against her mouth. "You've put a spell on me, bewitched me. A devil-woman is what you are. My devil-woman!"

There was an undercurrent of anger in Clay's words that did not match the sweetness of his kisses.

Could it be, Yana wondered, *that Clay is as unhappy about the volatile reaction between us as I am?*

It didn't make sense to Yana. Not from what she knew—or thought she knew—about Clay McKenna. He was always in control of himself and the world around him.

In a dreamy lassitude, she felt the buttons of her gown, running down the back, being unfastened. She tilted her head to one side, exposing her neck invitingly. Clay kissed her cheek, then neck, bending Yana further backward, forcing her voluptuous body to conform physically as well as emotionally to his wishes.

"Clay . . . Emma . . . she'll come back."

"Emma knows better than that," Clay rasped. He curled his fingers into the black silk, sliding it down over Yana's shoulders. "She left you alone with me, Yana, and she won't return unless we ask her to. You don't really want to be rescued, do you?"

Yana had to move her hands away from Clay's chest for him to slide her gown down further. She slipped her arms out of the sleeves with slow deliberation. When she looked into Clay's face, she smiled. For once, she was not going to question herself or her actions; she wasn't about to doubt herself, or Clay, or think about anything.

"Make me feel what I felt before," Yana whispered, holding lightly onto Clay's shoulders as he bent to push her gown past the sweeping curve of her hips. "Take me to that place again, Clay."

Yana stepped out of the silk gown, leaving it crumpled and discarded on the floor.

Clay straightened and took a step away from Yana. Though he wanted to appear calm, completely at ease with the acceptance of what they were doing, he could not hide the vein pulsing feverishly at his throat. The fire in his ebony eyes suggested to Yana that Clay was as incapable of controlling his desires as she was.

"I've undressed you before," Clay said, taking another step backward so that he could see all of Yana. "This time you must do it yourself."

Yana was self-conscious now that Clay wasn't touching her, kissing her. With him at a distance, she was able to think clearly—too clearly—and a blush stole up her neck, coloring her cheeks. She looked down, her weight shifting nervously from one foot to the other.

"Don't be scared," Clay said, the sound of his voice shattering the silence in the room. "You have no reason to hide. I've never seen a woman so enticing as you."

Yana caught the top bow of her corset between her fingers. She waited, searching inside herself for the courage to do what she felt was necessary.

"Go ahead, Yana. Don't be scared. It's me. It's just me and you . . . alone together."

She pulled at the bow, unknotting it. And then, with trembling hands, she tugged loose the criss-crossed bindings of her corset. Unconsciously, as the corset opened, Yana turned slightly away from Clay to hide herself.

"Don't . . . please, Yana . . . I want to see."

Hurry! Hurry, before you shake so much he'll laugh at you! Hurry, before your courage runs out! thought Yana.

"Slow down. There's no need to hurry."

Yana ignored Clay's wishes this time. She didn't dare slow down because if she did, she might stop. With artless haste, Yana rid herself of her clothing, lastly balancing unsteadily on one foot as she peeled her stockings, still attached to the garters of her corset, off her legs.

167

And then Yana was naked. Naked and vulnerable, she crossed her hands one over the other, keeping them modestly low. She struggled to control her breathing, knowing what she wanted, too nervous and ashamed to adequately put her wants into words.

"Come here," Clay whispered. Then, in a more commanding voice, he said, "Come to me, Yana."

She walked across the room to him, naked and frightened, driven by Clay's indomitable will, drawn by a force that she did not fully comprehend.

"Look up at me."

Yana did as she was told. When she looked at Clay, she was struck once again by the flawlessness of his features. But she also saw that the control he'd been maintaining was an enormous strain on him. Yana felt a sense of victory.

"It's your turn." Clay took Yana's hands and raised them to his mouth. He kissed the fingertips, then brought her hands to the top button of his shirt. "It's only fair.

"Only fair."

Yana watched her fingers working the ivory buttons of Clay's shirt. She worked down to his belt, then stopped. To go further was dangerous— unavoidable, exciting, but definitely dangerous.

She pushed her hands inside Clay's shirt, touching his bare chest, taking pleasure in the feel of his hard, rippled muscles. Her hands crept up to Clay's shoulders. Finally, though she wanted to allow her hands more time to explore, she knew she must comply with Clay's demands and the whisperings of

168

her own need.

She took off his jacket, careful not to touch Clay with her body. Yana dropped the garment to the floor. When she looked up again, she saw Clay's deadly revolver strapped beneath his left arm in the holster. She grimaced, moving backward a step, the sight of the gun bringing back images that Yana wished would remain deeply buried in her subconscious.

Clay noticed the way Yana reacted to the sight of his revolver in the shoulder holster. He quickly removed the weapon and holster, letting them drop lightly to the floor at his feet.

"Now you can continue," he said lightly, a faint smile returning to his mouth, making his eyes glitter.

Yana wished Clay would touch her. Whenever he did, she couldn't think, all she could do was feel. And right now, *thinking* was making Yana uncomfortable, anxious, anticipating what she knew would happen *later*.

"Come on, Yana, show a little courage," Clay said teasingly. "After all, fair is fair."

To her extraordinary surprise, this strange game Clay was playing with her had turned erotic. Yana helped Clay off with his boots, then removed his shirt, and finally, with tantalizing leisure, unsnapped his trousers and slowly, one button at a time, unbuttoned his fly.

Clay groaned audibly as Yana pushed his trousers down, averting her eyes at the appropriate time, kneeling briefly to tug the garment down to his

169

ankles and help him step out of it.

He's been toying with me. But now he wants me as much as I want him.

Yana stood, smiling coolly, looking straight into Clay's eyes. Her gaze drifted downward. Clay was flagrantly, beautifully aroused.

"Satisfied, Mr. McKenna? I have done everything you requested."

"Yes you have . . . but I'm a long way from satisfied. That will come much, much later."

Clay, stepping backward so his eyes never had to leave Yana's, sat in the overstuffed chair again. He reached out a hand for her.

"Come to me," he said, his voice hoarse with tension.

Yana's knees trembled, her heart pounding. She straddled Clay's heavily muscled thighs. She was moist, heated, achingly ready for him. She touched him, and Clay sighed.

Their gaze never wavered as Yana guided him into her.

Clay's hands were at her bottom, pushing upward and then relaxing to coax Yana into the rhythm he wanted. When she began the movements on her own, a smile curled his mouth, a smile that was too infuriatingly triumphant for Yana's pleasure. She rose up enough to release Clay from her velvety confines. Clay's eyes opened wide in shock.

"You can only take what I freely give you," Yana whispered, her own hunger for pleasure rapidly escalating, yet the need to put Clay's arrogance in perspective also acute. "Is that understood, Mr. McKenna?"

Not accustomed to receiving orders from women while making love—requests, of course, but never demands—Clay immediately began to protest. It was the look in Yana's eyes—flagrantly sensual, yet defiant of her own passionate hunger as well as of Clay's, if need be—that silenced him.

"As you wish . . . whatever you wish," Clay said softly, vaguely aware that he would make any concession, bend or break every personal rule, to be with Yana.

"Much better," Yana replied. She lowered herself onto Clay once again, taking in the full, fiery length of him.

Yana pushed the fingers of her right hand into Clay's hair, pulling so that he was forced to look up into her eyes. "Now you must do what I tell you," she purred sultrily.

Her left hand circled her breast. The nipple was peaked, eager for attention. Yana lifted the breast invitingly, her eyes glowing as she raised and lowered herself.

"Now kiss me, Clay, and you must be very, very good or I will be displeased. And you don't want to displease me, do you, Clay?"

Yana hugged his face to her breast and felt the pressure building inside. She purred softly, knowing Clay could release that pressure and take her to a world where nothing existed but pleasure.

Chapter 9

"You wanted to see me?"

Sorren picked up the coffee urn and reached across the small table in his office to pour a cup for his son. Clay closed the door behind him, then sat facing his father. Between them was a serving plate piled high with scrambled eggs, bacon, American fries, and toast.

Clay started filling his plate. Breakfast meetings were not uncommon for the McKennas. Breakfast meetings in Sorren's office, away from Shadow and the omnipresent Emma, were. Clay waited, knowing his father would talk in good time.

"You know there's been someone asking questions about us?"

Clay nodded, sipping his coffee.

"My sources haven't been able to put a name to him yet, but he was seen meeting another man." Sorren's gaze met his son's. "Antoli Pacca."

"Nico's assistant? How would he know anyone here?"

Sorren shrugged his shoulders. "From now on, be extra careful with what is said in front of Nico and Illyana. Until we get confirmation to the contrary, we work under the assumption that the Zacariouses can't be trusted."

Not trust Yana? It was a ludicrous idea to Clay, but he kept the thought to himself. Defending Yana would tip his hand, showing Sorren his real feelings for her. For now, that wasn't an admission Clay was ready to make to his father . . . or to himself.

"You've got men working on this?"

"Of course." Sorren scratched a match with his thumbnail, lit his cigarette, then reached over the table to light Clay's. As the flame touched the end of his cigarette, Clay's eyes met with Sorren's. "She's very attractive," Sorren said quietly, saying many things with those few words. "Don't let it blind you."

"Count on it."

"I'm counting on you for many things, Clay. Our family's got a lot riding on this deal. Let's make sure we don't get careless."

"You mean, let's make sure *I* don't get careless. You never let your guard down, do you?"

Clay sipped his coffee, wildly curious of what Sorren knew of his relationship with Yana. As a child, Clay believed his father could read his mind, knew all this thoughts and everything he did. Clay didn't believe that now, but Sorren was still the most dispassionately logical thinker he'd ever known.

"I'll keep my eyes and ears open," Clay said,

174

snuffing out his cigarette.

The meeting was over.

Nico had always loved mornings more than any other time of the day. As he rolled along the well-kept dirt road in the one-horse carriage, Nico could see why the McKennas were so attached to this land. It was fertile land, the kind that with sufficient rain and sun would grow any crop. And the people working the land, to Nico's considerable surprise, did not have the beaten, defeated look to them that was so common among laborers the world over. There was a brightness to their spirit, a vivaciousness. The businessman in Nico wondered what this joie de vivre cost the McKennas and how that cost translated into increased productivity.

The familiar sound of his daughter's laughter rang through the clear, cool morning air. Some thirty yards behind him, Clay and Yana were chasing each other on horseback, their faces beaming with youthful vigor, their eyes bright and shiny and full of affection.

Is Clay man enough for Yana? Nico asked himself, full of misgivings. *Man enough for my willful daughter when no other man has been?*

Nico watched Yana's hair flying behind her, like the mare's mane, as she went chasing after Clay. He could not remember a time when he'd seen his daughter so happy, her smiles and laughter so freely given, without affectation or guile.

Yana had apparently gotten over her differences

175

with Clay, and Nico wondered what those differences were. She had behaved so coldly whenever he was near her in New York. Nico wasn't entirely certain he was pleased with his daughter's change of heart. However competent a businessman Clay was, and no matter how mighty an American family he came from, he had the reputation of being a runabout. No father, least of all one as protective as Nico, could accept his daughter being taken in by the well-practiced charms of a known rake.

He turned his attention away from Yana. Nico knew from experience that his daughter's affections were short-lived. Since her early teens, she had worked her way through a series of young men, always finding each one "positively the most fascinating" man in the world. Three weeks later—at most—those same "fascinating men" were "crushing bores." Never for a moment did Nico have to worry that a young beau had gotten *too* close to his daughter.

Laughter once more drew Nico's gaze. Clay was in hot pursuit of Yana, heading away from the road toward the tidy, neatly arranged homes of the field hands and their families.

They look good together, Nico thought, then scolded himself. Yana had to marry a good Greek man if Nico was to maintain his standing among the elite in his country. It wasn't a good idea to entertain any other thought.

*   *   *

Virtually everything Yana had once believed immutably right and wrong, proper and scandalous, was now drifting in doubt. Since their ecstatic, unhurried lovemaking in the dressing room, Yana realized there was not a proper time and place for lovemaking—only the proper *man* for lovemaking.

"What are you doing?" Clay seemed a little cross as he reined in his stallion beside Yana's mare. They were between two small houses, hidden from Nico and the field workers. "Come on, Yana, I'm supposed to keep an eye on you *and* your father."

The look in Yana's dark eyes sizzled. "I prefer a monopoly. I want your eyes only on me." Side by side with their mounts facing opposite directions, Yana reached out to place her palm lightly against Clay's cheek. "You are a beautiful man, Clayton McKenna." She made a face. "Sometimes my English isn't so good. *Beautiful* isn't the right word for a man, is it? Too feminine for you rougish Americans. I don't care. To me, you are beautiful."

Clay leaned over in the saddle, slipping his fingers under her hair, hooking his hand behind her neck. He pulled her toward him until their lips met, warm and soft. A deep, low moan of pleasure escaped him. It occurred to Clay, in an oddly rational way, that he derived more pleasure just from kissing Yana than he had from sleeping with the other women he'd known.

"Is this why you lured me here?" Clay asked as he nibbled lightly on Yana's bottom lip.

Yana moaned a soft agreement. The tip of her

tongue traced the outline of Clay's mouth, then slipped between his lips. "I can't help myself," she whispered. "I know it isn't right of me, but I keep wanting you, Clay. More and more all the time."

She pulled away from Clay. Her dark eyes flashed right and left. They seemed secluded enough, away from unintended witnesses. When her gaze met with Clay's, there were no doubts to haunt her. Clay's need for Yana was as deep, powerful, and fathomless as Yana's hunger for him.

There was no need for words; their eyes said everything they needed to know.

I'm in love with her, thought Clay.

This realization came to him with frightening clarity. He had never intended to fall in love with Illyana Zacarious. Earlier, Clay had dismissed his near obsession with her as the answer to his need for danger and excitement. Since his father had expressly forbidden him to be with Yana, Clay naturally found her fascinating. But now, looking into her eyes, tasting her kisses on his lips, he understood the difference between love and lust—and realized that what he had with Yana was a spine-tingling combination of the two. The powerful epiphany triggered equal amounts of relief and anxiety.

"Kiss me, Clay," Yana whispered. "Kiss me one more time, then take me someplace where we can be alone."

Speaking from the heart was both rare and difficult for Clay. But as he looked into Yana's soft brown eyes, he heard himself begin to speak.

"Yana, I'm in—"

The gunshot cut through the air, silencing anything Clay was to say. A moment after the initial report, a volley of shots followed.

Clay's revolver was in his hand as he rounded the house and headed toward the melee at a full gallop. Nico was standing in the carriage when Clay first saw him. A split second later, he spun, falling onto the carriage seat, a spray of blood coloring the air pink.

There were four assassins that Clay could see. He thumbed back the hammer of his Colt, aimed at the closest masked rider, and squeezed the trigger. The assassin's arms flayed outward. He rolled backward, bounced briefly on his horse's rump for several strides, then fell heavily to the ground.

The horse pulling Nico's carriage panicked and rattled across an open field, scattering field workers already racing from the gunmen. Nico, bleeding and unconscious, slumped off the seat to the floor of the carriage, his life slipping away.

Clay sped forward, meeting the two remaining assassins' charge head-on. He fired again, missed, and thumbed back the hammer once more. Just as he had the last rifleman in his sights, he heard the dull thud of a soft lead slug hitting his stallion in the chest. With a screaming cry of agony, the animal's forelegs buckled.

Yana reined in her mare, seeing the carnage unfolding before her with numbing clarity. She watched as Clay's stallion went down hard, throwing Clay, who rolled on the ground as bullets kicked up dirt near his spinning form.

In a flash, Yana recalled the alley and how frightened she had been of the outlaws, then the confidence she had known when Clay entered the fight. But could he continue to fight against the odds and not die himself?

"Nooooo!" Yana screamed, watching horror-stricken as Clay had to scramble behind his own fallen horse to shield himself from the assassins' bullets.

Clay leaned over the stallion, the ugly black revolver in his extended hand held steady and sure. Another bullet struck the noble beast, stopping its agony. The gun in Clay's hand bucked and roared and the rifleman—the one who had fired the first shot at Nico—crumpled on his horse. He hit the ground and did not move again.

With his three cohorts dead, the last assassin wheeled his horse around and quickly disappeared into the pines from where he had first come, the sound of Clay's gunshots still ringing in his ears.

The nightmare continued for Yana, though later she would remember only fragments of what she had said and done.

Clay took Yana's horse to catch the runaway carriage. He stretched Nico out on the ground, and Yana cradled her father's head in her lap as he applied makeshift bandages to the old man's chest, shoulder, and thigh. Nico was alive, though critically wounded.

"He's dead," Yana whispered to no one, tears falling onto Nico's expressionless face. "Papa's dead and it's all my fault."

"He's not dead, and it's not your fault." Clay grabbed Yana forcibly by the upper arm, squeezing strongly enough to make her wince in pain. "I'm not going to let him die. But I need your help." Clay released Yana. He took a large piece of cloth given to him by an elderly field hand. He placed it over the bled-through bandage on Nico's chest. "Hold this in place tight." Clay took Yana's hand, placing it over the bandage. His jetty eyes, cold and hard as steel, met Yana's teary ones. "Do what I tell you," he said, quietly commanding, reassuring Yana that somehow he could make everything perfect once again. "I need your help, Yana. So does Nico. We all need you to be strong."

Clay issued orders to inform the "big house," as the ranch hands called his home, of what had happened, and to summon Dr. Cannell. A teenage boy took off at a dead run to do as Clay commanded.

He's so good at this, thought Yana bitterly. *Taking charge. Being in control. He knows just what to do because violence is a way of life for Clay McKenna and all the McKennas.*

Another field hand knelt beside Clay. Bandages were being made with bedding from the nearby houses. Clay wrapped one tightly around Nico's thigh, patching the entrance and exit wounds at the same time.

"Don't worry about his leg," Yana said, her tears having subsided. "He's been shot in the chest! Concentrate on that!"

Clay, very calm, shook his head. "The leg wound wouldn't kill him, if that's all he had. But he's lost a lot of blood. There's not much more we can do."

"What are you saying?" There was a shrillness to Yana's voice, an undercurrent of mortal fear.

Clay looked around, wishing there were more he could say to Yana, more he could do for Nico. Around him there were three field hands who had been wounded by stray bullets.

"I'll need you to help me with the others." Clay's voice was very hard, and Yana resented it. He was accustomed to taking command in crisis situations. This bloodshed, this seemingly random act of absolute violence, was nothing new to him . . . and Yana hated him for it.

"Go to hell!"

"Yana, other people have been hurt. I *need* your help."

Clay motioned for a young girl, probably not more than ten or twelve, to put her hands over Nico's bandages to keep the pressure on. Then he took Yana by the hand and pulled her to her feet. "He'll be brought to the big house soon. A rider has probably already been sent to fetch Dr. Cannell. I need you to be brave, Yana. I need you to be strong."

And though Yana had never before had to be brave in this way, something inside her took control. She found strength inside herself when she thought she had none, courage from a deep well that she had thought was empty.

Her hands were shaking so badly it was difficult to bandage wounds, but Yana did not let that stop her. She refused to let herself get sick, though the sight of so much blood made her stomach feel queasy. And when a young man needed Yana's help and strength, she was there to do all she could for him.

"It's going to be okay," Yana said to the young man, wrapping his forearm with a bandage. He had been hit by a stray bullet. Kneeling beside him was his young wife, who was very pretty and very pregnant. "The bullet went clean through," Yana explained to the young woman. "He's bled quite a bit, but the bleeding seems to have stopped. Keep holding the bandage in place. We'll bring him to a doctor as soon as we can."

"Thank you, ma'am," the young bride whispered. "Thank you. Thank you so much. I've never been good at doctoring."

Neither have I. But I have to be now. Clay's counting on me. Papa's counting on me. Even your husband and you are counting on me, and I don't even know your names.

"He'll be fine," Yana said. And then, despite the gravity of the situation, she forced a twinkle into her eye as she looked at the young woman, so much in love with her husband. "He's strong and he's handsome. He'll make strong, handsome babies. Trust me. I know about these things."

Yana didn't know about these things, of course.

183

Throughout her life, whenever these things had come up, there was always someone else to take care of the problem. Always someone on the Zacarious payroll whose job it was to make Yana's life as happy, simple, and trouble free as was humanly possible.

"Where the hell were you?"

Clay, sitting in a chair facing his father's desk, had to look up to see into Sorren's livid eyes. Sorren was standing, leaning on the desk, legal papers crumpled in his hands. Now that he knew his son was hale and hearty, that no assassin's bullet had drawn McKenna blood, his full wrath spewed forth uncensored.

"Well? What do you have to say for yourself?"

Clay shook his head, not knowing what to say. The truth didn't seem like something his father would want to hear.

Well, Dad, you see, Yana and I have patched up our differences lately and we just can't seem to keep our hands off each other. So Yana rode behind the track houses so her father wouldn't see us. We were just about to make love, and we would have, right out there under the sun and the trees with nothing but the grass for a bed. But we didn't make love because Nico got shot, and he's upstairs right now, dying if he's not dead already, and I know it's all my fault but there isn't a damn thing I can do about it now.

Sorren's tirade started again, then stopped when

184

the door opened and Shadow walked in. She closed the door behind her, then walked directly to Sorren's side.

"That's enough now, Sorren. This whole house can hear you." She patted Sorren's shoulder. He sat in his overstuffed wing-backed chair. "Clay, I don't know what happened, and frankly, I don't want to know. All that really matters is that you're safe now."

Clay leaned back in his chair, looking at his mother and father. Sometimes, when he saw them like this, he felt like an outsider. They were so close that nothing—not even a son—could get between them. So many times in the past he had seen them just like this—Sorren sitting at his desk with Shadow standing at his side, facing their problems together. They had fought so many battles together that now they nearly acted as a single entity.

Shadow, having calmed Sorren, continued to touch him, rubbing his shoulders as he spoke. "Mr. Zacarious is alive. Dr. Cannell said he was hit by five different bullets."

"What are the odds?" Clay asked.

Shadow frowned. She didn't like it when her son or husband were so coldly pragmatic. "Dr. Cannel gives him a twenty-five percent chance of making it through the night. If he's still alive tomorrow morning, his chances improve. Right now is the critical time because of the loss of blood." Shadow gave a small but reassuring smile to Clay. "Dr. Cannell said if it hadn't been for the treatment you gave Mr. Zacarious, he wouldn't have made it. Dr.

Cannel was quite impressed with what you did, considering you were using shirts and torn bed sheets for bandages."

"Yana helped. I couldn't have done it without her."

Sorren, not easily mollified, smoothed out a contract he had balled in his fists. "First aid should not have been necessary."

"Enough now," Shadow said quietly. She was the only person who could talk to either Sorren or Clay that way and not suffer the consequences. Certainly, she was the only one who could get them to stop fighting with just a word or a glance.

"You're right," Sorren said after a tense pause. "What's done is done. We have enough troubles ahead of us without dwelling on those in the past." Sorren rolled a cigarette before continuing, ignoring Shadow's disapproving look. "We have questions that need answers. For instance, was Nico the only target of the assassination? Who stands to benefit most from his death? Illyana? Antoli Pacca? The gunmen were apparently amateurs"—his eyes touched Clay's briefly, the glimmer of admiration in them unmistakable—"judging by how easily Clay . . . *dispatched* them."

"There had been four men. I'm sure of it. I only killed three."

Sorren nodded. "So you told me before. I've got men searching now. If this fourth man was as rank an amateur as I believe, he'll either be dead by now— killed by his employer to silence a wagging tongue—

186

or he'll have a pocketful of money. He'll spend the blood money fast and loose." Sorren made a face of disdain. Amateurs offended him. "If he's still alive, he shouldn't be too difficult to find."

Shadow continued to gently massage the muscles in Sorren's neck and shoulders. "There's also Yana. She and Emma had a talk. Nico's been trying to marry her off for a couple years now. No man she's met matched up to what Yana wants, apparently, since she's sent them all packing."

All except one, Clay thought guiltily, this turn of conversation disturbing him.

Sorren closed his eyes and allowed himself to relax as Shadow rubbed the tension-knotted muscles in his back. He said, "You think an unrequited lover would come all the way to Virginia from Greece to kill her, or kill her father to punish her? Why not have someone do the job in Pirias?"

"The men her father set her up with would all be well connected. They'd naturally have the money to do whatever they wanted, wherever they wanted. Doing it here would deflect suspicion."

"Makes sense," Sorren said. "But let's put that possibility aside for now."

Clay felt a chill go through him. Could it really be possible that someone would want to see his Yana— and now he thought of her as *his* Yana—dead?

"I think Nico was the target of the assassination," Clay said, a queer, uneasy fear suddenly growing inside him.. "Just Nico. Not Yana or me. Somebody paid the men to wait in the trees, someone who has

187

eyes and ears inside this house and has been spying on us unnoticed."

"Not likely," Shadow said, fully aware of the predatory instincts of both her husband and son. "One of you two would have smelled the danger. You always do."

"We always *think* we do," Sorren said quietly. "I'm not the man I used to be." Shadow began to say something, but Sorren shook his head, stopping her. She knew he had to accept at least part of the responsibility for Nico's wounds, even if it couldn't possibly be any of his fault. "For now, we've got to hope that Nico makes it through the night. Tomorrow I'll get the lawyers looking at the contracts we've already signed with the Zacarious Shipping Company. Then we'll know exactly what we're liable for as far as this venture goes."

Clay rubbed his temples. The day had been an unending nightmare, and it didn't help to know that sleep would not come easily to him. He cleared his throat to get Sorren to open his eyes.

"If Nico dies, who's in charge of the company?" Clay asked. "Yana? What about Antoli Pacca?"

"I'll check into that. It's going to be damned important to us. I don't know if I can trust Miss Zacarious, but I know I don't trust Pacca."

"Where is he now?" Clay asked.

"In the guest house. I've got Elijah watching him."

John Elijah was Emma's son. He was well over six feet tall, weighed over two hundred forty pounds, and was enormously strong. If he got his hands on someone, nothing less than Divine Intervention would free the man.

"Why don't you try to get some sleep, dear," Shadow said to her son. "It's been a long day, and tomorrow's going to be another hard one."

Clay nodded, rising from his chair. His bones ached all over. The smell of gunpowder and blood was still in his nose, and he couldn't seem to shake it.

"Good night," he said. At the office door, Clay stopped and turned to look directly at his father. For long seconds, their gazes locked and held. "I'm sorry I messed up, Dad. You gave me a job to do and I didn't do it. I failed my duty."

Clay left the room.

"Couldn't you have said something to make him feel better?" Shadow asked, still rubbing her husband's neck and shoulders. "Would that have been so difficult? You know he's going to punish himself much worse than you ever will."

Sorren sighed wearily. He tilted his head back, taking Shadow's soft hands into his own. "I know. I know I should have said something to him. I just . . . it's just so hard for me to be easy with him. I try. I really do. But then he gets so damn stubborn that I—"

"In other words, you've got a son who is just like his father, and that's what's so maddening. That's why you push him so hard." Shadow tugged on Sorren's hand. "Come on, it's time for you to go to bed, too."

"Where would I be and what would I do without you?"

"You'd be just like Clay, only older. Too handsome and too rich and smart and too easily bored . . . and just a little bit lost in this world that you keep trying to make sense of."

"Sometimes it doesn't make any sense."

"Then stop trying."

"I can't."

"I know you can't." Shadow squeezed her husband's hand, leading him toward their bedroom.

Chapter 10

Antoli Pacca tossed the brandy to the back of his throat, then swallowed it in a single burning gulp. He grimaced as the fiery liquor seared his throat, cursing that it wasn't ouzo.

Curse all the gods in heaven and hell! Curse the mothers and fathers and little children! And curse the incompetent Edward Danzer!

Antoli had waited for the good news—the news that Nico Zacarious was dead—at a small saloon in town. He didn't want to be at the McKenna ranch when the assassins struck. Antoli was afraid that his joy would be too great to contain. So he waited in the tavern for the good news. And he decided that when he got it, he would wait longer still—long enough so he could keep an expression of heartfelt sorrow on his face when he met with Yana to give his condolences.

"He's not dead?" Antoli asked, not believing what

he had heard. "They didn't kill him?"

Danzer shook his head, putting his hands up to quiet the Greek man's escalating temper. "Keep your voice down. I said he wasn't dead *yet*. My man promised me the old man got hit at least a half-dozen times. Zacarious is old. He'll never live through that."

"You don't know him like I do," Antoli shot back accusingly. "Nico Zacarious may be old, but he's got a strong heart. His will to live is enormous. If he is not dead now, he may not die."

Danzer gritted his teeth in rage. "Don't you worry, I've got plans to fix everything. Nico Zacarious is a dead man. He'll never leave the country alive."

Antoli shook his head. He didn't want to hear any more empty promises. "Enough of your talk! You say you can fix everything, but you can't even kill a doddering old man!"

In that moment, through the red fog of his rage, Antoli saw that Edward Danzer desperately wanted to kill him. But Antoli knew that was not Danzer's style; he paid other people to do such things. As he looked into Danzer's eyes, Antoli decided that when Nico was dead, he'd get rid of Edward Danzer, too. There was no way he could allow Danzer to live when this was done. Danzer was just a tool for a particular job, and when that job was finished, his usefulness would be over.

"Do whatever you have to do," Antoli said, forcing himself to be calm. "At this point, I don't care how you do it, just finish what needs to be done."

Danzer smiled malevolently. "You dance around your own words, Mr. Pacca. We're talking about killing your boss. It's called murder. While I have nothing against it, I do rather resent your high-handed, abstract approach. Don't for a second think you're above simple, common cold-blooded murder."

Antoli pushed himself out of the dirty booth. "I won't forget that, Mr. Danzer. And if you're an intelligent man, you won't forget it, either."

Shaking his head, Antoli snapped himself out of the bad memory. He poured another brandy and tossed it down his throat. He went to the window and carefully looked out between the curtain and the sill. The huge black man was still out there, silent and unmoving.

"Bastard," Antoli whispered to the shadowy figure outside. "I'll fix you, too. Someday, I'll fix all of you."

It galled Antoli that he should have to be afraid of a black man. He wasn't really afraid that the McKenna's had deduced his part in the assassination attempt. Even under the worst conditions, he couldn't have been found out yet. But the McKennas had put someone outside his door, presumably to protect him. A black man, no less. And that meant his movements were hampered. He was being watched.

Antoli poured three fingers of brandy into a glass and carried it to his bedroom. The dreams would be happy, even idyllic. Yana would beg him, absolutely *beg* him, to make love to her . . . in his dreams.

A drunken smile curled menacingly across Antoli's saliva-glistening lips as he headed for bed, comforted by his thoughts.

Yana sat cross-legged at the foot of her father's bed. Her eyes were puffy but dry as she watched his chest slowly and unevenly rise and fall. She had cried herself out. There were no tears left for Nico or for herself. For the most part, Yana just felt numb.

"I'm sorry, *Mbambaky*," she whispered. "I didn't mean for you to get hurt. I never meant to hurt you."

Yana's voice broke. She looked away from his ashen face, turning her eyes to the candles that burned on the nightstand.

He's so pale. Please, God, don't let him die.

"But I guess I've hurt you all along, haven't I? Mama died giving me birth, and you've been alone since then." Yana pulled her eyes away, fighting the hypnotic effect of the candles. She gazed at her father, willing him to open his eyes, willing him to live. "I've been a disappointment to you all along. I know that. Even if you've never told me, I guess I've always known."

Yana straightened her back, the way she knew her father would want her to, and managed a faltering smile.

"But things are going to change with us, *Mbambaky*," she said, using a favorite Greek expression of endearment to a father. "You'll see. I'll settle down and marry a fine young man . . . a good Greek man from a family you approve of. You just live,

194

Papa, and tell me whom you want me to marry."

Thoughts of Clay came flooding in, and again Yana's voice was choked off with a sob.

"I'm scared, Papa. I'm so scared. Please don't die."

Emma gave Clay a nudge, pushing him down the hallway toward his bedroom, away from Nico's door. "Leave Miss Yana alone for now," she whispered. "She's gots to be alone with her daddy at a time like this."

Clay walked slowly, keeping Emma at his side. He had opened the door to Nico's room, wanting to see if Yana would like a cup of tea. Yana never noticed the door open. For several seconds, Clay and Emma watched the young woman talking to her comatose father. And though they couldn't understand the Greek words that she spoke, Clay and Emma guessed their meaning.

"She's gonna be jus' fine," Emma said reassuringly, slipping her arm around Clay's slender waist, hugging him briefly. "An' so will Mr. Nico. I'll sees to it. So will Dr. Cannell. You know how powerful smart he is with doctorin'. Remember when you was jus' a baby, no more than six or seven, an' you broke your leg? He fixed you up right proper."

"I'm sure you're right, Emma," Clay replied with little conviction.

"Of course I'm right. Ain't I always right?"

Clay smiled wanly down at Emma. She'd been with the McKennas since before his birth, and he absolutely adored her.

"I'm right 'bout a lot of things. Like I'm right 'bout the powerful good feelings you got in your heart for Miss Yana."

Clay stopped. When Emma turned to look up at him, his face was grave. Emma reached up to place a loving, pudgy-fingered hand softly against his cheek.

"It's different with you this time, ain't it? Miss Yana, she ain't like them other ladies you tomcat aroun' with. I could see that right away. These ol' eyes o' mine don't miss much, an' what they do miss ain't worth lookin' at anyhow."

Clay wondered if Emma knew what had happened in the dressing room after she had left him alone with Yana.

"Do Mother and Father know?"

"'Bout you and Miss Yana? I can't rightly say. If they do, they do. But I ain't gonna be the one to tell 'em." Emma shook her head sadly. "You done got yourself in a mess o' trouble this time, Mr. Clay. You surely have. Now I don't know if it's truly love you got in your heart for Miss Yana, but whatever it is, it's somethin' truly special. An' near as I can tell, Mr. Nico's got his heart set on Miss Yana marryin' herself some rich Greek boy. An' if that ain't troubles enough, your mama an' papa ain't gonna cotton to the idea o' you mixin' your pleasure in with their business. They been turnin' a blind eye towards you an' your tomcattin' aroun', but they won't this time."

Clay, who had always suspected Emma was all-knowing and all-seeing, was now convinced of it. He asked her the question he'd never had the courage to ask Yana. "What does Yana think of me, Emma?"

"What you askin' me for? Ask Miss Yana that. She's the one doin' the feelin'."

"I'm asking you because you're the most intuitively intelligent person I've ever known." Clay added with a smile, "Besides, you're always right. You said so yourself."

"I don't know nothin' 'bout intui-whatever you said. I just knows what my eyes sees and my nose smells." Emma patted the back of Clay's hand, loving him, wanting nothing more than his happiness. "I thinks Miss Yana's got feelings jus' like you. She's all mixed up an' crazy inside. But she's crazy for you, Mr. Clay. Ain't no other way aroun' that. So you jus' gots to be real patient with her now 'cause she's in a powerful bad way. But there's gonna come a time when she'll need you. She'll need you real bad. You jus' wait for her to do the reachin', an' when she does, you give her some o' your strength."

Emma opened the door to Clay's bedroom and gave him a nudge. "You go to bed now an' get some sleep. Do what I say now, Mr. Clay, or you'll make ol' Emma powerful angry."

"We can't have that, can we?" Clay bent down and kissed Emma's cheek. "I don't know what I'd do without you."

Danzer leaned against the elm tree on the outskirts of town, waiting, hating, feeling the need to vent his rage becoming stronger with each second.

The McKennas had to die. All of them. Not just Clay and Sorren McKenna, but Shadow, too. Even the daughters, LaTina and the others, away at private schools, had to die. Not until every McKenna was expunged from the face of the earth and every trace of their foul bloodline had been thoroughly eradicated could he rest.

As surely as he believed the sun would rise in the morning, Edward Danzer believed that sooner or later Clay and Sorren would discover he had been behind the assassination of Nico Zacarious. And when that day came, Sorren and Clay would come for him, hunting him with slow, methodical precision.

Mortal enemies of the McKennas had a very short life expectancy, and Danzer knew it.

"Fools!" Danzer hissed, thinking of the men he had hired to kill Nico Zacarious.

It would have been better, though more expensive, to hire professional gunmen to do the assassination. But the information line that plugged straight into the McKennas like telegraph wires could never be silenced. Had the word gotten out that someone was in the market for professional killers, the McKennas would surely have found out about it. That forced Danzer to use alcoholic drifters and unemployed cowpunchers.

And where had that gotten him? Nico Zacarious was still alive. The McKenna mansion protected like a medieval fortress. Literally dozens of McKenna soldiers running around asking questions.

And there was Antoli Pacca. A hothead. His Greek temper made him a risk factor that Danzer hadn't calculated on in his plans to destroy the McKennas.

Antoli had openly challenged Danzer, insulting him, almost coming right out and threatening him.

Danzer had no doubt about what had to be done. A bullet in the Greek's ear and he wouldn't insult anyone again.

He heard the sound of hoofbeats coming from the east, moving closer at a canter. Danzer smiled. Soon the waiting would be over.

"You lied to me, you son of a bitch!" Paul Higgins spat, reining his roan gelding off the road, coming to a halt at the elm tree. "You said it would be easy! You said they wouldn't be expecting one damn thing!"

"Just relax. Tell me everything that happened."

Danzer appeared tranquil. The excitement going through him was thick with malice, but it did not show as he first calmed the would-be assassin, then coaxed him for details of the morning's activities.

"That's all of it then? Everything you can remember?"

Paul Higgins nodded vigorously. "That Clay McKenna was shooting like he had a Gatling gun in his hand instead of a Colt. And every time he shot, another one of us went down."

"Apparently, he didn't shoot at you."

For a moment, their eyes met. Danzer read the cowardice in the drifter's soul and knew beyond a doubt that when the other three assassins had made their charge at Nico's carriage, this one had stayed

199

back where it was safe, away from Clay McKenna's deadly Colt.

"He tried. Yeah, he tried for me, but I moved too quick for him. I was shootin' all the time and never let him get a bead on me."

You were running like the Devil himself was after you.

"So what about it, Mr. Danzer? You got the second half of my payment?"

"But Nico Zacarious isn't dead." It was only prudent to put up some resistance. To pay up too easily would draw suspicion. "I promised to pay you when the old man was dead, with a bonus if you killed his bodyguard at the same time."

"Yeah, but you didn't say nothin' about that bodyguard being Clay McKenna!" Higgins shot back accusingly. "Now I want my money and I want it right now!" Higgins's right hand hovered near the butt of the revolver at his hip. *"Now."*

Danzer looked him in the eye, smiling. "The old man's as good as dead, so I suppose you deserve something for what you've done."

Higgins smiled back, his body relaxing. His hand moved away from the revolver. "Good to know you're an honest man, Mr. Danzer."

Danzer reached for his money—or so Higgins thought. In the pale moonlight, Higgins saw the gleam of a knifeblade coming toward him. He tried to move out of the way, but the razor-sharp blade was already cutting through soft flesh. He tried to scream in rage, but the only sound to escape his lips was his final deathgasp.

Looking down at the corpse, Danzer said calmly, "I did say you deserve something for your trouble, didn't I?"

Edward Danzer rode toward town, enjoying the feeling of having tied up the loose strings of his life.

Chapter 11

Clay was thankful that breakfast was not a solemn affair. Instead, it was a strategy session, a time for the McKennas—Clay, Sorren, and Shadow—to discuss the possibilities of what the immediate and long-range future held in store for them.

"Clearly, the possibility that someone is trying to prevent the agreement between the Zacarious Shipping Company and McKenna Enterprises from going through must be explored," Clay said, addressing his mother and father. "So, who benefits if we don't go into business together?"

Sorren shook his head, sipping coffee, thinking.

Shadow said, "I think it had something to do with just Nico. Why would anyone want to destroy the arrangement? It would provide many jobs in both Greece and the United States. Cotton growers and tobacco growers like ourselves would profit by it through expanded distribution points. I just don't see why that would threaten anyone."

"I'm inclined to agree with you," Sorren said, his eyes unfocused, his voice even, detached. "Everyone from dock workers to field hands to growers in the U.S. would benefit from the deal. And in Greece, there's the wineries that would profit by it, as well as the optics companies in Germany and Switzerland. That encompasses a lot of people. Why destroy something like that?" He shook his head. "No, I think this was definitely an act of revenge. It was against the Zacariouses, not against the McKennas."

Sorren leaned back in his chair as Emma entered the room. She ladled another helping of scrambled eggs onto his plate, then did the same for Clay.

"Even if this is just against Nico," Sorren continued, "it looks bad for us. Never good to have something like this on your own land. It's not just bad business, it's bad form."

"It's not your fault," Clay said, still feeling guilty for having run away with Yana when he should have stayed with Nico, where he could have protected the unarmed Greek businessman.

"No. Not completely. Some blame must surely rest on your shoulders, but not all of it. You weren't there when the first shot was fired, but if it weren't for you, Nico would most certainly be dead now." Sorren let his gaze land briefly on Clay. The tension between them that had existed the previous night had almost completely vanished. "You weren't there when the first shot was fired. That was an error. But you repelled the assailants when they made their charge. You killed three of the four. That's to your credit."

Shadow, who felt that *taking credit* for killing three men—even if they were murderers—was not something a gentleman should do, wanted to protest, but did not. There was the very real possibility that her family was in the early stages of a war, and her husband and son were better equipped to handle such matters.

"What's the possibility of Nico having done business in the U.S. before?" Clay asked. "What if he cheated someone in the past? He's an influential man and word gets around fast. This certain someone who was cheated discovers that Nico Zacarious is back in the United States, and the first thing he does is hire an assassination squad. It's just our lousy luck that it happens on our land, when we're trying to finagle a deal with him and his company."

"That's a possibility."

Shadow said, "I'll look into that. I know a hundred wives in Washington whose husbands have connections. They know of every business transaction between American business interests and foreigners, and will know if Nico's done business here before."

Clay looked at his father and smiled. He knew how uneasy she was whenever there was talk of violence. But in discussing their family business and solving business problems, she was an absolute equal to Sorren. In some ways, she was even better at negotiating than Sorren was, usually because so many men found it impossible to argue ably with a woman.

"I'm glad the girls aren't here," Shadow said after a pause. "Someday, we'll all be able to work on . . . these types of things . . . together. For now, though, it is best they get an education."

Sorren chuckled, thinking of how his eldest daughter, LaTina, would love nothing more than to be in the middle of a good business fight. LaTina was just like Clay—intelligent, willful, and sometimes impossibly stubborn. She wouldn't back down from a fight if the odds were one hundred to one against her—a tendency that Sorren couldn't help but admire, even as he occasionally lost his temper with his daughter.

"Thank goodness they're not here," Clay said. "LaTina would be under my feet the whole time. I don't need her causing me aggravation."

Shadow chuckled, knowing better than to take Clay at his word. He missed his sisters—particularly LaTina—constantly. No matter how many women openly adored Clay, nothing compared to the adoration of his sisters.

Sorren, ever the pragmatist, cleared his throat, signaling it was time to get back to business.

"Do we have a consensus then? We work under the premise that the attack was directed solely at Nico, and that if we are to do business with him, we must determine if this was an act of revenge, or if Nico is the victim of enemies and needs our help and protection. We must above all answer this question: What did Nico do to bring this upon himself?"

Yana whipped into the room, skirts flying, her face

red with rage.

"How dare you say such things about my father when he's lying in bed right now, more dead than alive? What kind of people are you, anyway?"

Yana looked at each of them in turn. She had been standing outside the door for several minutes, listening to the McKennas talk of their troubles, hearing them assign guilt and blame to Nico, daring to suggest that the assassination was something he had actually brought upon himself.

Clay said quietly, "Yana, I don't think you quite understand—"

"Don't patronize me! I understand that you three are sitting here discussing my father as though he were nothing more than a machine, a tool for you to use to increase your personal wealth! You talk of him in terms of profit and loss! You are so quick to blame my papa for getting shot. Do you really expect me to believe that you have no skeletons in *your* family closet? No associate who feels cheated? Don't you have enemies of your own?"

The hatred Clay saw in Yana's eyes surprised him. This wasn't just hurt she felt, this was a threat to her and her father. When she turned her eyes to him, he saw the betrayal she felt, from him and his family.

"Yana, it's not like that. Really, it isn't," he said. "This has been a very confusing, tragic time for all of us. We're grasping at straws. We're guessing, that's all. We just want to know what happened and why."

"My father got shot, that's what happened! He's lying upstairs now, unconscious." Her voice cracked, and for a second Yana's anger decomposed into sorrow. "Go look at him." Yana spoke softly, her voice laced more with fear for her father's life than anger for the McKennas. "Just look at him . . . he's so pale . . . so pale."

Clay started to get out of his chair. He didn't care if his mother and father saw him holding Yana, he had to take her into his arms. He had to let her know that no matter what happened, he would never let anyone hurt her. He had to look into Yana's eyes and convince her that she was the most magnificent thing that had ever happened to him, and that if her father's death pushed her away from him, the tragedy would be doubled.

But the icy, contemptuous look that Yana shot Clay stopped him in mid-step.

Let Miss Yana come to you, Emma had said. It was wise advice, and Clay sensed that if he were ever to become a part of Yana's life again, he would need to follow it.

Yana composed herself and quickly asked Shadow, "Can you please have some food brought to my father's room?"

"Of course," Shadow replied. "I'll have Emma make you some—"

Shadow stopped talking. Yana had walked out of the room.

"I want men with rifles on the rooftops there and there," Clay said, pointing to the guest house and the northwest corner of the main house. "Good men. Men we know we can trust."

John Elijah nodded. A Winchester repeater was cradled in his enormous arms. "I'll take that spot there myself," he said, looking at the main house.

"You were outside all last night, weren't you?"

John Elijah nodded. He seldom spoke, but his eyes said he wouldn't mind spending another night outside if Clay felt it was necessary.

"Make the security arrangements, then get some sleep," Clay said. "You've got to be dead on your feet by now. I want you fresh and alert for tonight."

"Yes, Mr. Clay." John Elijah looked away. Clay, sensing more was to be said, waited impatiently. A man couldn't hurry John Elijah along with his words. "You really think they'll try again, Mr. Clay? I looked at the men that tried and failed. They were no-goods. Seems to me they failed pretty bad. Three out of the four got themselves killed. And we've got our guard up now, Mr. Clay."

Clay shrugged, studying the tall black man's handsome profile. John Elijah was twenty years older than Clay, and in many ways he had always been like an uncle to the younger McKenna.

"What do you think happened, John Elijah?" he asked, trying to coax the words out. "I can hear the wheels turning."

"I think somebody wants us to look bad, Mr. Clay. If it was just that Greek man who needed killing, and I was the one that wanted to kill him, I sure wouldn't do it the way they did."

209

"I'm not sure I get your point."

Another lengthy pause, then, "The McKennas are rich and powerful. They've got themselves rich and powerful friends, and rich and powerful enemies. I believe the same can be said for Mr. Zacarious."

"Uh-huh. But I still don't see what you're getting at."

"What's all these rich and powerful enemies doing hiring a bunch of no-goods to do something like this? You'd think professional men would be hired, wouldn't you? Even then, it wouldn't be a gang, it would be just one good man with a rifle. He'd sit back a hundred or hundred-fifty yards, he'd squeeze the trigger just once, and that would be the end of it."

John Elijah turned, walking slowly with his head down, his eyes unfocused on the ground at his feet. Clay walked with him.

"You've been talking about business dealings and all that sort of thing. Well, what if it ain't a business thing at all? If it was business, then there would be more money in it, wouldn't there? No, Mr. Clay, I'd say whoever was behind this isn't in the same league with the McKennas and that Greek fellow. Whoever is behind this is poor, mean no-goods."

Clay cursed himself for not having thought of that on his own. Although John Elijah's analysis didn't necessarily hit the bull's-eye, it was a possibility that Clay and his father hadn't yet explored.

"Get some sleep," Clay said. "I get the feeling we're all going to have some long days ahead of us."

"I get the feeling you're right, Mr. Clay. That I do."

When he awoke, Antoli felt like someone had split his head in two with an axe. He splashed his face with cool water and stumbled around the guest house for an hour before getting dressed.

Is Nico dead yet?

He doubted the old man had died, though Antoli desperately wanted to be wrong. If Nico had died, someone would have come to him to give him the news. After all, Antoli was Nico Zacarious's right-hand man, his personal assistant. Surely that would warrant some priority.

What if someone came to the door and I didn't hear because I was so drunk when I went to sleep?

That could be explained. A man can be excused for imbibing too much when a revered leader has been shot. Nico is like a father to me, Antoli would tell them. The shock of discovering he had been shot was too much. He'd had a drink or two—maybe more than that, he didn't remember exactly. Such a thing can be forgiven, can't it?

The thought brightened Antoli's spirits. His head was still throbbing hideously, but the prospects of stealing the Zacarious fortune and destroying what remained of the Zacarious family added color to his cheeks.

He looked at himself in the mirror over the washbasin. His eyes were yellow, sick-looking.

If nobody came last night, Antoli thought, *I can tell them I couldn't sleep at all.*

He smiled. He might even get some sympathy for his haggard appearance.

It was a bright afternoon, the sunshine stabbing Antoli with painful brilliance. He squinted his eyes, looking around the compound. He cursed softly in Greek when he saw the stern faces of the men and noted the rifles and carbines many of them carried. Midway between the main house and the riding stables, Antoli saw Clay talking with the gigantic black man who had stood outside his door the previous night. Antoli cursed the black man's soul, then automatically added Clay's name to the imprecation.

When Clay and the black man parted company, Antoli headed toward Clay, putting on his best expression for the occasion.

"Good afternoon, Mr. McKenna," Antoli said. A weak smile ruffled the corner of his mouth, the smile of a sad man who is trying to make the best of a bad thing. "Is this a good time to talk, or should I talk with your father?"

"Talk?" Clay eyed Antoli suspiciously. "What do we have to talk about?"

"Our business arrangements, of course. I'm sure that Mr. Zacarious would want—"

"He's not dead, Antoli."

Antoli Pacca swallowed his rage. The Americans were so quick to call everyone by first name. They obviously didn't realize that first names should be saved only for a special few, to make the critical

212

distinction between business associates and close friends.

"Yes, and for that we are all grateful, Mr. McKenna," Antoli said, hoping Clay would follow suit. "Nevertheless, I am sure that Mr. Zacarious would not want this unfortunate incident to get in the way of his plans."

"Oh?"

Antoli looked away for a moment, wishing on his partner's grave that the buffoons who had attacked Nico had been skilled enough to kill Clay, as had been planned.

"I was just going to see him. How is he?"

Clay's aggressive stance was undisguised. He had seen Antoli casting glances—covetous, lustful looks —at Yana when she wasn't aware of it. He didn't like Antoli, and he wasn't in the mood to pretend he did.

"Unconscious. Still unconscious. But Dr. Cannell said his condition is more stable than last night. His chances are improving all the time."

The doddering old man doesn't even know when it's time to die! thought Antoli with acidic intensity.

"Just the same, I would like to see him," Antoli said, giving Clay another smile in the vain hope that it would win him some sympathy. "Just to see him will give me comfort, even if Mr. Zacarious doesn't know I am in the room. You must understand that."

Clay said nothing. Antoli felt a slow, creeping fear work up his spine.

"How is Illyana taking this? It must be such a shock to her. But then, it is a shock to everyone, is it not? Who would want to hurt a man like Mr.

213

Zacarious? So kind and generous with the people."
Antoli moved a little to his left so that Clay's head
blocked the sun. His headache had returned with a
mighty vengeance. "Perhaps we can talk later.
Everything is in chaos now, but plans must be made,
agreements settled. Isn't that the way it should be,
Mr. McKenna?" Antoli asked.

"Yes, I think it is," Clay replied. He smiled
humorlessly, making Antoli shiver. "I just don't
know if you've got the authority to speak for Mr.
Zacarious."

Antoli walked slowly toward the main house,
hating Clay with a passion that astounded even him.
Usually it took longer for Antoli to develop a hatred
deep and consuming enough for him to want to kill a
man.

At the main house, an elderly Caucasian maid in a
starched uniform greeted Antoli at the door. Antoli
started to move past her when a cowboy, his clothes
clean but well-worn, his hand on the butt of his
revolver, stepped in quickly behind the maid.

"I am Mr. Zacarious's assistant," Antoli said,
fighting against his growing indignation. "If you
had been here earlier, you would have known that.
Now please step aside so that I may see Mr.
Zacarious."

"He's sleeping," the cowboy said.

Antoli looked at the man. He found it incompre-
hensible that some unshaven cowboy had the
temerity to stand in his way.

The final indignity came moments later, when

214

Emma arrived on the scene and gave the approval for Antoli to go to Nico's bedroom. Antoli could not fathom how a family as powerful as the McKennas could allow a black woman such authority. He knew now why Edward Danzer had spoken at such great lengths about the disgusting McKennas. Sorren McKenna marries a squaw, and then a black woman rules the roost!

He let himself into Nico's room. Illyana, who had been sitting at Nico's side, stood and crossed the room to Antoli. Her face was pale and drawn, with dark circles under her eyes. When Antoli looked at Illyana, all he saw was a very attractive woman who was excitingly vulnerable.

"How is he doing?" Antoli asked. He put his hands on Yana's shoulders, but she twisted sharply, shrugging him off and taking a step backward to be out of reach. "Yana, I only want to help. You know that."

"Keep your voice down," Yana whispered. She glanced over at her father as though afraid she'd woken him. "What are you doing here?"

"I wanted to see if there's anything I can do to help." Antoli assumed a hurt expression for Yana's benefit. "He is a friend to me, Yana, not just my employer. I wish you would see that. What has happened hurts me gravely." And then, calculating her emotional weakness, he said, "I love him, too, Yana. He has been my mentor, my teacher."

Yana's tenuous hold on her emotions began to slip, and Antoli made the most of it. He took her by

215

the shoulders again, and though she struggled, he pulled her against his chest, then wound his arms tightly around her.

"It's a terrible thing that has happened," he said in Greek, hoping the use of her native tongue would help to crumble Yana's resistance. "Terrible for all of us. So we must stand together and be united, Yana. You know that Nico has always counted on us to support him. Surely, you know that in your heart. And Nico will feel that unity between you and me, and he will know that he is a part of that unity and that we are here for him."

Yana stood with her hands at her sides, crushed against Antoli's body. She didn't have the strength to fight him, and his words touched too close to her heart for her to even want to fight.

Antoli felt Yana's body relax slightly, a loosening of the tension in her muscles. He felt the fullness of her breasts pressing against him and smelled her distinctly feminine aroma. With his right hand, he stroked her hair, letting his hand slide down her back. His desire to take her forcibly, then and there, was intense. Only knowing that someday soon he would have Yana at his mercy stopped him from acting immediately to satisfy the cravings of his body and soul.

"It's okay to cry. You can lean on me if you need to. I'm here for you, Yana, just like I have always been there for your father." He dipped his head down and very lightly kissed the top of Yana's head. "You can trust me, Yana. I am here for you now."

Chapter 12

"You recognize him, Mr. McKenna?"

Clay looked at the corpse. He had never seen the man before. "There are drifters moving in and out all the time."

The sheriff, who had sent a rider to the McKenna homestead the moment the body had been found, made a grunting sound to indicate he knew all about drifters and the trouble they could get themselves into.

"Anybody know who he is—was?"

The sheriff said, "His name was Higgins. He was in town just a couple of weeks. He worked for a week at the saloon cleaning up, sweeping the floors and such. That's all we knew. Plenty of folks saw him drunk at one time or another."

"Just because he got drunk doesn't mean anything."

The sheriff grimaced, wondering if the comment

was directed at him. His drinking was well known among the local population.

"You figure he had something to do with the gunplay at your place?"

Clay shook his head. He wasn't interested in letting the sheriff know of his suspicions. Though Clay hadn't gotten a good look at the fourth assassin—the one that had escaped his immediate lethal wrath—he strongly suspected Higgins was that man. But the sheriff had never been known for his ability to keep secrets or to find criminals. Besides, Clay had been raised to believe that McKenna problems were best solved by the McKennas, and he was far more interested in discovering who had paid the gunmen rather than the identity of those who actually did the shooting.

"No," Clay said finally. "I'm sure he was with some of his drinking buddies and they got in a fight. Somebody pulled a knife and that was the end of the fight. That's the way it looks to me. Thanks for alerting us anyway, sheriff. It's appreciated."

The sheriff shifted a wad of chewing tobacco from one side of his mouth to the other. "No trouble at all, Mr. McKenna. You know I'm only trying to clear up this case."

He had a look of disdain on his face. The murder of a drifter did not cause him to lose any sleep. However, having a guest of the McKennas shot on McKenna land had a way of making him look very bad indeed, and the sheriff had no intention of losing his comfortable job. As long as the case remained open, a dark cloud was over the sheriff's head.

"You figure maybe somebody figured out this Higgins fella was in on that trouble you had at your place, Mr. McKenna?" the sheriff asked. "Maybe somebody wanted to do you a favor by putting an end to this Higgins guy?" The sheriff smiled, warming to the idea. A simple man, he liked simple, tidy solutions. "Yeah, Mr. McKenna, that seems to me like what happened here. Somebody just up and did you a favor by killing this fella."

Clay, fully aware of the sheriff's desire to close the case, nodded his acceptance of the story. The sheriff, enormously pleased that he could now report the case closed—and glad that he could brag about solving the crime—thanked Clay, then went to the undertaker, who was waiting to take the corpse.

Yana sat at the breakfast table, feeling refreshed and happy. Yesterday had been the first time since the shooting that she'd slept through the night. Residual darkness from a week of sleepless nights still clouded her eyes, but other than that, her face was as untroubled and exuberant as ever.

"Good morning," Yana said to Clay's parents.

"Morning," Sorren answered. "You're looking very nice this morning."

"Thank you." Yana added a smile to her thanks.

She was mildly disappointed that Clay was not yet at the breakfast table. She had particularly hoped to make an entrance for Clay, wanting to thaw some of

219

the ice that had formed between them since Yana's outburst against all the McKennas eight days earlier. Since that time, her passions had cooled, and she saw the McKennas in a fairer light. At the same time, the McKennas—with Shadow, not Clay, in the fore-front—had come to understand that whatever Nico Zacarious's past sins, none of them justified lethal retribution.

"How's your father feeling today?" Shadow asked.

"He was still sleeping when I looked into his room this morning." Yana smiled her thanks again at Sorren, this time for filling her delicate china cup with steaming, aromatic coffee. "Last night, just before I retired for the evening, we talked for over an hour. He was in wonderful spirits." Her smile faded slightly as she remembered how her father's energy had suddenly waned. "He gets tired so fast now. It never used to be like that. Papa always loved to talk." Yana rolled her eyes, her vacillating moods concern-ing her father's health once again on the upswing. "Some people think Papa loves talking *too* much."

Emma, who had just entered the room with a silver tray laden with eggs, breakfast meats, orange juice, and slices of apple, made a clucking sound with her tongue as she began filling Yana's plate.

"Listen to me, missy," Emma began. "There ain't no such thing as too much talkin'. When a man's talkin', a lady knows what's goin' on between his ears. But when a man ain't partial to talkin', a lady's gotta guess what a man's thinkin'. Take Mr. Sorren and Mr. Clay, for instance. They're a-thinkin' all the time, but they ain't always talkin'. That can make 'em mighty difficult to be around sometimes."

"I can vouch for that!" Shadow said with a laugh.

Clay stood at the doorway, a half smile tugging at his mouth. It was the closest Clay had come to smiling since Yana had said she hated him and had blamed him for Nico's brush with death. Emma, as usual, was dead on the mark. In the past eight days, Clay hadn't said five words to Yana, and not much more to anyone else. When he did speak, it was little more than terse orders given to the men handling security at the ranch.

"We would all probably talk more," Clay said. "But Emma, with you talking all the time, you don't give Dad and me a chance to get a word in."

Emma huffed indignantly, pointing at Clay's empty chair with a serving spoon. "Your breakfast is gettin' cold. Now hush up an' put your behind on that chair 'fore I paddle it with this."

Emma shook the spoon menacingly at Clay, who leaped into the chair with comic haste.

Clay's shining gaze met Yana's and held for a moment before he broke the contact. *She looks gorgeous. She hasn't looked this good since before the shooting. Since about one second before I was about to say I love her.*

Her beauty tugged at Clay, conjuring up memories that were bittersweet. The same beauty that had made Clay forget that his first duty—to himself and to his family—was to protect Nico also made him feel a little weak inside. It was a force, an attraction, which he found impossible to resist.

No, Clay's coldly logical mind amended, it wasn't Yana's fault that he was so distracted by her beauty. He had allowed himself the distraction—the sweet moment of dalliance with Yana—and because of it, Nico had been shot. The blame rested squarely, heavily on Clay's shoulders.

Never before had he allowed his amorous inclinations to interfere with business or with his family responsibilities. Now, as he wrestled with the demons of guilt, he had a sinking feeling he was losing.

A thousand times since that hideous moment when he'd first heard the gunshots, Clay had asked himself whether or not he could have prevented Nico's shooting if he'd remained close to him instead of following Yana behind the track houses. Each time Clay asked himself that weighted question, he faced the same answer: maybe. He might have saved Nico from shedding a single drop of blood. But maybe—and he grasped at this possibility with pale hope—he might not have made one whit of difference in the final outcome.

"You're particularly quiet this morning, dear," Shadow said to Clay. "Is something wrong?"

"No." Clay took a bite of juicy Italian sausage. He suddenly found it difficult to look at Yana when she was smiling. It was easier being near her when she was sad or angry—she wasn't nearly so tempting.

Shadow began telling Clay the latest news on Nico's health, then stopped and urged Yana to do it.

The stumbling, drastically abbreviated version that Yana gave Clay caused Shadow and Sorren to exchange suspicious looks.

"How far do you think it's gone?" Sorren asked his wife shortly after breakfast.

"How far what's gone?" Shadow replied, feigning innocence, hoping for once that she misunderstood him.

Sorren frowned, shaking his head in mock exhaustion. "Precious, you are many things in this world—and almost all of them exciting, I might add. But dumb you're definitely not."

"Almost?"

"Sometimes you can be the most frustrating woman in the entire world!" Sorren slipped his arms around Shadow's waist, pulling her firmly against him. She pushed against his chest but didn't put up much of a struggle, though she had a pout on her lips. "But only sometimes. Other times you are positively . . . *exhilarating!*"

"You're going to have to do much better than that to squirm your way out of this one, Sorren McKenna."

Sorren chuckled warmly, thinking of dozens of very pleasurable ways he could show his wife just how exciting he found her. But sadly, this was not the time for such thoughts, even if Shadow was looking especially appealing this morning.

"You know I *could* do *much* better, my love, but

it'll have to wait until later," Sorren whispered, his voice softly intimate. "Now answer my question."

Shadow, looking up into Sorren's face, opened her eyes wide in a mockery of innocence. "But what question was that, dear?"

Sorren's arms slackened around Shadow, and after a moment he stepped away from her. His eyes and tone became serious once again.

"Clay and Illyana . . . do you think they've got something for each other?"

This time, Shadow answered. "Oh, they've got eyes for each other. I've no doubt about that. And they have surely had some words together. You saw how uncomfortable she was when she had to talk to Clay." She paused. "What you really want to know is whether they are lovers or not."

"Well?"

"I don't know." Shadow chuckled softly. The thought of her son being with a young woman as clearly strong-willed and independent as Illyana Zacarious was not without its humorous side. "Why don't you ask Clay? He'd probably remember if he and Yana had made love."

Sorren looked crossly at his wife. "Don't make light of this. We don't know how Nico will react if our son and his daughter have been sleeping together. And though you try hard to ignore the facts, our son is something of a profligate."

"Profligate? Sorren, that's one of the more gentle ways you've ever described our son. And as far as ignoring Clay's . . . well, his indiscretions, that isn't

MORE PASSION AND ADVENTURE AWAIT... YOUR TRIP TO A BIG ADVENTUROUS WORLD BEGINS WHEN YOU ACCEPT YOUR FIRST 4 NOVELS ABSOLUTELY *FREE*
(AN $18.00 VALUE)

Accept your Free gift and start to experience more of the passion and adventure you like in a historical romance novel. Each Zebra novel is filled with proud men, spirited women and tempestuous love that you'll remember long after you turn the last page.

Zebra Historical Romances are the finest novels of their kind. They are written by authors who really know how to weave tales of romance and adventure in the historical settings you love. You'll feel like you've actually gone back in time with the thrilling stories that each Zebra novel offers.

GET YOUR FREE GIFT WITH THE START OF YOUR HOME SUBSCRIPTION

Our readers tell us that these books sell out very fast in book stores and often they miss the newest titles. So Zebra has made arrangements for you to receive the four newest novels published each month.

You'll be guaranteed that you'll never miss a title, and home delivery is so convenient. And to show you just how easy it is to get Zebra Historical Romances, we'll send you your first 4 books absolutely FREE! Our gift to you just for trying our home subscription service.

BIG SAVINGS AND FREE HOME DELIVERY

Each month, you'll receive the four newest titles as soon as they are published. You'll probably receive them even before the bookstores do. What's more, you may preview these exciting novels free for 10 days. If you like them as much as we think you will, just pay the low preferred subscriber's price of just $3.75 each. *You'll save $3.00 each month off the publisher's price.* AND, your savings are even greater because there are never any shipping, handling or other hidden charges—FREE Home Delivery. Of course you can return any shipment within 10 days for full credit, no questions asked. There is no minimum number of books you must buy.

4 FREE BOOKS

TO GET YOUR 4 FREE BOOKS WORTH $18.00 —MAIL IN THE FREE BOOK CERTIFICATE T O D A Y

Fill in the Free Book Certificate below, and we'll send your FREE BOOKS to you as soon as we receive it.

If the certificate is missing below, write to: Zebra Home Subscription Service, Inc., P.O. Box 5214, 120 Brighton Road, Clifton, New Jersey 07015-5214.

FREE BOOK CERTIFICATE

4 FREE BOOKS

ZEBRA HOME SUBSCRIPTION SERVICE, INC.

YES! Please start my subscription to Zebra Historical Romances and send me my first 4 books absolutely FREE. I understand that each month I may preview four new Zebra Historical Romances free for 10 days. If I'm not satisfied with them, I may return the four books within 10 days and owe nothing. Otherwise, I will pay the low preferred subscriber's price of just $3.75 each; a total of $15.00, *a savings off the publisher's price of $3.00.* I may return any shipment and I may cancel this subscription at any time. There is no obligation to buy any shipment and there are no shipping, handling or other hidden charges. Regardless of what I decide, the four free books are mine to keep.

NAME

ADDRESS _____ APT

CITY _____ STATE _____ ZIP

( )
TELEPHONE

SIGNATURE _____ (if under 18, parent or guardian must sign)

Terms, offer and prices subject to change without notice. Subscription subject to acceptance by Zebra Books. Zebra Books reserves the right to reject any order or cancel any subscription.   029002

the way it is. I simply choose to not dwell on Clay's less appealing traits.''

Sorren looked at his wife, loving her desperately, amazed that after all these years she still loved him.

"Would it really be so bad if Clay and Yana feel something special for each other?" Shadow asked.

Sorren shrugged. "I just don't want him getting bored with her in a week or two. I don't want him hurting her. She's very young, you know."

Shadow smiled broadly. "Yana does not strike me as the type of woman who becomes boring in a week or two, or a year or two, or even twenty. And as for her age, she is a year older than I was when you and I became lovers."

Sorren grimaced. What scared him most was that he remembered all too well what he was like when he was Clay's age. And Clay, to Sorren's occasional consternation, was just like his father.

"Come on, let's get to my office. Yana and Clay should be there by now, and we've got a lot to deal with. Yana's talking on behalf of her father, I've been told.''

Yana was shaking her head. She heard Clay and Sorren sigh wearily. She ignored their exasperation. She was determined to negotiate as fiercely as her father would.

"Come up with another ten percent of the operating capital necessary to outfit the first ship," Clay said, leaning over the big oak table in his father's office. "Then, after that, we'll split all the costs fifty-fifty for building the two new ships."

"Not good enough," Yana replied without hesitation. She was also leaning over the table, looking at the numerous sheets filled with numbers. Her eyes traveled slowly from Clay's over to Sorren's, then back again, challenging the McKennas to defy her.

"The first ship will be outfitted by the Zacarious Shipping Company at our dockyards in Pirias," Yana continued. "When the work is completed, we'll take the first load of optics and wine to the United States ports. You'll receive the goods and immediately begin reselling them. That means you'll be making profit first—by about three months—using Zacarious money." She smiled, softening the hard-line effect of her words without changing their meaning. "It's only right that McKenna Enterprises puts up a little more money in the beginning, to right any inequity."

Sorren put up his same defense—that if the partnership was to be equal, then all expenses must be equally shared.

Yana shook her head, sending her dark hair fluttering against her high cheekbones. For only a moment her eyes, holding a hint of mischief, touched Clay's. "After all," she said, looking at Sorren but speaking to Clay, "it's only fair."

"You did what?" Antoli Pacca shouted, his eyes wide as saucers, his mouth open as he looked at Yana, who stood in the foyer of his guest house.

Antoli hit himself just above the ear with the heel of his palm, then shook his head, using the ancient Greek superstition to get the foolish words out of his mind.

"It's a good deal, Antoli. I'm sure Papa will think so, too."

"You should have sent for me. I should have been there when you were negotiating. I would have prevented this from happening."

Yana did not bother saying that that was precisely the reason she had negotiated without him.

Antoli threw his arms up, then slapped his sides, thoroughly disgusted with the young woman who thought she could fill a man's shoes.

"Your papa is never going to agree to this deal, Yana. It looks bad for the company and for the Zacarious family name to have a woman doing a man's work."

Yana's anger flared at Antoli's words. She had discovered that in America, women were treated far more equally than in Greece. Of course, America still had a long way to go before it achieved real equality between the genders, but at least here it was generally considered unacceptable for a man to beat his wife and daughters. In Greece, many men felt their womenfolk were their personal chattels.

Antoli continued to rage. Yana held her tongue, not out of any real respect for Antoli, but for her father's sake. She had taken matters into her own hands by negotiating with the McKennas. Although

227

her father had given his approval to her speaking on his behalf, it was generally understood that Antoli, who'd been at Nico's side through a hundred similar discussions, though none on quite as grand a scale, would be there to act as Yana's safety net should she misstep.

"I will talk with Sorren McKenna myself," Antoli said firmly, stepping closer to Yana. "He would be a fool to think we would let him take advantage of us this way! He cannot expect us to honor any agreement reached without either Nico or myself there."

"*I* was there and *I* negotiated the deal, Antoli. It's a good deal." Yana wanted to scream at Antoli, but it wouldn't be appropriate. Whether she despised the little sycophant or not, he was her father's professional right hand. It could be dangerous to underestimate Antoli's influence. "Just take a good look at it before you reject it out of hand."

Antoli walked within an arm's length of Yana. He felt two searing desires burn through his veins: to take her pretty little throat in his hands and squeeze the life out of her, and to slide his fingers into the bodice of her American-fashion gown—which by Greek standards was brazenly low-cut—and rip her clothes off. But, at least for now, Antoli could do neither.

"I worry about you, Yana," he said softly, patronizingly. "I just don't want to see these arrogant Americans take advantage of you."

He reached to take Yana's face into his hands, but

she moved quickly away from him.

"Don't!" Yana said sharply. "I don't like it when you touch me."

"What about when the McKenna boy touches you?"

"That is none of your business! You have a filthy mind to even think such a thing!" Yana strode purposefully to the door. She stopped and turned toward Antoli, her jaw set defiantly, her brown eyes dangerously alive. "I came here to inform you the deal had been agreed upon, Antoli. I didn't come here to ask for your blessings or your permission."

She left the guest house with a triumphant spring to her step.

Alone, Antoli felt it all coming undone. The years of working at Nico's side, anticipating the old man's moves and moods, learning the way he thought so that when the time came to strike, Antoli would be fully prepared—it was all in jeopardy now. Nico was getting stronger with each passing day, and instead of placing his vice president in charge of Zacarious Shipping while he recovered from his wounds, it seemed all too apparent that Yana was now the one giving orders.

They were gathered around Nico's bed. Nico, never one to shy away from being the center of attention, was propped up in bed with a mound of pillows against the thick, solid oak headboard.

He had lost a considerable amount of weight. His

cheeks were gaunt, almost concave. His eyes lacked the brilliance they'd had before the shooting, and they seemed sunken into his skull. Nevertheless, compared to his appearance a fortnight earlier, Nico appeared in the peak of health.

"I have much to say to all of you," Nico began, his voice very nearly as strong as normal. "We still do not know who was behind the attempt to kill me. The men who did the shooting are dead now—thanks to Clay. But those men were only pawns in a much larger chess game."

Illyana half sat on Nico's bed. She patted his leg through the blankets, not entirely pleased with having to live through the shooting once again but happy to see her father in fine spirits.

Nico smiled at his daughter, pausing in his rehearsed speech. "Because the McKennas have been able to find a common ground with my Illyana, the Zacarious Shipping Company and McKenna Enterprises are about to embark on what I am positive will be a profitable venture for our companies and our countries.

"It is time now for this venture to begin, but I am an old and weak man. I am recovering my health. That much is true. But Dr. Cannell has forbidden me to travel. For once, I am in accord with his diagnosis. No matter how much I want to believe otherwise, I know that my health will not withstand such a voyage."

Nico sighed, and Yana suppressed the smile that tried to dance across her mouth. Her father loved theatrics, and he was making the most of his captive audience.

"I am sending my daughter back to our home in Pirias. From there, she can begin the work needed to renovate the first ship." Nico looked at Yana, smiled, then turned his attention to Antoli Pacca. "And you, my friend . . . you have always been there for me when I needed you. I need you again, Antoli. I need you now as I never have before. I need your experience and wisdom. I ask you to do for my daughter what you have done so ably for me. Be her eyes and her ears. Counsel her when she is in doubt. Support her when she makes decisions. Will you do this for me, Antoli?"

"Of course, Mr. Zacarious. You know I will do anything you ask of me."

"I know that, Antoli. I have always known that."

Clay, standing beside his father, shifted his feet nervously when Nico's gaze slid over to him.

"And for you, Clayton, I have a most important request. I want you to travel with my Illyana. Be her bodyguard. Whoever—"

"Mr. Zacarious, sir, I don't think that is such a good idea," Clay interrupted hastily. "I don't speak the language. Besides, I really don't have such a good track record as a bodyguard. You got shot, remember?"

Nico wiggled his palm, shaking his head. "You speak nonsense. We both know what happened when I was shot. If not for you, those rabid animals would have emptied their guns into me, then spit on my

231

corpse. Instead, they are being eaten by worms, and I am here now."

"But, Mr. Zacarious—"

Nico waved a hand to silence Clay. He looked at Sorren and Shadow. "Of course, I should have asked you first. Will you give your permission? Your son is a very capable young man. He is the kind of man I need to protect my Illyana."

Shadow was smiling as she said, "If that's what you really want, Nico, then you have our blessings. However, it's really been quite some time since Clay's asked for our permission to do something."

"Not that denying our permission ever changed what he did anyway," Sorren muttered wryly.

Nico continued, his voice steadily becoming weaker. "Whoever had me shot is still out there. When Yana takes my place as the leader of Zacarious Shipping, she will be at risk. I do not like the thought of placing my daughter—my only flesh and blood— in danger. But if I do nothing, if I let my wounds kill the business Sorren and I set out to do so long ago, then whoever had me shot, whoever the vile, cowardly animal is that wants to see me die . . . then that man will have succeeded."

Nico's tone grew raspy, soft. He continued with some difficulty. "I cannot allow this faceless, cowardly man to win. I am Nico Zacarious. I am old and tired, but I will fight because I have always fought. I will not retreat because I have never retreated." He had to force the words from his lips now, the last of his strength nearly spent. "I am a fighter, and so is Illyana. That is the way it has always been . . . and that is the way it must always be."

Yana, her eyes glistening with unshed tears, patted Nico's leg. "Be quiet now, *Mbambaky*. No more talking. We can talk later. Rest now. Take a nap and save your strength."

Nico did not hear his daughter's words. He was sleeping, his breath coming in shallow, sporadic inhalations.

"It's time for us to leave him alone," Shadow whispered. "Emma will look in on him later. He'll be fine, Yana. He's just very tired right now."

Chapter 13

Antoli's rage was so great he doubted he could contain it, though he prided himself on his ability to hide his feelings.

Immediately after leaving Nico's bedroom, Antoli had told Yana in the hallway that she had his total support. Then he made a beeline to the guest house and the bottle of ouzo he had waiting there.

Alone, quietly, between gulps of ouzo, he cursed God, Nico, Illyana, and Clay, and made a vow to personally kill Edward Danzer. If Danzer had done his job properly, Nico would be dead now and he, Antoli, would be running Zacarious Shipping instead of Yana.

The words Nico had spoken rang in Antoli's ears, repeating themselves hideously, tormentingly.

Does that old fool think I worked this long just to be a slave to his daughter?

Antoli vowed that the day would come when he

would feel Nico's throat in his hands. Nico would be looking into Antoli's face when that happened. And when death at long last claimed Nico, Antoli's face would be the last one he saw. And after Nico, there would be Illyana, and the things he would do to her would make her plead for death. . . . But now there was Clay to contend with. Even in Greece, there would be the McKenna man and his goddamn revolver.

"I think we should talk," Clay said, standing alone with Yana in the hallway near her bedroom door.

"Yes," she replied quietly, without much enthusiasm. She took a step toward the bedroom, then stopped abruptly. There was a time when she would have gladly, even happily, brought Clay into her bedroom. But not anymore. "Where can we talk in private?"

They said nothing until they were in the library and the door was closed safely behind them. Clay sat in his favorite reading chair near the eastern windows, where he had spent so many cozy hours, curled up in the sunlight. Though he tried to appear calm, his whole body was taut, like an overwound watch mainspring.

Yana paced slowly in front of the windows.

"What did you want to talk about?" Yana's voice was calm, her tone casual. Tension was making her feel queasy, and she was not altogether certain that she wouldn't get ill. "You called me in here. Surely you must have something to say."

As tokalo! You little fool! You're babbling like a schoolgirl!

Yana pushed the thoughts from her mind. She inhaled deeply, forcing herself to think calmly as the speed of her pacing increased to that of a caged animal.

"You deserve congratulations," Clay began, avoiding the real reason he needed to talk with Yana. "I never thought you would get Dad to come up with the extra ten percent advance money. You're a lot tougher than you look."

Yana stopped pacing. "Yes, I am. Are you?"

Clay gave her a half smile that held more sadness than humor. "Probably not."

"Did it surprise you that I wouldn't back down when you and your father tried bullying me?"

"We weren't trying to bully you. We just wanted the best deal we could get. You had to expect as much." Clay pulled the makings for a cigarette from his coat pocket. "But to answer your question . . . yes, it did surprise me that you held your ground. The McKennas have a way of—"

"Always getting what you want? Yes, I've noticed that about you." Yana's eyebrows raised above her slightly mocking eyes. "It's not entirely one of your more appealing traits." Yana looked at Clay studiously, and the pseudo-serious quality in her voice became stronger. "I suppose that's an unfortunate side effect of living the life you have. Scores of women throwing themselves prostrate at your feet—"

"Yana, it's not like that."

"—and being the gentleman that you are, you don't just let them lie there feeling foolish. No, not Clayton McKenna. You gallantly sweep those poor young ladies up in your strong arms and carry them straight away to your bedroom." The sweet memory of making love with Clay in the fitting room flashed painfully across the surface of Yana's mind. "That is, of course, if your bedroom isn't too inconvenient. If so, any other room will do just as well, won't it?"

Clay scowled, realizing he and Yana were angry with themselves and taking it out on each other, angry for being vulnerable to the ways of the flesh and the whisperings of the heart, angry for letting Nico get shot . . . but knowing this did not soothe his troubled soul.

Clay blew a stream of smoke toward the ceiling. "This isn't getting us anywhere."

"Perhaps not," Yana said blandly. "But it does feel rather nice to see you on the defensive for a change. This is probably good for you—to see how the rest of us feel most of the time when we're in the company of you McKennas."

Clay's patience was quickly reaching its limit. "Listen to me, Yana. I don't know what's brought on this little spat of yours, and quite frankly, I don't *want* to know. I called you in here to tell you that we're going to be spending a lot of time together, so we've got to remember what's really important to us and our families at all times. When we . . . when *I* forgot what was really important, your father ended

238

up getting shot and very nearly died because of it."

Yana turned away from Clay. From the high windows she saw the men with rifles cradled in their arms, all strategically positioned to defend the main house against an all-out assault from armies unknown.

The harsh sight reinforced Yana's certainty that her romantic involvement with Clay could only lead to catastrophe. She had to end it now, before it was too late, before she couldn't find the strength to walk away. *Yes*, she thought, *best to end it in a way that Clay will understand. He could never understand the truth.*

"Don't worry, Clay, I won't fall apart without you. It was nice being with you. I'll give you that much. You really do know how to make a woman feel pretty, feel wanted, feel—" Yana caught her lower lip between even teeth, biting to cut off the next word. She had very nearly said *loved,* and that would just never do. "Well, let's just say that my time with you showed me many things. Please try to understand that if I don't want to stick around long enough for you to leave me, it's really nothing personal." She smiled at Clay as though he were a child who needed everything explained to him and still couldn't grasp the facts at hand. "Papa taught me to be a survivor, Clay. And if there's anything certain about you, it's that your romantic involvement with a woman never lasts."

"What the hell are you talking about?" Clay asked, his voice rising with tension. "Make sense!"

When Yana turned her face toward his, her rich brown eyes held a distant quality, and Clay could have sworn, then and there, that he'd never seen her before in his life.

"Your time is up," Yana said, her voice cold, emotionless. "It's over, Clay. I'm sorry if I'm disturbing your usual way of doing things. How many good-bye speeches have you given in your life? You must have it down to an art by now."

Yana saw the muscle in Clay's jaw flicker as he clenched his teeth. She had cut through his armor, going straight to the open nerves that every person jealously, zealously protects.

"In the long run, this will be good for you," Yana said with malice born of anger and disillusionment. "It'll teach you that, contrary to what you want to think, there is at least one woman who can walk away from you." She saw the rising anger in Clay, could feel his rage and could only guess what would happen if that anger was unleashed. "Have I hurt your pride by leaving first? Don't worry, your reputation will not be tarnished. I'm not going to kiss and tell. And should anyone ever find out about what has transpired between us, I will say nothing and everyone will feel sorry for me because they'll know that you seduced me, then decided to turn your affections to someone else. After all, that's what you always do, isn't it?"

After this, he'll hate me for the rest of my life.

Yana didn't want to continue twisting the knife into Clay. It was cruel, and she was not, by nature, that way. But she did not trust her own conviction to stay out of his arms, so she had to count on Clay being so angry that he wouldn't want to hold her.

"Nothing to say?" Yana issued a short, high false laugh. "That surprises me. I thought you'd be quicker on your feet than this."

Clay's eyes were glittery black jewels that frightened Yana, but she refused to look away. Just a few more well-chosen barbs, she knew, and she'd never have to worry about Clay wanting to hold her, touch her, make love to her.

"You're becoming a disappointment, Clay."

"Go to hell!" Clay spat. "Go straight to hell!" He laughed hollowly, bitingly. "You're not the only one who is surprised. I knew you had a lot rattling around in that pretty head of yours, but I never thought you were this much of a mercenary! What's wrong? Afraid you'll lose your inheritance if Nico finds out you lost your virginity to an Indian? Can't let that happen, can you?"

Yana felt herself falling apart inside. She was convinced she was doing the right thing, but that didn't make her actions any easier.

"Think whatever you like." Yana turned away from Clay, heading for the door. "But it'll be best for all of us if you keep your thinking geared toward business."

"By all means." Clay's tone dripped venomous sarcasm. "I wouldn't have it any other way."

Yana left the room without looking back, hiding her face—and her tears—from Clay.

Chapter 14

For several days afterward, Yana stayed either in Nico's room as he instructed her on the things that she would need to do while at the helm of Zacarious Shipping, or she stayed in her room. She declined all offers to take meals with the McKennas, choosing instead to eat alone.

Yana struggled to keep her mind only on the new responsibilities that had suddenly and unexpectedly been thrust upon her, but her thoughts regularly drifted back to Clay. Sometimes she thought of what it had been like being with him in New York. Other times she recalled fondly how exciting it had been to hide her affection for Clay while Nico was around. But whenever these pleasing thoughts came to mind, they were invariably followed with the too-vivid memory of her last private meeting with Clay in the library, where she had done everything she could to make him hate her, and he had let her know that she had been an unqualified success.

Nearly a week had passed before Yana accepted Shadow's invitation to take a ride around the estate.

"What was Clay like when he was young?" Yana asked Shadow. It was important for her now to know everything about the man she had forced out of her life. She hoped she didn't sound too obvious in her intention, but the quick look that Shadow gave her let Yana know her interest in Clay was duly noted.

"What age? How young?"

Yana shrugged her shoulders. "I don't know. You pick an age and tell me."

Shadow smiled at the young woman, wondering once again if Yana had what it would take to make her son settle down with just one woman. Shadow reached into her jacket pocket, took out a cube of sugar, and gave it to her mare.

"Clay was always a wild one. From the very beginning, I could see that he would be just like his father." Shadow and Yana walked their horses along the banks of the winding stream that cut through the grazing field. "He was our first, you know. And, I suppose we spoiled him a little."

"A little?" Yana asked suspiciously.

"Okay, we spoiled him a lot. When I became pregnant with Clay . . . it wasn't entirely a good time for Sorren and me."

"You were having troubles with your marriage?" Yana felt guilty for asking such a personal question, but she needed answers.

244

"No. It wasn't our marriage. In fact, that was the only solid thing we had going. It's really a long story, too involved to get into now. Suffice it to say that there was a time when Sorren was working as . . . in a rather strange capacity for the government, and we had to live under assumed names. We had to travel for quite some time. There didn't seem to be anything permanent in our lives. Nothing, that is, except our love. Then Clayton came along and it just seemed like everything started to fall into place."

The words seemed strange to Yana. She had always seen her own birth as the cause of so much unhappiness, such intense loneliness because of the death of her mother. To see the birth of a child as a beautiful and unifying event was strange and reassuring to Yana.

Having a child doesn't have to cause loneliness and guilt, thought Yana.

It was a comforting thought. For the first time in many years, Yana began to question whether her fears had merit, whether the guilt she had taken upon herself was justified.

Yana walked slowly beside Shadow, her thoughts chaotic, her palms clammy with cold sweat as she clutched the reins tightly. She decided that Emma was right; Clay *was* too often closemouthed about himself, about the *real* him.

"Clay was a pretty normal boy, I suppose," Shadow continued. "He seemed to have a peculiar flair for finding trouble, but he also had a way of getting out of trouble." Shadow smiled and sighed.

Time had softened the frustration she'd felt toward Clay's youthful exuberance. "In school, he pretty much did whatever he wanted to. When he studied, he did wonderfully, especially in the math and sciences. And then, just like that"—Shadow snapped her fingers—"he'd decide he had more important things to do than . . . How did he put it? Waste my days with my nose in a book? . . . and he'd completely forget about his studies altogether."

"He must have been . . . it must have been difficult for you at times."

"*All* the time, not just *some*times," Shadow said emphatically. But her ebony eyes betrayed the lie. The joy Clay created more than outweighed his whimsical annoyances.

Shadow was silent for a few moments. Yana left her alone with her thoughts, hungry for more news about Clay, yet knowing she mustn't pry too blatantly.

"Everything seemed to come so easily to him. His studies . . . sports—"

"Women?" Yana interjected cautiously.

Shadow smiled crookedly, giving Yana a sideways glance. "Yes, even women, I'm afraid."

Has she fallen completely in love with Clay, Shadow wondered, *or is she just interested? Many young women have found Clay fascinating, but only from a distance. They realize Clay's life flame blazes too hot and know they'd get burned if they got close. How much should I tell Yana? How much about Clay does she even want to know?*

"Were there . . . many women?" Yana asked

quietly, not looking at Shadow, speaking in the same tone she would use to discuss the weather or Clay's school sports record. She knew the answer, but she wanted to hear what Shadow had to say anyway.

"I really can't answer that question." Yana glanced at Shadow. She didn't have to voice her doubts for Shadow to know them. "I'm serious. I really don't know about Clay's . . . escapades, or whatever you want to call them. He didn't bring his female friends to the house, didn't introduce them to Sorren and me. We'd hear that Clay had been seen at this ball or at that dance with a girl, but he never brought them to meet us. I asked him to, of course—every mother wants to know the company her son is keeping—and Clay always promised he'd bring so-and-so by the house, but he never did."

It surprised Yana that Shadow was being so candid, so open about Clay. In many ways, the entire McKenna clan could be very secretive. It didn't surprise Yana very much, though, to find out about Clay's secrecy when it came to his lovers. After all, wasn't she just another one of his secrets? But who was he trying to protect? Himself? His amour's reputation? His parents?

"Well?" Shadow asked pointedly.

Yana, caught in her own thoughts, hadn't heard Shadow's question. "I'm sorry. My mind's been going in a thousand different directions lately."

When she met gazes with Shadow, the older woman seemed to look deep into her. Yana turned away, quickening her stride just slightly as she followed the banks of the creek.

"I don't doubt that with all that's happened, there are times when you feel confused. With your father having that accident and you suddenly in charge of a company like Zacarious Shipping . . . it can play on your mind."

"I'll have Antoli to help me. He's been with Papa a long time. He knows everything."

"Nobody knows everything," Shadow replied quickly. Then, in a gentler tone, she said, "You will have Clay with you, too. He has a very practical head for business. Very . . . pragmatic."

"Yes. Clay is nothing if not pragmatic."

Shadow's mare dipped her head to munch on sweet green grass. Shadow used the delay to stop walking. She turned so that she faced Yana directly.

"I love my son. I love him more than you'll ever know. But I also know what he's capable of, Yana. He's—he's like the man I fell in love with long ago . . . my husband." Shadow looked at Yana, trying to see her as Clay would. She could understand why her son would be attracted to the young woman. "Clay is one of the strongest people I've ever known. Strong here." Shadow tapped a forefinger to her heart. "Strong inside. But if you try to squeeze him too tightly, he'll slip away. Squeeze him tight and he'll run, just as surely as I'm talking to you now."

"Clay and I have nothing . . . I mean, we're not—" Yana said, stumbling for words, finding it necessary to deny that Clay's presence in her life had changed it completely.

"You're telling me that you and Clay aren't sweet on each other?" An eyebrow arched dubiously. "I find that rather hard to believe."

"Sweet? I don't understand."

"You might not understand English expressions, Yana, but you must surely understand my doubts. I've seen the way you and Clay snipe at each other, and I've seen the way you look at one another when you think the other isn't looking. The only thing that causes that comes from right here"—Shadow again tapped her heart—"and denying it isn't going to change a thing."

Yana smiled sheepishly. Trying to lie—or at least not tell the entire truth—was difficult with Shadow. She was a parent, and just like Nico, she had heard all the stories, all the weak excuses that a child can put forward.

"What do you think your father would do if he knew you've got feelings for Clay?"

"I don't know," Yana said, part of her still wanting to deny that Clay meant something special to her, and part of her glad that the truth was out. "He can be very stubborn at times."

"Yes, I'm sure he can. So can Sorren. But that isn't always such a bad thing. There are times—and maybe you'll understand this when you get older—when it takes a stubborn man to make things right."

Yana wondered why she did not let Shadow know that whatever feelings Clay might have had for her were all in the past, all before their loud, abusive confrontation in the library.

"But to get back to my original question," Shadow said, pushing right into Yana's thoughts. "Do you think Clay will be trouble for you when you go back home? I know what your father said, what his request was. But we can hire an army of bodyguards for you if you don't want Clay going with you back home."

"Why do that?"

"Because you think my son is handsome, and probably quite charming. But there's also something between you two—and I'm not going to pry or ask questions about what that is—that's put you at odds with one another. If you'd rather Clay not travel with you to Greece, I can arrange it so he won't."

The words were issued so calmly, so coldly, that it was difficult for Yana to remind herself this was Clay's mother she was talking to.

They can all separate their feelings from their actions, these McKennas. They're kind people, but they're hard. Hard on themselves . . . so rigid . . . so logical and emotionless.

Yana knew this was her chance for the perfect exit. With just a word to Shadow, Clay would be replaced by nameless, untempting bodyguards. Then she could put an ocean between herself and Clay, and her mental turmoil would finally, blissfully be over.

No, she thought, that wasn't true. Her mental processes might be clearer, but there wouldn't be much bliss in her life.

"You don't have to worry about Clay and me," Yana said quietly, not entirely sure if she was lying to Shadow or not. "I'll admit that we have had eyes for

250

each other now and then, and we have had some cross words. But we're too much alike to—how did you put it?—to be *sweet* on each other."

Shadow nodded her head, brushing a long tendril of ebony hair away from her cheek. "Whatever you want," she said softly, seriously. "I only want to see that you are happy, and I'm not entirely certain that Clay is the man who can make you happy. And there's always the business."

"Yes, the business. I'm afraid that's going to take up all my time. I won't be able to worry about affairs of the heart."

"Of course not," Shadow replied, her doubts registering in her tone. "I'm sure you will do whatever is best for everyone."

Chapter 15

Yana felt the difference the moment she sat down at the small table in Sorren's office. When she'd been invited to have her morning meal in Sorren's office instead of at the breakfast table, she hadn't realized the importance of the seemingly insignificant invitation. Now, with Sorren pouring her a cup of coffee, and Shadow and Clay smiling at her, she knew that her relationship with the McKennas had changed.

Illyana Zacarious was now an insider. She'd been invited into the inner circle. She was one of them.

"I trust you slept well?" Shadow asked.

Yana wondered if there was more to the pleasantry than its surface meaning. What would Shadow think if she knew that Yana was—or at least had been—her son's lover? Would she treat her differently if she knew the truth?

"Yes," Yana answered at last. She smiled sheepishly. For the most part. I kept thinking of all the different things that must be done when I get back home."

Clay, sipping coffee, eyed Yana over the rim of the cup. "Think there will be trouble with the board of Zacarious Shipping? Problems with you being inexperienced and a woman?"

"I can see that the small talk is over." Yana paused to look at each McKenna in turn. She wondered how angry Clay was with her and whether he secretly hoped she would have trouble.

The McKennas waited patiently for her answer. Yana sensed that nothing less than the complete truth would suffice.

"Yes. At least initially. At home, it's not like it is in America. Not like it is in this house, anyway. It's all right for a wife or daughter to work in the family business. It's even expected. But to run the business? To give orders to men and expect those orders to be followed?"

Yana smiled, shaking her head, thinking of the incredulous looks she would receive when the foremen and managers of Zacarious Shipping first learned that their leader was now the little girl who used to play with dolls in Nico's office.

"You'll have to take charge immediately," Shadow advised. "And once you take control, never back down, never show any doubt or weakness. That doesn't mean you can't ask for advice, ask someone for an opinion. In fact, if you're a good leader, a confident and competent leader, you'll regularly seek out your best men for their knowledge. But never"—

Shadow's eyes grew dark and hard with conviction—"allow anyone to question whether you are in control."

"You sound like you speak from experience."

"I do." Shadow glanced at Sorren, affection and pride shining in her countenance. "I am a woman with the added disadvantage of being half Kiowa Indian. Early on, when Sorren and I first started McKenna Enterprises, there were problems with some of the men."

With a smile, Sorren interjected, "Not for long, though. After you fired my vice president, protests became rather . . . muted."

"He didn't just challenge my authority, he tried to embarrass me."

Sorren, who had defended Shadow's actions at the time, shrugged his broad shoulders. "He was a good man as far as numbers and cost estimates were concerned. Too bad he couldn't work for a woman."

"Obviously, his loss to the company wasn't that great," Yana observed.

She felt more confident now. If Shadow could fight and win respect in a man's domain, then she could, too. It *was* possible to win. Not easy, certainly, but possible . . . especially with a strong man at one's side.

For nearly an hour they talked business—all of them. Nobody ever quite completely finished a sentence without someone else cutting in, finishing the thought, disputing or confirming an idea.

Yana quickly learned the rules: Say whatever you

want, hold any opinion you like—just be able to defend it with cold, hard, undeniable facts. Emotions, gut feelings, were treated with universal disdain. Each idea was a survival of the fittest; only the strongest ruled.

"I'll use the men Papa has used in the past to do the initial renovations on the *Jenco Seafarer*," Yana said.

"That's the first ship we're using, correct?" Clay asked.

"And you're sure you can do the renovations with the money we've agreed upon?" Sorren asked.

"Pretty sure. Within a seven percent margin for error." Yana looked straight into Clay's eyes, almost defying him to say the seven percent was too large. "Before anything goes over projected costs, though, I'll check with Clay." It wasn't easy for Yana to keep the smile from her face when she concluded, with just a touch of sweet, teasing mischief, "That is, of course, if Clay has the authority to speak for McKenna Enterprises."

Clay grit his teeth but said nothing. Sorren, who couldn't believe Yana could be so cheeky, looked at her blankly. Shadow, with an absolute deadpan expression, said, "Yes, Yana, we have complete faith in Clay's judgment. He has total authority."

Yana looked at Clay. For just a second, she wasn't entirely certain he wouldn't attack her right there in front of his parents.

It's going to be an interesting voyage back to Greece! And when we're there, how will Clay like it

256

when he's in my land, in my home, struggling with customs that are as foreign to him as his are to me?

"Clayton McKenna and I will be leaving for Pirias in three days," Antoli said, finding it difficult to keep his temper in check when he was with Edward Danzer. "We'll be traveling with Illyana to Greece. Nico will remain at the home of Sorren McKenna." Antoli leaned across the table to emphasize the importance of his next words. "That means that you still have the chance to finish the job we agreed upon."

Edward Danzer refused to be intimidated by Antoli. Though Danzer would sacrifice his left arm to see the destruction of the McKennas, he saw no particular reason to ingratiate himself with Antoli Pacca now. If Nico Zacarious's death helped destroy the McKenna empire, that was fine. But Edward Danzer had no personal grievance against Nico, so he had no particular reason to risk his neck to satisfy another man's desire for revenge.

"When I am back in Greece, I will be able to control Yana," Antoli continued, leaning back in the saloon's bentwood chair. "Clay doesn't speak Greek. He doesn't know our way of doing things. He doesn't understand our life. He will be lost, completely lost. And Yana is going to be lost as well when she gets home. She will find out that just because her father *says* she can run the company, that does not mean she can." Antoli's face became more animated, while his

257

eyes grew distant and unfocused as he thought about the troubles Yana would soon face. "Suddenly, Yana will find that workers who had been reliable will not show up for work. Supplies she purchases will end up stolen. Expensive items will get broken or won't be installed properly. . . . And when renovation costs have doubled or tripled expectations, when Sorren McKenna and Nico Zacarious are at each others' throats, they will turn to the one man in Greece who can right the wrongs and put Zacarious Shipping back on course. And when I get control of the company, that will be the beginning of the end for Nico Zacarious. The beginning of the end for all the Zacariouses . . . and their fortune will be *mine!*"

Edward Danzer looked across the table at Antoli's blatant lust for power and wondered, without haste or any great malice, when he should have the man killed.

When the bureaucrats from Washington had summoned Sorren, his reaction was simple: I don't dance to your tune anymore. If you want to talk to me, you know where I live.

Consequently, the three well-dressed, middle-aged men who stood in Sorren's office were not in the best of spirits. Neither was Sorren, but it didn't show. His face held no expression at all as he stared at them over his desk.

Sorren was seated, but he'd had the other chairs in his office removed to keep the bureaucrats from the

Special Branch standing. After years of on-again, off-again service with the War Department and its functioning arm, the Special Branch, and with various other even less savory elements of the government, Sorren had learned how the game was played . . . and as always, he played to win.

"Mr. McKenna, you must understand that we—and I'm speaking for the country here, not merely myself or the Special Branch—are very interested in seeing continued cooperation and free exchange between the United States and all other friendly nations." The speaker—he'd introduced himself as Smith—was heavyset, powerfully built, and apparently well educated. Sorren guessed him to be a retired field agent who had settled down to a desk job once he had a wife and child. "However, Nico Zacarious is a businessman of . . . shall we say, dubious ethics."

"No, we shall not say that," Sorren said calmly, his eyes cold and unwavering as he stared at Smith.

"He has contacts with known criminal elements in Greece," Smith said. "The SB is very concerned about that."

"Yes, that's true. Would you like to personally vouch for the character of every man who collects a salary from the SB?"

"That's hardly a fair analogy, Mr. McKenna."

"Mr. Zacarious's contacts and associates are of no concern to me, Smith. Only Mr. Zacarious's character and honesty, as well as his ability to build ships, are of importance to me."

Sorren felt a tickle in the pit of his stomach. He wasn't sure where Smith was trying to lead him. He didn't trust the man, and he knew from his own experience that it was part of Smith's job to not trust him.

The smaller man with the prematurely bald pate, who stood uncomfortably beside Smith, said, "Of course, Mr. McKenna, we understand your feelings exactly. This is America, after all, and a man has the right to earn a dollar however he can—provided it's within the law, of course. What we are primarily concerned with is the type and nature of the business we are promoting with other countries. Nico Zacarious is a man who has contacts with organized criminal elements in his home country. While he's here, on your land while you work on future business projects, there is an attempt on his life." The SB man's voice became quieter, harder. "Now, it doesn't take a genius to figure out something underhanded is going on."

Sorren smiled, but the expression wasn't friendly. "Are you accusing me of underhanded business practices? If that's not what you're doing, I suggest you start saying exactly what you're doing here and what you want from me. I'm giving you exactly five minutes."

The big man—Smith, if that was actually his name—was trying to calm the escalating tensions in the room when Clay walked in without knocking. He walked past the three SB men, then leaned against his father's desk, studying the visitors with curious amusement twinkling in his dark eyes.

"What's going on, Dad?" Clay asked, never taking his eyes off the strangers.

"I'm not sure yet. These men seem concerned about some of Nico's less aboveboard business acquaintances. Perhaps they are concerned that we're bringing illegal elements into the country."

Clay issued a crooked half smile, mirroring his father's. He wondered idly if any of the three had read his SB dossier, then chided himself. *Of course they have. These are company men shackled to a desk. They read everything about everyone. They love dirty details.*

Clay thanked the Fates once again that he hadn't stayed with the SB for very long.

"There's no reason for anyone to get angry," Smith said placatingly. "No reason to accuse anyone of anything. The government is concerned, that's all. We would like to improve our relationship with Greece, if possible. However, we don't want to open Pandora's box. We don't want to have some long-standing feud from Greece make its way to the United States."

Sorren looked at Smith, rather liking the man despite the circumstances. Smith was probably very much like himself—a little unhappy about no longer being a field agent, yet willing to make the sacrifice of a desk job to raise a family. Among the three men from the SB, only Smith seemed to have any real inner strength. The other two men, Sorren guessed, were weak, intelligent, annoying little men who

261

enjoyed prying into other people's lives.

Smith's eyes went from Clay to Sorren, sizing the McKenna men up, wondering how far he could press the issue without it blowing up in his face. He had gone through their files carefully, wanting to know everything he could about Sorren and Clay. Sorren was something of a legend at the SB, and Clay would have been one if he'd stayed in longer. They both followed their own rules and did whatever was necessary to get the job done. This philosophy made the McKennas awesomely, frighteningly efficient.

"We would like you to keep your eyes open—both of you," Smith continued. "We don't yet know exactly what we need you to report. However, having Greek shipping tycoons attracting assassination attempts doesn't do much to diminish our reputation in Europe and the Mediterranean for being a savage nation."

Sorren, who had married an Indian, and Clay, who had Indian blood, stared at Smith coldly. After a moment, suddenly realizing his horrendous choice of words, Smith grit his teeth and turned his head away. At that moment, Clay was sure that Smith had been a field agent; no bureaucrat or politician would have ever made such a terrible faux pas.

"I know what you're thinking, but it's not what I meant!" Smith said in a rapid-fire manner, violently angry with himself. "I didn't mean what you're thinking."

"You have no idea at all what we're thinking," Clay said levelly.

Sorren, pointedly, removed the thick gold watch from his vest pocket and pressed the stem to open the facing. The engraving on the inside cover read: "To my husband, who alone understands—Shadow." The engraving reminded Sorren how wise it had been to distance himself from his past.

He looked at Smith and said, "You're running out of time."

"We just want you to let us know what you see, what you hear. What you are doing—fostering trade with one of the most powerful and influential men in all of Greece—can be very beneficial for the country. We just want to make sure that there are no—negative effects from such a union. You can understand that, can't you?"

Clay lit a cigarette, his eyes thin slits as he looked at the three intruders. "Mr. Zacarious is staying here at the house, under heavy security. Miss Zacarious, who is in charge of her father's business until he is healthy enough to resume his position, is traveling back to Greece to begin the initial stages of the McZac Import-Export operation." It surprised Clay how quickly—and unconsciously—he went back to speaking the language that the SB hierarchy seemed so fond of. "I'll be going with her to act as McKenna Enterprises' man on the scene and to personally supervise Ya—Miss Zacarious's security."

Smith nodded his head slowly, his eyes hard but approving. "That's good to hear." His body seemed to uncoil, as though a great weight had suddenly been lifted off his shoulders. "I was certain that you two would know how to handle such delicate matters." He looked at Sorren. "Good choice to send your son along to keep an eye on things. I guess in some ways we never really do retire from the service, do we?"

Sorren's face was impassive as he asked, "How long have you been behind a desk?"

"Not quite a year." Smith grinned crookedly with embarrassment. "Is it that obvious?"

"How's the family?"

Smith smiled proudly, not entirely unhappy that Sorren could read him like a book. "My boy has his first birthday next week. The missus is due with number two in the fall."

Later, when the SB men had left his office, Sorren poured bourbon for himself and Clay.

"They think I'm going to Greece to spy on Zacarious Shipping." Clay made a growling sound in his throat. "Damn them! I suppose they'll want reports from me, too!"

"I'm sure they will. That doesn't mean you have to do what they want. We're not working for the government now." Sorren sipped his bourbon, pleased with the way it felt going down. "They did bring up some good points, though. Nico might be a liability for McKenna Enterprises. We can't say for certain what he's been into. I want you to be careful at all times. If there are people out there trying to topple Zacarious Shipping, then Illyana is next in line." Sorren's gaze met his son's. All their fighting, all their arguments, didn't diminish the love they shared. "I don't want you getting hurt. If for one second you think this deal's going to blow up in our faces, you get the hell out of there."

"If we pull out now, we'll lose a bundle."

"I've made and lost fortunes before. You're the only son I have."

Chapter 16

The sound of the waves lapping against the solid hull of the ship, the smell of the ocean, the feel of water beneath her—it all helped to calm Yana's soul.

She had always loved the water. From her earliest days, she had been around ships that traveled the seas. As Nico Zacarious's daughter, the sea was as much a part of her blood as her name or her heritage.

Yana sat in her private chambers, tea laced with rich honey beside her, as she thought about what had happened to her since she arrived in New York so long ago and what lay ahead of her.

I've got to think like Mbambaky.

Even Yana had to admit that she was woefully inexperienced. She knew how her father thought—or at least was convinced she did—and she knew about ships. But she had never concerned herself with actually running Zacarious Shipping. It had always been assumed that the man she married would carry that mantle. Yana would play the wife of the tycoon, the socialite, the philanthropist.

And there was Clay. What exactly was she going to do with Clay, and all the crazy and chaotic feelings she had for him?

It wasn't easy to cast him out of her life. When she had decided that she could not allow a union of personal and professional involvement, it had seemed a perfectly natural decision to make. Life had taught her the price of love and the guilt that went along with someone else paying that debt.

It was the wise move, Nico would surely have said, if he had any inkling of what had really transpired between his daughter and Sorren McKenna's son.

But the words that Shadow had said kept ringing hauntingly in her ears. Perhaps it *was* possible to mix the two. After all, Shadow and Sorren had done it. Though Yana was convinced that Shadow was an extremely strong woman, quite capable of standing on her own two feet and making intelligent decisions, it was highly doubtful she could have run the companies of McKenna Enterprises under her direct control without Sorren there to back her up. At least in the beginning.

Will I need a man to stand beside me, just like Shadow?

There was Antoli Pacca, of course. Once Nico's right hand, now he was Yana's. But Yana had never warmed up to Antoli, though she had tried. And when he looked at her and thought she didn't notice, his covetous glances made Yana's skin crawl and feel clammy. But when Clay looked at her in just the same way, her skin tingled.

Could Clay be the man at her side?

That was a possibility. But he knew nothing at all about how things were done in Greece. His straightforward I-don't-let-anything-or-anyone-stand-in-my-way style was as likely to hinder operations as help them. Antoli, on the other hand, was well versed in the circuitous maneuverings the Greek culture dictated.

Shadow had given Yana the chance to put an ocean between herself and Clay, and she'd refused it. Now, for better or worse, she had to live with the fact that he would be near her, day after day. She would see his face, watch him as he walked, see his half smile and . . .

. . . and nothing. Yana shook herself from the pointless reverie. She could not allow anything or *anyone* to interfere with the business at hand. Clay was a distraction, but only if she allowed him to be. If she saw him as just another man, just one more cog in the wheels of commerce that would give Zacarious Shipping a foothold in the lucrative American market, then he would be a valuable asset.

But if Yana allowed herself to think with her heart, if she let her preoccupation with Clay cloud her business judgment, then it was entirely possible she could make bad decisions that would destroy everything Nico had spent his lifetime building.

What was it Sorren had said? Business is business? Yes, that was it. Clean and simple. Mix the two and a person courts disaster.

I made the right decision. Clay and I had our time together. I learned from it. I felt beautiful things because of it. For a time, I felt closer to Clay than I have ever felt to anyone, even Papa. But that time is over with. Too many people have already been hurt by love. I promised Papa on his deathbed that I would marry a Greek man. I can't go back on that promise now.

Suddenly, Yana felt quite miserable and alone, and not even the gentle rocking of the ship could alter her mood.

Clay looked out the porthole, trying to ignore Antoli's droning voice. The man annoyed Clay for a couple of very good reasons and countless petty ones. Among the latter was his thick Greek accent, which had begun like a mosquito buzzing near his ear that first only annoyed Clay slightly and now made him want to swat Antoli, just like he would the bothersome insect. Why Clay found Yana's accent somewhere between adorable and sexy was something he couldn't explain and didn't even want to question.

Topping his list of perfectly reasonable explanations for disliking Antoli was the way the Greek man hungrily eyed Yana whenever she was in the room and didn't notice his rapacious stare. Occasionally, Clay wondered whether Yana and Antoli had ever been involved romantically, but he always dismissed the thought. Antoli just didn't seem like Yana's type, and the entire notion of seeing them together—even in his mind's eye—was repulsive to Clay.

Clay had been looking for someone or something that he could vent his anger on since Yana had issued him his walking papers and he had said she could, for all he cared, go straight to hell.

No style. No style at all, old boy. She knocked you right out of the saddle, and all you could come up with was a third-rate rejoinder.

He thought about her constantly. For a while he had held onto the slim hope that somehow, once on the ship and headed for Greece, he would find enough to occupy his thoughts. The wish had proven futile. Alone in his lavishly appointed stateroom, all too aware that Yana was in the next one, thoughts of her haunted his every moment.

What is she wearing now? he would ask himself, staring at the carved teakwood ceiling as he lay in bed, certain that he wouldn't find sleep soon. *Does she ever think of me?*

Clay was angry with Yana for casting him aside. He was angry with himself for being so vulnerable. He was furious with Yana for exploiting that vulnerability to meet her own ends. But most of all, he was angry with whoever was responsible for the fact that he still wanted her.

Clay was quite convinced—in the irrational manner that sometimes seems like perfect logic to the emotionally distressed—that someone else was responsible for him still wanting Yana, since he knew

271

she was nothing but a mendacious, coldhearted, shrewd debutante who could never love anyone but herself and her own precious inheritance.

For a while, he tried hard to convince himself that the only reason he wanted Yana back was so he could get her into bed again, then boot her out of his life. Once he did that, *he* would be the one in control, the one who made the decisions concerning himself and Yana.

The only problem was that even Clay knew it for the lie it was, no matter how much he wanted to believe it was the truth.

Clay hated this new feeling of powerlessness over his own life. Yana had decided—for the two of them—that it was best to sweep their private history under the rug and ignore it. She wanted the reality to become a dream, illusory and quickly forgotten. What *he* wanted didn't matter, though she'd made the choice that, at least in theory, affected them both equally.

Lying in bed, waiting for sleep night after tormenting night, Clay's thoughts traveled in chaotic, aimless directions, quite unlike his usually ordered thoughts.

On the first night aboard ship—and by midnight he had memorized every intricate detail of his stateroom ceiling—Clay was quite convinced that Yana had made good on her word to cast him out of her life without another thought. And though she might have the right to do whatever she felt was best for herself—even if that meant treating Clay like some kind of expendable commodity—the least she could do, if she was any kind of woman at all, was to have some doubts about her decision to leave him. The absolute *least* she could do was to think about him once in a while and maybe miss a night or two of sleep.

It was in the futile hope he could lose himself in work that Clay found himself in a room with Antoli, looking at blueprints for the *Shadow* and *Despina*, the ships that would be built by Zacarious Shipping and that would, if calculations were correct, make them all even richer than they already were.

"You agree then that this retainer wall can be moved back at least ten meters?" Antoli held his finger on one of a dozen blueprints that were unrolled on the table in Clay's stateroom. "Clay, are you listening to me?"

"Yes, I'm listening. I'm thinking."

Antoli, who had sensed a change in the emotional chemistry between Clay and Yana, allowed himself a momentary smile behind the American's back.

"Is it the retaining wall that occupies your mind, or something else?"

Clay turned away from the porthole. He wondered if the contempt he had for Antoli showed in his eyes.

"Of course it is the retaining wall I'm thinking about. That, and the hundred other decisions that have to be made before we can put one ship in the water."

Clay looked straight into Antoli's eyes, wishing the little Greek man would call him a liar. Clay didn't require an earth-shattering excuse to unleash his temper. Most any excuse would do.

"I don't mean to pry," Antoli explained, smiling a little, being deferential and obsequious with Clay. He thought Clay would appreciate such fawning behavior, not realizing the man had no respect for bootlickers.

Angry with himself, his world, and everyone in it, Clay decided it might be best if he really did throw himself wholeheartedly into the work. He wouldn't be happier, he realized, but at least he would be productive.

"It is agreed then? We move it ten meters to the stern, like I suggest?"

Clay looked down at where Antoli's finger made contact with the blueprint. A sudden memory tickled his distracted mind. His eyes narrowed in concentration, intent on the blueprint for long moments before his gaze traveled upward to lock with Antoli's.

"I was under the impression that retaining wall is a closed issue. We talked about that back at the ranch, and even more recently—two nights ago—right here, with Yana."

"Yes, of course. But I think if you'll listen to me, you will see that it is not in our best interests to have this wall built where it is drawn."

"Yana explained why it is important the retaining wall be placed there." Clay thumped his finger against the desk, hitting the blueprint with sudden certainty. "We discussed this with Yana."

Antoli gave Clay an oily smile. "Yes, yes . . . but

274

let's not give Nico's little girl too much"—Antoli rolled his eyes theatrically, searching for the appropriate English word—"credence? Authority? Whatever it is, she does not need it, because she does not truly understand the shipping business. She is Nico's little girl and he loves her, but he knows—and you and I *surely* know—that Yana cannot be in charge of an operation as complicated as this one."

Insults threatened to explode from Clay's lips. He kept his mouth tightly shut, waiting for Antoli to take enough rope to hang himself.

"When Yana talks, we must be polite and listen to her, yes? But we mustn't take her too seriously. She is having fun thinking she is in charge of Zacarious Shipping. It makes her feel good, very important. But she is only a woman—and a young woman at that." Antoli patted Clay's forearm, signaling they must be comrades in the charade. "I will—"

"You will *what?*" Clay's eyes bore into Antoli.

Antoli had been ready to say that he would run Zacarious Shipping, with Clay's help. Now, looking into Clay's dark eyes, he thought better of it. A little more genuflection now would assist him in the long run.

"I will help you run Zacarious Shipping, of course. You must be the leader in Nico's absence. Whatever you do not understand, whatever you need help with, always know that I am here at your disposal."

Nico's got a Judas in his bed, Clay thought, remembering the doubts that Sorren had had about Antoli.

"We don't have to make any decision right now," Clay said, turning his attention away from Antoli and back to the blueprints. "There are plenty of other wrinkles that must be ironed out."

Clay roamed the ship, apparently aimlessly, moving in a desultory manner. He drew the attention of several women on the ship. Some of them eyed him coyly as he passed by, resplendent in his coal-gray suit that concealed the holster and revolver under his left arm. Other women eyed him more openly. A woman, now in her mid-thirties, who at sixteen had married a man twenty years her senior, gave him a come-hither look that was beyond misinterpretation. Clay merely smiled, nodded in acknowledgment— no sense in being rude or burning bridges, especially since Yana had made it clear that he was a free man now and capable of pursuing his own amusements— and kept right on walking.

Only his eyes gave his casual appearance away. They were jetty black, steely, moving often though he seldom turned his head.

He had a great deal on his mind as he searched for Yana. What exactly he planned to tell her—if ever he had a chance to be with her alone—Clay hadn't yet decided.

He didn't like the idea of being a tattletale. However dangerous and disloyal Antoli Pacca was to Zacarious Shipping in general and to Illyana

Zacarious in particular, Clay wanted Yana to find out for herself. If he told her, he'd feel like a schoolboy running to the teacher to tattle on who had written the nasty words on the chalkboard.

Clay had just rounded the entrance to the captain's office when he heard her voice. He stopped for a moment outside the doors, his ears pricked for the slightest nuance in her speech that might suggest she was flirting with the captain. It galled him to think that he could experience jealousy but he did, and Clay's limited ability for self-deception remained silent.

No, he thought after a moment, she's talking business with the captain. Nothing more than business. Doesn't she ever stop working?

Clay entered the captain's room. When Yana saw him, she smiled. The captain, a tall, rangy man with a physique similar to Clay's, though he was considerably older, had to drag his gaze from Yana to see who had entered the room. Clay immediately disliked the man.

"Is it possible for me to have a moment of your time?" Clay asked politely, though he felt a strong urge to take Yana forcibly by the arms and hold her in place so he could say all the things he needed to tell her. "There's something that's come up that I think you should know about."

Yana's eyes narrowed slightly. "Of course. If something has come up, I'd like to hear of it." She turned to the captain and smiled up at him, triggering more irrational urges that bordered on blatant violence in Clay. "Please excuse me, Captain. You know what it's like with ships. There's always something that needs looking after."

"Yes, always something." The captain's eyes, cobalt-blue and wizened from years at sea, flashed in Clay's direction for only a split second before returning to Yana. "Perhaps, in your busy schedule, we can talk more again sometime . . . sometime soon."

"I'd like that."

She doesn't waste any time finding a new man to feed her ego.

Clay swallowed the thought distastefully, reminding himself for the umpteenth time that he had to separate feelings from logic.

When they were out of the office, walking slowly along the foredeck with many other passengers, Yana looked at Clay with eyes that reflected her concern. "What's wrong? Did you find something in the blueprints that we missed?"

Clay cleared his throat, looking away from Yana toward the sea. A little voice inside his head, which sounded suspiciously like his father's, whispered, *It's neither manly nor honorable to be an informer. Sometimes, in business, I have found it prudent to use informers, but I never really respected the men who do it.*

"Clay, what is it?" Yana prodded.

"How well do you know Antoli?"

Yana's brow furrowed. "He's worked for my father for a long time. Years. His personal life has never

278

been of any concern to me, if that's what you're asking."

"I wouldn't trust him if I were in your shoes," Clay said, forcing the words out. "He's not the loyal servant you think he is."

"You have something specific to tell me?"

"No." It was as far as Clay could go. He had warned Yana without actually tattling on Antoli. "It's just a feeling I have." With just a touch of anger in his tone, Clay added, "You believe in feelings, don't you?"

Yana looked away, not wanting another confrontational discussion with Clay. She noticed an attractive woman, younger than herself, looking at Clay out of the corner of her eye. When the woman looked at Yana, her expression became vaguely disappointed.

"I believe in some feelings, not in others," Yana said finally. "If you have something substantial— something more than vague allusions—I wish you'd tell me now. If not, I'm afraid you sound rather petty."

"I'm not a petty person, Yana, and my suspicions of Antoli are hardly trivial." He looked at Yana, thinking he must surely sound like a jealous, spurned lover. "Just watch yourself around him. That's all I'm asking you. He can't be trusted. Believe me."

Yana chuckled softly, a pleasant little sound that came from her lips and, in happier times, had pleased Clay immensely. Hearing it now, he felt like she was mocking him and his concern.

"He's dangerous, I'm telling you." Clay clenched his teeth, knowing he mustn't get angry but feeling that emotion rising to the surface anyway. "Behind all his smiles and all his sycophantic behavior, he's a calculating man who is not looking out for your best interests."

"And you *are* looking out for my best interests. Is that what you're trying so hard *not* to say?"

Yana looked at Clay, enjoying the fluid movement of his steps, liking the way his gray suit fit him, recalling fondly and lamentably how she had slowly taken his clothing off in the dressing room before making passionate love to every inch of his beautifully responsive body.

"Clay, if this is about our decision . . ." Yana began, stopping when the words became too difficult. She bolstered her willpower and continued. "It is best for both of us that we bury the past."

"You've already made that point abundantly clear too many times. I haven't the damndest idea why you felt it necessary to . . . aw . . . to hell with it!" He wheeled around and began to walk away.

"You wouldn't understand, Clay."

He stopped. "Sure I understand, Yana," Clay replied sharply and bitterly over his shoulder. "I understand perfectly well. A woman's got to set her priorities, she's got to be practical. And you, my lady"—Clay's venom was poisonous now—"are *nothing* if not a practical woman."

She had never intended to tell Clay the real reason

280

she had to deny the things they had shared together. The demons in her soul were too real to ever easily put into words. So when Yana began talking about her childhood, she looked at the deck of the ship beneath her feet instead of at Clay, listening to herself as though it were someone else speaking.

"It wasn't your fault that Papa got shot," she said in a whisper. "If I hadn't ridden away, you wouldn't have followed me. I should have stayed by Papa, like he told me to."

Clay wanted to take her into his arms. He wanted to shoulder all the blame for Nico's brush with death. But he knew, at least for now, that he must remain quiet and listen to Yana, and allow her to bridge the chasm that separated them.

"I should have known all along that we couldn't . . . that if we were ever together, something bad would happen. First my mother, now Papa." Yana closed her eyes briefly and her steps faltered. She got back in stride quickly, and when she looked up at Clay, her eyes were soft and sad, weary with a world that seemed so hostile to her happiness. "If we were together . . . if we stayed together . . . how long would it be before you were the one to be hurt?"

"I still don't . . . Your mother? What does she have to do with this? With us?"

"She has everything to do with us," Yana continued in that distant, numb tone. "You can't love someone without hurting someone else. Didn't you know that?"

"No, Yana, I didn't know that. And I don't believe

that, either. It's nonsense. People protect the people they love. They don't hurt them." Clay wanted to promise that he would never hurt her, but he knew she would never accept the help, the comfort that he wanted so much to give. "*I* protect the people I love," he continued, making his words more direct, more personal. "I wouldn't knowingly or willingly hurt someone I love, and neither would I let anyone else hurt that person."

Yana's eyes told Clay she knew secrets about the world that he did not. She smiled sadly at him, then very slowly explained how her birth had caused her mother's death and her father's lifelong loneliness. She finished the story with a brief explanation of her deathbed promise to Nico to marry whomever he wanted her to.

Clay remained silent as Yana spoke, beginning to understand at last the demons that haunted her. He looked at her profile, remembering what it was like to hold her close and feel her in his arms, to smell the special fragrance of her skin and feel her responding as they made love.

"So, you see, we just can't be," Yana said in a whisper.

"It doesn't have to be that way. Not if we don't want it to be," Clay replied.

"Yes it does, Clay. That's part of the reason we can't stay together. What's happened . . . Papa getting shot . . . the guilt . . . it's all so much stronger than we are. You just don't understand that yet."

You don't understand that I'm in love with you,

Clayton McKenna. I didn't even know that until just now. But I do love you, and that's why I can't have you. Wanting to love you nearly killed Papa. And if I did love you, eventually you'd be the one who gets killed. I love you too much to let that happen, Clay . . . and that's what you can never understand.

Clay took Yana's hand in his, forcing her to stop walking, turning her so that she faced him. He grabbed her by the shoulders, bending slightly so that their faces were closer.

"You are throwing away something beautiful, Yana. I don't know if there is anything I can say or do that will convince you of this. But I'll tell you this right now. I'm not someone you can easily toss aside. What we have together isn't something you can deny. You can't just pretend it doesn't exist."

It? Clay thought bitterly, hating his inability to say precisely what he felt in his heart. *It is love. Why don't I just tell Yana I love her? Why? Because of all the sweet words I've used to seduce women, love is one word I've never used. Because all along I've known love is something special, something I didn't have with those other women . . . something I didn't have until Yana.*

"Yes, I can, Clay," Yana whispered, looking up into his ebony eyes. "I can, because pretending that you and I have never touched each other, never felt anything for each other . . . it's the right thing to do. It's even more than that, Clay. It's my duty. Aren't you the one who is always talking about how important duty is?"

283

Chapter 17

"Dinner was wonderful," Yana said, tilting her head back to let the breeze play with her hair.

Clay, standing beside Yana on the fantail of the ship, sucked in his breath as he looked at her. Against the backdrop of the ebony night sky of an evening at sea, illuminated only by the light that shone from the promenade deck, she looked more beautiful to him than ever before.

It's just the time I've spent without touching her, the forced celibacy, that's making me feel this way, Clay thought, hoping it would reassure him that Yana wasn't really that desirable, that she didn't really beguile him.

But she was there for him to see in a mint-green velvet dress, trimmed with darker green lace around the dramatic neckline and ruffled white lace at the wrist cuffs and the skirt hem. Yana stood leaning against the safety railing, one foot up on the lower railing, looking toward the stern of the ship, her back toward the water.

Her creamy bosom, pressed together and held high, full, and enticing, drew Clay's eyes. His insides tightened at the erotic vision. When his gaze pulled upward, Yana's high cheekbones, silky skin, and large, soft eyes made Clay ache for the days when she could laugh with him and smile at him . . . and be so bold as to insist that he make love to her.

Clay rolled a cigarette, hoping it would calm him. He lit it, then struck a casual pose.

Yana had been perfectly polite in the three days they had been at sea. Clay had tried to see Yana alone, if only for a few moments or for a single meal, but Antoli was always there, always underfoot, always preventing Clay from talking intimately with her.

Tonight, Yana had insisted again on discussing nothing but business, from the hors d'oeuvres to the after-dinner coffee. Then, when Antoli excused himself, promising to be back shortly, Clay suggested an evening walk around the deck. He was surprised when Yana agreed.

"I've always loved being at sea," Yana said. A warm breeze pulled strands of dark hair from her coiffure. She pushed the tendrils away from her face, tucking them behind her ear with a faintly annoyed expression. She had no idea how enticing she appeared.

Clay cleared his throat, pulling his eyes from Yana with some difficulty. "I've never spent much time on the water." Clay turned, facing the sea, looking at the glimmering stars. "I've always been a lot more at home on the back of a horse than on the water."

"A cowboy?" Yana grinned without looking at Clay. "Some of the men who work for my father read the translations of your American novels. What do you call them? Anyway, you don't seem like a cowboy to me."

"Dime novels," Clay answered. "And I'm not a cowboy. Cows interest me only if they happen to be cooked medium rare, take up most of a dinner plate, and are accompanied by a large potato with lots of butter and a lettuce salad." Clay chuckled. "I'm no cowboy. A horseman, maybe. But I'm definitely not a cowboy."

"We have few cows in Greece. Many sheep and goats, though. Makes for good Gouda cheese."

Clay frowned. "I didn't think of that. I guess my diet's going to change when we get to Pirias."

Yana looked beneath her lashes at Clay, wondering if he was still susceptible to whatever charms she possessed. It didn't matter, though, since what she had once had with Clay was gone, she reminded herself. Just the same, Yana wondered if Clay, seeing her in profile, still had the same overpowering desire to take her into his arms—a desire that had once seemed so strong he could not control himself.

"Don't worry, I'll make sure you don't starve, even if you don't have steak twice a day," Yana said. "Emma would never forgive me if you lost even a single pound."

Like a flash, Yana saw Clay's body in her mind's

eye. Naked, powerful, the muscles moving sleekly beneath his skin, like some sensuously predatory jaguar, seducing her with maddening ease. From where would he even lose a pound? His body was perfect just the way it was, all sinewy muscle and sensual grace.

"Emma's actually a very forgiving person. She just thinks that unless people are as heavy as she is, they're on the verge of emaciation." Clay laughed softly. "She'll never change . . . thank goodness. She's always been there for me, for my whole family."

"And for me," Yana said softly. "You love her a lot, don't you?"

"Yes. It's hard not to love Emma, though she does occasionally get to be like a blanket that's too warm. No matter what you do, you can't throw her off." Clay smiled to himself, his eyes fixed on a distant wave. "Not that I wouldn't freeze without it, you understand."

Clay's smile widened as he thought how nice it was to talk with Yana about something other than tariffs and import regulations.

"I had someone like that in my life, but she's gone now. My Grandmama Zacarious . . . I miss her."

Clay turned so that he could look at Yana. He wanted to touch her face, to explore her delicate contours with his fingertips. Instead, he gripped the safety railing tightly to keep his hands away from her.

"You don't talk about your childhood," Clay said softly. "Actually, you haven't talked about anything but work in quite a while."

Yana smiled softly, apparently finding some amusement in the statement or simply pleased that her professional manner had been duly noted. Anger, stark and primitive, began to bloom in Clay's soul like some poison fruit produced by a beautiful flower in a moment of aberrant evolution. Clay felt his anger build, each second heightening the rage inside him. Yana was teasing him, finding amusement in the fact that he still wanted her and she, quite obviously did not want him.

I miss her.

The thought struck Clay forcefully, and he mentally staggered from the impact. Never before in Clay's life had he *missed* a woman. He'd missed some aspects of this woman's or that woman's sexual proclivities, to be sure. He had on occasion wished he could sleep with a former mistress one more time, just for old time's sake. He had done all those things, but he'd never missed the totality—her mannerisms, her smile, her way of looking at life—of a woman before.

Clay grit his teeth as he concentrated on holding his anger and confusion in check. His forearms, beneath the white silk shirt and tweed jacket, bulged with exertion as he gripped the safety railing.

"Is anything wrong?" Yana asked sweetly, showing a mild degree of concern. "You've got the strangest look on your face, Clay. It's almost . . . frightening."

"Nothing is wrong. Nothing is troubling me."

The words came out clipped, as if out of a Gatling gun. Clay smiled tightly at Yana. "Not one damn thing is wrong with me. You should know that better than anyone else."

"You *are* angry, Clay. Have I done something?"

"You haven't done a damn thing." The sudden desire to use foul words, to shock Yana and offend her inbred sense of decorum, was strong in Clay, but he resisted the urge.

"Is it the ship? You don't have to be embarrassed by a bout of seasickness. It happens to most people when they spend time on a ship for the first time. Especially right after a meal."

"It's not seasickness." The anger now showed in Clay's eyes, glittering with menace. He knew it was wrong to be so furious with Yana, and he realized that fighting his rising anger was a losing battle. "It's you, Yana."

"Me? What could I possibly have done to offend you? If I've said something . . . I certainly didn't mean to. I apologize if I've—"

"Shut up!" Clay stepped away from the railing, moving so that he had Yana between himself and the side of the ship. "Or should I say *as tokalo!* That's the Greek word for it, isn't it?"

Yana, her face the loveliest expression of curiosity Clay had ever seen, looked at him silently, her head shaking almost imperceptibly. She simply did not understand Clay's mercurial mood swing.

"Yes, Clay, that's the right word for it. But why tell me to shut up after asking me to come out here for a walk? Walking in silence doesn't strike me as entirely entertaining."

"But, then, *entertainment*"—Clay drawled the word out lasciviously—"is off the menu with you and me, isn't it, Yana? At least that's what you want me to believe."

Yana looked away for a moment. She hadn't expected this from Clay. Wasn't he the man who had left dozens of women behind?

"Is this kind of anger really justified?" Yana had expected better from Clay. "If you're not happy about the way things are, I'm sorry. I'm sorry for you and I'm sorry for myself. But I thought it was agreed that we couldn't . . . you know what I'm saying. I made a promise to Papa. That promise was made when we didn't know if he was going to live or die. Don't you see that I've got to honor that promise now?" Yana's eyes held Clay's. "We had an agreement."

"*You* came to that agreement by yourself," Clay said, quietly but hotly, conveniently forgetting that there was a time when he had planned to give a farewell speech to Yana.

"Clayton . . ." Yana sighed, feeling herself crumbling inside, feeling the arctic cold she had kept inside thawing precipitiously. "We tried and we failed. You don't like failing and neither do I. But the simple, sad truth of the whole mess is that whenever we're together, we do something to self-destruct. We can't help it, I suppose. Maybe it's just the way we are. I'm nineteen years old. I should have married three years ago. How old are you, Clay? How long ago should you have married?"

"I don't see how that's got anything to do with you and me," Clay said, clutching the safety railing on either side of Yana, his face now very close to hers, his acute senses picking up the delicate fragrance of her skin.

"It means that we don't do what everyone else expects of us. You've avoided marriage and so have I. How could two people like that possibly expect to have any happiness together?"

Yana was leaning backward, arching over the railing, trying to keep her face as far away from Clay's as possible. She had seen him in many different moods in their time together, but never had she witnessed anything quite like this. It wasn't so much rage that she saw in his glittering dark eyes as it was helplessness. Yana understood that for a Mc-Kenna to feel helpless was foreign, and something that could trigger a head-on, all-out assault against any perceived threat.

"That's the most idiotic excuse for logic I've ever heard!" Clay hissed.

Yana put a hand up in the small space that separated her body from Clay's. The hand was steady, though her blood was racing faster all the time.

"Touch me, Clay," she said quietly, offering her hand. "Touch me and you'll feel how things have changed with us. You'll feel the difference when nothing happens."

But Clay McKenna did not touch Yana's hand. He

was young and strong and had enjoyed a long history of beautiful women fawning over him. So when Yana, the one unattainable woman in his entirely attainable life, smiled and suggested that she would feel nothing at his touch, it was all much more than a hot-blooded, hot-tempered McKenna man could take.

He swept Yana up in his arms, crushing her to his body. Clay's mouth came down hungrily, slanting over Yana's smaller, softer one. He kissed her almost harshly, demanding that she respond to the kiss because if she did, it would be proof that all her coolly delivered dialogue had been a bunch of shabby lies.

Yana realized all this instinctively and without resentment. She knew precisely what Clay wanted from her and that she should slap his face for being villainously abusive in both words and actions.

But the sensations came back to Yana in a splendid rush that she felt all over her body, from the top of her coiffured head to the tips of her slippered feet. All the things that Clay had introduced to her senses—the pressure of his solid chest against the sensitive firmness of her breasts confined in a bodice, the taste of his mouth against her own, his tongue as it slipped between her lips and touched her own, his hands, one against the small of her back, the other between her shoulder blades to press the full length of her body against him—came back with a vengeance, heightened by the time she had forced herself to avoid Clay's embrace, heightened further still because she knew

293

what ecstasy followed his intimate kisses.

The kiss was long and wet, and Yana would not have protested for one moment had she been anywhere but on the deck of a ship where God-knows-who could walk by at any moment. Passion aside, discretion was still in order.

With her hands against Clay's chest, Yana pushed away, turning her face aside to end the breathtaking kiss. The facade of conviction that she had been able to maintain—the bald-faced lie that she no longer cared for Clay—had been destroyed with a single kiss.

"Clay, not here," Yana said, her voice quavering a little. She looked into his eyes and, most irritatingly, saw triumph shining there. "This isn't the place to be kissing, no matter how boldly people think they can act on ships."

Clay was smiling, his arms still around Yana. "Who would even notice us? We're not the first two people who have kissed on a ship deck at night." Clay tried to pull Yana to him again, but she resisted. "Come to my room," he whispered, the timbre of his voice familiar, triggering impulses within Yana that she had thought no longer existed.

"I've got to think." Yana extricated herself from Clay's arms, sighing softly when his hand—apparently accidentally, though she doubted it—passed lightly over the lush swell of her left breast. "Clay, please don't ask things like that."

She took a step back, feeling the need to be far away from him, safely locked alone in her stateroom so she could try to make sense of her chaotic, disquieting thoughts.

"Just give me some time," Yana continued softly. "I've got to be alone." And then, knowing Clay was anything but a patient man, she said, "For once in your life, please try to be patient."

She left in a rustle of fine fabric, leaving Clay behind to stand alone on the deck, staring out to sea at the darkness, reliving once again in his mind's eye all the glorious memories he had of a fiery Greek heiress named Illyana Zacarious . . . and dreaming of all the spendid memories to come.

Yana pulled the brush through her hair, closing her eyes, enjoying the feel against her scalp. In New York, after making love to Clay and with her hair a mess, he had insisted on combing out the tangles.

"I caused them, after all," he had said, taking the brush from her hand and turning her around on the bed so that her back was to him. "Just relax now and let me do this."

Brushing her own hair now clarified Yana's memories, sharpening them, making them more precise. It was not what Yana wanted, of course. She had hoped that time away from Clay's tender kisses would dull the memory, lessen the ache.

On the stand near her was the jade necklace that Clay had bought her. She picked up the cool metal, weighing it in her hands. Slowly, as though the necklace itself were a living thing that might protest, she brought it around her neck and hooked the clasp. When she looked at herself in the mirror, the jade stone gleamed in the light, nestled coolly in her bosom just above the lace-trimmed edge of the soft white silk nightgown.

The knock at her stateroom door made Yana jump. She had been lost in her dreams, in her memories. She instinctively reached for her robe. The nightgown was another of Clay's gifts and the bodice was, even by American standards, scandalously low-cut. The garment shimmered, all finely sewn white silk that defined every curve of her upper body, flowing smoothly in a wide skirt that showed the full, tapering line of her strong thighs when she walked.

Clay's come for me, thought Yana with a smile. *I wouldn't go to his room, so he's come for me.*

She held the robe in her hand, knowing the appropriate thing to do was put it on before answering the door. But she dropped the robe back on the chair and walked slowly toward the door, her heart accelerating, her palms suddenly moist.

Yana opened the door wide, standing there for Clay to see, knowing from experience what his reaction would be. Hadn't he nearly gone out of his mind in Virginia when he'd seen her in the nightgown?

Only it wasn't Clay at the door.

Yana recoiled from Antoli, crossing her arms over her scantily covered bosom. She turned away from him, rushing to the chair for her robe. With her back to him, she quickly put the modest robe on, tying the sash tightly around her waist. When she turned back to Antoli, she was shocked to see he'd entered her quarters and was about to close the door.

"Don't!" Yana said, much louder than she had intended, a shrillness to her voice that frightened her.

Antoli smiled as though he'd done nothing wrong. Desire glittered in his lidded eyes. Yana held her robe closed at the throat, though she was suitably concealed.

"Why have you come here?" Yana demanded, anger and authority ringing in every word. She had been caught off guard, but she'd regained her composure quickly. "What do you think you're doing?"

"I only stopped by to make sure that you are well," Antoli said subserviently. "I thought that perhaps you would like me to bring you some tea from the galley?"

"That won't be necessary." Yana saw the desire Antoli felt, and it made her feel somehow unclean. "Everything is fine. Please leave now, Antoli, and we'll talk tomorrow at breakfast."

"As you wish." Antoli paused at the doorway, wanting one more look at Yana. "If there is anything you need, my room is just down the hall. All you have to do is ask."

"Thank you, Antoli. I will remember that." Yana tried to smile but couldn't. "Thank you . . . now please leave. It is late and I'm about to retire."

"Of course." Antoli's gaze traveled up and down

over Yana, touching her as though she had not put on the protective robe. "Sleep well." He closed the door behind him as he left.

Yana rushed to the door and locked it.

Was this what Clay was trying to warn me about? That Antoli has dirty thoughts for me?

Yana had noticed Antoli looking at her surreptitiously in the past. She'd thought it rather comforting that Clay was concerned for her safety. She wasn't worried about Antoli, though. She knew exactly how to keep servants in their place, and no matter how high Antoli Pacca had clawed his way up in Zacarious Shipping, he was still just another servant.

Yana went back to the small bench seat in front of the dressing table, removing the robe as she walked. As she resumed brushing her hair, she wondered why Antoli's desire for her made her feel fouled, why his unspoken thoughts and wishes were dirty in her thinking, when the same thoughts, from Clay, made her skin feel sensitized to the possibilities of pleasure.

She had escaped this time, she thought. She had, at the moment she'd opened the door, been willing to go back on her decision, been willing to compromise her own convictions to be with Clay. Instead, she had given Antoli a sight of her that he would probably never forget.

Yana smiled. Poor Antoli, he was never quite good enough. Even her girlfriends in Pirias had laughed quietly among themselves whenever he was around. He saw himself as a power in Zacarious Shipping and believed that power would serve as an aphrodisiac to Yana's friends. He did not realize that they saw him as Nico Zacarious's valet and nothing more.

Antoli paced the small confines of his cabin, which was considerably smaller than the staterooms Yana and Clay had. In his hand was a razor-sharp knife with a curved blade. He always kept the knife with him, thinking he would use it to cut the tongue out of any man who dared insult him. But Antoli had never once drawn the knife on a man, though he had suffered many insults. The only time he had ever threatened anyone with the knife was when a prostitute in Athens had laughed at him after their business transaction ended almost as soon as it began because Antoli was unable to control his desires. As Antoli had negotiated a price with the woman, he'd promised her she would enjoy it so much she should pay *him*. Business began and ended in less than a minute.

"Slut! Bitch!" Antoli hissed. He waved the knife in midair, pantomiming all the vicious things he would eventually do to Yana. "Flaunting herself like a whore for McKenna!"

Antoli's first conclusion was that Yana had opened the door, showing herself in the sheer white nightgown because she had kept her passion for him a secret all these years and could contain herself no longer. He wanted to hold onto that belief, but the disappointment in Yana's eyes at seeing him, plus the way she had frantically gone for her robe, told Antoli that he was not the evening visitor she had hoped to see.

The notion of Yana letting Clay touch her—or, even worse, her hands on him—sickened Antoli. His Indian blood would surely taint Yana for all time. There would be the smell of Clay on Yana's skin if he touched her. Antoli was certain of it because he'd known sailors who had traveled to North Africa and slept with native women. When the sailors returned to port in Pirias, the dark-skinned women had left an indelible odor on the indiscreet sailors. The thought that such a fate might happen to Yana, at least before he could have her, nauseated Antoli.

Could the stain of Indian blood be passed onto Antoli if he slept with Yana after Clay?

Still pacing, Antoli pondered the question. He didn't like the idea of going around the rest of his life with the smell of Indian on him, no matter how much he wanted to drive himself viciously into Yana and hear her screams while he took her.

Antoli banged his shin against the one small chair in the room. He cursed loudly and gave the chair a savage kick, sending it flying across the room to slam against the wall and causing pain to lance up his leg like a lightning bolt exploding in his brain.

Antoli cursed some more. He didn't have to worry about Yana hearing him. His room was far away from hers—though Clay's room was right next to Yana's.

Limping, Antoli went to his bed—a single,

whereas Yana and Clay each had double-wide beds, he noted—and massaged his bare, throbbing foot. He kept the knife beside him on the bed.

The pain in Antoli's foot crystallized his thoughts. He had to get to Yana before Clay did. Since he couldn't control Yana and couldn't trust her not to behave whorishly with Clay, Antoli's options were limited. He had to kill Clay—and quickly. The body could be disposed of overboard and no one would be the wiser. Things like that happened on ships all the time.

He would have to be cautious, though. Other men had tried to kill Clay and they'd died for their efforts. Antoli knew he must get close to Clay first, get Clay to trust him, just as he'd gotten Nico to trust him. Only then could Antoli make his murderous move.

Antoli picked up the knife, touching his fingertip to the point. A drop of blood formed on his finger. Antoli made a mental note to wash his hands very carefully after he cut Clay's throat from one ear to the other, to make sure none of Clay's Indian blood stayed on his own skin for too long.

In such matters, a man couldn't be too careful.

Antoli sucked the blood from his fingertip.

Clay stood with his arms hanging at his sides, looking at Yana's door. He wasn't sure if he was simply cowardly—not a pleasant revelation for a McKenna man to even contemplate—or if he was trying to summon, without really knowing it, an

301

unseen power that would make Yana open the door.

"Damn weakling schoolboy," Clay murmured disgustedly, damning himself for not making his presence known and for waiting in his own stateroom for over two hours, laboring under the pathetically misguided belief that Yana would come to him.

Clay raised his hand, an inch away from putting knuckles to wood.

I'm crawling back to her. It's humiliating and unmanly.

"Shut up and leave me alone," Clay whispered, answering the annoying voice in his head.

He knocked on the door. The memory of himself at fifteen, standing on a neighbor's porch about to escort the daughter of the house to school, flitted painfully in his mind. Clay wondered if he looked as juvenile as he felt.

"Yes?"

Yana's tone sounded wary, a little defensive. It occurred to Clay that she might not even open the door for him. The idea of talking to a door brought on fresh waves of potential humiliation.

"Who is it?" he heard her ask. Then Yana rattled out a stream of words in Greek. Clay could not tell if the words were meant for Antoli, who would understand them, or if she was cursing at him, Clay, in her native tongue, knowing that he would have no idea what she was saying.

"Yana, it's me, Clay. I've got to talk to you."

He stared at the brass door handle, mentally

302

willing it to turn downward, disengaging the latch. Clay was holding his breath. In his mind's eye, he could see Yana, only a foot away on the other side of the door, standing in silent concentration, thinking whether she should open the door and speak to him face to face or shoo him away like he was a bothersome adolescent.

He heard the click of the bolt being slid back, then his hopes soared as the handle turned downward. The door was opened a mere ten inches, and the face that had haunted all of Clay's dreams appeared in the opening.

Yana's hair was down, not pinned up as usual. Dark tresses cut diagonal lines across her forehead, framing her face, highlighting the size, color, and the softness of her eyes.

"I just wanted to talk to you," Clay said quickly, hoping he sounded considerably more mature than he felt. "I didn't get you out of bed, did I?"

Yana shook her head, sending her silky hair swirling around her face. In the ten minutes that had passed since Antoli's intrusion, she had regained her composure and her better judgment. She wasn't going to fling the door open wide, and she wasn't going to let Clay step one foot inside her stateroom.

"Do you have a minute? This really won't take long."

"Can't this wait until breakfast tomorrow?"

Clay had absolutely no idea what he was going to say next. When he was in his own room, contemplating going to see Yana, he hadn't been able to think of any good excuse for disturbing her. With characteristic confidence, Clay assumed he would think of some clever white lie along the way. After all, it wasn't like he had ever been tongue-tied with women.

None of his past experience with the fairer sex prevented Clay from standing in the hallway with a blank expression, mutely admiring the classic Greek perfection of the face—and that was all he could see of Yana—that stared back at him, no doubt waiting for him to be witty and clever and . . . well, Clay McKenna-like.

"I was just about to retire. Unless this is very important, I'd like to discuss it tomorrow at breakfast," Yana repeated, paused a beat, then said, "When Antoli is with us . . . he should hear whatever is so important."

It was at that moment, just when Yana was about to close the door, that Clay saw the heavy gold links resting lightly against her pale neck. He had only seen a gold chain exactly like that once before—on the jade necklace he'd bought for Yana.

Clay put his palm against the door and pushed. He pushed slowly but forcefully against Yana's half-hearted resistance, until the door was open wide.

"I think you'd better leave," Yana whispered.

For a second, Clay stood in the doorway, staring at the heavy jade stone resting between Yana's breasts. Then his eyes went over her, taking in the fullness of her bosom and noticing, with a connoisseur's appraisal, the rounded shape and size of her breasts and how the silk held them as though they were, like the jade resting between them, infinitely priceless jewels. The silk pinched in at Yana's waist before flowering out over her hips.

Clay stepped into Yana's room and kicked the door closed. "I can't," he said simply, then reached for her.

Chapter 18

"Clay, don't," Yana whispered, stepping backward, realizing that she had allowed herself to fantasize and now had to deal with the real-life consequences. "You shouldn't be in here."

Clay shook his head, his gaze incandescent with intent. Weeks of self-denial shone in his dark, hungry, predatory eyes.

"I know that eventually you'd wear my necklace. Have you been wearing it at night—only at night, so I'd never see it on you?" He advanced slowly, crossing the spacious stateroom toward Yana. "You shouldn't have done that. There's no need to hide from me. No need to hide anything from me."

"I haven't been hiding anything from you." Yana cleared her throat, struggling for a less tremulous tone. "This is the first time I've put it on since you gave it to me in New York."

"I don't believe you."

"Then don't," Yana replied quickly. "It's the truth, whether you want to believe it or not." Yana crossed her arms over her bosom. "I don't care what you choose to believe."

"I don't believe that, either."

Clay stepped closer to Yana. His hands were at his sides, but he burned with the desire to take Yana into his arms.

"Would I be overstating the obvious to tell you how beautiful you look?"

Yana sighed, unable to look up at Clay, not wanting to hear his lovewords, however flattering they were.

Clay slipped his finger inside the slender strap of pale silk at Yana's shoulder, pulling the fabric away from her flesh. He worked his hand slowly up and down inside the strap, not touching Yana, enjoying the feel of silk.

"Don't do this to me, Clay. I told you . . . I just can't."

Her words had no influence on Clay. He continued sliding his finger against the inside of Yana's shoulder strap. The motion caused the bodice of the silk nightgown to rise and fall, and though he did not touch her breasts, it seemed to Yana that he was caressing them.

"Yes, you've told me many things. And I've tried to understand your superstitions and all your reasons for staying away from me. So now, Yana, it's time I told you some things. It's time for you to be a little understanding."

Yana looked up at Clay, her curiosity piqued despite herself. Her eyes said she would listen. Her better judgment said that the more time she spent with Clay, the more likely it was she would fail to fulfill the promise she'd made to her unconscious father.

"You worry about Nico, and whether you can run Zacarious Shipping and protect his—your—business interests if I mean something more to you than—than either of us ever intended."

"That's right."

Clay released the strap, letting it snap against her skin. Her breasts trembled when the tension was released. Yana moaned softly as a wave of warmth went through her.

"You had never been with a man before me." Clay's fingertips grazed against the back of Yana's hands, which remained crossed over her bosom. "Your father has chosen some of the finest young men in Greece—all of them wealthy, all from prominent families—in hopes that you would marry one of them."

"Clay, we both know all of this. Why go through this? It serves no purpose."

"Yes, it does. I'm proving a point." Clay's fingers curled gently around Yana's wrists. He pulled her hands apart and inhaled deeply at the vision revealed to him. "You wanted nothing to do with those men because you knew they weren't what you were looking for. Me? I'm like that necklace . . . I'm made for you. Maybe neither of us knew it at first, but we both know it now."

Clay lowered Yana's hands. He slipped his fingers inside both shoulder straps and tugged them over her shoulders until they were at her upper arms. The lace edging of Yana's nightgown slipped fractionally lower on her bosom, still holding and concealing her breasts. But any lower, and she would be bared to Clay's seductive gaze.

"You were waiting for me all along, Yana. You didn't know it, but you were. That's why you made love to me. That's why you will make love to me again." Clay smiled. "You just can't help yourself."

Yana felt the truth in Clay's words. She had shown personal discipline with every man she'd ever met . . . except one. And then, under Clay's touch, she'd experienced a desire that was stronger than her will, more powerful than her fears of intimacy. She wanted, at that moment, to remove her nightgown and show herself to Clay, knowing full well how he would react to seeing her.

"Throw your superstitions aside, Yana. Your father will understand."

Yana crossed her arms over herself again, and her eyes became cold and hard. "You're not confident, you conceited Clay McKenna. You talk like you're the only man in the world, and that what you believe is what *everyone* must believe. You're wrong, Clay. You belittle my ways and call them superstitions. Weren't you the one who took out your medicine bag and burned a hawk's feather to make sure Papa wouldn't die? What if I said your Kiowan beliefs were

310

silly superstitions?''

Yana pulled her straps once again up to her shoulders. She welcomed her growing anger. When she was angry with Clay, she thought clearly. At other times . . . his touch only clouded and confused her thoughts.

"I'd say you were right." Clay placed his hands on Yana's shoulders, giving her a smile, more convinced than ever that if he could not get her back into his life, there would be a void that would never be filled. Her smooth skin was soft and warm against his palms. "I'm arrogant, egotistical, and often insensitive. But none of that really changes anything." Clay's hands slid down the silken surface of Yana's shoulders, pushing the straps with them. "We *must* be together, Yana . . . don't you see that?"

For long moments, Yana looked into Clay's eyes. Her power to deny Clay, to deny herself, to hold true to the promise she'd given Nico while he lay in a coma, the vow she'd made so many years ago to never allow another child to live with the same guilt that she lived with, slipped through her fingers like sand in an hourglass.

"*Se agapo,*" she whispered. Then, in English, she repeated, "I love you."

She saw the shock—and pleasure—register on Clay's face. Only then did she fully realize what she had said.

Yana pulled her arms through the straps of her nightgown, exposing her breasts, wanting to see the pleasure in Clay's face when he looked at her,

311

needing the tantalizing sensations she felt when he touched their risen crests.

Yana took Clay's hands in hers. She brought them to her mouth, kissing both palms before placing his hands on her breasts.

"I love you," she whispered, sliding her arms around Clay's neck, pulling him down to share a tender kiss. "I love you so much."

Tears of joy burned in Yana's eyes as she kissed Clay, opening her mouth to his inquisitive tongue. She didn't want to cry, afraid it would destroy the mood, afraid Clay would be displeased with her for her tears. Wasn't he always disgusted with weakness in himself and others? And wouldn't he see her tears as a sign of weakness?

They shared a long, tender kiss. Clay's hands erotically kneaded Yana's breasts while his tongue explored her mouth. Before the series of kisses had ended, Yana had regained control of her emotions enough to keep the tears in check.

Yana turned her face down and wiped her eyes quickly, smiling, feeling a little embarrassed. Clay took her face in his hands, tilting it up to his.

"You don't have to hide anything from me, Yana." He kissed her lips, then kissed the tears from her eyes. "No more secrets, no more fears."

Clay took Yana's hand in his. He turned, walking toward the bed that awaited them, taking her with him. At the bed, Clay turned Yana around, pushing her until she sat on the mattress. He sat beside her, an arm around her shoulders and kissed Yana as his free hand went to her breasts. He eased her backward until they were reclining together on the bed, their legs over the edge.

"I love the way you touch me," Yana purred, wriggling toward the center of the bed, trembling softly when Clay caught one erect nipple between a finger and thumb.

Yana pulled Clay to herself, needing the feel of his weight upon her. He kissed her, his mouth pressing hungrily against hers, his hand sliding from one breast to the other. Yana returned the kiss, her tongue playing against his, sliding along his lips, slipping into his mouth.

She felt silk gliding up her legs and realized Clay was pulling up her nightgown. His fingertips crept sensually upward, trailing along her satiny inner thigh. Yana feasted on his mouth, biting his lower lip, anxious for his fingers to touch her more intimately yet knowing that this delay, this languid exploration, heightened her anticipation and eventual satisfaction.

"You'll never get rid of me again," Clay murmured against the arch of Yana's throat. He said it possessively, and the truth of his words pleased him.

After his initial, almost irresistible desire to have Yana immediately, he had regained control of himself. Once before he had pressed his desires upon Yana and later had promised it would never happen like that again. It was a promise Clay would die before breaking.

In a mood that was both selflessly caring and

coldly self-serving—Clay wanted Yana to remember this night for a hundred years—he was determined to be more sensually skillful than ever before.

He captured the crest of her breast between his warm, moist lips, flicking his tongue against the tip while his fingertips continued to swirl enticingly higher on Yana's thigh.

Yana wondered, then, if it was possible to go mad, quite completely insane, with desire for a man. She writhed on the bed, not wanting to think about how unladylike her pose must appear, unable to concern herself with anything but the heated, wet mouth on her breast and the touch of fingertips that crept with tantalizing slowness closer and closer to the core of her need.

And when, at last, Clay's hand reached the juncture of her thighs, Yana gasped, her back arching, rapidly peaking, her cry of ecstasy muffled against his mouth.

He brought her to the edge of the abyss with his hands, then sent her free-falling over the brink with his mouth, holding tightly onto Yana as her body was wracked with spasms of ecstasy, his arms like steel hands around her thighs to keep them apart.

Afterward, breathing deeply, her nightgown bunched into a circle of expensive silk around her stomach, Yana reached for Clay, pulling him up so that the fabric of his shirt was cool and smooth against her heated flesh and she could look into his eyes.

Clay smiled at Yana—a bit too arrogantly, as

though there had never been any doubt in his mind that he could bend her will to mold to his desires—and she thought it was entirely unfair for so many advantages to be heaped upon one man. But she loved Clay and she had told him so, and he hadn't disappeared like a puff of smoke at her impassioned confusion. She loved him because he was arrogant and charming and simply too damn handsome. She loved him because he was endlessly stubborn and amazingly talented. And most of all, she loved him because he made her feel loved—not just satisfied sexually, but *loved*.

Yana kissed Clay lightly, her fingers fumbling with the top button of his shirt. She wanted to tell him that she loved him, but she kept silent for fear he would think she loved him for his lovemaking alone.

There were a few awkward, stumbling moments while Clay and Yana, each trying to remove the other's clothes hastily, felt the sensuality of the stateroom start to fade. Clay finally rolled off the bed and rid himself of his clothing, while Yana pulled back the blankets and slipped between the crisp linen sheets.

"Ohhh!" Clay sighed, his naked, muscular body pressing against Yana when he'd gotten between the sheets with her. "You have been in my every thought. I tried to forget about you, but I couldn't. I couldn't do anything but think about you, and remember how happy I am when I'm with you and how miserable I am when I'm without you."

"Don't talk about that now," Yana said. "That's

all in the past. That's all yesterday."

Clay, resting on one elbow to look down at Yana, brushed a dark strand of hair away from her mouth, then kissed her lips softly. Though the need to satisfy his own intense cravings for Yana bubbled inside him like an active volcano, the desire to savor this precious moment and to convince Yana that she was not just another of his amorous conquests was even stronger.

"Promise me you'll never leave me again. Promise me you'll stay forever," Clay demanded, the seriousness in his own voice shocking him. He was not asking Yana to stay the night; such appeals had been issued before to many others, sometimes to women whose names he could no longer remember. This time, forever *meant* forever.

Yana felt tears threaten her once again. She willed them away, closing her eyes, looping her arms easily around Clay's middle, pulling him on top of her.

"I promise," she answered in a whisper. "Forever and always. Now love me, Clay. I need you now. I need to hold you and feel you inside me, a part of me."

Clay was propped against the headboard of Yana's bed, his leanly muscular body splendidly naked, a faint, rather drowsy smile on his lips. He was watching Yana eat the cubes of various meats, cheeses, and fruits he had procured during his hasty trip to the ship's galley.

"Making love makes me hungry," Yana said, munching on a piece of delicious cheese of undetermined type. "Doesn't it make you hungry?"

"Sometimes."

Yana looked at Clay, taking pleasure in his nakedness and thinking that she shouldn't, wishing mildly she could be so comfortable with herself and with Clay that she could lounge naked and not be embarrassed. Sitting cross-legged on the bed, she had a blanket wrapped around herself.

"What are you looking at?" Yana asked, her insecurities never too far from the surface when she was with Clay.

"You," Clay answered, his devilish half smile spreading to a full grin. He plucked a grape from Yana's plate and popped it into his mouth. "I like watching you eat. Everything you do is so sensuous. Especially when you eat. It's not necessarily sensual or sexual, but it's decidedly sensuous. You take such extraordinary satisfaction in the most mundane things."

Yana chuckled and dramatically tossed a piece of sausage into her mouth. "Trust me, Clay," she said between bites, "you are not mundane."

"That's nice to hear, but that's not what I was talking about."

Yana's brows pushed together, and for a few seconds she studied Clay, looking at him as though she'd never seen him before. "Are you always so sure of yourself? Are you really as confident of yourself as you seem?"

317

Clay looked down at his naked body, shrugged, then turned his gaze upon Yana. "Obviously, I'm not hiding anything from you."

Yana slapped him on the stomach. It was like slapping a wall.

Clay laughed lightly, savoring Yana's companionship even though they had only recently completed a second satisfying lovemaking session. In his other romantic liaisons, he'd had little desire for the woman's company after his lust was thoroughly sated.

"You lay there as naked as the day you were born, without a care in the world, so at ease with yourself even with me here." Yana turned her face down, searching for words, trying to make sense of her own thoughts. "We've just made love—"

"Twice," Clay interjected with a roguish smile.

"It was beautiful, but I would still feel uncomfortable lying naked like that in front of you."

"You shouldn't," Clay said. He pulled another grape from Yana's plate and ate it. "Most women would kill to look the way you do. Every man worth his salt would kill to look at you." Clay paused meaningfully, his eyes trailing down his body slowly. After making love twice in succession, his body was—in his opinion—lamentably relaxed. "I, on the other hand, am not showing you my most . . . flattering self."

Yana's eyes followed Clay's gaze. She blushed and turned her face downward. Her body still tingled deliciously from the ecstasy Clay's aroused manhood brought her. It was almost a relief that he finally

318

seemed to have had his fill of her—at least temporarily.

"That's sort of what I mean," Yana said softly, moving pieces of cheese and sausage around on her plate, unwilling to look up or let her eyes meet with Clay's. "I don't think I could ever let you look at me unless I was at my most flattering."

"I can't imagine you ever looking anything but spectacular," Clay said, his voice suddenly a little hoarse. The sheet around Yana had come loose, exposing nearly all of the erotic curves of one luscious breast. And beneath that, Yana's beautiful legs, crossed under her, were there for Clay's unhindered, unhurried inspection. "Someday, when you feel more confident and comfortable with me, you won't feel any need to hide yourself."

"Maybe . . . I hope so."

Clay reached out, taking the edge of the bedsheet in his fingers and moving it to the side, exposing Yana's breast completely. He could tell that this sort of thing was still troublesome to her, and in a way, it added to her charm.

"Yana, if only you could look at yourself through my eyes, then you would know that you have nothing to be ashamed of." Clay watched the blush color Yana's cheeks, a sign of innocence, in stark and erotic contrast to the single, heavy breast within his arm's reach. "Come here," Clay said huskily.

Yana's blush brightened. "Clay . . . you can't be serious."

But all Yana had to do was look at ClayMcKenna to know that he was very serious.

Chapter 19

It had been the grandest three weeks of Yana's life. Being in her native country and living in her own home once again made her feel more at ease when she was with Clay. Her confidence, as Clay had predicted, increased daily.

As Yana showed Clay the sights of Athens, the ancient city became almost magical and gave her new pleasure, heightened by his unrestrained enthusiasm to see each new sight.

Yana's early fears that she could not shoulder the responsibilities of running Zacarious Shipping proved unfounded. She accepted her inexperience, after some initial setbacks, as a temporary condition. Once she accepted the fact that she was not Nico and lacked his experience, Yana began making her decisions with more assistance from Antoli and Clay. Though the men quite obviously did not like each other one little bit, Yana decided it was not necessary for Clay and Antoli to be best friends for them to do what was best for Zacarious Shipping and McKenna Enterprises.

Yana sipped her tea, looking out the large windows of her father's office. She was sitting in his chair behind his desk, looking at the dockyards three stories below. Somewhere down there, Clay was overseeing the renovations under way for the *Jenco Seafarer*, the first ship in the newly formed company, McZac Import-Export.

Thinking of Clay brought a dreamy smile to Yana's lips and made her eyes shine softly. For three weeks, Yana had spent every night with Clay and had awoken every morning to see him beside her in bed. Though his clothes and luggage remained in one of the many guest bedrooms, he stayed with Yana. Clay did occasionally mess up the blankets in the guest room for the benefit of the servants.

Living together without the benefit of marriage—living in sin, it was called—was unthinkable in the Greek community, even among the financial elite, who tended to have a more cosmopolitan spirit than the working classes. The house servants, however, knew that to cast any disparaging looks at either Clay or Yana for their indiscretion—which was well known despite the mussed bedding in Clay's room—would mean immediate dismissal by the mistress of the house. Without a letter of introduction to a future employer, the dismissed servant would need to find a new line of employment, which was bound to be more strenuous and less profitable.

Yana was reasonably certain that word of her sleeping arrangements wouldn't travel from Pirias to Virginia. And if it did, she would just have a very serious talk with Nico and he would simply *have* to understand, because Yana was happier than she ever had been in her entire life.

When she heard the knock at the door, Yana groaned, disappointed that her reverie must come to an end. After pouring over yesterday's new problems and writing down a series of suggestions to solve the troubles, Yana had set down her pen and allotted herself ten minutes to sip her tea and daydream. She had only been allowed four minutes. Being in charge of a company, Yana was discovering, was much more work than she had thought it would be.

The ornately carved teakwood door opened and Mr. Beddickow, Nico's personal secretary of many years, stuck his head inside. "Mr. Pacca is here to see you, ma'am. Shall I send him in, or do you want him to wait?"

Yana knew that Beddickow resented working for a woman instead of Nico, and as she looked at him, seeing his thinly disguised annoyance at her sitting at Nico's desk, she wondered once again whether the old man would cause enough aggravation to prompt his replacement.

"I've got time to see him now."

"Yes, ma'am," Beddickow said with just a bit too much respect in his tone; it was sarcasm more than anything else.

"Mr. Beddickow?"

"Yes, ma'am?"

"Please remember that your continued employment here does not depend on your liking me or your job. It does, however, depend on me liking you and the work you do. Do you understand me?"

"Yes, ma'am." Beddickow's eyes hardened for only a second. "I'll send Mr. Pacca in now."

Antoli came storming into the office, puffing from the long, brisk uphill walk from the dockyards, his face flushed with anger and exertion. Even before he said a word, Yana wondered what Clay had done to infuriate the Greek man so. Only Clay could make Antoli this angry.

"This time that cowboy has gone too far! I can't work with him another day!"

"Settle down, Antoli, and tell me what the problem is now."

Yana's markedly bored tone did not in the least improve Antoli's disposition. He stepped up to the desk where he had spent so many hours helping Nico make decisions, slamming his fists down hard enough to rattle the crystal ashtray Yana had purchased for Clay's benefit. The remnants of Clay's last cigarette were still in the ashtray, a reminder to Antoli of the American's intrusion into Nico Zacarious's sanctum sanctorum.

"I don't mind doing business with the McKennas, but do we need to have them here? That cowboy doesn't know anything about ships!" The veins in Antoli's neck stuck out as he glared at Yana. "Clay McKenna is going to single-handedly push us over budget and behind schedule!"

Yana listened to Antoli's compalint of how Clay had countermanded his order for the workmen not to build a secondary compartment on both the starboard and port sides near the captain's quarters. During a previous meeting, Antoli had argued against the change while Clay had argued in favor of it, stating that it would provide a safe storage for the most expensive wines, insisting that there was a market for the product. The topic had been tabled so Yana could give it further consideration. She had decided in favor of the change, had told Clay to have the workmen go ahead with the proposed changes to the original blueprints, and had never bothered informing Antoli, knowing that he would sulk childishly after once again being voted down.

"He's doing exactly what I want him to do," Yana said when Antoli paused to take a breath. "You don't like the idea because it was Clay's."

"He doesn't have any experience in shipbuilding. He has said so himself!"

"Regardless of his inexperience, it is still a good idea."

Antoli slammed his fist down on the desk again. His face had become even redder. The workmen had taken to Clay's leadership quickly, while after many years, they still looked upon Antoli as Nico's high-paid, relatively powerless parasite.

"Maybe if you spent more time with me at the dockyards and less time in bed with Clay, you'd see that I am right!"

Yana was too stunned to even yell at Antoli. She sat motionless, looking up at him, hating him, pitying him because he would never be anything more than another man's lackey, knowing that the only female companionship he ever had was with the prostitutes in Athens.

"Then you don't deny it," Antoli said, gaining confidence when Yana did not respond. His face twisted into an ugly sneer. "You soil your soul with an American savage. You know as well as I do who and what Clay's mother is."

"Get out of here," Yana whispered, a lethal rage building inside her. "Get out of here now before I say things that I shouldn't.

Antoli couldn't keep his mouth shut. He knew he had already gotten away with more than could be expected, but he wanted to humiliate Yana, to punish her for sleeping with filth like Clay McKenna while she turned her nose up at him.

"Think of what you're doing to yourself, Yana. Think of what you're doing to your honor . . . if you have any left." Antoli placed his hands on the desk, leaning forward, his tone suddenly more paternal than condescending. "Think of what this would do to your father. The bullets have not put him in the grave, but this—this would break his heart, and that would surely kill him."

"I told you to get out of here," Yana said, her voice even, level. "And do not speak to me of my father! Didn't you ever wonder why my father never wanted you and I to marry? Of course, you know why. We both know why. You're insignificant, Antoli. You always have been. Your presence here at Zacarious Shipping is a convenience to my father and myself . . . but don't for a second think that you are indispensable.''

Yana stood, pushing the chair back, not wanting Antoli to look down at her metaphorically or literally. She said, "Don't ever come in here talking like that again. You're just jealous because I want Clay and not you." Yana issued a small, derisive laugh. "Don't you think I'm aware of how you look at me? I know you want me, and what makes you so furious is that the thought of you ever touching me makes me sick! Run along now, Antoli. You've outstayed your welcome here.''

Yana looked straight into Antoli's eyes, feeling her power consolidate, knowing that she had shamed him to the core of his being and that he could never forgive her for it.

"You talk of my father and what he would do if he knew that I am in love with Clay. . . . Well, think of what Nico would do if he knew his trusted right hand, his confidant, had insulted his daughter. Think of that, Antoli, before you open your mouth the next time.''

Nico was not a young man. Nevertheless, in the intervening months since the assassins had cut him down, his strength and stamina, his appetite and general well-being, had all slowly and steadily improved with time . . . and with Emma's continuous barrage of food and attention.

He sat on the wide rear porch of the McKenna main house, a small glass of rich red wine near him, holding the letter he had received from Yana in his lap. The setting sun was brilliant orange, and a cool autumn breeze made Nico pull the wood blanket a little tighter around his shoulders.

Nico's conscience toyed with the letter, making him think about his daughter and her relationship to Clayton McKenna.

In previous letters, information about what Antoli and Clayton were doing in Greece was evenly matched. Yana wrote about how the two men were helping her with her new responsibilities and how they were so valuable to her in these troubling times.

But this letter was different. Yana wrote glowingly of the renovations to the *Jenco Seafarer* and how the cargo ship would soon be ready to set sail. She wrote in vivid lauguage of Clay's ever-increasing knowledge of the shipbuilding business. She went to great lengths to describe Clay's close relationship with the workers at the shipyards and how the laborers clearly respected him and his judgment.

So when Yana, in the letter, eventually got around to informing Nico that she missed her father and wished he were at her side, the sage old man was suspicious.

Nico didn't need to have Yana write that she had grown close to Clay. He could sense it in every word she wrote. Centuries-old customs of social propriety were not easy for Nico to completely cast aside, no matter how much he respected Clay McKenna and the entire McKenna family.

Clay McKenna was not Greek. He wasn't even Mediterranean. He didn't practice the Greek Orthodox religion. His mother was part American Indian.

A nightmare vision of a wedding with dancers wearing nothing but eagle feathers and his beloved Illyana dressed in Kiowan garb and chanting to the sun god flashed hideously in Nico's mind.

"Don't think about it," Nico whispered, needing to hear the sound of his own voice to bring him back to the present, to take him out of his self-induced nightmare. "They're not savages."

It was not easy for a man, born and bred into the elite of one of the oldest civilized cultures in the world, to see another culture, particularly one as young and foreign as the American Indian, as being equal. But still, inherited prejudice notwithstanding, Nico found the notion of the McKennas as in-laws not intolerable. It would be an embarrassment to him as far as his friends and business associates in Pirias and Athens were concerned, to be sure. But what did Nico care about their opinion? In all of Greece, he had not met a businessman who was a match for Sorren McKenna and a young man with the character of Clay.

Nico smiled, his moods vacillating, wondering how far Yana's relationship with Clay had progressed since she had written the letter, dated nearly six weeks earlier.

He heard the sound of footsteps behind him on the porch and turned his head to greet Shadow with a smile.

"How are you doing?" she asked pleasantly, returning Nico's smile. "Is there anything I can get you?"

Nico looked at Shadow, wondering how he could ever have thought of her as a savage. She was, in a navy-blue ruffled dress, the height of sophistication. The aristocratic chiseled planes of her face spoke of two cultures—the white man's and the Indian's—taking the best from both to create a magnificent woman.

"Actually, I think I have everything I could ever hope for."

Shadow looked at Nico a little strangely, knowing there was something else on his mind but polite enough to not inquire as to what it was.

"If you need anything . . ." Shadow replied, letting the sentence die away.

Nico's gaze held Shadow's for a moment. He smiled finally and said, "We are lucky to have such good children, no?"

Shadow nodded her head. "We are lucky to have such good children, *yes.*"

Edward Danzer read the letter a third time and cursed under his breath. Antoli Pacca spoke English much better than he could write it.

"Idiot," Danzer hissed, thinking of Pacca. "I

330

should never have become involved with him."

The gist of the letter, as near as Danzer could decipher, was that Antoli was concerned with when the next attack against Nico Zacarious would take place. Didn't the damn fool realize that Sorren McKenna had hired an army of men to protect the compound? It was impossible to get anywhere near Nico now, and apparently, he hardly ever left the house. When Nico did, it was always with several highly paid bodyguards.

Danzer felt his dreams of destroying the McKenna empire slowly slip from his grasp. He had lived with the dreams so long that to feel them move further and further beyond his reach was as disturbing as if he'd discovered he was not really his father's son. A truth does not suddenly become a lie for Edward Danzer.

In his more rational moments, Danzer knew that he would never have his land—land the McKennas now owned—back. They had stolen the land for all time. But he could still make them pay, and pay dearly . . . with their lives.

"Idiot," Danzer muttered again, picking up his glass of whiskey to sip it, this time cursing himself. His involvement with Antoli Pacca had jeopardized his lifelong dream of revenge.

Perhaps, he thought, revenge could begin with one of the children, one of the girls in private schools. Where were they? England? France? How difficult would it be to find out? Maybe Antoli, who worked with Clay every day, could discreetly ask questions.

But what if Clay discovered that Antoli had had

something to do with Nico's shooting? What if he questioned Antoli, and Antoli told Clay about Danzer's part in the scheme?

The thought made Danzer's hands shake.

"Damn them all," Danzer whispered, sure of little more than one truth: At least some of the McKennas would die before his role in Nico Zacarious's shooting was discovered.

Chapter 20

Contrary to Antoli's expectations and to his considerable disappointment, the renovations on the *Jenco Seafarer* were finished on time. The work did go slightly over projected costs, but this was primarily due to eleventh hour changes that, in the long run, would more than make up for the additional expenditure.

Antoli had paid three men—working from the inside as carpenters—to sabotage the production, but their destructive usefulness was not worth his out-of-pocket expense. Clay McKenna, whose fuse for incompetence was notoriously short, had spotted the problem quickly and summarily fired the three laborers.

After that, as the sailors are fond of saying, it was easy sailing.

The changes to the *Jenco Seafarer* were behind Yana now, and even as she clipped on a flawless two-carat diamond earbob, her mind was filled with concern for the construction of the *Shadow* and the *Despina*—so named after the wives of Sorren and Nico—ships that would complete the newly formed McZac Import-Export fleet.

Yana looked at herself dejectedly in the mirror. Her luxurious auburn hair was done up in a delicate coiffure, held in place with jewel-encrusted gold combs. At each temple a slender curl of hair swirled down her cheeks. She didn't like the style at all.

"Will you stop it? You look gorgeous," Clay said, tying his necktie.

Yana scowled at Clay through the mirror. The gala event taking place at the Zacarious mansion would be attended by the political and business leaders of Greece, as well as by moguls from Italy, Sicily, Germany, Austria, and Switzerland. Tomorrow McZac would become a reality, and the party tonight was in celebration of that event.

Yana wanted everything—positively *everything*— to be perfect for the occasion. The success of McZac could well depend upon the opinions that were formed tonight at the party.

"Come on, leave your hair alone or you'll undo everything your lady did for you." Clay stepped up behind Yana, placing his large hands, which were now lightly callused from the work he had personally attended to on the *Jenco Seafarer*, on Yana's shoulders.

"You don't understand how important this is for me," Yana said. "Everyone expected me to fail, and this party is going to prove that I haven't failed at all." Clay began massaging the muscles in Yana's neck, and she felt the familiar warmth of his touch radiate through her. She closed her eyes briefly. "Don't do that now, Clay. This is a very important evening for me . . . and we haven't got time."

Clay's hands continued kneading the muscles in her neck and shoulders. Yana sighed, summoning her willpower.

"I'm serious . . . we haven't got time for this kind of nonsense."

"Nonsense? I'm hurt."

"You're not hurt, and you know this is nonsense because nothing can come of it. Our guests are going to begin arriving at any minute and I've got to be there . . . *we've* got to be there. You know how important it is to greet them at the door."

Yana reached up to take Clay's hands into her own, stopping the seductive massage before it would melt her resolve to be the perfect hostess. She looked at Clay in the mirror, marveling at how dashing he looked in a black tuxedo with a white ruffled shirt. Not one man in a thousand, she thought, could look perfectly natural in both work clothes and a tuxedo.

"You're just being insecure again," Clay said mildly, tempering his tone so that Yana wouldn't take too much offense at his words. "There isn't going to be a man here tonight who will not want to get in on this deal." Clay slipped his hands out of Yana's, then resumed working at getting his tie just right. He, too, knew the importance of making a good first impression. "The word has been out for over a month now that McZac Import-Export is going to be the most efficient, fastest fleet going. Even if the old guards who run this country don't like the idea of a woman running the company, they'll know a good thing when they see it."

Clay chuckled softly, imagining the surprise of the businessmen in their clubs throughout Europe as they exclaimed about how Nico Zacarious's little girl had pulled off the business coup of the decade.

Clay smiled at Yana's mirrored reflection and said, "Money, my love, speaks a language that every guest we have tonight is going to understand."

"And you're not going to try to speak Greek to anyone tonight, are you, darling?" Yana looked at Clay warily. It was more a statement than a question.

"Wouldn't dream of it."

"Promise?" Yana was suspicious. Clay was learning most of his Greek from the laborers, who tended to speak in a language infinitely more colorful than Yana—and polite company, for that matter— thought proper. Clay had been known to use the wrong Greek word on occasion, like when he and Yana had been in the finest restaurant in Athens and he had decided to order for himself. Instead of ordering a beef steak, he'd suggested the waiter do something to himself that was quite probably impossible. The waiter, along with the restaurant management, had not been amused. "Come on, I want you to promise me, Clay."

"I promise . . . but only if I can extract a promise

from you in return."

The timbre of Clay's voice, rich with intimacy, deep and mellow and full of memories, made Yana shiver with pleasure for a moment.

"Stop it now," she said, her tone sounding more critical than she really felt. "You know this isn't the time for that."

"How could I forget? You haven't stopped telling me."

But as Clay busied himself with the rest of his wardrobe, Yana was smiling to herself in the mirror. Tonight would be a glorious, glamorous evening. She would prove herself as the leader of a proud and resourceful company . . . and she would cap the evening off in just the right way, with just the right man.

It was Clay's third Scotch, and as he leaned back against the staircase railing, he studied the many guests milling about the Zacarious mansion ballroom, idly wondering who he would throw out first and which of the male guests would present the most problem.

The party had begun on time. The guests, arriving to see Illyana Zacarious and privately speculate among themselves whether she was, in fact, running Zacarious Shipping or merely acting as a figurehead, arrived in order of curiosity and ascending social rank. Clay knew, for example, that the Baron and Baroness Klaus von Horst had traveled all the way from Prussia for the ball, yet had waited in their carriage for more than an hour so they could arrive "fashionably late."

For his part, Clay had thus far been nothing less than charming. He discussed his previous business experience with the men who were curious about such things, and smoothly slipped out of the amorous trap set for him by the widow Andolini, who owned one of the finest wineries in Italy and, obviously, intended on adding Clay to her list of acquisitions.

It wasn't so much that Clay strongly suspected many of these smiling guests secretly wanted to see Yana fail that galled him, though this was the excuse he had initially given himself. What was wearing on his nerves and becoming steadily more intolerable as his Scotch consumption continued was the way that every man at the ball had, at one time or another, undressed Yana with his eyes. The only exception to the Lust For Yana rule, Clay observed wryly, was the Austrian general who owned half an optical company and wanted to possess his partner's extremely young, very attractive, and slightly inebriated wife.

It annoyed the hell out of Clay that he now wrestled with the two-headed, sharp-toothed demon of possessive jealousy. The fact that none of the guests had actually done anything more than look covertly at Yana did not keep Clay from speculating whether he would get his point across more effectively by throwing the French mayor out the door or through the oceanside windows.

As Yana approached him, making her way through the throng of guests, Clay looked at her as objectively as he could. The midnight-blue gown was not entirely to his liking, he decided. The front buttons went completely up to Yana's throat. In Greece, it would cause a scandal for a woman to show her forearms, much less have any kind of décolletage.

"You're not getting into any trouble, are you?" Yana asked Clay through a smile, just in case someone was watching her.

"Of course not, love," Clay answered.

Yana would have felt better about Clay's ready answer if he didn't have that maniacal twinkle in his eyes that suggested he was going to make something happen and that he didn't particularly care what it was, just as long as it created a hell of a stir.

"They want you, you know," Clay said softly, his eyes roaming over the soft planes of Yana's face, once again astonished at his luck in having a woman like her in his life. "Every man in this room wants you."

"You're talking nonsense," Yana scolded. "I've known many of these people my entire life. They're curious to see the changes in me, that's all." Yana looked away, scanning the crowd. "What about Herr Krueger? He has no designs on me."

Herr Krueger, on his next birthday, would turn eighty.

"Not so, my lady. Herr Krueger is a bit like a dog chasing a carriage. He has a goal in mind, but it would probably kill him if he ever got what

339

he wanted."

Yana chuckled softly. "You're a rascal. Now mind your manners, don't let the widow Andolini get her lusty little hands on you, and be your witty and celver self for our guests."

"Your wish is my command," Clay said softly, his ebony eyes letting Yana know that he was in the mood to receive some very interesting commands from her.

Stephanos Kristinovacious watched Yana cross the room, his eyes following every graceful move of her voluptuous body. She looked more beautiful than ever, and Stephanos wondered why he felt this way, since for all outward appearances, Yana seemed exactly the same as she had the previous year, when his father and Nico Zacarious had tried to arrange a marriage between their children. Everything had been set for the wedding, which would have joined two of the most powerful families in Greece.

Stephanos's teeth clenched as he thought of his humiliation at learning Yana had cancelled the wedding a mere week before the event. She had, quite simply, decided that she didn't want to be married, not to Stephanos or to anyone else, and that was that.

In the clear, hard-edged memory that such pain produces, Stephanos could still hear the partially hidden laughter of his friends when they learned that he had been unable to control his fiancée. To be unable to silence a woman in Greece was tantamount to losing one's masculinity. Perhaps the worst of it was that Yana's father had added the crowning blow: He refused to force Yana to marry Stephanos, and he didn't even whip her for her contemptible behavior.

How exactly is Yana different now? he asked himself, watching her as she spoke with the magistrate of what Stephanos considered an insignificant district of France. Could she, perhaps, be a woman now? Had she finally allowed a man to touch her?

Looking at the crowd, Stephanos spotted Clay McKenna standing alone near the stairway. His pose was casual, his body relaxed as he leaned slightly backward. Yet even so, there was something about Clay that suggested a primitiveness, a readiness to strike out at any moment. Stephanos noticed that Clay was a head taller than most of the men in the ballroom, his height made even more significant by those ridiculous boots he wore. And unless Stephanos was greatly mistaken, there was a gun in a holster beneath Clay's left arm, hidden by the tuxedo.

"Oh, Paulo, look at that fellow over there, that American," Stephanos said to his companion. He and Paulo shared the common bond of both having been spurned by Illyana. "What in God's name does he have on his feet?"

Paulo chuckled condescendingly. The boots, of shiny black leather, were pointy-toed and high-heeled. Neither of the men had ever seen western riding boots before.

"I haven't the foggiest, but I've heard that he's an Indian."

341

"Oh, really?" Stephanos drawled. "I thought he was an American."

"Not an Indian from India . . . he's a savage. You know, a red man."

Stephanos made a face of disgust. "It's amazing he hasn't shown up here with feathers in his hair. You've read about what those savages from the States are like, haven't you?"

Paulo gave a trilling laugh, then abruptly swallowed his laughter when Clay fixed him with a dark, unnerving stare. Turning his back to Clay, Paulo whispered, "Can you believe the nerve of Yana bringing something like *that* to *this*? If Nico were here, the old man would keel over dead on the spot."

Stephanos was slightly less daunted by a look from Clay than his friend was. He looked at Clay, speaking out of the side of his mouth to Paulo, "You don't suppose that Yana and he have—?"

"Never! With Yana? Never!"

The idea that Yana would want a crude Indian from America rather than either of them, both wealthy young Greek men from prominent families, was unthinkable.

Stephanos sighed dramatically. "Poor Nico. Yana will never be a proper daughter."

"You don't have to worry about a thing, Mrs. Andolini," Antoli said, moving just an inch closer to the older but still attractive—and extremely wealthy—widow. "I've got everything under control with McZac."

342

Mrs. Andolini's large dark brown eyes opened wide, impressed. "Then you're really running Mc-Zac, not Illyana?"

Antoli shrugged nonchalantly. "I wouldn't really want to put it quite that way. Let's just say that Nico and I have worked together for a very long time, and though he loves his daughter very much, he also realizes he has obligations to his company and his valued clients. If it pleases Illyana to have a title, well . . ."

"Mrs. Andolini's eyes went once again over to Clay, and a burst of white hot hatred burned through Antoli's veins.

"So you see, Mrs. Andolini," Antoli continued quickly, trying to regain the widow's attention, "you can count on McZac Import-Export to take your finest wines to the United States safely and quickly."

"Yes, yes, of course. Tell me something, Mr. Pacca. How much do you really know about that Clayton McKenna? He seems like a very mysterious man. I think I'd like to get to know him a little better before I commit to any long-term arrangements with Mc-Zac." Mrs. Andolini batted her lashes for Antoli's benefit, as though it were difficult for her to discuss business. She was a shrewd and tough woman, though she tried to hide it. "Surely you can understand my wanting to know as much as I can about anyone I do business with, can't you, Mr. Pacca?"

*　　　*　　　*

Margarite will never change, thought Yana acidly, talking with one of her oldest friends—or enemies. Yana wasn't sure which label Margarite wore.

"He's a very attractive man, Yana," Margarite purred, rolling her eyes expressively, looking over Yana's shoulder to Clay, who was talking cordially with several men not far away. "I can't imagine how you can concentrate on work when he's around all the time."

"I manage," Yana replied, wishing the conversation would turn back to the harmless trivialities of the latest New York fashions. "All it takes is a little discipline, which some of us have."

Margarite was not offended by the thinly veiled insult. "But discipline has always been our problem," she said gaily. "That's why neither of us are married."

Yana knew all about Margarite's two-year marriage, the rampant infidelities on both sides, and the scandalous divorce. It had been the hottest topic of conversation, from chic salons to tawdry saloons, for an entire winter.

"How has discipline been *our* problem? What's that got to do with us not being married?"

"You've got too *much* discipline, and I haven't got enough!"

Margarite laughed again, a little too loudly, making Yana wonder exactly how much wine she'd consumed.

"He's coming this way," Margarite said excitedly, immediately switching to English. "Quick, tell me something about him! Something I can surprise him with." Margarite leaned close, pressing her cheek against Yana's to whisper conspiratorially, "Men *love* it when you surprise them."

Yana felt strangely angry at Clay for having attracted Margarite's attention, though he had not, to the best of her knowledge, actively sought it. Yana did not want to stand around and watch Margarite try to seduce Clay. And she was also annoyed that Margarite had blithely assumed Clay had not directed his considerable charms at her, Yana.

"Ladies . . ." Clay said, stepping up to the young heiresses.

Yana felt like scratching Clay's eyes out when she saw his effect on Margarite. She was positively swooning.

"Hello, Mr. McKenna," Margarite said in a sultry purr. "I'm so glad we'll finally have a chance to talk." Margarite dipped her lashes seductively. "When we were introduced earlier, you seemed so busy."

"Yes . . . well, now and then we all must mix business and pleasure, work and play." Clay smiled at Margarite, and Yana wondered to whom he had directed that remark. "There were some men who needed my attention. A minor inconvenience, that's all."

"I understand completely," Margarite replied.

Yana rolled her eyes. Margarite had never spent more than three minutes in her father's office unless she was asking for yet another advance on her already extravagant living allowance.

Clay turned toward Yana and winked. Yana had been with Clay long enough to know exactly what the gleam in his eyes indicated.

To Margarite, Clay said, "Would you care to step out onto the south balcony for a little fresh air? It's getting so . . . warm in here."

Even before Yana could speak, Margarite took her by the arm and said rapidly, "We simply must talk more later. I mustn't take up any more of your time than I already have. I just know that *everyone* here wants to talk privately with you."

It was a dismissal, plain and simple. And Clay, curse him, obviously had no intention of changing any of Margarite's plans. Clay's smile to Margarite was perfect—gracious, suggesting he was pleased to be in her company, but not gauche enough to be openly libidinous.

"Excellent," Clay said, taking Margarite's arm in his, turning her away from Yana toward the balcony.

Yana stood in stunned silence, unable to believe what she had just seen with her own eyes, watching Clay's broad, tuxedo-clad shoulders as he eased through the crowd with Margarite on his arm.

The look in Clay's eyes—the look that Yana had come to recognize so readily and that always made her heart race wildly—was not solely directed at her. Whatever doubts Yana had had about Clay's faithfulness, she had hoped that at the very *least* he would be discreet about his indiscretions.

One second before Yana was about to make as

hasty an exit from the ballroom as she could without drawing too much attention to herself, Clay turned and headed back toward her without Margarite on his arm, that easy smile still playing on his lips.

"I suppose you think this is funny," Yana hissed.

"Relax. It's not what you think."

"Just because I wouldn't . . ." Yana moved closer, aware of the curious, malicious minds all around her who would love nothing more than to gossip about this kind of thing. "Just because I wouldn't . . . when you wanted to, you're running off to the balcony with the first woman who . . . with my friend?"

"I'm inclined to doubt Margarite is much of a friend, but you'd be more aware of that than I."

Clay's abominable cheerfulness fanned the fires of Yana's anger. "Shouldn't you be running along? Margarite is as impatient as you are, from what I know about her inclinations toward the wrong sort of man." Yana looked into Clay's humor-brightened eyes. "Why did you come back here, anyway?"

"I want you to meet me in your father's wine cellar in exactly ten minutes." Clay's eyes did a quick, appreciative dance over Yana. "We can't have our guests watching us go up to the bedroom together, can we? But if everyone sees me go outside with Margarite . . . ?" Clay's smile did dizzying things to Yana. "Be there in ten minutes . . . and be ready for me."

"Good Lord, Clay, you can't be serious," Yana exclaimed. It wasn't easy keeping her voice down.

Clay nodded his head and Yana shivered. "Clay, listen to me. Everyone who McZac needs is in this house right now. If we get caught . . ."

"That's part of the excitement of it. That's also why we're going to the wine cellar and not up to our cozy, comfortable bedroom." Clay glanced to the balcony, where Margarite waited at the doorway with a look of hungry impatience. "I'm going to make sure plenty of guests see me walking around with Margarite. That'll give you time to get downstairs unnoticed. By the time I get there, no one will make the connection between the host and hostess being away from this gala gathering at the same time."

It was the most preposterous thing Yana had ever heard. It was also professionally dangerous, marginally wicked, and probably completely immoral.

"I won't be there." Yana shook her head slowly, wondering how she had ever seen anything redeeming or worthwhile in Clay.

"If you're not there, you'll disappoint us both a great deal. Don't let fear get the best of you, love. I know you better than you think." He winked at Yana. "Ten minutes."

And then he was gone again, disappearing as abruptly as he had appeared.

Yana fumed, angry at Clay for his wicked ways, mad that he would even *think* she would consider an amorous tryst in a wine cellar while she should be playing hostess to the people who were necessary for McZac Import-Export to be successful.

Baron von Horst approached Yana, asking her

348

several trenchant questions concerning the *Shadow* and the *Despina*, but she was in no mood to give him her full attention, even though moving his merchandise would be a great boost for McZac.

"So you really think Zacarious Shipping can be operating at full capacity, with a three-ship fleet, within two years?" he asked suspiciously.

"I don't think it, Baron von Horst, I know it."

"And what does your father think?"

Yana, who was already angry, was irked by the question. If she had been Nico's son instead of his daughter, von Horst would never have thought of asking such a question.

"My father is the driving force in this company, Herr Baron von Horst," Yana said sharply, forcing herself to say the words she knew he wanted to hear but unable to put the diffident tone in her voice that would truly have pleased the stodgy, sanctimonious old millionaire. "But, of course, that goes without saying."

"Of course."

"Of course," Yana mimicked curtly. "Now if you will please excuse me, I'd better check on the wine. I wouldn't want anyone getting thirsty."

Baron Klaus von Horst smiled at Yana. He was pleased with her responses to his questions, glad to hear that Nico was still in control of Zacarious Shipping, and happy to see that Nico had apparently been able to control his renegade daughter.

Yana headed for her father's private wine cellar. It was necessary for her to cozy up to von Horst and tell him all the drivel he wanted to hear, but it damn sure wasn't necessary for Yana to be obsequious for Clay's benefit. He needed to be told what he could and could not do, and Yana decided that now was as good a time as any to put Clayton McKenna in his place.

She wasn't completely down the poorly lighted stairway before Yana sensed that the quickness of her step and the drumming of her heart had nothing to do with anger. Clay, curse his seductive ways, had ignited a fire inside Yana even before the party had started. The effect of his eyes, his words, his sometimes humorous and sometimes intimate tone in the bedroom while Yana fussed with her hair, was like a burning match thrown onto the dried pine needles of a forest floor. The little match might seem harmless enough at first, but two hours later it had caused an inextinguishable forest fire.

Yana rushed past the large general wine cellar. She wrinkled her nose at the faintly musty smell. It was a minor distraction, instantly forgotten. She continued on to her father's private cellar, where he kept the wines that he personally enjoyed, whether they were the most fashionable ones or not, as well as the wine he made himself, which he especially prized, though it wasn't very good.

Throwing open the door, Yana stepped inside. A single candle dimly illuminated the small room. Clay, cast in half-light and shadows, leaned against the small single bench upon which Nico did his bottling. A lighted cigarette dangled from his lips.

"I was afraid you wouldn't come," he said. He

350

dropped the cigarette and crushed it beneath his boot. "I was afraid this wouldn't be as important to you as it is to me."

"You're a fool to think that," Yana whispered, her mouth dry, her body feverishly ready for all the exquisite pleasure that Clay was so skilled in giving.

Yana rushed into his arms, pressing her body against him so adamantly that she forced him to bend backward over the bench. She kissed Clay wildly, opening her mouth invitingly, immediately receiving his tongue in response. Clay's hand forced its way between their bodies to slide over the curve of one breast. He squeezed it, pressing his fingers into the firm, resilient flesh through her gown, fanning the flames of a passion in Yana that had long ago become inexorable.

"We shouldn't," Yana said in a breathy rush of words. Her hands told quite another story. She reached down and squeezed Clay, feeling his strength and power through the silk of his trousers. Her trembling fingers had a difficult time working free Clay's buttons.

Yana moaned when Clay turned her around so that she was leaning against the small bench, the pressure hard against her buttocks. She didn't care. The disquieting contact of hard wood against her was nothing compared to the harshly erotic hand manipulating her breasts through her gown or the mouth covering hers, which tasted faintly of Virginia tobacco and good Scotch.

"This is madness," Yana said, her voice almost a

whimper, maybe a plea for help, maybe a plea for fulfillment.

There was no need for preliminaries, for the deliciously erotic, satisfying dalliances that Clay so willingly gave and Yana so gratefully received. The foreplay had been done in their minds, unconsciously, in the intervening hours that separated Clay's suggestive comments in their bedroom prior to the party and the moment when Yana leaned into his hand to force her breast more firmly into his palm, heightening the sensation.

"Hurry, Clay!" Yana whispered, pushing open his tuxedo, her mind in a whirl, her experience in such matters limited to bedrooms and long hours where time was not a factor, where, in fact, time often stood still.

The skirt of her midnight-blue nightgown was raised high, and the drawstring of her pantalets unknotted.

Strong fingers cupped Yana's bottom. With Clay's assistance, she gave a slight hop, partially sitting on the edge of the wooden bench.

"The most exciting woman in the world," Clay whispered, his eyes hot with desire for Yana.

Yana reached for Clay, taking him into her hands, guiding him, crying out in ecstasy as she felt that first aching thrust that swept her into a vortex of rapturous sensations.

Chapter 21

The next morning, Yana awoke to find herself alone in bed. Momentary panic gave way to a distant memory of Clay saying he wanted to check something on the *Jenco Seafarer* before the workmen arrived.

Lying back down again, Yana smiled dreamily, recalling her adventurous tryst with Clay in her father's private wine cellar—she was certain she would never again go there without remembering what had happened—and how many verbal agreements she had made for shipping to the United States through McZac.

No doubt about it, Clay's dream, born of a restless mind and spirit, would prove to be a success from the very beginning.

Yana's dreamy smile faded suddenly as the tickle in her stomach, which she had at first dismissed as lovemaking afterglow, took on a decidedly sour turn.

I didn't really have that much to drink last night, she thought, struggling to justify the nausea that was very rapidly becoming stronger, rising steadily. *I'm not going to get sick* was her next thought, followed immediately with, *Oh, God! Yes I am!*

Yana rushed out of bed, hunched over, hands covering her mouth, fearful that she wouldn't take it to the toilet in time, wondering what she would tell the servants if she couldn't, wondering even more what she would tell Clay if the servants told him.

Yana patted the cool water from her face with a thick towel, then looked at herself in the mirror. She was pale as a ghost.

It was the wine. I had too much to drink at the party. And it could be nerves, a letdown from the pressure I've been under.

Yana closed her eyes for a moment, thinking that she had sipped at the same glass of wine all night. The only time she had been light-headed at all was when she had frantically made love to Clay in the wine cellar, and again after the last guest had been ushered out and she had made love to Clay in their bedroom, this time much more leisurely.

She looked at her reflection in the mirror again. Her time with Clay and his hard-boiled pragmatism had made self-delusion difficult at best, and usually impossible.

I'm not sick, I'm pregnant.

*   *   *

Yana was not in the mood to sit through another fight between Clay and Antoli. Unfortunately, she had no choice in the matter because the three of them were in Nico's office—her office now—going over the blueprints of the *Shadow* and the *Despina*.

"Illyana, you must listen to reason," Antoli beseeched, turning away from Clay. "You *must* see the wisdom of my plans and the foolishness of his."

Yana held up a hand, cutting Antoli off before he could say more. "Before you go on any further, I want the two of you to try to work this out without me."

"But, Yana, surely you—"

"Give it ten more minutes." Yana pushed herself out of the chair. Why did her legs suddenly feel so weak? "I'm going to get some air. You two work out a compromise position and we can all talk about it when I get back."

When Yana's eyes touched Clay's, she saw his silent accusation. Answering what had remained unspoken, she said, "I'm not running away from my problems and I'm not shirking my responsibilities. I just think it is important for you two to learn to work together."

Yana left the office before either man could draw her into the argument.

On the pier, with all the familiar sights and smells surrounding her, Yana placed her hand lightly on her stomach. She could not feel the baby inside her, but she knew the child was growing, growing just a little every day. Her child. Clay's child.

He had to be told. He had the right to know.

355

But how would Clayton McKenna, a man given to sexual intemperance, a man known for his inability to stay with just one woman, accept the knowledge that he was about to become a father?

Yana had no idea how Clay would react. He spoke quietly and seriously about family and duty. He also had spent his entire adult life pursuing women while avoiding creating a family himself. It was a mixed message given to Yana and every woman who had succumbed to Clay's charms or had openly sought them.

"Damn," Yana muttered, watching the blue waves gently slap against the thick wooden pier beams. She smiled, realizing she had used Clay's favorite epitaph.

As Yana stared at the water, oblivious to the curious looks she received from the laborers who maintained a respectful distance, she thought how odd it was that her old childhood fear—which had lived within her breast until this very moment—could have vanished without a trace, like a puff of smoke.

For as long as Yana could remember, she had felt guilty that her birth had caused her mother's death and her father's subsequent loneliness. She had lived silently with that guilt and had vowed to stay away from men so that no other child would have to bear such a heavy burden. But now that she was pregnant, planned or unplanned, married or not, the fear had simply disappeared. Illyana Elani Despina Zacarious had a responsibility to live, to help her child grow

356

into a fine adult, and nothing was going to prevent her from sharing each day, each precious moment, each new revelation in a world that was so new, with her child.

Yana smiled, but it was a troubled smile. She had grown up without a mother. Would her own child, the one now slowly growing in her womb, grow up without a father?

The manner in which society would react to Yana's giving birth without benefit of marriage had no impact on her. Whether her so-called high-brow friends, all born into wealth and influence, accepted her and her child of mixed blood mattered little to Yana. Truth be known, Yana had never really liked her friends. She hadn't really chosen them on her own. Instead, her father's wealth and social position had chosen them for her, and Yana had passively acquiesced because she hadn't known any better.

No sense in thinking about what anyone will say, at least not until Clay finds out he's going to be a father.

Yana suddenly felt irritable. Until Clay finds out? If he really loves me, he'll know instinctively, she thought. Fathers are always supposed to know, aren't they?

Yana was convinced of Clay's reaction to hearing that he was to become a parent. And what was it Shadow had said? Squeeze Clay too tightly and he'll run? He'll run like hell and she'll be alone with her baby, but never for a second will her child feel any guilt.

No, Yana thoughtfully amended, not a parent, a father. No . . . even that wasn't entirely correct. Nico was a father. That's what fathers were to Yana, and Clay bore no resemblance to Nico Zacarious whatsoever.

"Damn," Yana muttered. "Why tell him at all?"

"Pardon me, ma'am?" a passing workman asked. He carried a thick wooden beam on his shoulder and was sweating profusely under the weight of his burden.

Yana looked at the man, blinking her eyes for a second to clear her thoughts. "Get some help carrying that," she said, feeling emotionally removed from her surroundings. "It's too heavy for you to carry alone. You'll hurt yourself."

Later, in taverns throughout the city, the story would be embellished and repeated, and the word would go round that Illyana Zacarious truly cared about the welfare of the men who worked for her.

Clay couldn't understand the change in Yana. Was she angry because he'd left their bed so early in the morning, without waking her? She certainly couldn't be angry with him for instigating their tryst in Nico's private wine cellar. Yana had proven at the time that she was his emotional equal in adventurous spirit. Her ardor had matched, if not surpassed, his during their all-too-brief encounter.

So what was bothering Yana? Why was she treating him like an invader into a private world that she suddenly had no intention of sharing?

"Will you just get off your high horse for a minute and listen to me?" Clay demanded, his jeweled gaze glittery with rising anger. "I *do* have a voice in the decisions we make."

The look of condescending acceptance Yana gave Clay drew a laugh, curt and deprecatory, from Antoli. Clay balled his hands into fists, wanting desperately to punch Antoli, then throw him out of Yana's office so he could talk privately with her.

"Of course, you do," Yana said with infuriating indulgence, drawing another pleased laugh from Antoli. "But just for a change, why don't you do something my way without fighting me tooth and nail every step of the way." Yana's tone dropped until it was barely audible. "Or maybe it just bothers you to take orders from a woman?"

"Don't use that patronizing tone with me."

Clay glared at Yana over the desk, wondering what had changed between them, unable to understand why she was jumping at every opportunity to convince him that she didn't need him at all.

His gaze shifted from Yana to Antoli. The Greek man looked as if it was taking every ounce of willpower he possessed to keep from cheering on the escalating argument between Clay and Yana. For a second, Clay envisioned the pleasure he would take in backhanding Antoli. He closed his eyes, aware that such thoughts occasionally led to actions.

Yana said something to Antoli in Greek, speaking

359

rapidly, knowing it was beyond Clay's limited understanding of the language. It was the final straw, the breaking point for Clay. He pulled his corduroy jacket from the back of his chair, jammed his arms into the sleeves, and pulled the garment around his chest to hide the big-bore Colt revolver under his left arm.

"Play your stupid games, Yana. But play them without me."

Antoli, snickering, said, "Do be a good loser, Clay."

Antoli had intended on saying more, on twisting the knife into Clay's heart, but in the blink of an eye he was laying unconscious on Yana's office floor. For one blinding instant, Antoli was aware that he had gone too far, that he had needled Clay beyond the level of acceptance and even Yana's presence in the room couldn't save him. Then the big right fist was headed straight for his nose, and there was just no way in the world he was ever going to avoid those knuckles. Pain exploded in Antoli's brain as his head snapped back and the sharp crack of his nose breaking filled the sun-slit confines of the office.

Antoli Pacca never felt himself hit the floor, nor did he hear Clay slam the door on his way out.

Margarite had spent a foul, sleepless night, and she was not in good spirits as she stepped down from her carriage at the front doors of the Zacarious

Shipping Company.

Clay McKenna, with his dark good looks, his tall, lean, muscular body, and his easy-going manner, had sparked Margarite's interest. When she had spoken with him at the party, and particularly while they were alone on the south balcony, Clay had seemed quite willing to return that interest. But then, infuriatingly, Clay had proven himself to be not only well-bred and charming, but frustratingly polite, elusive, and manifestly proper as well.

Margarite had very little interest in having another polite conversation with Clay. She had done everything short of throwing herself into his arms and tearing at his clothes in hopes that he would save his proper behavior for proper debutantes like Illyana Zacarious, and still she hadn't been able to draw the kind of response from Clay she wanted.

"It was a horrible, terrible time for me," Margarite had whispered, leaning into Clay, feeling mildly irked that he hadn't even put his arms around her when she had done everything she could to indicate that, in the very least, she wanted him to kiss her. "My marriage was one long nightmare. Who could blame me for searching for comfort wherever I could find it? You wouldn't blame me, would you, Clay? You would give me comfort, wouldn't you?"

"Who could possibly blame you?" Clay smoothly replied, sidestepping both Margarite's comment and her advance, moving so she couldn't trap him against the balcony railing.

So now, looking up at the imposing building of

Zacarious Shipping, Margarite was determined to get some answers from Yana about the enigmatic Clay McKenna. Yana had to know at least a little something about Clay, Margarite figured. And since Yana had never shown any particular desire for men—transitory interest in boys aside—she should not object to imparting whatever hidden facts she possessed about Clay.

Margarite did not like believing that Clay might not want her, so there had to be *something* that was keeping him from making the advance she clearly would not object to.

A wife back in the United States, perhaps? No matter. Margarite had dealt with such trivial problems before. After all, she hadn't determined whether she was looking for a husband or just an end to her boredom.

So troubled were Margarite's thoughts, despite the headache she still had from her wine consumption the previous night, that she did not see Clay until he bumped into her at the doorway to Zacarious Shipping.

"Clayton!" Margarite exclaimed, stumbling slightly, taking a quick step backward down the marble stairs and away from the collision.

Clay didn't smile when he saw Margarite. "Good afternoon," he said brusquely. "Yana's in her office."

Margarite felt a sudden pang of self-doubt when Clay didn't greet her more pleasantly. She didn't necessarily need or want his fawning adulation, but a

362

smile would go a long way toward bolstering her confidence.

"What makes you think I'm looking for Yana?" Margarite felt small and intimidated by the angry American who glared down at her. She heard herself swallow, her eyes locked with Clay's.

She saw the recognition of her invitation register subtly in Clay's dark eyes. It was nothing more than the slightest softening of his features. The right corner of his mouth pulled upward mirthlessly.

"I've got my carriage here . . . if you want to go somewhere. . . ." Margarite's voice was soft, and she wondered where all her confidence had gone.

Margarite felt her first true glimmer of hope when Clay muttered "Damn her" under his breath and glanced up at Yana's office window. When he looked at Margarite again, he shook his head in negation of something she did not comprehend and said, "What the hell, why not?"

It wasn't an outpouring of emotion, but it was acceptance, and that was good enough for Margarite to continue. She smiled, waving a slender lace-gloved hand toward the carriage.

"Shall we?" Margarite asked, her courage and confidence in her own allure escalating by the second.

"What did you expect? You've been challenging him constantly from the very first day we got back home," Yana said without even a trace of sympathy in her voice. "I'm surprised he didn't break your nose before this. You know what kind of man Clay is."

"He's a savage," Antoli replied, his words muffled through the handkerchief he held against his broken and bleeding nose. "He's a rabid dog. I'll have his hide for this."

Yana shook her head sadly. "He broke your nose for laughing at the wrong time. What do you think Clay would do if you actually became a threat to him?"

"Whose side are you on? I'm the one who was attacked!" Antoli groaned, trying to slow the flow of blood from his nose. "That crazy madman tried to kill me!"

Yana turned away from Antoli, then looked back at him again unsympathetically. "If he had tried to kill you, you wouldn't be around to curse him. Trust me."

Antoli's masculinity was offended, but he kept his mouth shut. Yana was not in the least bit concerned with his pain.

He looked at Yana and wondered why he hadn't smelled Clay's fouling touch on her beautiful, silky smooth flesh.

Things were going from good to bad in a hurry for Margarite, and she wasn't sure she knew how to change the downward slide her time with Clay was taking.

First he had insisted on going somewhere to have a drink, though Margarite had suggested they go somewhere private so they could talk. Once ensconced in the finest café in Pirias, Clay made it abundantly clear that for reasons he refused to discuss, he was furious with Yana and a good drink was all he really wanted.

Clay's anger made Margarite more determined than ever. It had never occurred to her that a man as ostentatiously virile as Clay would be interested in a silly virgin like Yana for very long. He might, in the short run, find her beauty alluring, but that interest would soon flag because Yana's bed was a cold and lonely place that she shared with no man.

Margarite had been courted by many men in her life, with infuriating regularity by those in the rare atmosphere of the social elite who only turned their eye to her after being spurned by Yana. But what if Clay had succeeded with Yana where all others had failed?

The thought of stealing from Yana the man who had deflowered her—of stealing Clay right out of her bed—added rare spice to the feast of the senses that the tall American seemed to promise.

"I don't know what Yana has done to make you so angry," Margarite said softly. The waiter started her way, but Margarite stopped him dead with a look that warned she had better not be disturbed. She looked at Clay again and, her voice dropping slightly, used a style of flirtation that had gotten her the men she wanted in the past. "Or maybe it is something she *didn't* do."

Margarite placed her hand lightly over Clay's on the table. He moved to take his hand away, but she squeezed tightly enough to keep him in her grasp.

"If your quarrel with Yana has to do with ships, I can't help you. But if it has more to do with what Yana hasn't done, then I think you and I can be very beneficial to each other."

Clay pulled his hand away from Margarite's, rising swiftly, like some gigantic eagle taking flight, all power and fluid grace.

"I'm sorry, Margarite. I shouldn't have come here." Clay's mouth was pressed into a severe, thin line. He was violently angry with himself for his loss of control with Antoli and for Yana's mystifying behavior toward him. "I'm afraid I've misled you. I really didn't mean to. Perhaps it would be best if I left."

Outwardly unflustered but inwardly enraged that once again she seemed to be losing to Illyana Zacarious, Margarite smiled pleasantly. Only her eyes, cold as ice, gave notice of her inner, hidden feelings. "Would you like to use my carriage?"

Clay shook his head, glad that this ill-fated encounter would end abruptly and bloodlessly. "I think the walk will do me some good. Maybe I can clear my head."

Margarite smiled, her mouth shimmering and sensual, her eyes bitter, frozen pieces of ice. "Whatever you want," she replied amiably. "Better run along now. . . . Mustn't keep dear Yana waiting."

366

The treacle malice was expected, and Clay was glad to receive it because it reaffirmed his general opinion of Margarite. Without a backward glance, he walked out of the café, having no idea at all where he was going next, not realizing the kind of enemy he had just made.

Chapter 22

The sitting room was dark, the single lamp on a small table turned low to cast pale yellow light over the small, frightened woman in the large wing-backed chair.

Yana jumped when the clock above the fireplace on the mantel chimed softly. She settled back into the chair, too frightened to be angry. The clock chimed three times; it was three o'clock in the morning. She had been sitting in her father's chair for two hours, waiting for Clay to come home.

Her concern had started to grow at nine o'clock. At that time, Yana was merely angry with Clay for storming out of her office after knocking Antoli out cold. *He's a man, she told herself. He needs to blow off a little steam. So what if he hasn't told me where he's going? I'm his lover, not his mother. Clay's a grown man. He can take care of himself.*

By midnight, anger was still the predominant

emotion Yana felt, though fear for Clay's well-being had begun to shoulder its way through her ire. Clay was in a strange land. He didn't know the dangers he could get into here in Greece. Something bad could have happened, Yana told herself. And though she didn't want to think of it, her haunting belief—that people who loved her eventually paid a horrible price for that love—kept winding its way through her mind, like a poisonous, engulfing, choking vine.

By two o'clock, Yana was no longer angry. She was willing to forgive Clay any transgression—past, present, or future—if he would only return to her, healthy and happy, in one handsome piece.

Yana cautioned herself against being too hopeful. She'd seen Clay drink, and though he occasionally got a little tipsy, she had never seen him truly drunk. It was unlikely that Clay had imbibed too much and was now in a hotel bed, snoring away, sleeping it off, oblivious to the concern he was causing. Unless, of course, he wasn't sleeping *alone* in that hotel bed . . .

Yana didn't want to question the probabilities of that scenario, either. If he was with another woman, there was nothing Yana could do about it now. She didn't even want to know the answer. Ignorance, Yana thought practically, might not be bliss, but there's no inherent comfort in knowledge, either.

As the clock finished chiming, Yana was willing to accept Clay's return in any fashion, drunk or sober, a celibate or profligate. Whatever problems there were between them could be solved just as soon as Clay returned.

This heartfelt attitude vanished at precisely four minutes after three, when Clay walked through the front door, looking weary and bedraggled and still appealing, registering surprise when he saw that Yana had waited up for him.

"I'm touched," Clay said, a hard smile on his face. "You stayed up. I never knew you cared."

Yana was in no mood for Clay's sarcasm. She exploded out of the chair, angry at Clay for finding this amusing. When she closed the distance between them, she smelled the brandy and, in a flash, recalled the wonderful, stolen evening they had shared in Clay's bedroom in Virginia, when he had off-handedly stated that brandy always tasted better after making love.

"You're drunk."

"I've been drinking; I'm not drunk. There's a difference."

"Tell someone who cares. I'm in no mood for semantics." Yana swept past Clay, no longer willing to spend a single moment with him, cursing herself for ever having been concerned for him. He caught her by the elbow as she rushed past, twisting her around so she faced him. "Take your hand off me," Yana spat, her voice as sharp-edged as ice chips.

"What's wrong? I'm a little late." Clay issued a half smile that for once had no effect on Yana whatsoever. "It's not really a major offense, is it?"

"I'm going to bed."

"A capital idea." Clay released Yana's arm. He pulled at his tie, which was already loose.

"Alone." Yana said the single word fiercely. She had spent the night waiting for Clay to return, waiting alone with her fears and her insecurities and her imagination running unfettered. She had no intention of sleeping with the same man who had caused her to live through that nightmare.

Clay chuckled softly, still finding it humorous that Yana had waited up for him. His confidence in his own abilities to stay alive under any circumstances was so unshakable that he found it absurd anyone would be frightened for his safety.

"Sorry it's so late." Clay shrugged his shoulders, looking down at Yana, still thinking he could smooth out whatever wrinkles there were in his relationship with her . . . not knowing that she had been afraid her child would never know his father. "I haven't had a curfew in quite a while. It'll take some getting used to."

For long moments, Yana just looked at Clay. Was this really the type of man she wanted as the father of her child? A reprobate? A man known for his all-night parties and his ability to fill those parties with the most beautiful and available women?

"You scared me," Yana said softly. "I was worried about you."

"Don't be," Clay said simply, as though by saying it Yana had not spent hours worrying about him. "I can take care of myself."

"You can also sleep in your own room tonight."

For a fleeting moment, Clay's eyes hardened, becoming thin, angry slits that glared down at Yana.

Then he grinned crookedly and shook his head. "Have it your way. Sleep alone, if that's what you really want."

Clay had started to walk away when Yana asked, "Who were you with?"

Clay turned back to Yana, rolling his eyes. "Listen, Yana, it's very late. I'm really in no mood for an argument, and I'm not accustomed to justifying to anyone where I've been and what I've done." He put his hands on his hips, accentuating his leanness, shaking his head slowly. "It's been a long night for me. I've walked through every street in Pirias. I just don't feel up to a fight with you right now."

"Who was she?" Yana asked, wanting desperately to hear a denial from Clay.

"I wasn't with anyone," Clay replied, conveniently forgetting that he had been with Margarite. "Now, if you'll excuse me, I'm going up to *my* room to crawl into *my* bed . . . all by *my*self."

Yana watched Clay walk out of the room. She felt terribly alone, more alone than ever before in her life. She placed her hand lightly on her stomach and wondered if there would ever be a right time to tell Clay he was about to become a father.

If he had spent the night walking, he would have protested more. He wouldn't have wanted to sleep alone. If he hadn't been with a woman, he would have fought to defend himself. He didn't do anything of the sort. Damn you, Clay. Damn you to hell.

*   *   *

Antoli could hardly breathe through his nose. Both of his eyes were black, the tiny veins beneath them having burst at the same time his nose broke. It was small consolation to him that Yana, for the first time since taking over the helm of Zacarious Shipping, arrived at the office late. She looked angry and tired.

"What do you want, Antoli?" Yana asked, tossing her sable coat onto the sofa and sliding into the chair behind the desk.

"I want to know what you intend to do with Clay McKenna. Are you sending him back to the United States?"

Yana shook her head. "You know that isn't possible. He's a partner—a full partner. He's got just as much right being here as you or I do."

"Are you saying that because you don't want an empty bed?" Yana's head snapped up, and Antoli, feeling emboldened by her apparent weakness, looked straight into her eyes. "It's a legitimate question, Yana. Are you making foolish decisions because you're sharing your bed with Clayton McKenna?"

If she had felt stronger, she would have told Antoli exactly what she thought of him. Instead, she smiled coldly at the little man and said, "Go somewhere. I don't care where you go, I just want you out of my office. I can't talk seriously with a man who looks like a raccoon."

The blood seemed to drain from Antoli's face, making his eyes look even darker. He rose slowly, as though he had to use great effort to keep from leaping at Yana.

"You mock me, Yana, but I would never treat you the way McKenna does. I would never disgrace my own father the way you do." Antoli moistened his lips. Saliva glistened on his mouth. "Someday you will be sorry that you have not treated me with the dignity that I deserve."

"Someday I'll also be gray-haired and old, but that day isn't coming soon, so why worry about it? Leave now, Antoli. I simply can't look at you a moment longer."

At the door, with calculated malice, Antoli turned to Yana and said, "Perhaps you and Margarite can compare notes. Beddickow told me that when Clay left here yesterday, he left in Margarite's carriage. Don't you find that interesting? I certainly do."

Antoli could have hit Yana in the stomach and it wouldn't have had as powerful an impact on her as his words did.

Chew on that information, you bitch! he thought, waiting at the door, not wanting to miss a second of Yana's turmoil.

"Get out," Yana said, the timbre of her voice lacking any semblance of confidence. "Get out of here now and don't ever come back."

"I'll be in my office." Antoli reacted as though Yana hadn't said a word. "If you want to talk, you know where I'll be."

*   *   *

375

It was nearly noon before Margarite pushed open the curtains of her west bedroom window. Her head was pounding, and she cursed herself for having had too much to drink two nights in a row. In her bed, his naked body tangled in the sheets, was the Italian sailor she had settled for after Clay had left her.

"Wake up," she said irritably. She slapped his foot, which was dangling over the edge of the bed. "Wake up, I said. You've got to get out of here. I want you out in ten minutes."

The sailor groaned, rolling onto his side. He rubbed his beard-stubbled face, then his eyes. When he looked at Margarite, he smiled lewdly. "Already? Don't you want to have some fun before I go?"

He reached for Margarite. She slapped his hand away, stepping out of his reach. In the clear light of morning, through red-rimmed eyes, the sailor did not seem nearly as exciting and dangerous as he had the previous night, when Margarite had been frustrated and had drank several glasses of potent red wine.

"Leave," she said, her voice hard, authoritative. She'd given similar commands many times in her young life. "I want you out of here by the time I get out of my bath."

Margarite was feeling human again when the maid entered her bedroom and informed her that Illyana Zacarious was in the waiting room.

"Really?" Margarite drawled, smiling for the first

time that day. She sat at her dressing table and looked at herself in the mirror. She wasn't pleased at what she saw. "Tell her I'm a little busy right now. Give her some lunch if she'd like. It'll take me thirty minutes, then I'll see her."

"Yes, ma'am." The maid whisked away, but not until she had cast critical eyes toward the bed sheets and blankets pulled free of the mattress. It looked like there had been a fight on the bed.

It wasn't an easy feat to get ready in just thirty minutes, but Margarite did. She pinched her cheeks to put some color in them, then clipped on the cameo brooch at her throat. Her hair was brushed and pulled back away from her face, held with a simple green ribbon. It wasn't her best appearance, but it would do for the audience she had.

"Good afternoon," Margarite said, walking into the waiting room as though she hadn't really made Yana wait a half hour. "What brings you here, Yana? You so seldom grace my house with your presence."

Yana had no desire for polite banter. She looked at Margarite and wondered how they could ever have been friends. Private boarding schools had held them together, but they were older now, and Yana saw no reason to continue the charade of their supposed friendship.

"I have just one question for you," Yana said. "Did you—"

"So harsh!" Margarite interrupted. "Please, Yana, whatever you have to say can be said politely, can't it? After all, there's no reason we have to talk like drunken sailors, is there?"

"I'm sure you're more versed on drunken sailors than I am, but that's not why I've come here."

Margarite sat on the settee and poured herself a cup of tea. "I see. . . . We're going to take the claws out for this, then. Very well. . . . What is it you wanted to see me about? I'm a very busy woman, and I'm not entirely inclined to spend my time with someone filled with so much"—Margarite's eyes were cool, faintly amused—"vitriol."

"Where were you last night?"

"I don't see as how that's any of your business."

"I'm making it my business. I want to know."

"And I don't *want* you to know." Margarite smiled. She was thinking that this might be fun. Illyana wasn't usually in such a powerless position. "I guess that leaves us at an impasse, doesn't it? Oh, well . . . it's been nice talking to you. I'll have the butler see you out."

Margarite rose from the settee, knowing the conversation wasn't over but wanting to see what Yana would do next.

"Sit down." Yana stood, moving to block Margarite's exit from the room. Never before had she threatened someone with physical violence like this, but she was ready to wrestle Margarite to the floor to get the answers she'd come for. "We're not finished yet."

Margarite looked into Yana's eyes. She saw the desperation there, and it made her smile. "Very well, Yana. Whatever you want. I'm not given to accepting orders from anyone, least of all from you. But I'm also not inclined to involve myself in fisticuffs like a commoner, so I suppose I shall listen to you." Margarite sat, crossing her legs delicately at the knee. She picked up her tea, sipped it, then looked at Yana over the rim of the cup.

"Where were you last night?"

"I was home." Margarite's eyes dipped a moment, her lashes lowering and then rising, hinting that she had spoken only a half-truth. "For most of the evening, anyway."

"With whom?"

"You really don't expect me to answer that, do you? I mean, I may not be quite as virginal and virtuous as you, but I'm hardly given to discussing the men I choose to . . . share my time with."

"Were you with Clay last night?"

Oh, God! This is going to be better than I dreamed, Margarite thought. A fresh burst of anger at Clay bloomed inside her. If he hadn't left her alone in the café, she wouldn't have spent the night with a nameless Italian sailor who needed a bath, a shave, and some instruction on the fine art of sexually pleasing a woman.

"I asked you a question," Yana whispered, her eyes burning with hatred.

Margarite looked at Yana. Her mind toyed with the way to play the scene to her best advantage. She wished there was time for her to rehearse so that she could do it just right, for maximum, crippling effect.

"I . . . Yana, you've got to understand that it

wasn't something I had planned," Margarite said, her voice very soft, her eyes cast downward in mock humiliation. "I had come to see you yesterday. It was so grand to see you at the party, and I thought perhaps we could have lunch together. I ran into Clay and he said he needed to get away—those were his words, 'get away'—and he seemed so desperate. Yana, I'm sure you know what Clayton can be like, so charming and considerate." Margarite looked up, meeting Yana's gaze briefly. "I didn't know that you and he . . . If that's the case, I'm so terribly sorry, Yana. I truly am. If I had only known . . . if you'd only told me . . . I never would have let him . . ."

Margarite kept her eyes cast downward as she heard the footsteps moving away from her. Not until she was certain that she was alone did she allow herself to smile.

Even though Clay inherently possessed a great deal of energy and had conditioned himself from an early age to make do with very little sleep, it still didn't mean that three hours was sufficient to make him feel refreshed.

"Yana's not here? Why not?" he asked, standing at the doorway to Antoli's office.

"You should know that better than me."

Clay smiled, seeing Antoli's black eyes. "Sorry about yesterday. You shouldn't have laughed. Bad timing on your part."

"Burn in hell."

"Probably." Clay couldn't be insulted by a man he had no respect for. What difference could it make if Antoli disliked him? Antoli's insults meant as little as his compliments. "Any idea where she is? I want to find her."

Antoli looked straight into Clay's eyes. Beneath the desk, he felt the knife in his pocket. "She doesn't want to see you. She wants you to go back to your own home and leave us alone."

"I doubt that."

"It would be best for everyone. You're not needed here. You only get in the way. Nobody wants you here."

"I doubt that, too. Are you going to tell me what I want to know or not?"

"You can get your throat cut if you're not careful."

Clay shrugged his broad shoulders. "And you can get your teeth kicked down your throat. But that's neither here nor there. Where did Yana go?"

"We don't act like savages here. Go back where you belong."

Clay walked across the office. He leaned over Antoli's desk and said, "Bad choice of words."

Antoli was reaching into his pocket when that big right fist, for the second time in two days, connected solidly with his nose. Antoli toppled backward, taking the chair with him and hitting the floor hard.

"You just never learn, do you?" Clay asked the unconscious man on the floor as he massaged his knuckles.

In the reception area, Clay said, "Mr. Beddickow,

Mr. Pacca asked me to tell you that he doesn't want to be disturbed.''

Beddickow, who had heard every word spoken in the office, said, "Yes, sir, Mr. McKenna. Are you leaving?''

"Not far. I'm going down to the dockyards. I want to see how the boys are doing on the *Shadow*.''

"Then you won't want me to get you ice for you hand?''

Clay shook his head and smiled. He could see that Beddickow shared his contempt for Antoli. "Naw. It feels kind of good, actually.''

Chapter 23

"What's the letter say?" Shadow asked impatiently.

Letters from Greece were always greeted with excitement at the McKenna household. This one, from Yana, was written in Greek. Sorren, Shadow, and Emma waited anxiously for Nico to read through the letter once, then give them the translation.

Nico finished the letter but pretended that he hadn't. This one was different from the previous letters. There wasn't a word in it about Clay. Not a word about Antoli. Unlike her usual lively accounts, it was a cold recitation of the facts, and that worried Nico.

He cleared his throat, keeping his eyes trained on the fine, delicate handwriting. "The celebration for the *Jenco Seafarer* went very well, Yana says. There are almost enough orders for the first vogage. She suspects the *Jenco* will set sail before the end of the month."

"Wonderful!" Shadow exclaimed. She patted Sorren's knee, saying in a lightly scolding tone, "Didn't I tell you Clayton would do just fine? Didn't I tell you he would handle everything?" And then, realizing her omission, she said to Nico, "And Yana, of course. This would never have gone so smoothly without Yana."

Nico nodded, then turned his attention back to the letter in his hand. What about Yana? What had happened to the glowing words that used to describe her time with Clay?

Shifting his weight on the sofa, Nico grimaced. His hip throbbed painfully, but he tried to keep the discomfort from showing on his face. He fooled no one.

"Can I get you anythin', Mr. Nico?"

"No, Emma, that won't be necessary. I'm fine."

"You ain't fine, Mr. Nico. You's in pain and I sees it." Emma went to the liquor cabinet and poured a small glass of the rich port wine that Nico seemed to favor. She handed the glass to him, her wizened countenance stern. "I told you you was pushin' yourself too hard, Mr. Nico. I told you and told you, and still you had to push yourself. Then you up an' fell and hurt your hip, and now you're moanin' and groanin' with pain."

Sorren said, "He's not moaning and groaning, Emma."

"Maybe he ain't, but that's only 'cause he's tryin' to

384

fool me, Mr. Sorren." Emma pushed a stool in front of Nico and carefully raised his foot, placing it on a pillow. "You just sit there nice and calm now, Mr. Nico. You let ol' Emma take care of everything."

"Do I have any choice?" Nico asked, unsuccessfully hiding a smile.

"None at all, Mr. Nico. None at all."

Nico laughed, but it was an uneasy laugh. It wasn't the pain in Nico's badly bruised hip that weighed heavily on his mind, it was Yana. Across the ocean, there was something wrong with Yana, and Nico couldn't rest easy until he was certain she was safe and happy.

In the past two weeks, Antoli's eyes had gone from black to the sickest-looking green Clay had ever seen. He would have found more humor in it had there been someone to share his humor with. Clay and Yana hadn't exchanged ten words—ten civil words, anyway—since their tête-à-tête after his three A.M. return the night he had aimlessly wandered the streets.

The craziest thing of all, as far as Clay was concerned, was that he was being blamed for cheating on Yana. Of all the times in his life when he had, in fact, cheated on a woman, he'd always been able to talk his way out of suspicion and back into her bed, if not into her heart. Now, when he was laughably innocent of the charges, he found himself confronted by a woman who didn't want to hear any excuses or explanations.

After several frustrating attempts to break through her resistance, Clay gave up and began to match Yana's hardheadedness with equal measures of his own. If she didn't want the truth, he wasn't interested in giving it to her.

Let her think what she wants, Clay mused bitterly. *She's already branded me guilty, and there isn't anything I can do to change her mind.*

Now, looking down at the work being done on the *Shadow*, Clay idly consulted Antoli. "Have you noticed anything strange about Yana lately?"

"What do you mean?" Antoli asked resentfully. He didn't like being summoned to Clay's office. The bad blood between them still existed, though they tried to present a rosier picture of their relationship whenever Yana was around.

"She comes in late now. She never used to do that. And in the morning she's looking so drawn, so fatigued." Clay's eyes were on the workers in the shipyards, but he wasn't seeing them. In his mind, he was looking at Yana and remembering what she had once been like in the morning, all full of youthful exuberance, zealously embracing the new day. "I've tried to talk to her about it, but she won't tell me anything."

"Perhaps she's simply beginning to understand what everyone else has known all along?" Antoli's tongue slithered around his mouth to moisten his lips. He couldn't resist an insult. "Maybe she's just recovering from her contact with you. Did you ever stop to think of that?"

The insult ran off Clay's back like rain. He gave it neither thought nor answer. "Something is wrong with her, and I just don't know what it is. Hmmmm . . . You've known her most of her life. Has she ever had any medical problems? Has she ever acted like this before?"

And so the conversation went, with Clay not caring if he received insults from Antoli, wondering what was wrong with Yana, wishing she would allow a conversation that did not directly and specifically involve work.

As Clay turned away from the window, Yana stuck her head into the office. She smiled at Clay, but it was a courteous smile, fundamentally no different than the one she gave to Antoli.

"Sorry I'm late," Yana said with feigned cheeriness that didn't fool Clay. "I was up late last night going over the figures. Can we meet in my office in ten minutes?"

"Of course," Antoli replied quickly.

Clay said nothing.

Mr. Beddickow cleared his throat to announce his presence at the doorway to Yana's office. When Yana looked up, flanked by Clay and Antoli, Beddickow said, "I'm sorry to bother you, ma'am, but there's a man here who says it is urgent that he talk to you."

"Who is it?"

"His name is Dorretti, ma'am. He's a sailor."

387

Yana's brows furrowed. She saw no particular reason to interrupt her busy schedule with problems that should rightly be handled by managers or foremen. "Tell Mr. Dorretti that I am extremely busy right now. If he would like to make an appointment, it might be possible to see him sometime later in the week."

"Yes, ma'am. I'll send them away," Beddickow replied, clearly not at all happy with having to deal with sailors.

"Them?" Yana said quickly, before Beddickow could close the office door. "Who's with him?"

"Two of our men, ma'am. Georgi and that Swedish fellow you brought in last month."

Yana felt the quickening of her heart. She nodded her head to Beddickow, saying, "I'll see them. Please have them wait just a moment."

"What's going on, Yana? If this is something about McZac, I've got the right to know."

Yana looked at Clay for a moment, thinking, *You've got the right to know, just like you've got the right to know you're going to be a father. But people forfeit rights when they act the way you do, Clayton McKenna. Even rights have to be paid for.*

"This is a private matter," Yana said, somehow emphasizing the fact that Clay was no longer allowed to know such things. "It's personal."

Clay said nothing in reply to Yana's comment. How much more personal could two people get? He had shared Yana's bed and her heart. His lips tightened across his teeth, and Yana could see that he

388

was biting back words he wanted to say.

"Now if you two will please excuse me, I'd like to find out what these gentlemen want from me," Yana explained. Clay turned and walked out quickly. Antoli hesitated. "You, too, Antoli. Now."

Beddickow ushered the three men in. Dorretti was wedged in between Swede and Georgi. There was puffiness near Dorretti's left eye, and the right side of his jaw bore the unmistakable red mark of knuckles.

"Afternoon, Miss Zacarious," Georgi said, standing rigidly at attention. "We're real sorry to break in on you like this, but you said if we heard anything, we should let you know right away."

"That's correct." Sitting behind her desk, Yana's hands, hidden from the men, were balled into tight, nervous white-knuckled fists. She could feel the blood drain from her face. "What have you found out? What have you heard?" she asked as though the news were trivial, when in truth her future happiness might well hinge on what they told her.

Dorretti started to speak, but Swede slapped him on the back of the head. Yana cringed inwardly, never liking violence of any sort. To the Swede, she said, without great reproach, "I don't believe that will be necessary. Mr. Dorretti seems polite enough."

The big blond Swedish shipbuilder, who had at best a limited knowledge of Greek, nodded his understanding. Georgi said, "This man here's been braggin' 'bout spending the night with that lady you told us about."

"Mrs. Andropolous? Margarite Andropolous?"

"That's her, Miss Zacarious."

Yana's mouth felt dry. It seemed as though there were no longer any air in her breezy office. She asked, in as calm a voice as she could manage, for Georgi to tell her everything he knew.

Dorretti, it seemed, on the evening after the gala party for the completion of the *Jenco Seafarer*, had been walking from one dockside tavern to another when a very lavishly appointed carriage stopped beside him. A young woman, quite attractive, spoke with Dorretti for several minutes, then invited him to go with her. Dorretti spent the night with her, he said, not leaving until the following morning, when she made it quite clear that she was not interested in seeing him again. She gave him a gold coin for his time and his silence.

"You don't work for Zacarious Shipping, do you, Mr. Dorretti?" The Italian shook his head. Yana smiled and replied, "Good. You're not trustworthy. That woman gave you money to show the consideration of silence. You're exactly the kind of man all women despise."

"He's whale dung, all right," Georgi said, then grimaced at his choice of words. "Begging your pardon, Miss Zacarious. Didn't mean to offend you."

"That's quite all right, Georgi." She paused a moment and added, "Everyone makes mistakes now and again."

"He's telling the truth, too, Miss Zacarious. Me and Swede talked to him before we brung him here. He's telling the truth, and that's a fact."

Yana looked at the swollen cheek and eye on Dorretti. She could just imagine how the big Swede and Georgi had verified the veracity of Dorretti's claims.

"Did you hear anything else?"

Georgi nodded his head, glancing sideways at Swede before answering. "Dimitri—he's the old carpenter been working for me an' your papa upward of fifteen years now—saw Mr. McKenna that same night you was concerned about. He was walking down near Dimitri's home off the bluff."

"W—what time was that?" Yana asked, cursing herself for stammering, not wanting these men, though they were clearly loyal to her, to know how much she needed answers.

"Dimitri said he got up in the night to"—Georgi stopped himself before uttering another wrong word, blushed, then continued—"do his nightly duty. He don't know exactly what time it was, but after midnight, he figures. Maybe closer to one or two."

Yana thanked Georgi and Swede, promising them that their discretion and loyalty would not be forgotten. She instructed them to put Dorretti on the first ship headed out of the harbor. Dorretti looked as though he were going to protest this eviction from Greece, but Swede put a huge hand on the Italian's shoulder, and the idea of leaving Pirias no longer seemed quite so bad.

Dorretti had spent the night with Margarite. If Clay had made love to Margarite, he'd never have had the time to walk the considerable distance to and from the bluff. Not by three A.M.

"You stupid fool," Yana mumbled, not sure if she was insulting herself or Clay.

Clay *had* been telling the truth. It was Margarite who had lied. But why? Yana didn't want to know the answer to that question. The workings of Margarite's mind were beyond logic, as far as Yana was concerned.

Very slowly, Yana pushed herself out of her chair. She stood before the open window, breathing in deeply, feeling her body cooling down.

Yana lightly placed a hand on her stomach. The morning sickness was abating some, but the start of each day was still unpleasant for her. But she could accept whatever discomfort her pregnancy caused as long as Clay was with her.

"I think it's time your papa found out about you," Yana said to the growing child inside her.

She patted her stomach, not knowing if Clay would accept the news she was about to give him, but secure in the knowledge that he had not been unfaithful to her, as Margarite had maliciously claimed.

Yana walked out of the office and said to Beddickow, "Will you please have my carriage readied. Mr. McKenna and I will be leaving shortly."

"Mr. McKenna has gone down to the dockyards, ma'am. He said you could find him at the *Shadow* if you wanted him for anything."

A slow, knowing smile, the first of its kind in weeks, curled Yana's mouth. "Oh, yes, I want him for

392

something special."

Clay saw the change in Yana, though he had no idea what had happened between the time he'd left her office so she could attend to "private" matters that didn't include him and the time she'd shown up at the *Shadow* in her personal carriage.

"Hi, sailor," Yana said, leaning out the carriage door window. "Can I give you a lift?"

Clay, surprised, just looked at Yana for a moment, enjoying the shining joy he saw in her eyes and wondering what had put it there.

"Well, sailor, I'll ask again," Yana said, her voice dipping softly, suggestively. "Can I take you anywhere?"

Clay nodded, still wary but pleased with the change. It had been three long weeks since he'd foolishly agreed to get into Margarite's carriage. He couldn't help but wonder if his life would turn upside down again if he got into Yana's carriage.

Yana opened the door for him. After Clay got in and closed the door, Yana tapped her knuckles against the roof. "Drive on," she called out.

"What's going on? Why the sudden change?" Clay asked, his voice cool and level.

"What makes you think something's going on? You're so suspicious of everything."

"It helps me stay alive. Besides, you're hardly one to talk. You define the word *suspicious*."

Clay pushed himself into the corner of the carriage, keeping his distance so that he could see Yana better. She had changed clothes, he noted. No longer was she wearing the staid gray, high-necked, long-sleeved woolen dress she had on that morning. Now she wore the light blue silk dress he had made for her in Virginia, the one with the U-shaped neckline that Yana had explained showed far too much bosom to be acceptable in Greek society. She had also rearranged her hair, abandoning the tight, severe bun that Clay had said wasn't her most attractive style. Her lustrous auburn hair was brushed free, the bangs combed back away from her forehead, with dark spirals of silky hair framing her cheeks.

"What's going on, Yana? I thought you weren't talking to me."

"That's not true, and you know it," Yana replied, her voice barely above a whisper, the intimate purr still in every word she spoke. "That's never been true. Even when we've had our . . . little misunderstandings, I've always talked to you."

"True. You asked me questions concerning the ships. You talked about finances." Clay shook his head, then pushed fingers through his ebony hair, pushing it straight back off his forehead. "But that isn't talking, that's conducting business. There's a big difference, and you know it."

Undaunted by the battle-weary suspicion in Clay's dark eyes, Yana waved her hand, signifying that whatever had happened in the past meant nothing now.

She looked away from Clay, through the window of the carriage. Outside, dozens of men worked on the skeletons of ships that would, in time, become the *Despina* and the *Shadow*. Seeing the workmen made Yana question whether she could go through with her hastily thought-out plan to break through Clay's self-erected iron wall.

"I assume there's a reason you're keeping me away from my work," Clay said, neither bored nor anxious, merely stating a fact that he would like verified.

Yana looked back toward Clay and felt the flutter of her heart. Even during the past three weeks, when she had been convinced he was a lecherous man who could never be trusted—even if he *was* the father of her child—the sight of him had always affected her powerfully, conjuring up images and feelings from the past that she hoped would eventually fade.

"Of course, there's a reason, Clay. You should know me well enough by now. I've got a reason for everything I do. You may not *like* my reasons, but they are reasons nonetheless."

"Are you going to get to the point or not?"

"You're so *impatient*," Yana scolded mildly. "You've always been that way, though, haven't you?" Yana laughed nervously, feeling herself running out of time, sensing Clay's notorious impatience for such things. *Hurry, you fool! You're losing him once again!* "Why—why didn't you let me know you were telling the truth?"

"The truth about what?"

"The truth about not sleeping with Margarite."
Yana gazed into Clay's eyes, then looked downward.
She did not see the slightest forgiveness or under-
standing there.

"I told you I hadn't slept with her. You said I had.
Since I had no way of proving anything, and since
you had already convinced yourself of my guilt, I saw
no particular reason to waste my breath. I don't like
arguments that have no purpose. Your mind was
already made up. What was the point?"

"But when Margarite said you'd been together—"

"She said *what?*" Clay exclaimed.

"Why didn't you protest more when I accused you
of being with another woman?"

Clay's voice was low but hard as steel as he said,
"People believe only what they want to believe."

Yana reached across the space that separated them
in the carriage, placing her hand lightly on Clay's
knee. His eyes went to her hand, then up to her face,
but he made no move to pull away from Yana.

"I talked with a man named Dorretti. He says—
and I think he's telling the truth—"

"Get on with it, Yana."

"—that he spent the night with Margarite. The
same night, incidentally, that I thought you had
slept with Margarite." Yana squeezed Clay's knee,
hoping for some kind of favorable response from
him. She received none. "And there is a trustworthy
workman, Dimitri. He saw you walking that night.
If you were walking, at some time past midnight,
somewhere near the bluff, you couldn't possibly have

been at Margarite's at any time past midnight. The two areas are too far apart."

Clay shrugged his shoulders, still impassive. "I could have hired a coach."

"Two weeks ago I had Georgi question every coachman in Pirias."

"You had me investigated?" As a matter of principle, Clay disliked the thought of anyone investigating him.

Yana looked straight into Clay's eyes, challenging him now, reminding him that she, too, had wealth and all the power that goes along with it. "You didn't take any hired coach. You were on foot, just like you said. And you didn't sleep with anyone that night—"

"Including you," Clay said frostily.

"—as you said. The only person who seems to have lied is Margarite."

"She's very bitter," Clay said. "I think she likes hurting people."

"She and I have been competing against each other our entire lives."

"And since she loses too often, she took the opportunity to hurt you while she could," Clay said, finishing the thought.

"Margarite has many men." Yana's hand slid higher on Clay's leg, her fingers caressing the solid muscles beneath the fabric of his trousers. "But I only have one. . . . I have you, don't I, Clay?"

"Do you?"

The hardness in Clay's voice did not match the mischievous twinkle in his eyes; his anger at being falsely accused was quickly fading in the face of more pressing matters—namely, figuring out what to do with the woman next to him, whose hand was slowly creeping sensuously up his thigh.

Yana swallowed the lump in her throat, searching for the same adventurous spirit that had compelled her to meet Clay in her father's wine cellar when there were dozens of influential guests upstairs.

"I'd like to think I do, even though I sometimes make mistakes, jump to conclusions that I shouldn't." Yana pushed her hand higher on Clay's leg, her fingernails scratching lightly against the inside of his thigh, caressing him through his trousers. "But you wouldn't hold a mistake against me, would you?"

"I might. It all depends on what the mistake was."

"You're not making this easy for me."

"And I don't intend to, either."

Yana slid closer to Clay. She slipped her left hand around his neck, her fingers pushing through the thick, silky mane at the nape. Her right hand continued its slow, circular movements, inching fractionally higher with each revolution.

"Remember back . . . long ago . . . the first time when we were together in New York?" Yana pulled lightly at Clay, trying to get him to lean toward her so she could kiss him. Though Clay resisted, Yana was undaunted. If he wouldn't come to her, she would go to him. "You saved me that day, there in that dirty alley. And then later, when we were alone in the carriage, and I was so frightened and you were so cool, as though nothing could ever frighten you, do you remember what happened then?"

Clay nodded his head but said nothing. Yana's right hand had reached the juncture of Clay's powerful thighs, her fingers soft as a feather, trailing along the thick, burgeoning length of him. Yana watched his face, seeing the passion coloring his cheeks, though he tried vainly to be aloof to the illicit pleasure she was providing.

"And remember how you had told me later that you didn't like being—how did you put it?—left behind?"

Yana stifled a small sigh when she felt Clay's manhood throb beneath her fingertips.

He still wants me, she thought with satisfaction. *Whether he wants to want me or not doesn't matter. He's no more immune to me than I am to him. Nothing has changed . . . fortunately.*

"Do you remember that?" Yana asked, feeling courageous from her influence over Clay. She flicked open the top button of Clay's trousers. "I thought you would. As a matter of fact, I recall you being rather *disturbed* with me for . . . leaving you . . . behind."

Clay, pushed into the corner of the carriage, looked away from Yana, out the window. Workmen—men he knew, men who took orders and instructions from him—were busy with their labors, constructing the supports and hulls for the *Shadow* and the *Despina*. As the carriage rattled along the cobblestone street, some men turned to look, some nodding their heads in greeting.

Clay gasped softly when the last of his buttons was unfastened and Yana's small, trembling hand reached inside to grasp him firmly, boldly, with greater conviction and purpose than ever before.

"Damn it, Yana, do you know what you're doing?" Clay asked, looking at her with a glazed, excited, confused glint in his ebony eyes.

"No," Yana replied, her heart racing, her hand sliding up and down over his thick, aroused staff. "I don't. But I'm learning, Clay." Yana kissed Clay's mouth lightly, her tongue flicking against his lips fleetingly. "I'm learning fast. Very"—she kissed his neck—"very"—she kissed his chest, sliding down in the carriage—"fast."

Clay felt the warmth and wetness of Yana's mouth surround him. He closed his eyes, moaning softly, vaguely understanding, as pressure built inside him from Yana's magic, that in every sense of the word he had met his equal.

Chapter 24

"I never thought I would feel this kind of contentment again," Clay said softly, stroking Yana's hair.

Yana murmured, saying nothing, more asleep than awake, enjoying the dreamy warmth of Clay's naked body next to her own.

He was lying in her bed—*their* bed, once again—with Yana's head on his naked chest.

The intervening hours between the ride in the carriage and the first sighting of the morning sun had been filled with passion, tenderness, and elucidation. Clay's stubborn refusal to defend himself against the charges of infidelity had been deemed, by a unanimous consensus of two, foolishly pigheaded, embarrassingly masculine, and thoroughly unwise.

And, by mutual agreement, Yana's virtually groundless yet cast-in-stone belief that Clay was guilty of any and all charges brought against him was deemed paranoid, self-defeating, and generally damned silly, since any fool, and certainly a wise man—Clay insisted he fit the latter category; Yana, sipping wine, abstained from voting on the flimsy pretext that it was four-thirty in the morning—could see that Yana was not only the most beautiful woman in the world, but also the sexiest, most erotic, adventurous, and spine-tingling one. With that going for her—and, at this point, Clay reminded her once again that he considered himself a wise man and not a fool, though this was not an inarguable point— Yana had to be quite silly to think that he could ever want another woman's bedroom companionship.

Yana then suggested Clay prove his desire. After all, such a declaration was empty without action to verify the claim. Clay insisted he had spent the better part of the past fifteen hours or more trying his level best to prove exactly that.

"You said your love for me was undying," Yana whispered, an impish twinkle in her eyes.

"Yana, there is a critical difference between undying and inexhaustible," Clay replied. "Unless you grasp that critical difference, I'll end up in critical condition in a hospital somewhere."

Yana pouted, her lower lip pushing out prettily. She rolled over in bed, turning her back to Clay and pushing her naked behind against his hip. She sighed a long-suffering sigh.

Clay, though passion-weary and bathed in perspiration, discovered that with the proper inspiration, he could, in fact, prove his desire for Yana once again.

"You're not serious," Yana said softly as Clay pulled her on top of him so that she straddled his lean hips.

"There's no turning back," Clay said, his eyes bright and alive as he pulled Yana down, needing to kiss her as he felt himself slide deep inside.

"No turning back . . . ever," Yana purred, meaning it more than she'd ever meant anything in her whole life.

As the sun first sent its rays through the curtains and into the bedroom, Clay was feeling a little sore and infinitely satisfied, complete in a way that he had never been before. He was, in fact, happier than he had ever been in his life, and most strangely of all, this revelation did not cause even a glimmer of misgiving.

"I love you," Clay whispered, continuing to stroke Yana's hair softly. He kissed the top of her head. "Yana . . . I am deeply, passionately, hopelessly in love with you. I'm telling you this so that you'll understand why I refuse to ever again spend a night without you." He chuckled softly, the sound reverberating through his chest. "I hate to sound dictatorial, and I know how much you hate being told anything, but I really must insist on this one issue. I simply *cannot* spend another night of my life without you."

He listened to her breathing as it quickened and knew that she had heard him. He would tell her

403

again later, when she was fully awake. He was talking to hear himself now, to taste the nourishing words of devotion on his tongue.

Yana raised her head from his chest. Clay looked into her eyes, and what he saw froze the blood in his veins. In Yana's eyes he saw stark terror.

"Oh, no," she whispered, turning away, pushing herself out of bed. "No, no, no!" she cried, rushing out of the bedroom, hunched over with her hands covering her mouth.

When Yana returned to the bedroom, she was pale and wan. She had a large bath towel wrapped around herself, and she refused to let her eyes meet directly with Clay's.

"I'm all right now," she whispered, sitting on the edge of the bed.

Clay rolled onto his knees, moving behind Yana. He placed his hands lightly on her shoulders. "Are you sure?" Yana nodded. "You're positive?"

"Don't push me on this, Clay."

"Is there anything I can do? Anything I should know?"

Yana closed her eyes, her head down, her face away from Clay's. This was the moment she had dreaded. This was the moment of truth, the time when she would find out what was *really* inside Clay McKenna, the man she loved, the man whose words, spoken softly in a bedroom, could not be taken at face value.

404

"Clayton . . . I'm pregnant."

Yana waited for a response, but none came. Each second crept by like an eternity. She turned violently and said, nearly shouting, "Can't you hear? I said I'm going to have a baby!"

And all the damn fool did was just sit there and smile.

For the longest time, Yana just looked at Clay, not quite understanding why he was smiling like that. And then, youthfully exuberant and yet manfully strong, he took her into his arms tenderly and kissed her.

"We're getting married." It was a declarative statement from Clay. "Now. Immediately." His eyes twinkled and he kissed Yana's forehead, then placed his hand carefully on her stomach. "I'm going to be a papa. I'm going to be a *great* papa, and we're going to have *great* children."

"What about me?" Yana asked, smiling broadly now, a world of worry suddenly lifted from her shoulders.

"You? Oh, yeah. You'll be a great mama, too." He grinned sheepishly. "Didn't mean to leave you out. You are rather important to this whole process."

"I love you, Clayton," Yana whispered, hot tears of happiness spilling suddenly from her eyes. She kissed Clay on the mouth, wanting to feel his arms around her. Instead, Clay leaped to his feet and stood in the center of the bed. "What on earth are you doing?"

"We're getting married," Clay said, hands on his

hips. He apparently had forgotten that he was, with the exception of having a bit more hair, just as naked as the day he was born. "We're getting married now, right here, right now! In this bed! In this very bed!"

Smiling, laughing softly, tears of joy still shining in her eyes, Yana asked, "Don't you think you should get dressed first?"

Chapter 25

Had the enceinte bride-to-be been poor and not from one of the most famous and influential families in all of Europe and the Mediterranean, perhaps it wouldn't have been so easy to arrange a wedding in the largest Greek Orthodox church in Athens at a moment's notice.

With the combined weight of the McKenna and the Zacarious names, along with a sizeable donation to the church from Clay, it was soon determined that Clayton McKenna was indeed a practicing Greek Orthodox and that Illyana Zacarious hadn't missed a Sunday service in years. The priest, whose duties included seeing to the soup kitchens so the poor and homeless could eat and have shelter, took a pragmatic approach to the problem of Clay's religious affiliation, deemed the groom-to-be duly baptized, and efficiently arranged the ceremony, pacified by his thoughts of feeding the hungry for weeks with Clay's beneficence.

The church was empty except for the priest, Yana, and Clay. Clay memorized the Greek vows and spoke them slowly and precisely, his words echoing softly through the huge, old, empty church.

Yana, in a lavish white wedding dress adorned with countless pearls, felt proud of herself when only two tears trickled down from her eyes as she said her vows. She tried not to cry, but Clay looked so proud and so handsome in his gray suit, and her happiness was so marrow-deep, that she simply could not contain the tears.

They dashed jubilant letters off to their parents in the United States, explaining that they were now husband and wife and would be having a baby later in the year.

"Think your father will accept me?" Clay asked after Yana finished reading him her letter to Nico.

"He will. It might take a while for him to get used to the idea, but he'll accept you." Yana folded the one-page letter neatly, then tucked it into the envelope with Clay's letter to Sorren and Shadow. "How could anyone who knows you *not* love you?"

"I can think of several good reasons for not loving me."

"So can I, but I'm your wife now, so I'm not supposed to think of things like that."

They had their honeymoon on the French Riviera, taking the largest suite, shutting the door on the world outside, sharing their love with no one but themselves.

Sorren sat stiffly, his jaw clamped tightly shut, waiting for Nico's reaction. Nico had his letter from Yana in his lap. Sorren held Clay's version of the same letter. The air in the office seemed absolutely motionless, and Sorren was sure he could hear the beating of his own heart, the heady rush of blood flowing through his veins.

Waiting for Nico's reaction to the letter, Sorren thought of his own daughter and wondered what his reaction would be if a young man—a young man he trusted—impregnated one of the McKenna girls.

Sorren knew exactly what his reaction would be: He'd want to throttle the unconscionable cur of a man and would tell his daughter she couldn't leave the house for a month of Sundays.

When Nico lifted his face up from the letter, there were big, glistening unshed tears in his eyes. "My baby is going to have a baby," he whispered. "I'm going to be a grandpapa."

"Don't you worry, Nico, Clay is going to treat Yana right." There was a sharp edge of anger to Sorren's voice. He had completely misread the tears in Nico's eyes. "He married her, and he's going to take care of Yana and the child. They'll never want for anything. I promise you that. Yana and the child will never have to worry about—"

Sorren's words were abruptly cut off when Nico's

face slowly transformed from stunned confusion to beaming paternal pride. Sorren, still afraid that his son had done something Nico could never forgive, looked over at Shadow to gauge her reaction. She was smiling even more broadly than Nico, if that were possible.

"He will be a son." Nico made the prediction with the authority of a man who believed he actually could command the sex of his grandchild. "A fine son, strong and true." Nico looked at Shadow, then over at Sorren. Slapping his palms loudly against the padded leather arms of the chair, he said exuberantly, "With Yana as his mother and Clayton as his father, and with the three of us as his grandparents, how can this child, this fine baby boy, ever be anything less than the leader of Greece?"

Sorren, whose heart was beating once again now that he was sure Nico wasn't looking to put a shotgun in Clay's ribs, laughed easily, letting the tension flow from his body. He hadn't yet figured out what he himself thought of the wedding and his grandchild-to-be.

"I had thought the president of the United States would be a nice position for our future grandson," Sorren said. He looked over at Shadow, who stood at the corner of his desk. "Precious, do we have any really good champagne on ice? This is an occasion that requires only the very finest champagne."

"I'll see what we've got cold," Shadow said softly. She went to Sorren and kissed him on the cheek. Whispering so only her husband could hear, she said,

"I told you Clay was an honorable man. I said that all along."

"I know you did, and I've never doubted it. I'm sure Clay and I will get along much better now." Beneath the desk, where Nico could not see, Sorren patted Shadow's knee, and his eyes brightened with amorous amusement. "You know, you look pretty good for a grandmother."

"Oh, you!" Shadow exclaimed, slapping Sorren lightly on the shoulder. "I'll go see what champagne we've got cold."

Sorren held the champagne bottle upside down over his glass in a valiant effort to get out every last drop. He set the bottle on the floor, beside the three previous bottles Shadow had brought in. He and Nico looked at the empty bottle, as though it had somehow greatly disappointed them both.

"I think a toast is due," Nico said, slurring his words slightly, his eyes rolling around a bit before settling on Sorren's face. Nico raised his glass high overhead, spilling champagne as he waved his arm theatrically. "To my beautiful daughter and her new husband, Clayton McKenna."

They clinked glasses, spilling more wine onto the leather-covered sofa cushions between them. It was the fourth time they had drank to that same toast. As the champagne disappeared, the originality and wit of the toasts diminished.

Shadow walked into the office, open bottle of

champagne in hand, a disapproving look on her face.

"Haven't you two had enough yet?" she asked, directing her question to Sorren but including Nico in her ire.

"We're getting there, Precious, but we're not quite there yet." Sorren took the bottle from his wife, then replenished his glass and Nico's. "You should stay here, Precious," Sorren continued, his diction perfect, though he was a long way from being sober. "Nico and I, as concerned grandfathers, have been unable to decide whether the future McKenna should lead Greece or the United States in the next century, so we've been concentrating our intellectual energies—"

"Such as they are at the moment," Shadow cut in with equal portions of humor and annoyance at her husband's condition.

"—on the child's education. Nico says there are several very fine universities in Greece—it does have a long history of advanced intellectual achievements—but I think that England is really the only place for a complete university education."

Shadow took Sorren's glass from his hand. She sipped the wine, enjoying the icy tingle of the liquid as it went down. "It's a shame such good wine is getting swilled like slop. If I'd known you were going to drink like this, I wouldn't have bothered with our best wine."

Sorren very seldom drank to excess and, because of this, knew that his wife's anger wouldn't last long. He took Shadow's free hand in his. "I suppose you're going to say that Nico and I should mind our own business and let Clay and Yana make such decisions."

"Exactly."

Nico started to laugh, then Sorren joined in. Shadow finished the champagne, then handed the glass back to Sorren. "When you've finished mapping out the life of your first grandchild, please try not to make too much noise when you come to bed."

Before Shadow left the room, Sorren and Nico were at it once again, arguing with comic seriousness about where the child would study law.

"Is it terrible of me to wish we didn't have to go back?" Yana asked, standing on the balcony of their three-room hotel suite overlooking the blue waters of the French Riviera. Clay was standing behind her, gently pulling a brush through her hair.

"I wish we could stay here too, love, but duty calls." Clay eased the hair away from Yana's nape, then bent low to kiss her behind the ear. "Someday we'll have time for more leisure."

"I wish that someday was right now. I love it here."

"Then we'll just have to buy a home here. I'll get a lawyer working on it right away. How large would you like the chalet to be?"

Yana laughed softly, not yet fully accustomed to Clay's generosity. He had, thus far during their honeymoon, bought just about everything that had caught Yana's eyes. Their suite was crowded with brightly wrapped packages from the delightful French boutiques and shoppes. Yana couldn't even remember all that Clay had bought her, and when she suggested that perhaps a little moderation was in order, Clay dismissed this casually by saying, "Let me have my fun. I *like* buying my *wife* gifts."

Yana tilted her head to the side, inviting more kisses. She heard the brush rattle against the marble balcony floor, then felt Clay's strong hands slide under her arms and around her waist. He pulled her against himself, placing a palm lightly over Yana's stomach.

"How's the baby? Kicking yet?"

Yana laughed softly. "The baby is just fine, and I seem to be finished with the morning sickness. And, no, the baby isn't kicking yet and won't for quite a while. I told you that yesterday."

"I know, but I thought something might have changed since then. The baby is a McKenna, you know. We're not like everyone else."

Yana laughed again, a light, easy, carefree laugh. She had not thought it was possible, but Clay was just as excited about the child as she was. He was doggedly determined to fully accept all the responsibilities of his impending fatherhood. Since there wasn't a child yet for him to dote over, he busied himself with buying gifts for his developing progeny. In the suite there were two rocking horses, three cribs, and a vastly varied assortment of clothes, some of which would not fit the child for two or three years.

"I want it to always be like this for us," Yana said softly, looking out at the sailboats on the water, her head resting against Clay's chest. "For the very first time in my life, I feel truly happy. And . . . it's like I know that nothing—nothing from now on—can ever take away my happiness."

"Your pleasure," Clay said, the timbre of his voice deeply sensual, his hand sliding up from Yana's stomach to gently cup her breast, "is my number one priority."

Chapter 26

Antoli wrote the check carefully, savoring the experience, the feeling of power it gave him. It was the seventh check he'd written from the Zacarious Shipping Company account since Clay and Yana had gone on their honeymoon. The only problem was the check was for just two thousand drachmas. It was the ceiling limit on business checks without a countersignature from Illyana. Clay hadn't yet been added to the bank records as Illyana's husband.

"Another withdrawal, Mr. Pacca?" the teller asked.

"Trying to get everything in order for Miss Zacarious's return."

"Don't you mean Mrs. McKenna?"

"Yes, of course. Mrs. McKenna." Antoli grinned crookedly at the teller, wishing she'd keep her damn mouth shut and mind her own business. "With all the romancing she's done lately, I've been pretty much running the company."

The teller just smiled, which told Antoli that she didn't believe him. As she began counting out the cash, she stopped in mid-count and looked at Antoli.

"I've seen the man Miss Zacarious—I mean, Mrs. McKenna—married. He was in here a while back. He's *very* handsome, don't you think?"

Antoli was tired of everyone telling him how lucky Yana was that she had married Clayton McKenna. "Just count the money and let me be on my way," Antoli said curtly. "I got work to do."

The teller recounted the withdrawal. She handed the money to Antoli, then wrote herself a note to tell the bank president that Antoli Pacca had drawn the maximum amount of money out of the Zacarious Shipping Company account every day since the celebrated, though private wedding of Illyana Zacarious to Clayton McKenna.

Antoli walked slowly back to Zacarious Shipping, a faint smile on his lips as he thought of the grand irony that Zacarious Shipping money would be used to destroy Illyana, Nico, and Clay. It would pay the men who would kill them all.

Antoli shook his head, amending his thoughts. He couldn't kill Nico. That would be a pleasurable event, but Nico's death would not enhance Antoli's personal fortune, and however much he wanted to see Nico's blood spilled, he wanted to line his pockets with Zacarious money first.

His smile broadened as Antoli thought about how much more money was in the Zacarious Shipping Company account at the bank and in Nico's personal account. Hundreds of thousands of drachmas, all waiting for the right signature to be withdrawn. Antoli wasn't certain yet where he would redeposit the money once he got it. Perhaps Switzerland. He'd heard bankers there had a way of keeping their priorities in line with their depositors' wishes and maintaining strict confidentiality.

As Antoli walked slowly, his mind drifted to Clay. The American had proven to be a constant annoyance to Antoli. Though Antoli wanted desperately to kill Clay, he'd never been able to get close enough to accomplish his dream. Antoli's knife had never been removed from his pocket because Clay McKenna had never let his guard down, not in all the time the two men had spent together.

Antoli hawked loudly, then spit on the ground. Clay had broken his nose twice, and this had done something to Antoli's sinuses. He hadn't been able to breathe comfortably for weeks now.

I'll kill him for breaking my nose. And when Clay and Yana are dead, there won't be anyone left for Nico to turn to but me.

Antoli walked on, greater confidence in his step, assured that he had hired professionals to do the work that he couldn't do himself. Real professionals, not amateurs like Edward Danzer had so stupidly hired in Virginia.

After all this time, year after bitter year, Antoli was so close to revenge he could taste it sweet on his tongue.

*　　　*　　　*

Edward Danzer picked up his key from the sleepy old man behind the desk, then made his way up the stairs to his thirty-cents-a-night room.

All the sacrifice had been worth it, he thought. Living in transient quarters in Washington, watching every penny he spent, saving his money so that he could buy the information he needed to get his revenge on the McKenna family. It had all paid off because tonight, only an hour earlier, for fifty dollars he had bought the information he needed. LaTina McKenna was living in London, England, where she was attending one of the universities.

Danzer had saved enough money for a ticket to England. The fare would about tap him out, but he wasn't worried about that. Once in England, he would find LaTina, kill her, then busy himself with such mundane matters as making enough money for food and shelter. First things first though. Kill LaTina—begin the downfall of the McKenna empire—then get on with life.

His steps were weary as he rounded the corner of the stairs, needing to go up one more flight to get to his dingy little room.

Danzer was smiling as he thought about the activities of the evening. He had bought the information concerning LaTina's whereabouts from John Elijah, Emma's eldest son. The transaction had reaffirmed Danzer's belief that all blacks were untrustworthy.

He inserted the key into the lock, stepped into his tiny room, then closed the door behind him again. In this hotel, a man couldn't be too careful. There were thieves everywhere, even if nobody had anything worth stealing.

Danzer struck a match, lighting the one small lamp, spreading a sickly yellow light across the room. He peeled off his jacket, turned toward his bed, then froze.

"Mr. Danzer," Sorren McKenna said, "I'm glad to see you've made it home. I've been waiting for you."

"W—what are you d—doing here?" Danzer stammered, his face suddenly drained of all color.

In the pale glow of the lamp, the planes of Sorren's face were harshly etched in light and shadow. He stood, broad-shouldered and lean-hipped, dressed from head to toe in black. When he spoke, his voice was calm and even.

"My man, John Elijah, is faithful to me. But, you see, I needed him to put my mind at ease. I had thought you were behind my problems, but I wasn't really sure." Sorren's voice became softer, sounding like death. "You are a threat to my family."

Danzer began to tremble. "You can't prove a thing," he said, his voice a high-pitched whine. "There isn't a judge in the county who'll believe you."

Sorren smiled. It was a frightening thing for Danzer to see.

"Mr. Danzer, in this case, *I am the judge.*"

Clay's thoughts were on Yana and the growing

child inside her womb, when the open carriage pulled to a halt beside him at the pier. There were two men inside, and one look at them told Clay these weren't sailors, they were criminals.

"Mr. McKenna, there's someone who wants to see you," the man holding the reins said. "Will you please get in? We'll take you to see him."

The Colt was nestled in its holster beneath Clay's left arm. Yana, he knew, was at the office. With his primary concern—Yana's safety—out of the picture, Clay was more inclined to discussion than he otherwise might have been.

"Who wants to see me?" Clay asked, quite certain that if either man in the carriage went for a hidden gun, he could drop them both before they ever got off a shot.

"I can't tell you that, sir."

"Then I'd rather not go."

"It's important, sir."

"So is my time. If your boss wants to see me, he knows where he can find me." Clay said the words without much malice, remembering how his father had warned him that Nico sometimes associated with men who were on the wrong side of the law.

"Mr. McKenna, the safety of you and your wife is at stake," the man in the carriage said. Clay noticed that both men made a point of keeping their hands in clear view. "In fact, your safety can only be guaranteed if you come with us."

Clay felt the tightness in the pit of his stomach, a strange sort of empty feeling that made him feel sharp.

"Would you like to explain that?" Clay asked quietly, stalling for time, his mind reeling with the possibilities of what could happen.

"I'd like to, sir, but I can't. If you get in the carriage, nothing bad will happen to you or Mrs. McKenna."

Very quietly, so there would be no misunderstanding, Clay said, "You promise it with your life. You'll be the first one that goes down."

The driver nodded, and Clay saw his throat bob as he swallowed his nervousness. Clay's concern lost its knife edge. If these men meant him harm, they wouldn't go about it this way. They'd let guns do their talking, just as the men in Virginia had when they cut Nico down.

"You're not carrying a gun, are you?" Clay asked.

Both men shook their heads. Clearly, they felt naked without their weapons. "Boss's orders," the driver explained.

Clay smiled coldly, and it put a chill in the two men. "In that case, I'll get in. But remember one thing: No matter what, you two will be the first to die."

The two men kept their eyes trained forward. At the outskirts of Pirias, the carriage came to a stop before a dilapidated warehouse badly in need of new wood and paint. Clay jumped out immediately, his face grim, his eyes bright and alert. The weight of his Colt in its holster, heavy beneath his left arm, felt good, reassuring.

"This way, Mr. McKenna," the driver said. He turned and walked toward the warehouse, keeping his hands out unnaturally far from his sides. He would not get shot in the back because he'd thoughtlessly reached into his pocket for a cigar.

In a strange way, Clay respected the man. He had a lousy job to do, but he did it quietly and efficiently, without complaining. He was a professional. Clay didn't care for the man's profession, but he did respect the professionalism he had demonstrated.

The warehouse smelled of rotting fish and rotting, seawater-soaked wood. The vast interior was completely empty except for five men, kneeling on the muddy floor, their hands and feet bound with short pieces of rope, dirty rags tied over their mouths. Two other men, well-dressed, flanked a third man who was older, perhaps in his fifties, with ebony-black wavy hair that had gone silver-gray at the temples and a large aquiline nose that hooked downward at the tip.

"Good morning, Mr. McKenna," the older man said. "Please excuse the melodramatics required to bring you here. I assure you, it was quite necessary."

Clay walked forward, all his senses alert. He did not recognize any of the five men kneeling with their hands and feet bound, nor did he recognize anyone else.

"You know my name," Clay said, stepping up to the leader. "Mind giving me yours?"

"My name is Alexi Konstantini. I hope that we can be friends." Alexi's sharp eyes went over Clay. He nodded his head approvingly. "Nico has gotten lucky. From all I've heard of you, Mr. McKenna, you're a fine man. The men in the dockyards respect you. That's quite an accomplishment. They respect few men, and no outsiders."

"I hope you haven't brought me here just to flatter me."

"I have brought you here to warn you." Alexi waved absently toward the bound prisoners on their knees. "These"—his face twisted into an ugly scowl—"*things* have been hired to kidnap Mrs. McKenna and hold her for ransom. Once the ransom was received, they were to kill her. Later, you were to be killed, too."

A vein pulsed hotly in Clay's temple. It was the only outward sign that he'd heard the threat on Yana's life.

"I am ashamed to admit that these men have, on occasion, been employed by myself. Nothing serious, mind you. Unloading ships at night, minor smuggling operations, that sort of thing. Just the same, I feel somehow responsible for their behavior." Alexi turned away from Clay, indicating he wanted the American to walk with him away from the group. "Your father-in-law, Nico Zacarious, has been my friend and business associate for many years," Alexi continued as Clay matched his step. "Nico is a good man. He understands the way things get done. I'll admit that he and I haven't always been on the best terms, but we always know where the others stands. We always know that whatever we do, whatever

decisions we make, it doesn't involve our families."
When he looked over at Clay, Alexi's dark eyes were
fiery bright. "A man's family is sacred."

"I agree," Clay replied, feeling perspiration make
his white silk shirt stick to his back. "A man can and
should be held accountable for what he does. But
whatever he does, it doesn't include his wife and
children."

Alexi smiled, nodding his head approvingly.
"Nico is a fortunate man to have a son-in-law who is
so wise."

They stepped through a creaking door, into the
sunshine and the fresh air. The squawk of seagulls,
so common in Pirias, somehow seemed out of place
to Clay. It was a common sound on an uncommon
morning.

"The things in there have been hired by a man they
have not met. I only found out about this because
they were trying to recruit more men from my ranks.
Fortunately for all of us, an honest man came
forward and told me what was happening." Alexi
shook his head sadly, as though he were the parent of
misbehaving children. "I will take care of these men.
I believe they have told me everything they know, but
I must be certain. When they have finished, they will
no longer be a threat to any man's wife."

Clay wanted to protest, since it was clear that Alexi
would have the men killed when he'd finished with
the questions.

"You've got courts here," Clay said cautiously.
"Can't the law handle them?"

"Mr. McKenna, you are an intelligent man, and I sincerely hope that you and your lovely wife stay in Pirias. You are the kind of man that makes this little village a good place to live. But you are not in America. You are in Greece, and here we do things differently." Alexi patted Clay's shoulder, looking up into his eyes. "I will do what is necessary with those things in there. It is what Nico would do for me; it is what I will do for him and for you."

"Those 'things,' as you put it, are men."

"They are things. Men do not accept money to kidnap women; men do not agree to kill women. Men don't do those things, only animals." Alexi turned away from Clay, looking out to sea. "I brought you here so that you would know what has happened and why. You see, Mr. McKenna, whoever hired those animals in there could have hired more men." Alexi glanced quickly at Clay, his eyes saying he was holding back his anger. "I understand your lovely wife is with child. Perhaps you can visit your parents in the United States until the child is born. Think of how happy it would make Nico to be near his daughter when his first grandchild comes into this world."

Clay's heart thumped against his ribs, and only his training at hiding his inner feelings prevented his expression from changing. Alexi Konstantini knew about Yana's pregnancy. He either had spies inside Clay's house, or he had paid off Yana's personal physician to get the information. Either way, it made Clay nervous.

And what about the possibility that Alexi was bluffing? The men bound and gagged in the warehouse could actually be stooges who would be released the moment Clay was out of sight. It could be a ruse to get Clay and Yana out of Greece.

Clay looked critically at the well-dressed man standing with him, then dismissed his doubts. The kidnapping plot was no hoax. When you hold real power in your hands like Alexi Konstantini, there is no need to bluff.

"I don't know who you are, and frankly, that tells me I shouldn't trust you," Clay said in an even voice, not at all cowed by Alexi's display of power and intimate knowledge. "But since I can see no good reason for you to lie to me, I'll believe you. At least for now." Clay straightened his shoulders a little, towering over Alexi, looking down into his eyes. "If anything happens to my family—anything that you've caused—I'll come looking for you . . . and I'll find you. Do you understand me?"

Alexi Konstantini smiled. He was not troubled by the threat, though he took it seriously. "Mr. McKenna, I expect nothing less from you. These are troubling and dangerous times we live in. Until I can be sure that there is not another group of men who have been hired to do this foul deed, it is best that you return to the United States with your bride. Don't you agree?"

They walked back through the warehouse. Clay kept his eyes away from the five kneeling, bound men, knowing what their fate was, hating them for what they had agreed to do for money, thinking he should try talking Alexi out of having them assassinated, yet knowing in his own mind that he would kill all five of them himself, without a moment of regret, if they posed a threat to Yana and his child.

"I'll have you brought back to Zacarious Shipping now, Mr. McKenna," Alexi said. "If I find out who hired these men, I'll inform you immediately."

Clay said, "Thank you."

"We live in a dangerous world, Mr. McKenna. Be on your guard."

Chapter 27

Antoli cursed violently under his breath when he heard that Clay and Yana had returned from their honeymoon a week early. He had hoped to write several more checks from the Zacarious Shipping account. At least he had enough for the down payment for the mercenaries.

Sliding out a back door of the Zacarious offices, he took several deep breaths to calm himself. The earliest Yana could find out about the bank withdrawals was tomorrow morning, and even that wasn't a certainty. She might not concern herself with that until several days later, after she had inspected the progress made on the *Despina* and the *Shadow*. By that time, if plans went as Antoli passionately hoped they would, she would be kidnapped and Clay would be scrambling to come up with the ransom.

Everything in Antoli made him want to run, but he

kept his feet firmly planted in one place. He closed his eyes. *What is the best course of action now?*

A word of advice Nico had given him years earlier came back, and Antoli smiled because he knew the old man was right.

"Always confront the opposition," Nico had said. "Don't let them come to you. If you do, they've got the upper hand."

He took a final deep breath, squared his shoulders, and stepped back into the Zacarious Shipping offices.

Antoli took the stairs two at a time, heading straight for Yana's office. He touched his knife, feeling its contours through the fabric of his trousers. With any luck at all, he would use the knife soon, just as he had always planned.

Antoli rushed into the outer offices, moving past Beddickow, who raised his head and seemed about to say something. Antoli didn't have time to listen to anything a secretary had to say.

"Yana, it's so good to have you back," Antoli said, bursting into the office without knocking first.

Yana was standing near her desk. She did not seem overly pleased at seeing the senior vice president. "Hello, Antoli. How have operations been in my absence?"

"No problems at all." Antoli sat in the chair facing Yana's desk, then got to his feet again almost immediately. He was nervous, edgy. Yana's return was unscheduled, and he didn't like making decisions on the run. "I took care of all the little things that came up. You know how it is. There's always something."

"Yes," Yana said, sounding bored with Antoli. "Where's Clay?"

"He went to look at the ships." She sat at her desk, smiling to herself. "He's never been one to sit behind a desk unless he absolutely has to."

Antoli paced the office, moving back and forth, irritating Yana.

"The honeymoon went well, I take it?"

"Yes, very well."

"You should go home," Antoli said quickly, finding it impossible to appear calm. "There are a thousand wedding gifts for you. As soon as the news got out that you were married, gifts started coming in from everywhere." Antoli walked to the window and looked out. "Maybe you should go home and see what you've gotten."

And when you're home, my men can show up and take you away. If I can keep Clay here at the office, all you'll have are those bumbling butlers to protect you!

"I'll see them all in good time. Right now, I've got more important matters to attend to, like running Zacarious Shipping." Yana swiveled in her chair, turning toward Antoli. She said dryly. "If you'll excuse me, I have a great deal to do. I'd like some privacy."

Antoli watched the open carriage come to a stop outside Zacarious Shipping. Clay McKenna stepped out onto the street. After a moment, Antoli recog-

433

nized the carriage; it belonged to Alexi Konstantini.

What would Clay want with a criminal like Konstantini? Antoli had hired Konstantini men to kidnap Yana, but he'd kept his own identity a secret, wearing a mask when he made the first payment. Alexi Konstantini couldn't possibly know what Antoli had planned, he thought reassuringly.

Yes he could! Curse all the gods in heaven and hell! Alexi Konstantini has found out, and he's told Clay!

"Yana, why don't we both go to your home and see those gifts? Wouldn't you like to freshen up some?" Antoli was speaking fast. He reached into his pocket for his knife. "Come on, I know you'd like to bathe and rest before getting back to work."

Yana's attention was focused on the pile of notes on her desk. She thumbed through them, recognizing Georgi's barely legible handwriting. Distractedly, she looked up quickly at Antoli, then back to her work.

"Antoli, the only thing I need right now is for you to get out of my office and leave me alone. I don't mean to be rude, but I really must insist that—"

The hand gripping her dress at the shoulder was strong, and this surprised Yana. When she looked up at Antoli, the point of his knife was just inches from her face.

"Do what I tell you, and you won't get hurt," Antoli whispered. "Get up."

"What is this, Antoli? Have you completely lost your mind?" Yana could not take her eyes away from the knife.

434

"We're getting out of here now, and if you give me any trouble at all, I will kill you."

There was a quiver in Antoli's voice, but Yana knew that he meant every word he said. The hatred she saw in his eyes was so clear, so easy to read, that she couldn't understand why she had not seen it earlier. As she got slowly to her feet, she remembered how Clay had warned her not to trust Antoli.

Clay couldn't have known Antoli is like this. He would have done more than just warn me; he would have stopped Antoli long ago.

Antoli kept his hold on the shoulder of Yana's dress as he pushed her out of her office. When Beddickow saw the look on Yana's face, then the knife that Antoli held to her back, he gasped but did not rise from his chair.

"I won't say anything," Beddickow promised. "I won't tell anyone, Mr. Pacca. You can trust me."

Yana looked at her secretary, and with her eyes she called him a coward before she was pushed through the outer office doors.

"What do you want?" Yana asked, feeling the needle-sharp point of the knife against her back as she walked down the stairway. "I can't help you unless you let me know what you want."

It surprised Yana that she felt so little fear. She knew her life was in jeopardy. The hand at her shoulder, the knife at her back, the wild-animal hatred she saw in Antoli's eyes, told her that. But somehow, for reasons she did not truly understand, she knew that it would be all right in the end. She had

Clay in her heart, and she had his child growing inside her, and perhaps more than anything else, she had confidence in herself. She could do whatever was necessary.

"Easy, Antoli . . . just take it easy," Yana said quietly as they descended the rear stairway of the Zacarious Shipping Company offices. "I'll do anything you want."

"Shut up," Antoli hissed, his eyes darting around, his ears pricked for the sound of footsteps. Clay had to be coming. And when he came, he'd bring that deadly revolver with him. But would he use the gun if Antoli held a knife to his wife's throat?"

Antoli sensed that his life was tied to Yana. As long as he held her hostage, Clay couldn't do a thing.

Once they were outside, Antoli's fear increased. There were countless places Clay could launch an attack from. Antoli saw the Zacarious mansion, which graced a cliff overlooking the ocean, high up on the rocky terrain less than a mile from the offices. At that moment, the Zacarious mansion looked to Antoli like a fortress that would protect him from Clay. It was, however, an uphill walk the entire way.

Years of riding horses and daily walks through her father's beautiful gardens had kept Yana in good shape. The same could not be said for Antoli. By the time they were halfway to the house, Antoli was gulping in air loudly. The one time Yana had dared look over her shoulder at him, she saw sweat streaming down his face despite the cool weather.

"Keep going," Antoli said between breaths.

"Why, Antoli? This doesn't make any sense."
Yana started up the hill, then cautiously looked over
her shoulder again. "You know that my father would
give you anything you could ever want."

"Shut up!" Antoli gasped. His exhaustion aged
his features, and Yana realized that Antoli had been
drinking much more than she had previously
suspected. "Just keep walking." Antoli prodded
Yana along with the knife.

Behind them, over Antoli's head, Yana saw a tall,
lean man step out into the sunlight at the rear door of
Zacarious Shipping. *Clay!* Even from the distance
that separated them, Yana could see him reach inside
his jacket and withdraw the revolver he always kept
with him. On their honeymoon, she had chided Clay
for having the gun with him everywhere but in bed.
Now she was thankful for it. Clay started up the hill
toward them. Afraid that Antoli would see the
direction of her gaze, Yana turned back toward her
house.

"I'm nobody's charity case, Yana," Antoli said.
The closer to the Zacarious mansion he got, the more
confident he felt. In all his years of service to Nico,
Antoli had been invited to the house only a couple of
times. That was just one of a thousand insults and
slights that Antoli was going to make Yana pay for.

"What do you think Nico really is, Yana?" Antoli
continued. They were very near the house now. An
explosive mixture of fear, confidence, and the sense
of power he felt at having the knife touch Yana's back
was making him feel talkative. "Do you know how

437

your father got his money? He stole it. He stole every stinking drachma of his money, Yana. Mostly from my family."

Yana listened, not believing a word of Antoli's story, thinking she had to say whatever the madman wanted to hear.

"If that's the case, Antoli, there's no reason why we can't reach some kind of settlement. Yes, a settlement. Just let me know what you think is fair, and I'll have our attorney—"

"Shut up, you whore!" Antoli released the shoulder of Yana's dress. He slipped his fingers inside the back of the neckline, balling the fabric into his fist. He could feel the warmth of her smooth flesh against the backs of his fingers.

When they reached the house, Antoli said, "Open the door. If I have any problems with your servants, I'll kill you."

He's crazy. Dear God, Antoli's completely crazy.

Talking with a criminal did not disturb Yana overmuch. Trying to reason logically with a madman did.

Yana's hands were shaking as she opened the heavy oak door to her home. Before she stepped through the doorway, Antoli pushed her against the jamb, holding her there with more force than was necessary. He laughed softly, menacingly.

"Clay's coming, Yana. He's coming for you."

He's coming for you, too, Antoli. Clay will kill you for this. She said, "Good, Antoli. When Clay gets here, he can get you whatever you want. All you have to do is ask and it's yours."

"Shut up!" Antoli hissed, panic swelling inside him at the sight of Clay—his greatest enemy— making his way rapidly up the hilly terrain. Antoli squeezed the haft of his knife tighter, keeping the deadly point of the blade touching Yana. "Get inside. We're going to your room."

"No, Antoli! You don't want to do that!" Yana tried to twist round, but Antoli slammed her against the door frame again. "Please, Antoli, not there," Yana sobbed, thinking of how many beautiful memories she had with Clay in her bedroom, and how if Antoli forced himself upon her there, he would not only violate her body, but her memories, too.

They went through the sitting room and past the ballroom, then up the wide stairway to the bedrooms. The servants, to Yana's relief, were apparently busy elsewhere in the house, and she and Antoli made it to her bedroom door without being seen. This situation was best handled by herself and Clay, Yana thought.

At her bedroom door, Yana stopped again, fervently hoping that there was some small amount of humanity in Antoli, a vestige of basic decency, that she could appeal to.

"Antoli—"

"Get in!"

Yana gasped when the point of the knife was pushed through her dress, touching her skin for the first time. It surprised her that she didn't feel more pain. Yana sensed then that she could not confront

Antoli again. Her fear of being violated by Antoli could not take priority over the child—Clay's child—growing inside her.

She opened her bedroom door and Antoli pushed her in, kicking the door shut behind them. He gave Yana a hard shove, causing her to fall to her knees on the thick carpet.

Antoli locked the door, then turned to Yana. Seeing her on the floor, her face pale with fear and her coiffure untidy, gave Antoli a surge of adrenaline, a sense of power, that he had waited his entire life for. He leaned against the locked door, holding the knife loosely in his hand in clear view of Yana. She would not forget that he held the power over her life and death.

He smiled at Yana. When Yana pulled her feet beneath her, Antoli smirked, shaking his head. He liked having her kneeling in his presence. After years of groveling to satisfy Nico's wishes, Antoli intended to make the most of this moment. He couldn't take the time now to do to Yana what he had always fantasized he would. Clay would show up at any second, and Antoli couldn't afford to have his concentration divided—not with an opponent like Clay McKenna. But perhaps later, once Clay had been disposed of, there would be time to force Yana to turn his violent fantasies into satisfying reality.

"What are you going to do?" Yana asked quietly, sounding much more in control of her fears than she felt. "I can't help you, Antoli, until you tell me what you want."

When Antoli stepped closer, Yana turned her face down. She couldn't look up at him. His eyes glowed with sadistic pleasure. She could see into his soul, into his demented mind, and the sight sickened more than frightened her.

Antoli roughly removed a tortoiseshell comb from Yana's hair, pulling several strands from her scalp in the process. He tossed the comb against the door. "Take your hair down. Take it down for me, just like you do for that stinking Indian you spread your legs for."

Yana pulled the combs from her hair, then shook her head. Rich waves of shimmering auburn hair tumbled over her shoulders. Antoli groaned lustfully, deep in the back of his throat, reacting to Yana's fear, helplessness, and beauty.

From downstairs, they heard Clay call out Yana's name. She looked to Antoli, not sure what he wanted her to do next.

"Call him." Antoli moved behind Yana. He reached down, entwining his fingers in her thick hair. He pulled her to her feet, enjoying the sharp cry of pain she issued.

"You don't have to hurt me," Yana said, grimacing when Antoli tugged her hair again, inflicting pain without cause or purpose.

"Call him. I swear I'll cut your throat if you don't do everything I tell you."

"Clay!" Yana shouted. "Clay, I'm here in the bedroom!"

Antoli snapped his left arm around Yana's neck,

her throat in the crook of his elbow. He brought the point of his knife to Yana's ear. They heard Clay's boots stomping against the stairs, then down the hall.

"Tell him if he shoots through the door, he'll kill you first."

Antoli's breath was hot against the back of Yana's neck, making her feel nauseous. She called the words out to Clay, doing as she was told, trying to stand still, to calm the furious beating of her heart, to steady her trembling knees.

"Yana, are you okay?" Clay asked from the hallway. "Has he hurt you?"

The arm around Yana's neck tightened, as did the pressure of the knife against her throat. For a second, Yana closed her eyes and said a prayer for the protection of Clay and her unborn child. Antoli rubbed himself lewdly against her bottom as he pushed Yana closer to the door.

"Back away from the door, Clay!" Antoli hissed, spattering saliva on Yana's cheek. "Make one wrong move and I'll cut her throat." To Yana, he whispered "Open the bolt. I swear, I'll cut you bad if you do anything wrong."

Yana worked the locking bolt free of its cylindrical housing. Antoli jerked her backward, his forearm hard against her throat. Yana coughed and sputtered, grabbing Antoli's arm for the first time to lessen the pressure.

"Open the door!" Antoli said. He laughed nervously, a shrieking, cackling sound that did not resemble anything human. "Come on in, Clay. The three of us can have a little party. But the first time I can't see your hands, I'll cut her face! I'll cut her pretty face!"

Clay opened the door slowly, pushing it wide. He stood in the opening, feet spread to shoulder width, eyes dark and emotionless, hands hanging loose and ready at his sides.

"You okay?" Clay asked quietly. Yana nodded, then coughed when Antoli's forearm tightened over her throat. "Just be calm. I'll give him whatever he wants, then he'll let you go."

"You don't look like such a dangerous man now," Antoli said. The sadistic power he held over Clay and Yana was exhilarating, intoxicating Antoli in a way that the ouzo and prostitutes never had. "Easy now, open your coat, take out your gun, and drop it to the floor."

"I haven't got it with me."

Antoli growled, pushing the knife against Yana's cheek. "Don't lie to me! Do as I tell you or I'll kill her! Do you *want* to see me kill her?"

"No, that's why I left my gun outside." With his left hand, Clay opened his coat, revealing the empty holster. He held his right hand out to the side, showing he was unarmed. "I left my gun outside. I'm no threat to you, Antoli. There's no reason for you to hurt Yana. Let her go and—"

"Shut up!" Antoli laughed softly. His tenuous grasp on his sanity had failed him at last, now that he could feel Yana's body against his own, could sense

443

her fear, and could look at Clay and know with gratifying certainty there was nothing the American could do to hurt him.

Antoli rattled off several insults, directing them at Clay but speaking of Shadow and her mixed-blood heritage. When the insults had no apparent effect on Clay, Antoli took his left arm away from Yana's throat, placing his hand over her breast for Clay to see.

Yana refused to feel the groping hand at her breast, and she looked straight into Clay's eyes. *Don't let him take away your logic, Clay*, she said with her eyes. *I'm strong enough to withstand this, and so are you. Be strong, my love, and we can defeat him together*.

"Is she good, Clay? Does she treat you like a good whore should?"

Clay nodded, hating himself for doing it yet knowing that Yana's life depended upon him pacifying Antoli.

"This is what you're going to do, Clay," Antoli continued, feeling invincible now. "You're going to go to the bank and withdraw all the money from the Zacarious Shipping account and from Nico's account. You won't tell anyone why, because if you do, I'll kill her, Clay, and you know I will."

"Anything you say," Clay replied, knowing that he lacked the authority to withdraw money from the accounts. "Just don't hurt Yana while I'm gone."

Antoli cackled again, his hand brutally squeezing her breast. "Hurt her? Clay, while you're at the bank,

444

Yana's going to delight me with all the tricks you've taught her. Isn't that right, Yana?" When she didn't reply, Antoli prodded her with his knife. "Isn't that right, Yana?"

"Yes, that's right, Antoli." Yana looked at Clay, counting on his understanding, on his ability to choose reason over emotion when necessary. Cold reason was their only hope. "I'll bet she's real good. Is she, Clay? Does she know how to satisfy a man?"

Clay nodded. He felt the Colt tucked into the waistband of his trousers at the small of his back, wondering if he had the skill and speed that would be required.

"Yes, she knows what to do," he said, but the tone of his voice had changed slightly. "She knows when to be on her knees."

Antoli laughed harder than before, loving the crude comment by Clay. And he was still laughing when Yana twisted inside his arm, catching his knife hand by the wrist with both her hands to keep the blade away from her as she dropped to her knees. His laughter died as he watched Clay pull the revolver from behind his back with blinding speed and fire in one smooth motion.

Antoli's last thought was that once again he had lost to Clayton McKenna.

The single gunshot echoed painfully in Yana's ears. She never looked back, knowing that Clay's aim was deadly, needing no confirmation of his lethal skill.

"Tell me you're all right," Clay said frantically as

he knelt beside Yana, searching for knife wounds that did not exist. Yana nodded. Clay swept her up in his arms and carried her out of the room. "I was so afraid. My God, Yana, you'll never know how much I love you." He kissed her, then looked into her eyes as he carried her down the hallway. "You are so brave," he said softly, in a tone of awe.

"You've taught me how to love," Yana whispered. "That's taught me how to be brave, Clay McKenna. And we're going to have a strong, brave, loving child."

Clay walked down the stairway with Yana in his arms, past the stunned servants.

"Lots of children," Clay said with a twinkle in his ebony eyes. "Lots and *lots* of children."

"Don't I have a say in this?"

"Sure you do. But remember, I'm a McKenna, and we like to have our own way."

"I'm a McKenna, *too*, and *don't* you forget it!"

"For all time," Clay whispered.

Yana took Clay's face lightly between her palms. She kissed him softly and said, "For all time."

Epilogue

Nico bounced Nicholas on his knee, smiling at the infant. Nicholas made gurgling noises and blew bubbles happily in response to his grandfather's facial antics.

For Nico, the world had suddenly become a friendly and loving place. He no longer felt the need to attack life. He was happy with his success and had turned over the helm of the Zacarious Shipping Company to Yana without a backward glance. Clay was busy running McZac Import-Export, though with Yana's pregnancy, he would need to run both companies until the most pressing of Illyana's maternal duties were met.

Looking over at Yana, Nico's smile broadened. He'd never before seen any woman radiate such pleasure at being pregnant. Yana simply glowed with happiness.

"Nico, there's a carriage here for you," Clay said, a

sly grin on his face.

It was the widow Bartolo. She had at one time been married to an Italian businessman who did shipping with Nico. Mr. Bartolo had died several years earlier. Recently, Nico had spent a good deal of his spare time—and now that he had retired, that was all of his time—with the widow.

"Thank you, Clay," Nico said, half reluctantly handing his first grandson over to his father.

Clay bent over so that he could whisper into his father-in-law's ear without being overheard by Yana or the Greek servants. "Nico, is this getting serious between you and Mrs. Bartolo? Do I hear wedding bells in your future?"

Nico grinned. "Only God can tell the future," he said with a smile.

Pausing at the balcony, looking out to sea, Nico felt a deep, satisfying contentment. His daughter had married a good man, and she would in three months bear her second child. Business was sailing along as usual . . . and the widow Bartolo was beginning to think that maybe marriage wouldn't be such a bad state of affairs. . . .